Books by Stephen Vizinczey

IN PRAISE OF OLDER WOMEN

THE RULES OF CHAOS

AN INNOCENT MILLIONAIRE

AN
INNOCENT
MILLIONAIRE

AN
INNOCENT
MILLIONAIRE

Stephen Vizinczey

The Atlantic Monthly Press
BOSTON / NEW YORK

FIRST AMERICAN EDITION

LIBRARY OF CONGRESS CATALOGING IN PUBLICATION DATA

Vizinczey, Stephen, 1933–
    An innocent millionaire.

    I. Title.
PR6072.I9138   1985   823'.914   84-45816
ISBN 0-87113-015-7

MV

PRINTED IN THE UNITED STATES OF AMERICA

Thanks are due to
Dr. M. M. Fisher and Professor Philip Anisman
for their comments on matters of
Medicine and the Law.

Apart from artists and politicians who have left their stamp on the age, all characters in this book are fictitious and any resemblance to actual persons living or dead is purely coincidental. The chronology is also fictional, and there are many deliberate anachronisms. Though most of the action takes place during the 1960s, the novel is not an account of any particular decade but a portrait of the modern world. The past is drawn against the background of the present. The Washington monument to the Vietnam War dead, unveiled in 1982, casts its shadow over earlier years.

AN
INNOCENT
MILLIONAIRE

1

A Bitter Thought

August 22, 1963, Toledo, Spain

I am looking at the towers and battlements of Toledo, the ancient capital of Spain, which stands on top of the hill across the ravine, and I have decided to make a note of all the important events of my life so that people will know what I have been through.

    But will they bother reading it? I'm probably wasting my time. What's the use? Men are not brothers but strangers and no one is interested in anybody's story. People just do not give a damn about each other.

MARK Niven was fourteen years old when he wrote this first entry in his diary and he meant every word of it, for he never added another line.

The diary itself is a solid book bound in blue morocco leather with a Toledo sword embossed in gilt on the cover; evidently he thought it was too expensive a thing to throw away.

Making a Killing—the 19th Century Origins of a 20th Century Drama of Greed, Love and Malice

The province of Peru —
the chief and richest in the Indies . . .
ZÁRATE

THE beginning of this contemporary story dates back to 1820, to the South American wars of independence against Spanish colonial rule, and has a great deal to do with José Francisco de San Martín, the Liberator of Argentina, Chile and Peru. Fate never picked a nobler character for the inadvertent cause of a series of crimes.

Born in 1778 in the viceroyalty of the Rio de la Plata, which is now Argentina, this great enemy of colonialism was the third son of a colonial official, the lieutenant-governor of the province of Yapeyú, who distinguished himself by remaining poor in a post that offered ample opportunities for stealing. The father's integrity compelled the sons to fend for themselves from an early age — a privilege in disguise, ensuring that they would exercise their intelligence and courage to the utmost while they were still young enough to grow and improve. One must start early to become a great man.

José de San Martín got as far as North Africa by the age of fourteen, a brave ensign under fire, fighting the Warrior Bey of Mascara at the walls of Oran — though this was already comparatively late in his military career. He entered the army at the age of twelve after two years of formal training at the Seminario de los Nobles in Madrid, where he learned all manner of skills and was jeered at as a *criollo,* a Spaniard born in the Indies. People should beware of insulting children: they will get their own back one day. Though an apparently loyal officer for over a decade, fighting against the Moors in North Africa and Napoleon's troops in Spain, the *criollo* turned into the greatest scourge of the Spanish army once there was a chance to liberate his native continent.

2

When he returned to Buenos Aires at the age of thirty-four, San Martín soon proved to be the most competent leader of the rebel cause, accepting "none but lions" to serve under him. He became a successful revolutionary, which is a rare enough phenomenon, but what sets him apart from most great men of history is the fact that in spite of his victories he remained immune all his life to the temptations of power. An avid reader of the French *philosophes* and the Latin historians, a thinking soldier, simple in his habits and extravagant in his aims, General San Martín had a passion for liberating countries but no desire to rule them.

As the handsome and brilliant general who had driven the royalist forces out of Argentina, the country's best-loved hero commanding the best troops, he could have seized power in Buenos Aires at any time during 1814, but he chose the path of immortal glory instead. Leaving the regular army behind, he had himself appointed governor of the remote western province of Cuyo, which he set out to civilize by founding libraries and planting trees — while also recruiting and training four thousand gauchos to wrest Chile from Spain. As luck would have it, he succeeded. After two years of preparation for a march which was to rank in military histories with Hannibal's crossing of the Alps, he led his army across the Andes through snow and clouds and, taking the Chilean royalists by surprise, captured the capital city of Santiago. Then he made a blunder.

He took pity on the defeated enemy troops and let them run. Months later they came back with reinforcements from the viceroyalty of Peru and scattered his army to the winds. It seemed Chile was no sooner freed than lost again. But gathering together the living, San Martín made up for past mercies and wiped out the royalist forces in the battle of the River Maipú on April 5, 1818.

The jubilant Chileans wanted to proclaim him their king or president, whichever he preferred, but San Martín declined, wishing to get on with the liberation of Peru. Always persistent but never in a hurry, he spent two years organizing a new expeditionary force and building a fleet for a seaborne invasion. At the same time he addressed manifestos to the Indians and Africans of Peru, vowing to abolish slavery and forced labor and calling on them to avenge their miseries.

Peru, and what is more to the point, its capital, Lima, one of the richest cities in the world, faced certain war and possible revolution. It was a historic moment of agonizing uncertainty about the fate of immense fortunes. Ever since the time of the Pizarros the pickings of the continent that were not shipped to Spain had been hoarded in Lima, the City of the Kings. Now the fruits of three hundred years of plunder were in danger of being plundered. Was retribution, after all, a possibility?

BOTH the wealth and the guilt were practically limitless.

The treachery and massacres which yielded the legendary Inca treasures were only the foundation of Lima's riches. The surviving natives, used as forced labor, mined mountains of silver, gold and that valuable poison, mercury; they mined the sea for pearls and picked the coca leaves which were sold profitably for cocaine. And everything they produced passed through or stayed in Lima. Until well into the 18th century, the political and religious capital of all the colonies was also the center of all trade between Spain and South America, and this produced, in addition to everything else, the fabulous crops of political graft and commercial monopoly. In short, there was a great deal to be worried about as the danger of a reckoning became imminent. The poor were getting greedy, the rich were growing scared.

Some of the potentates of Lima decided to stake all they had on the waves and ship their fortunes to Spain. However, because the viceroy had impounded all Spanish ships for the defense of the colony, they could hire only foreign vessels, and with everything in warlike confusion, only one of these was loaded in time to set sail before Lima's port of Callao was blockaded by San Martín's navy — eight men-of-war commanded by another brilliant maverick, Thomas, Lord Cochrane, Tenth Earl of Dundonald. The British were on both sides: the ship that got away was captained by a Bristol man, one Thomas Parry. She sailed from Callao on August 10, 1820, the very day that General San Martín embarked for Peru.

A 230-ton brig which had carried coca leaf from Peru for over a decade, the *Flora* was laden on this voyage with weightier riches. There were 192 ironbound wooden chests aboard; to take just one example, the chest belonging to the Pardo y Aliago family of Lima contained 674 gold doubloons, a carved ivory jewel box and a cedarwood and ebony jewel box (contents: 7 necklaces, 5 pendants, 15 rings and 13 pairs of earrings, 11 brooches and 9 bracelets, all intricately fashioned of gold or silver and set with a total of 418 precious stones), a damascened Toledo sword in a gold-tooled leather scabbard studded with topazes and carnelians, and a chamois pouch containing 9 large uncut emeralds.

Altogether the *Flora* carried 29,267 diamonds, rubies, emeralds and amethysts, 11,254 pearls, most of them flawless, 743,050 gold doubloons with a smattering of escudos and piastres, as well as gold chains and medallions, gold goblets, bowls and platters, etc. etc. From the private chapels of Lima's leading families came gold and silver candlesticks and candelabra, crucifixes, ciboria, monstrances and chalices encrusted with pearls and precious stones or inlaid with enamels and lapis lazuli — most notably the Soldán y Unanue family's famous Cross of the Seven Emeralds blessed by Saint Pius V. The cargo also included 126 identical small-scale replicas of the life-sized statue of the Virgin in the Cathedral of Lima which was credited with saving the city from an earthquake in the 18th century; each of these was eighty centimeters high and weighed forty kilos of solid gold.

To conceive of this fantastic cargo, one must remember that profit in the colonies was usually converted into gold, pearls and precious stones — the most valuable currencies and the safest means of preserving fortunes. The gold Madonnas on the *Flora* were listed as the property of private individuals, not of the Church; the Virgin in solid gold was sacred twice over, as a holy object and as the best security in troubled times.

There were also seventeen tons of gold bullion on board, packed in wooden crates.

This immense fortune was now up for grabs on the open sea. And so it was that General San Martín's fight for freedom and justice precipitated a different kind of struggle, a no less deadly war for treasure, which is the subject of this narrative.

Apart from the crew, the *Flora* carried nineteen passengers: a papal legate, an official of the viceregal court and his secretary, and four ladies of the Spanish nobility with their children, seven boys and five girls, all under the age of ten. The passenger list may still be seen in the Archives of the Indies in Seville, along with the *Flora*'s manifest for the voyage, which records all the items of the cargo and their consignees, and also notes that Captain Parry had some twenty-seven tons of silver removed just before embarkation because he found the ship dangerously overloaded.

They sailed safely around Cape Horn, taking up supplies of food and water at several ports of call and departing unmolested in spite of the political conflicts, thanks to Captain Parry's diplomatic skill in presenting himself as a foreigner sympathetic to whichever party happened to be in control of the port. It was not until they sailed out of Recife and were on their way across the Atlantic to Cadiz that the captain finally allowed himself to be persuaded by his crew that they should keep the treasure for themselves. He turned his ship northwest to head for the Caribbean, and gave orders for the killing of the passengers.

An eyewitness account of these events is to be found in the Manuscript Library of the National Maritime Museum at Greenwich, in the form of a signed statement by Josiah Tyler, a cabin boy who jumped ship in Barbados and made his way to Bridgetown, where he gave himself up to the authorities. According to young Tyler's testimony, Captain Parry had tears in his eyes when he ordered his crew to murder the twelve children as well as the adults, to prevent any possibility of detection. *"'Tis a great pity there bain't no other way to keep the cargo!"* Tyler overheard him saying to the first mate. To spare the passengers the terror of knowing in advance that they were going to be killed, the captain wanted to have them strangled in their sleep, but the crew made a mess of it and "there were screams half through the night". Captain Parry was furious and cursed the men, and next morning gave each and every one of the passengers a proper burial at sea, conducting the services himself.

Soon afterward the crew dropped anchor in a deserted cove on Barbados to search for fresh water, and it was then that Tyler made his escape. The rest continued their voyage on a changed course; they were rich men now, with a new destination. The whole business came to nothing, for they went down in a hurricane a few days later; but as Tyler heard it before he jumped ship, the plan was to sail to the Florida Keys, where Captain Parry had friends he thought he could count on.

As for the passengers and the cargo, they could have safely remained in Lima.

San Martín did not march on the capital for ten months. With something of Kutuzov's distaste for battles and the same trust in the momentum of popular feeling, preferring maneuvers to bloodletting, he waited until the blockade forced the viceroy's army to abandon Lima, and even then would not enter the city until the people declared their independence from Spain. He assumed dictatorial powers as Protector of Peru for the duration of the war and the citizens suffered no loss of life or property, except through the abolition of slavery and forced labor.

San Martín also founded the National Library of Peru, but his plans for further reforms and the establishment of a constitutional monarchy under an English prince were up against more formidable obstacles than the viceroy's waiting regiments. Factionalism and corruption were all-pervasive; his most trusted aides were busy improving the world for themselves. Mustering the courage to admit that he could do no more, he left it all to Bolívar (who needed a few more years to become disillusioned) and retired to Europe at the youthful age of forty-six — a slight to subcontinental pride which caused much resentment.

ALL this belongs to the distant past, but there were immense quantities of gold and precious stones involved, and these last longer than flesh and bones — though, men, too, have a kind of immortality, at least in their actions.

The vile and noble deeds related here had fateful consequences for Mark Niven a century and a half later. Searching for the wreck of the treasure ship, he often wondered what he would be doing with his life if General San Martín had settled down to rule Argentina or Chile — if the potentates of Lima had not decided to ship their fortunes to Spain — if Captain Parry had valued his passengers more than his cargo and had kept his safe course for Cadiz, instead of sailing northwest into the path of the hurricane . . . but then, each man's life involves the lives of all men, each tale is but the fragment of a tale — the tale of mankind's history.

First Impressions

I must keep awake, because I'm on my own.
LAZARILLO DE TORMES

BORN in New York, Mark Niven was a much-traveled young man. He received the first great shock of his life in the city of Rome.

A sturdy five-year-old at the time, he was trying to close his suitcase, pressing the lid down as hard as he could on his left hand. It was a cheap fiberboard case with a sharp metal rim but at first he didn't even notice that he was hurting himself. Crouched on the floor of the narrow, airless room which stored the heat of the whole summer, he bent over the lid, pressing it into his fingers, as the Signora went on screaming at his parents about the *conto* and the *polizia*. He was anxious to finish packing and get away before the police arrived to lock them up.

His father was busy, trying to pacify both the proprietress of the pensione and Mark's mother, who had started to cry from sheer exasperation at the humiliating brawl. Unluckily her tears moved the Signora only to greater paroxysms of rage, scaring her into the terrible certainty that the Nivens would never have a single lira and she had lost fourteen days' rent for her two best rooms with a view of the waterfall of the Piazza del Popolo, for which she could charge extra — and in August, too, when Rome was filled with tourists! She would have needed to call down the wrathful justice of God and the avenging angels, but it was her cross to suffer a Roman temper without religious convictions, and her rage had the added force of despairing impotence in the face of her loss. Mark didn't understand many of the words but this only made their violent sound, unblunted by specific meaning, all the more menacing. Her shrill voice hit him like an electric current bolting through his brain. The woman was frantic, possessed by fury; she kept raising and lowering her arms, invoking retribution, and every ounce of her two hundred pounds trembled and swayed as if she were about to shed all the fat from her body. Nevertheless, she was the first to notice the boy. Still crouching by his suitcase, he stared at her with his huge dark eyes full of terror, holding his left hand by the wrist, as the blood from his fingers dripped on her good carpet.

Alerted by the Signora's abrupt silence, Mark's mother snatched him up and ran to the washbasin to rinse away the blood: he had cut his fingers to the bone. The water stung, starting the pain.

Fragments of this scene were the earliest events Mark could recall; it was as if he had just been born that afternoon in Rome. And what stayed in his mind with bitterest clarity, acquiring growing significance through the years, was the Signora's glazed look at the stains his blood had made on her property. Though he couldn't have put it into words he sensed right then and there that his fingers weren't worth so much as a piece of old rug to other people. It was his first intimation of man's indifference to man, and he convinced himself early in life that he couldn't rely on anybody, not even his parents.

AND yet, the very day after the trouble at the pensione where they couldn't pay their bill, they moved into a large stone villa off the Via Appia Antica, with five bathrooms for the three of them, a swimming pool, a maid for the house and a gardener to look after the surrounding citrus grove and orchard, which kept the rest of the world at a distance.

"What about the police?" Mark asked apprehensively as they were exploring the house.

"Police? What police?" his father inquired with a clown's exaggerated incomprehension.

"The *polizia,* you stupid!" the boy shouted, stamping his foot on the marble floor. This rash exertion rushed more blood into his bandaged hand; his fingers felt as though they were being torn apart, and he fell silent from the shock.

"Come on, Mark, you aren't still worrying about that woman, are you? She's *pazza,* she doesn't know what she's talking about. Anyway, that pensione was a lousy place! I decided to pay her off and get us something nicer."

Confusion was the last straw. Mark began to cry and had to be lulled to sleep by the maid, who was enchanted by the sturdy little boy with dark brown hair and thick, long lashes that cast shadows on his cheeks. *"Che bravo ragazzo — furioso, ma anche gentile!"*

No one can fuss over a child with so much enthusiasm as Italian country girls with round faces, and Mark soon realized that he could order Maria about and have the run of the house. This pleased him no end. He hated to leave the villa even for a few hours and screamed every time his mother took him back to Rome.

They made several trips to the Pronto Soccorso at the Ospedale San Giacomo to have his dressings changed, and she tried to take him sightseeing after the hospital, but Mark, worried that they wouldn't be allowed back into the villa again, refused to linger in the city and couldn't even be persuaded to go and look at the thirsty lion in Piazza Navona. He was unmanageable until they got into a taxi again, and only when they passed the crenellated towers of the Porta San Sebastiano leading to the Via Appia would he sit back and give his scowling face a rest.

Having his own orchard made him feel like a big landowner. With the help of the gardener, Bruno, who smiled through the white stubble on his brown face and bent down the branches for him, he picked peaches and plums with his good hand and took them to Maria, who put them aside in a special basket, as he would eat only his own fruit. The rest of the time he sat by the pool watching his mother swim (he couldn't go in until his fingers healed) or roamed around the big house, in and out of all the rooms — at last there was space for him to move about! And so he did, running up and down the marble stairs, checking the time on the various clocks, standing in the exact center of the Aubusson carpet, as if fearful that someone might pull it from under his feet.

"I hear you haven't counted the silver today," his father would tease him when he got home in the evening, always in a good mood since he had found a job.

It took Mark about as long as the bandage on his fingers lasted to get used to the idea that the splendid, spacious villa was going to be their home. Once he felt safe and settled, he began to worry about the heating for the winter, because he couldn't find any radiators.

"They're built into the floors," his father explained. "Anyway, we won't need them — we'll be leaving at the end of September."

The little face grew dark. "Leave this house?" he asked, scowling.

"Yes, we're moving back to Rome."

"No!" He clenched his fists and stamped his foot. "No!"

"You stamp your foot so much, it will fall off."

"I don't *want* to go," he sobbed, tears streaming down his cheeks.

"Good Lord, you don't think we could afford a house like this, do you? It was rented by a guy I know — he had to go back to the States sooner than he'd expected, so he let us stay here until his lease runs out."

"I don't care. You're not my friend!"

"It'll be nicer for you, you'll see . . . you'll have other kids to play with. And you have three more weeks here to swim and wander around."

"I don't want to!" shouted Mark, his heart breaking, and he would not say another word all evening, no matter how much they tried to cajole him. What was the use of liking a place if he had to leave it?

MANKIND, we're told, is divided into the haves and have-nots, but there are those who both have the goods and do not, and they lead the tensest lives. From the resplendent villa the Nivens moved into a dingy two-room flat in one of the thin concrete blocks which disfigure the suburbs of Rome, where no one can flush a toilet without everybody knowing about it, and once more they had to get used to being poor.

Such were Mark Niven's formative experiences, as his family kept exchanging opulence for penury, comfort for misery, traveling back and forth between England, Italy, France and Spain.

At times he felt that their very lives were in danger.

Once in Paris they lived on sardines, bread and cheese for weeks. There were evenings when he kept asking his mother for his supper and she kept saying *no*. Sometimes she refused him things because she wanted to teach him that he couldn't have everything in this world, or to punish him for tearing his clothes, but when she said *no* to supper, they were all punished. Once during a viciously cold winter in Madrid she fed him glasses of water all day. They seldom went hungry for long, but the memory of it preyed on his mind, and whenever supper was late he was seized by anxiety, wondering whether they would ever eat again.

When he questioned his mother about their future, she knelt down and squeezed him tightly as if wishing to protect him from some disaster. He loved to bury his nose between her breasts, warm even through her dress, but she would interrupt these rare moments by pushing him away abruptly as if she found something wrong with him.

"I wish I *could* tell you what's going to happen to us next!" she exclaimed. "Ask your father — *he* ought to know."

He didn't.

A short, stocky man with a massive head which bent forward and seemed to pull along the rest of his body, Dana Niven picked up his son and swung him in the air. "What are you worrying about?" he said cheerfully. "Something will turn up. Fear not, little flock, for it is your Father's good pleasure to give you the kingdom!"

When he was in a less confident mood he had a severe mouth and fierce eyes and looked angry, out of guilt, no doubt, when asked about their future. "We'll see," he declared in a stern voice. "It all depends."

And it always depended on the same thing — money. But money depended on nothing, nothing that could be foreseen or controlled: it was wild and unpredictable, changing their lives continually as a river changes the landscape; when it flowed the grass was green and they went on picnics, but when the source dried up there was nothing but water from the tap. Mark would wake in the morning hungry, scared that there would be nothing to eat and he would starve slowly and painfully before they had money again. He was ashamed of his parents. There was nothing so disgusting as people who had nothing to eat.

Certainly nobody wanted to have much to do with them.

"Couldn't you write to your dad?" Mark's mother asked his father accusingly one evening as they sat around the bare table thinking of food.

"He *cabled* us two hundred last month — I've ruined the poor man."

"Well, we can't ask Mother. We've spent all her savings — all she's got left is the house. And you know what my brother said the last time!"

His father raised his hands with a grin. "Relax — seek not ye what ye shall eat, or what ye shall drink, neither be ye of doubtful mind."

"What about George?" Mark's mother asked irritably. "He could help. He's a friend, and he's here."

"He says we can have dinner with them once a week, but he doesn't believe in lending money."

Her eyes grew big with surprise. "Did George really say that?"

"He doesn't want us to owe him anything. It would spoil our friendship."

"Oh, really?" she said, the color draining from her face. "I'll remember that the next time he tries to grope me."

"I told you to knee him in the groin."

She sat silently for a while, her cheeks reddening with fury as she thought about George. "He talks about running away with me, but he doesn't care whether I eat or not. . . . What an absolute shit!"

"Well, he's willing to feed you once a week."

She was so incensed, she couldn't sit still. She got up, paced the room, then stopped by the window, flung it open and took a deep breath to control herself. But unspent rage made her hysterical. "Come on, Dan, let's jump," she commanded in a determined voice, putting one of her legs over the windowsill.

Mark's father jumped to grab her arm — they were on the sixth floor.

"We'll soon be dead anyway, why wait!" She struggled to free herself from his grip. "Let's get it over with . . . let's jump!"

Mark ran to the window and threw his arms around his mother's waist to hold her back. He didn't want her to die!

"There isn't a single person in this whole rotten world who cares what happens to us!" she cried out despairingly, oblivious of the terror she was inspiring in her son.

Mark couldn't think of anything else for days. He would fasten his eyes on hapless strangers in the street and follow them with bitter looks, thinking, *there's another one who doesn't care!*

One day at school in Madrid he swallowed his shame and tried to talk a girl into sharing her lunch with him. Eyeing the fresh-smelling roll stuffed with butter and ham, he confessed that he hadn't eaten anything since the previous afternoon.

Immediately, she withdrew the sandwich from her mouth and moved closer to him on the bench, gazing at him with melting eyes. "What does it feel like?" she asked intensely.

Then, as she listened to Mark telling her about his hunger, she went on eating her sandwich. When she had finished her lunch, she asked Mark to let her listen to his stomach gurgling. This made him so angry and defiant that he charged her ten pesetas for it, and the same to all the other kids who were interested, and bought himself a roll from the proceeds.

MARK's father belonged to a profession in which there are scores of suitable applicants for every job and every job is strictly temporary. He was an actor, earning an uncertain living as a bit player in low-budget Hollywood movies made in Europe.

Mostly he died in films.

After perishing as a Christian martyr in an epic about the last sexful days of the Roman Empire, he would come back to life only to be killed again halfway through a Western filmed in Spain. In comedy-romances about Americans in Paris or on the Riviera he played the dim friend of the playboy hero, fading into oblivion with melancholy skill. It's all on late-night television.

Dana Niven was too intelligent not to loathe these monstrosities of the 1950s and too ambitious not to resent playing insignificant parts in them. But the ultimate humiliation was that even such small and dismal roles were hard to come by, and he was out of work more often than not. Several times the part he had been promised was given to someone else at the last moment. Occasionally his London agent got him a part in the West End production of an American play, but in spite of favorable mentions by reviewers his stage performances did not lead to better things. For the first eighteen years of his career this excellent actor was best known in the trade by a producer's witticism, "no woman would get wet pants watching Dana Niven".

Mark learned the full extent of his father's worthlessness from the violent arguments between his parents.

"I met so-and-so," the actor would say. "He thinks he has a part for me."

"Did he promise anything?"

"He couldn't promise anything — he doesn't have financing yet."

"No wonder he has a part for you."

"So he's a big talker, what can I do about it? That's all we've got to go on, love — phony promises from a bunch of phonies. But one of them always turns out to be for real. Remember the time . . ."

Barbara Niven was a pale, pretty redhead with slanting cheekbones which distanced her amber eyes; both the cheekbones and the eyes were easily inflamed by resentment. At the beginning of their marriage she had had boundless faith in her husband's talent, and now she couldn't forgive him for failing to live up to her expectations. She would listen to him with a peculiarly mixed expression of disdain and distress, as if she wished to dismiss him contemptuously and at the same time plead with him piteously to leave her alone. When she couldn't stand it any longer, she would interrupt him with an insult. "You're the leading actor in every picture they never make."

"What kind of a bitchy, irrational, insane remark is that?"

"I see you bought yourself a new shirt."

"If we had what you spend at the hairdresser, we'd be millionaires."

Like all insolvent couples, they reproached each other for every penny spent.

In fairness to Dana Niven, it must be noted that under the circumstances he was a model family man. Despising his colleagues who left their families with in-laws back in the States while they kept company with vagrant starlets and script girls, he would not part from his wife and son. "We're Catholics," he often said. "Lapsed Catholics, but Catholics all the same. We were married in church." He no longer believed in God, but as far as he was concerned people who had no use for religion because they didn't believe in God were the same sort of literal-minded fools who had no use for *Hamlet* because they didn't believe in ghosts. He saw a profound meaning in every Christian rite and myth.

"I believe in the Holy Family," he would declare, lifting his son above his head, then seating him on his knee. "It's all right to be on the run as long as we're riding the same donkey."

He made heroic efforts to keep his family housed, clothed and fed, spending almost nothing on himself and even giving up cigarettes and liquor in order to save money and keep in shape for his work. But all this counted for very little when they were running out of cash and no new supply was in sight. The couple had especially bitter arguments about his unfortunate name, which only made it more difficult for him to establish a public identity for himself, at the time when the English film star David Niven was at the height of his well-deserved popularity.

"People will have to take me as I am," he insisted. "I was born a Niven and I'm going to die a Niven. I don't care how many other Nivens there are. Let David Niven change *his* name!"

"Why don't you call yourself Saint Joseph?"

"Very funny."

Nor would he listen to suggestions that he should try some other occupation.

A talented linguist fluent in Italian, French, Spanish and German, who could have made a good living as a translator for some UN commission (all the more so as his knowledge was officially certified by a degree in modern languages from Columbia University), he wasted his expertise on the unpaid labor of translating plays in which he thought he could star. Worse, his choice of texts lacked practical wisdom: he translated only foreign classics no one wanted to stage. He was much taken, for instance, by Heinrich von Kleist (1777–1811), whose plays required a quick-witted audience. Producers, notorious for not wishing to exclude the slow-witted, showed no interest in a dead and difficult German playwright. Niven would have been better off translating bedroom farces, but to the despair of his wife he persisted in his odd preferences. A run of bad luck either breaks a man's spirit or inflames it, and Dana Niven bore his insignificance in an increasingly stubborn and cocky temper. The passions he had no chance of performing fed the passions of his pride; he would neither give up nor give in. But then, all artists who survive at all are geniuses in the art of endurance.

When Mark complained about their lot, Niven would silence him with a curt but deeply felt reply: "Life's tough, kid."

"That's a lie!" the boy muttered to himself.

Life was easy and grand — he had seen it with his own eyes, staying for short periods in the rich houses of his father's successful colleagues, and visiting the palaces of the European aristocracy with his mother. Thanks to Barbara Niven's enthusiasm for painting, sculpture and beautiful buildings, intensified by her need to get away from her husband, the boy in fact spent more time in palaces of priceless grandeur than many a poor prince.

The Villa Borghese in Rome made an especially profound impression on him. It was in this twin-towered summer palace, full of light and air, that he came upon the most fantastic apparition. A beautiful girl, slim and naked, was trying to tear herself away from a man who was seizing her from behind, clutching her smooth belly; she had just cried out, her mouth was still shaped in an O, her arms were raised for flight, but her legs were already turning into the trunk of a tree and leaves were sprouting from the tips of her delicate fingers. Even Mark's mother, who knew the story of the god who caught a nymph and held a tree, and had seen photographs of Bernini's rendering of this supreme moment of thwarted desire, couldn't help staring with amazement. Mark kept circling the thing, reaching out to grab Apollo's cold smooth white marble foot when he thought no one was looking. After this almost traumatic experience of joy and wonder he began to pay particular attention to trees.

More significantly, he grew increasingly fond of works of art, the glory of the rich, and developed a corresponding horror of everything ugly and cheap, finding his family's straitened circumstances ever more intolerable and unjust.

There were times when he summoned enough courage to talk back to his father: life wasn't hard for everybody.

The actor raised his eyebrows to high heaven. "What are you talking about? Do you think I'm having fun?'' he asked, speaking with more bitterness than his son could muster. ''You'd better take my word for it, kid. Life is tough — it can't be helped.''

The bliss of Mark Niven's boyhood was the daydream that he wasn't really his parents' child.

4

Money Is the Only Home

"For I have to go to England and be a lord,"
explained Cedric sweet-temperedly.
FRANCES HODGSON BURNETT

M ARK dreamed for himself the thrill of perfect surprise.
In the evening as they were having supper a messenger would
arrive — a beautiful Italian girl who introduced herself as the Contessina Giulietta Silvana Paolina Francesca Teresa Borghese. Greeting the
Nivens familiarly, she announced that what she was about to tell them
was going to be a shock. Mark's parents grew pale and silent, but he
went on sipping his tomato juice, unconcerned and unsuspecting.

"It's about you, Marco," the Contessina said, making eyes at him
and shaking her long jet-black, blond or curly titian hair (he invented
her in various shapes and colors according to his mood). She noticed
that he had a sad, suffering face, and wanted to kiss him on the mouth
as soon as they were alone. But Mark was rude to her at first. "I don't
even know you. What do you want?" She pleaded that she had good
news for him. "What news?" he asked skeptically, then thought hard
about the answer, carefully perfecting her reply until it had a whiff of
murder about it. "I imagine you'll be relieved to learn that you are not
the son of this no-good actor," she remarked with aristocratic nonchalance. The no-good actor gave her one of his black looks, but the Contessina was no more impressed than the producers who turned him down
at auditions. "He acts big at home," she observed, "but he's really quite
a useless person, isn't he?" Mark took exception to this and insisted
that she apologize.

To insult his father by proxy and come to his defense at the same time
was one of the very best parts of the daydream, allowing Mark to savor
the joys of both vengeance and magnanimity.

"Why should you try to defend him?" the Contessina demanded impatiently. "Doesn't he keep dragging you about from one place to another, giving you absolutely no say in the matter? He can't even look after you properly! Do you have the faintest idea what you're going to live on in a week's time? You don't imagine that your real father would treat you like that, do you?''

And indeed, had Mark not heard his mother telling the actor that if he were a *real father* he would have given up acting long ago? This always struck Mark as the supreme truth and inspired him to the thought that she wouldn't tolerate her husband's profession either, if she were a *real mother*. He was convinced that they would both have had greater consideration for their own flesh and blood.

The Contessina arrived to save him just in the nick of time.

"The fact is, *caro mio,* your name is not Mark Niven at all," she declared. "You are Il Principe Marco Giovanni Lorenzo Alessandro Ippolito Borghese, the future head of our family. And I have come to take you away from these people, so that you can assume your rightful position in the world."

Mark made a determined effort to keep his feet on the ground; he didn't want to get carried away. "You're crazy," he protested. "Go away, stop upsetting my parents. *Via, via!''*

"Don't you want the Borghese fortune?"

Of all the questions Mark imagined the Contessina asking, this was the one that shook him most. There was no doubt that the Borghese fortune would solve all his problems. The Contessina assured him that the Villa Borghese, along with the great Bernini's creations inhabiting it, would be handed back to him with the Italian government's apologies. "Of course the villa and park on the Pincio represent only a small, insignificant portion of your *patrimonio,''* she explained, and however reluctantly, Mark couldn't help listening to the dear girl's inventory of all the palaces, parks, forests, art treasures and secret Swiss bank accounts that would come to him. "Now that we've traced you, your worries are over," she said, "nobody will ever bother you about the rent. You'll own all the palaces where you want to stay. And if you don't already own them, you can buy them. Your *legali* will look after it."

Perhaps on account of the extraordinary impression Bernini's statues had made on him, Mark preferred to be claimed by the Borghese above all other rich and ancient families. Still, he wasn't pigheaded about it. In Madrid, for instance, after his walks in the Prado, he used to be visited by the Duchess of Alba. In England, after touring Syon House with his mother, he toyed with the idea of becoming the Duke of Northumberland. The duke's niece would materialize to inform him that he was the next in line.

"My dear girl," he told her firmly, "you're talking absolute rubbish. how could I be an English duke? I'm an American. I've seen my birth certificate with my own eyes, and it says I was born in New York City, in the state of New York." He related his mother's version of events, which was that he had been taken to London in a carrycot when he was three months old.

"A likely story!" scoffed the Hon. Lady Margaret. "You'd remember if you'd been there. Why, have you ever *seen* New York?"

There she scored a point. Mark had no memory of his native city, and the circumstances of his birth had always struck him as rather mysterious. Nor had he ever met his grandparents, who were supposed to live in Rochester, New York, or indeed any of his parents' relatives.

SINCE the Nivens wanted a multilingual education for their son, and in any case could not afford the private schools for Americans abroad, Mark attended the local schools wherever they went.

In the Italian school he sang *Fratelli d'Italia, l'Italia s'è desta* with Roman fervor; at the Ecole des Garçons in Paris, as a seven-year-old *citoyen aristo,* he proudly joined in the rallying cry of the revolution, *Allons, enfants de la patrie;* in London, he was an English lord imploring God to save his gracious Queen, to *Send her victorious, Happy and glorious* — and he often saw himself riding through the green and misty countryside with Prince Charles. Later he poured the loneliness of a much-dragged-about only child, his fear of being left out, into the Falangist song of allegiance to Spain:

> *Cara al sol*
> *con la camisa nueva*
> *que tu bordaste en rojo ayer*
> *Hallaré la muerte si me llega . . .*

But then they moved to Italy again.

> *Fratelli d'Italia, l'Italia s'è desta,*
> *Dell'elmo di Scipio s'è cinta la testa . . .*

Which was how, while enjoying all the advantages of travel, Mark also acquired an acute sense of dislocation. Where he was born he didn't stay, where he stayed he didn't stay long enough; he was from too many places and from nowhere in particular; he had no emotional address.

There were times, of course, when he felt safe and accepted his parents as legitimate. Their fortunes changed decidedly for the better when his father was finally given a leading part, the title role in a new version of *The Count of Monte Cristo,* to be filmed in Paris. It was no mere promise: the contract was signed and they received fifteen thousand dollars, with the additional sum of forty-five thousand dollars to follow on completion of the film. This was more money than Niven had earned in his entire life up to that moment.

The best thing was that they acquired a permanent home of their own.

It had belonged to an Olivetti executive who, unexpectedly transferred back to Milan, offered most of the furnishings for only ten thousand dollars to anyone who would take over his lease. The apartment was painted sky-blue and dove-gray, ivory and gold; all the paneling was finely carved, fluted and gilded, and everywhere there were mirrors. One of the most fascinating objects in the place was the big bed in Mark's parents' room, which had a canopy over it and gauzy curtains hanging down on all sides like a tent. His own room had something equally enthralling: a long, low velvet chair with a curved backrest, on which he could sit up and lie down at the same time. Curtains, cushions, upholstery, everything that was soft was made of silk or satin or velvet. The décor had in fact been inspired by Marie Antoinette's octagonal boudoir at Versailles, gratifying the Olivetti executive's taste for the style of the *ancien ré-gime*. His mother thought that it was "too much of a good thing", but Mark didn't find anything too much or too much of anything as he went about straightening the velvet cushions and studying his reflection in all the mirrors.

The rent was exorbitant, on account of the view: the apartment was on the fourth floor at 48, quai d'Orléans, on the south side of the Ile Saint-Louis, and the windows of the salon and Mark's bedroom faced Notre Dame to the right, and the river and the Left Bank straight ahead, with the dome of the Pantheon rising over the rooftops, emphasizing the immensity of the sky. It was the last grand view of Paris, just before the monstrous tower blocks were built. Mark felt that they were actually living inside the bright, clear sky that enveloped them from all sides, through the floor-to-ceiling windows and their reflections in the mirrors, which were placed precisely to create this effect. It was more exciting than flying: they were up in the air, yet there was no tilting and the earth stayed reassuringly close.

"We're rich, my pets," the actor said when he first led his wife and son into their new home. "We're safe and snug. From now on we can eat whether the phone rings or not."

Barbara and Dana Niven reacted to this unexpected turn of events by falling in love again.

Every day the boy could witness scenes between his parents which were utterly at variance with their former bickering. His mother would suddenly go and kiss the back of his father's neck, for no apparent reason. And one day he saw his father run out of the bathroom naked, waving a big fleecy towel like a bullfighter making passes with his cape, challenging her to charge him. She lowered her head and began puffing and snorting and ran at him, butting her head against his bare stomach; then they disappeared into their room with the tentlike bed, laughing.

Observing this incident, Mark felt elated and reassured without knowing why. And he himself got his share of all the hugging and kissing around the house. His mother pressed him to her breasts and showered him with endearments. "My heart," she whispered into his ear, "my dove, my prince, my lion, my pet, my sweet, my angel, my life, what a beautiful boy you are, you are, what a beautiful boy you are!" At first he was stiff, afraid that she would push him away again, but in their new home on the Ile Saint-Louis he could hang on to her, sniffing her body and perfume, for as long as he liked.

In the evenings they had dinner parties in restaurants, talking and laughing until well past his bedtime (especially when their party included a portly young actor-playwright from London named Peter Ustinov) or sat in their blue and gold salon, planning their future.

Mark's mother objected to the twenty-year lease, well aware of the problems they would face with his father becoming a star. "Dan, really, we can't stay in Paris all our life — most of your work from now on is going to be in Hollywood."

"So what? We'll be able to keep the place even if we aren't using it. It's only four thousand francs a month."

"*Only* four thousand francs!"

"Relax, love, I'll be getting a fortune for my next picture. And what could be more sensible than keeping a few apartments here and there, in exciting parts of the world? Mark, should we have nice little hideouts like this in all the places we've been to? Would you approve of that?"

"I didn't really like Madrid," said Mark, thinking of all the water he had drunk there.

"Very well, then, Madrid is out!" exclaimed the actor, rubbing his hands as if he had just won a fortune at roulette. Some scenes of the film were already shot and it was the gossip in the trade that *Monte Cristo* was going to be a great costume thriller which would make him an international star. "We'll have apartments in Paris, Rome, Venice, Barcelona, and a villa at Cap Ferrat. And to hell with *pensioni!*"

Mark loved every word of the conversation and everything about their new life: buying books and prints, taking riding and tennis lessons at a club in Neuilly, eating the world's most expensive strawberry tarts at a café on an island in the Bois. Still, what he liked best was staying at home in the apartment on the Ile Saint-Louis. It was an absolute joy to live on a small island yet right at the center of a great city. What he felt contemplating the visible evidence of this magic circumstance — stretched out on his gray velvet chaise longue by his floor-to-ceiling window, open to the river and the willow trees, the rooftops and spires — can be imagined only by readers who still remember the sublime moments of their childhood.

THE producer of the film, whom they could thank for their good fortune, dropped by for a drink every other day or so. A pale, bald man with tufts of hair above his ears and a melancholy smile, he paid little attention to Mark as a rule, but one evening he emerged from a confidential talk with Niven in the bedroom, took the boy's head between his moist hands and looked at him with soft eyes, like the priests in Spain.

"Mark," he said in the grave, quiet voice of true faith, "I want you to know one thing. Your father is the greatest actor alive. I'm not a man to pay compliments lightly, but he's the best there is. If I had to choose between Larry Olivier and Dana Niven, I'd choose Dana Niven any day."

The producer left swiftly before Mark had time to feel proud or to notice that his father's face had turned black — so black that his mother ran for ice cubes and placed them over his father's heart and on his forehead, fearing that he might have a stroke.

"Are you all right?" she kept asking him.

The film was off. The producer had come to deliver the news that the famous actress who played the heroine had withdrawn and the backers had cut off further funds.

As Niven was once more out of work and had less than a thousand dollars left from his original advance, he could not, of course, afford to keep the flat on the quai d'Orléans. To attract a tenant who would take over the lease immediately, he had to offer the furniture and fittings for half the price he had paid for them. Apart from the clear loss of five thousand dollars on the furnishings, which they had used for less than three months, Barbara Niven calculated that they had spent at least a thousand dollars entertaining people and over two thousand buying things they could easily have done without. They moved to a cold-water flat in Montparnasse and through the summer she often dropped whatever she was doing to exclaim despairingly: "If we'd only known that the first fifteen thousand was going to be the last!"

'Bon Dieu!' thought Mark, 'they're going to starve me!'

FOR weeks Mark had nightmares of a terrible hunger gnawing at his stomach. He dreamed of begging the soft-eyed producer for food, but the man shook his head sadly and went on eating his sandwich all by himself . . . he begged in the street, but people passed him by, shrugging their shoulders, and the terrible stone gargoyles of Notre Dame came to life, whipping the air with their long tongues and shrieking viciously, *let him die, who cares!*

But in the morning as he washed and dressed for school he would imagine that he was getting ready to leave for the airport: he would climb into his private plane and zoom away, leaving the Nivens to their own devices. The thrilling speed and ease of it all helped him through the day, and when he was in bed again at night he stared at the cracked and stained walls of his odiously drab little room picturing to himself a great hall richly hung with tapestries and thronged with his aristocratic relations, who could not understand how the young prince could ever have thought he had any connection with a poor actor and his wife. However, when he was left alone with his true parents, Mark had to admit that he was worried about how the Nivens would get along without him. "You know, *mon père*," he remarked to the Duc d'Orléans, "I feel badly about the Nivens. I'm sure they tried to do their best in their own way. Shouldn't we do something for them?"

"*Avec plaisir, Marc!*" exclaimed the Duchesse, running her fingertips through her auburn hair, "we'll invite them to dinner as often as you like."

"And we might let the poor woman cook now and then," the young prince suggested, emboldened. "She isn't bad when she has the money — she makes excellent *crêpes* and *tarte aux pommes.*"

"Ah, *très bien,*" approved the Duc d'Orléans. "Their trouble is," he added knowingly, "producers don't give the man a chance. I had my steward look into the whole thing."

"That's just it! You hit the nail right on the head. If he'd been given a chance, he and his wife wouldn't fight so much and he wouldn't have to worry all the time about his double chin."

"I'll tell you what we'll do," the Duc d'Orléans said, taking out his fountain pen and his Swiss checkbook. "I'll write him a check so that he can produce his own historical costume drama in Cinerama and Technicolor, making sure he can start over again if his leading lady quits."

"That would do it," Marc agreed enthusiastically. "He'd be all set after a wide-screen costume drama in Technicolor."

The Duc d'Orléans wrote out a check for fifty million Swiss francs right then and there. "I wonder — who should present M. et Mme Niven with this little token of our appreciation?"

"*Mais, ça va sans dire,* it must be Marc!*" the Duchesse declared. "He must go and give it to them in person."

Such happy fancies gave him courage to fall asleep.

Of course there were a great many other variations on the daydream. On days when he was fed up with girls, the messenger would be an elderly silver-haired lawyer. But whatever the details there was one constantly recurring element: Mark absolutely refused to believe that he could be an immensely rich aristocrat, that such a dramatic transformation was within the realm of possibilities. "A boy can't become a prince just like that," he protested. "It's all nonsense!" His mother would cry helplessly at having to part with him and his father would bite his lips, having lost all hope, while Mark still insisted that the whole thing must be some stupid joke. He allowed himself to be convinced only after being presented with numerous and incontestable proofs.

From earliest childhood Mark Niven dreamed of himself as a hardheaded, practical, down-to-earth realist. On occasions when he felt guilty about imagining things, he consoled himself with the reflection that after all he was dreaming about money.

5

A View of Toledo

My idea, having performed its acrobatic capers,
became a fixed idea . . . I cannot think
of anything in the world so fixed.

MACHADO DE ASSIS

ALTHOUGH the notion of a struggling actor's son that he was actually
a mighty prince has its funny side, in truth it was a very serious
business with far-reaching consequences both for good and ill. A child's
dreams are not idle fancies, they are the means by which he creates the
person he is going to become.

Indeed, who could fail to see that Il Principe Marco Giovanni Lorenzo Alessandro Ippolito Borghese was not going to be a mere victim
of his circumstances?

Most children who are subjected to extreme insecurity or deprivation
are blighted for life by the threats to their survival: panic dissolves their
inner strength and turns it to venom; they grow humble and sly, spine-
less and vicious. Not to blame yet condemned, molded for subservience
and betrayal, they conform according to their needs and pounce according to their opportunities. Such are the dregs of humanity, Shakespeare's swelling mob, the helpless but dangerous rabble, from whose
ranks Mark was saved by conferring upon himself the advantages of noble birth. He made himself a prince — and what does a true prince know
about servitude and compliance, pilfering, backbiting and twisting arms
to *get ahead?* He is already there. He has the privilege of honor, the
sword of an independent spirit, a multitude of generous and willful sentiments, the courage of great armies and the revenues of royal expectations to maintain them. A prince does not mix with the crowd, he has
no desire to get involved in sordid wrangles with indifferent or hostile
people; he covets nothing that is theirs, he wants only what is his by
birthright.

Mark did not disclose his dreams to anyone, but his father could guess

23

a great deal from the boy's fierce silences and his manner of bearing up to the solitude of travel.

"He'll end up doing something crazy with his life," Niven told his wife with deep apprehension.

"Look who's talking!" she retorted, blaming her husband and defending her child.

Shy and withdrawn by nature and habit, never staying anywhere long enough to make friends or keep them, Mark lived in his head. Through curiosity about his aristocratic forebears he became interested in history and, later, in romantic novels. History confirmed his conviction that he would have to look after himself, and romantic novels reassured him that it could be done. Historical figures who could also have been the heroes of romantic fiction were especially dear to him; General San Martín became his idol long before he figured out any connection between himself and the Liberator of Argentina, Chile and Peru. And he was enthralled by the character his father had nearly played in the film, Dumas' Count of Monte Cristo, who was betrayed and abominably persecuted, but found a fantastic fortune inside a rock in the sea. Mark didn't actually read Dumas' novel until after the film was canceled and they were banished from their home on the quai d'Orléans, but then it became his favorite book.

In turn, Monte Cristo's luck got him interested in books about buried treasure.

For a long time he couldn't quite decide whether he should be found by aristocratic parents or find a fortune on his own. In one respect this singular boy was not unlike millions: he longed for the good life without either slaving or stealing for it.

He was only fourteen when he set his heart on solving this insoluble problem.

The Nivens were spending the summer in Madrid, as Dana Niven had been hired for a few shoot-outs in a Western to be filmed on the plains of La Mancha, and on one of the actor's free days in August the family boarded a bus to take a look at nearby Toledo. It was during this sightseeing excursion that Mark decided, in a fit of bitterness, to stake his life on an unlikely enterprise. Despite his youth, it was a fateful decision. Sensible plans are often abandoned but senseless ones hardly ever; people persist in their most doubtful undertakings with the most obsessive determination. Obsessions grow from uncertainties.

As for the excursion to Toledo, Mark was pleased with his parents for thinking of it. The seat of ancient kings and Inquisitors General inspired him with the joy of recognition; he was delighted to find that its atmosphere of menacing splendor so faithfully reflected what he knew about its history, a chronicle of almost unrelieved horror from the time of the Visigoths to the 1930s Civil War. The somber buildings with their fortified entrances, the dark, twisting passages, the sudden spires, the whole uncannily beautiful city seemed imbued with the spirit of torture and bloodbaths. "No wonder El Greco painted people with long faces," remarked Dana Niven. In the cathedral, though, they were surprised by Narciso Tome's exuberant altarpiece which billows up to heaven, splitting open the distant roof, and is held up by two of the pluckiest little cherubs who ever shouldered fifty-seven tons of stucco and marble.

Mark also received presents, even though his birthday had been celebrated a couple of days earlier. After their visit to the cathedral they stopped by a secondhand bookshop and his father invited him to look and see whether any of the old books might interest him. From the pile on the trestle table outside the shop Mark chose a worn and bulky volume — bulky not because of its length but on account of the large typeface and thick pages, made of the sort of crude and heavy paper used for popular books at the turn of the century. It was a copy of Enrique Menéndez's pioneering work on sunken treasure ships, *Tesoros al Fondo del Mar,* the second edition, printed in 1908. Dana Niven never forgave himself for buying the book: it was the wrong present at the wrong time, and he brooded on the question of whether his son would have ended up the same way without it. But how was he to know, back then in Toledo, that there could be any harm in letting the boy have a dusty old volume which would help him to improve his Spanish?

"The worst of it is," he said bleakly, relating the incident many years later, on a film set in Marseilles, "I never wanted so much to make him happy. We both wanted to give him a special treat that day."

At a souvenir shop in the same street, which was so narrow that Mark, stretching out his arms, could touch the houses on both sides at once, his mother bought him an elaborately carved chess set with figures in medieval attire, and the diary in blue morocco leather with a Toledo sword on its cover. He never used the chess set, but he tried his hand at the diary later that day, expressing his conviction that "people just do not give a damn about each other".

Toledo was the right place for such a reflection, by no means a new one for the young misanthrope, and he could still be lighthearted about the bitter truth when they stopped in the Plaza Zocodover, the chief place of execution on the Iberian peninsula for over a thousand years.

"Take a really good look," Mark was saying in his usual way of sharing his historical knowledge with his parents, who were always keen to learn. "This square has probably soaked up more human blood than any other spot in Europe. See that arch over there? That's called the Puerta de Sangre. It was right here that King Pedro the Cruel used to burn women at the stake just because they refused to sleep with him. I'm not kidding. Any woman who wouldn't sleep with him was tied to a stake and burned to ashes." Then he added with the air of someone setting a trap: "I bet you think that's why he was called *the Cruel*, hey?"

"Why, of course," said his father, who played the straight man in this sort of conversation. "They couldn't have called him Pedro the Cruel for any other reason. Unless he did something even beastlier than that."

Mark grinned triumphantly. "You're wrong! They didn't mind him burning anybody. They called him the Cruel because he wouldn't let them massacre the Jews."

"But how cruel of him!" exclaimed the actor.

"Well, so much for people," Mark concluded cheerfully. So much for the species who didn't care whether the Nivens lived or starved.

They had lunch at the Parador Conde de Orgaz, a recently built replica of a 16th-century coaching inn on the crest of a hill on the other side of the river, where they could sit on the terrace and enjoy a panoramic view of the city. Set high on its great rock, ringed by its ancient walls and the River Tagus, solitary Toledo towered so distinctly apart from the rest of the world that it seemed not even time could touch it.

MARK's parents had brought him to the ancient capital to show him the wonders of the place and to tell him that they were going to get a divorce. It was at the end of their lunch, when Mark had assured them that he couldn't possibly eat anything more, not even another *bollo de crema,* that they finally broke the news. His mother was going to marry the jolly, rich Dutch architect whom they had met in London the previous winter and had been running into here and there ever since — alone or in the company of his two snooty daughters, who were now to become Mark's stepsisters.

"But we're Catholics!" Mark objected, his voice breaking. "You *have* to stay married. We've got to ride the same donkey."

The actor gave no sign of remembering. "These things happen," he said, straightening his back against the back of his chair. "People get divorced every day."

Mark was offered the choice of going to live with his mother and her new family in their comfortable home in Amsterdam or staying on the road with his father. Both parents insisted that his happiness came first and they would go along with his decision whatever it might be — which only convinced him that neither of them wanted him. Back in his hotel room in Madrid the next day, succumbing to terror and panic, he tore up all his handkerchiefs — the only things he could destroy undetected and not keep hearing about it — and such secret rages would recur for months. But in Toledo he refused to give his parents the satisfaction of showing that he was affected by the blow. "Well, at least I won't have to listen to you two fighting all the time," he told them. "It's a *relief.*"

Indeed, only moments later his mother started to argue that he should have been told sooner, before they came to Spain, and then the couple went off to quarrel in private.

Left by himself on the terrace, with the river far below and Toledo straight ahead of him in the sky, floating in the haze of the August afternoon heat, Mark wondered about all the times during the past year when his mother had gone sight-seeing on her own, telling him that he should stay home and study. She had lied to him. She loved a stranger more than she loved him. Jealousy made him experience the keenest sense of abandonment: he would never again daydream of imaginary parents. What was the use of rosy fantasies?

He took his presents from his mother's basket to see what he had, and after flipping through the empty pages of his leather-bound diary, searched the basket for a pen. Having found one, he started to write the story of his life, so that people would know what he had been through — but he wrote only a few sentences before deciding that nobody would be interested in his troubles. Then he picked up the old book his father had bought him and, wiping his eyes, read a paragraph here and there until he came upon the story of Captain Parry's ship, the *Flora*.

"Riquezas envueltas en horror y misterio," wrote Menéndez, giving a three-page account of the gold crowns and ingots, replicas of the Madonna of Lima and jeweled crosses, and noting that this floating treasure house was presumed to have gone down in the great hurricane of 1820, somewhere in the northwestern Bahamas. Racing through the chapter, Mark immediately knew that the *Flora* was *his ship.* (It was not until the next day that he started to worry about the possibility that someone might have found the wreck since Menéndez's book was published in 1908.) In his desolate mood, what enthralled him was not so much the description of the cargo as the revolting murders committed for it; they vouched for its value and made the treasures as real as if he had touched them.

'That's how it is, that's life,' he reflected, deciding to take diving lessons. 'People are monsters and I'd better get rich or I'll have to depend on monsters. I have to stop wasting my time.'

Having forsworn wishful thinking once and for all, Mark began to daydream about finding the bountiful wreck — distracted somewhat by the miraculous view of Toledo, suspended between heaven and the parched earth with its churches, monasteries and fortresses, pale gray, umber and gold in the shimmering haze.

Father and Son

Is he a serious person or just a fool?
DOSTOEVSKY

MARK chose to stay with his father, who managed to get a part in a Spanish television series as a wicked English lord, so that the boy could complete a full year in the same school in Madrid. Proud and relieved that his son was not deserting him, Niven soon had to face the fact that he was losing him just the same, as Mark began to lead his own life with a purposeful air. His room filled up with maps, wind charts, books on sunken treasure and Latin America — and he had very little time for conversation.

At first Niven thought it was a passing phase, a schoolboy's hobby, but school had become a tiresome waste of time for Mark now that there was something he really wanted to learn, and he spent his days in the archives of the Museo Naval in Madrid, reading the logbooks of Spanish ships that might have passed by the northwestern Bahamas in September 1820.

"Your mother will say I can't look after you!" Niven protested, after hearing from the director of the *gimnasio* Mark was supposed to be attending. "Don't be such a fool, please. It's impossible to find witnesses to an accident that happened at a busy intersection in the city last night, but you think you're going to find an eyewitness report about a shipwreck that happened hundreds of years ago —"

"It wasn't even a hundred and fifty years ago."

"— out in the wide Atlantic? In a *hurricane?*"

"Maybe after the hurricane. Lots of ships could have sighted the wreckage in the water or on the reefs. That would be recorded in their logbooks."

"I'm not going to let you drop out of school, and that's the end of it!"

Mark promised to reform but continued to play truant with as many excuses as he could think of, which were accepted without demur by his teachers; they didn't intend to wear themselves out trying to reform a transient foreigner. These *profesores* wore faded dark suits and were given to strumming their waistcoats with the dignified resignation of ill-paid gentlemen, and they listened to Mark's lies with boredom and a visible effort to appear credulous. 'They'd rather be somewhere else themselves,' Mark reflected. 'And if I stay poor I'll be like them, I'll have to spend my whole life in a place that makes me sick, just to keep myself alive.' His bright, intelligent eyes blazed with the flames of his resolution never to submit to such a fate.

In early December he disappeared with the money for his new winter coat. The police had no success in tracing him alive or dead. A week later he reappeared, with blue lips and running nose, half frozen but happy.

"Are you trying to kill me?" his father asked in a weak voice, cowed by nights of sleepless terror.

"I'm going to make it up to you, Dad," Mark said, hugging his father in a sudden rush of affection. "I would have asked you, but I knew you wouldn't let me go."

He had been in Seville, exploring the Archives of the Indies. "Just imagine," he said as his father was making tea for them, "they have a copy of the *Flora*'s last manifest. It's all true. There are a hundred and twenty-six solid gold statuettes of the Madonna of Lima in the hold. And seventeen thousand gold bars, each one kilo. That's seventeen tons of gold!"

"What, no diamonds?"

"Diamonds too — but diamonds are nothing, Dad! They're the most famous just because there are a lot of them — the world is full of diamonds. Emeralds are the real thing — they're the rarest and most beautiful stones. Did you know that the reason the Pharaohs were so rich was that they had an emerald mine? A girl at the Archives of the Indies told me that. We were talking about this famous cross, la Cruz de las Siete Esmeraldas. Seven emeralds as big as plums — and that cross is on my ship! It was blessed by St. Pius V in the 16th century — it says so right on the manifest because that makes it more valuable. It was just a simple gold cross with seven opals when St. Pius V blessed it. The emeralds are from Muzo in Colombia — they were put in two centuries later when the cross was taken to South America. I'll never sell that cross."

"But what will you do for a winter coat?"

Mark was taken aback for a moment; he still felt the terrible cold of the train. Then he shrugged defiantly, thinking of General San Martín riding through the icy mists of the Andes. "I don't mind the cold," he said.

Niven hoped the craze would pass once they left Spain, but when they got to Paris, Mark began to frequent the maritime archives and the Bibliothèque Nationale to look for references to the *Flora* in old logbooks and seamen's memoirs. He was the busiest young man. He earned money by selling the *Herald Tribune* on the boulevard de l'Opéra and bought an aqualung and scuba gear to practice diving in the Seine. To have fun, he went for long walks in the Louvre, just as in Madrid he had gone for walks in the Prado; strolling through palaces packed with great works of art had the sort of intoxicating effect on him that music has on others. At night, wanting to know more about the origins of his future wealth, he read Latin American history. On the wall over his bed were pictures stolen from library books — a portrait of General San Martín and a photograph of the statue of the Virgin in the Cathedral of Lima. On his visits to libraries he carried a razor blade in a matchbox, to cut out pages that interested him.

"I don't think it's such a great idea to grow up in dusty old libraries," the actor said to his son, who was looking more like him every month while becoming ever more distant.

"I dive a lot."

"Don't remind me."

"Anyway, libraries aren't dusty," Mark explained. "Librarians are fussy people, they dust things even with their handkerchiefs."

Thus passed nearly two years.

TRYING to cope with his adolescent son on his own, Niven had to bear the full burden of parental impotence. At times he felt tempted to beat some sense into Mark's head, but was restrained by the warning example of several of his colleagues whose children had disappeared for good. So he was reduced to fretting and nagging.

"You can't expect me to support you forever, you know," he said darkly.

"That's all right, I'll be a millionaire," replied Mark jauntily, pocketing his hands. "Quite apart from everything else, I'll have seven hundred forty-three thousand and fifty gold doubloons." (He knew the *Flora*'s manifest by heart.)

"Even if you find some reference to the wreck, which you won't, where will it get you? There are wrecks that were pinpointed on the map centuries ago and still nobody can find them!"

"You've been reading my books," Mark said with a grin. It was a serene and unconcerned grin, a rich man's grin, in fact — the kind of grin Niven saw on the faces of producers when he tried to impress upon them how badly he needed a job — the amiable, complacent grin of somebody who doesn't hear you but is willing to let you talk.

Staring at this grin, Niven grew disgusted with himself. He had sworn repeatedly that he would not argue, he knew that it was useless, yet he could not stop — and each time he was surprised that he made no impression! But no sooner had such reflections reduced him to grim apathy than another argument would occur to him and he would start up again, unable to accept the fact that nothing he could say would make any difference.

"If I were you," Niven said in a flat, colorless voice, bored by his own obstinacy, "I'd try to think of the big letdown, the bitter end all this will come to: You fill your head with gold coins, gold bars, emeralds, and some day you'll wake up to find yourself working in a gas station. I can't see anything else for you, the way you keep skipping school."

"Who needs it, sitting there all day wasting time? I pass my exams. You have a mania about school!"

"That's right. Your great-grandparents on both sides came from Scotland, and the Scots are fanatical about education. So you should be too."

"I speak four languages, what do you want?"

"I speak five and where does it get me?"

"Nowhere!" Mark shot back triumphantly. "And you have a degree from Columbia."

This was true and it riled Niven. "Sometimes I think if you were less bright you wouldn't be such an idiot!" he exclaimed, flaring up again.

Mark squinted as if to keep the insult out of his eyes. "You should be glad I don't drop acid or smoke or drink — you should be proud of me instead of criticizing me all the time!"

"If you want to do something crazy, why don't you be an actor? OK, let that go. But how about painting?"

Mark, who had moments when he felt ashamed of not being able to act or paint, blushed deeply and shot an angry look at his father.

"You fall in love with every Perugino woman you ever lay eyes on," Niven persisted, deciding that if he was doomed to be tormented with worry about his son, he would rather have him be an artist. "I'll never forget how excited you were when you and your mother came back from Firenze. So why don't you paint?"

"You only say these things to put me down!"

"No, I mean it. I think your trees were really good."

The boy raised his head with a mixture of belligerence and pride, daring his father to laugh at him. "I'll make my contribution to history in my own way."

"Well, at least you know you need talent to be an artist, that's something," sighed the actor.

"You fuss too much, Dad," Mark replied with the infuriating condescension of a sixteen-year-old who knew what he was about. "Relax."

Yet in many ways he was an ideal son.

Now that they were on their own they divided the household chores between them, each keeping his own room in order and taking weekly turns at preparing breakfast, washing the dishes, cleaning the apartment and going to the launderette. The problems of shopping for the best and cheapest coffee, yoghurt or soap were discussed between them as the weightiest matters. In all this the boy did his fair share before disappearing for the rest of the day.

Even his orderly habits, however, alarmed his father. Niven couldn't suppress the feeling that there was something profoundly unnatural about the methodical way Mark had settled down to trace a long-lost ship as if preparing himself for any normal profession with certain if modest rewards. It was this apparent unawareness that there was anything odd or unreasonable about the whole enterprise that scared Niven the most. When he was alone at home during the day he couldn't resist going into Mark's room — a room like the cabin of a studious petty officer, packed but neat, filled with maps, charts and other reminders of the sea. The sight of the aqualung in the corner made him break out in a cold sweat.

In the evening Mark would show up at their regular eating place, Chartier, carrying his notes and his thoughts, bumping into tables, or, worse, wielding a huge rolled-up chart. The diners ducked their heads, the waiters exchanged gleeful looks. Mark didn't notice. 'They think he's strange too,' Niven observed, 'and they don't even know him.'

Yet, though the waiters confirmed his own view, he tipped them less because of it.

ONE evening at Chartier Niven was seized by the extravagant hope that sex would save his son.

The grand old wood-paneled restaurant in the rue du Faubourg Montmartre, with its sawdust-strewn floors and its gaslight chandeliers now filled with electric bulbs, had been serving the best cheap meals in Paris ever since the Great Exhibition of 1869 and was still the most popular eating place for the poor but well-informed. It had also the additional attraction of an upstairs gallery along one side, where the Nivens always sat, if they could, at a table by the railing from which they could watch the crowd below. Niven, arriving late that evening, noticed Mark at their favorite table, ogling a big-breasted girl almost directly beneath him.

The actor was stopped by a pang of envy. His son was as stocky and broad-faced as he was, but the solidity of the impressively high forehead and wide cheekbones was softened by the liquid brightness of the eyes and the delicately curved lips, which were a maternal inheritance. 'I'd have been a star years ago with that touch of feminine charm,' thought Niven.

Sitting down at the table, he surprised Mark with a long question.

"Do you think I'm a malevolent old man who doesn't approve of anything you want to do? You think I don't want you to enjoy yourself?"

"No, not really — I'm sure you mean well."

Finding no appropriate response to this compliment, Niven hailed the waiter. After they were served he tried again. "I just wondered whether it isn't a bore for you to have dinner with me every night."

"We're friends, aren't we?"

"Sure, sure." Having looked around to check that no one nearby was speaking English, Niven pushed his plate aside and leaned closer to Mark. "But what if you want to get into a girl?" he asked straight out, to shake him up a little. "Play a game of tick-tack with her?"

"Mother was right, Dad, you have a foul mouth."

"What's so foul about *a game of tick-tack?*" asked Niven with sudden temper, withdrawing to his side of the table. "That's Shakespeare, you ignorant lout. I'm sick and tired of you putting me down all the time."

Mark bent his head, hoping that his father would understand that he was sorry and there would be no need to say it.

The actor was a man of violent feelings, but they burned away in his eyes, on his face, in his voice (which is perhaps why he was an actor) and his son's embarrassment was sufficient to pacify him. "What I mean is," he went on in a friendly voice, "if you like a girl and want to take her out, you don't have to worry about money. I'd be glad to give you some extra." The generosity of this proposal may be measured by the fact that Niven himself had affairs only with independent women who could and would pay their own way. Money seemed to go farther since his wife had left them, and he could provide two furnished rooms and regular meals even during his periods of unemployment, without the dramatic gaps of actual penury that had embittered his married life, but he accomplished this feat with a stinginess acquired by living for most of his working years on an uncertain income. However, he was quite prepared to make sacrifices in a good cause. "I can always let you have an extra sixty–seventy francs," he added after some rapid calculation.

"Don't worry about it, Dad," begged Mark. "I know some girls, we go for walks."

"Just let me know when you want me out of the apartment."

"Thanks."

"Listen, you'll soon be sixteen, that's just the right age. I suppose your grandparents would want you to wait until you're old enough not to get excited about it, but why miss out on the best time? Sixteen . . . you've no idea how lucky you are! *I* know because I'm getting on and I'm not like I used to be. I'm going to tell you something only a father would tell you. . . . After twenty, twenty-two, it's never quite the same for a man."

"I know, I know."

"Well, then, we'd better start by getting you a new jacket. Your wrists are running ahead of your sleeves."

"Thanks, Dad — honestly, though, clothes don't matter. I have enough clothes."

"You never ask me for so much as a new shirt," the actor said, getting annoyed again. "I really don't understand what you want that treature for — you're not interested in anything money can buy."

"That's not true. I want a lot of things."

"What, for instance?"

"I'll put up the money for a new production of *Monte Cristo*," Mark retorted promptly. "I'll buy a theater where out-of-work actors can come together and stage a play without worrying about rent or electricity bills. And I'll buy a lot of different places and keep everything we need in each of them, so we'll never have to pack and we can travel without worrying about leaving stuff behind. That was a good idea of yours — to have our own apartment or villa wherever we want to stay."

"I never said that," Niven protested.

"Oh yes you did — when we were living in the apartment on the Ile Saint-Louis — that time when it looked like you were going to be a star."

"So something I said got through to you!"

"I listen," Mark replied with a confident grin. "I'm also going to buy a Caribbean island and invite girls to come and stay with me."

"Don't make them wait too long," sighed the actor, giving up for the day.

BETWEEN the ages of fourteen and eighteen, traveling with his father and making side trips on his own, Mark spent most of his waking hours in the maritime archives of Seville, Madrid, Paris, Marseilles, Genoa and London, manifesting an extraordinary capacity for perseverance and a considerable talent for systematic research.

To find out what ships were in the area at the time, he read Admiralty and port authority records, acquiring an extensive knowledge of sea traffic between Europe and the Americas in 1820. To make sense of the ships' logbooks he found, he supplemented his Spanish, French and Italian with the language of the sea, studying old maritime charts and navigational instruments, trade routes, the speeds of sailing ships, the prevailing winds. Counting on finding some reference to the site of the wreck and anticipating that it might have shifted since 1820, he learned about the nature of undercurrents, changes in the seabed, erosion of the shoreline and the rate of growth of coral formations.

The actor's opinion that all his son's labors were utterly stupid and pointless was the sort of unfair exaggeration that characterizes parental anxieties. Becoming his own teacher and pupil, Mark developed the habit of looking for the connections between apparently unrelated facts and events, which is the *sine qua non* of thinking at all. His well-organized notes on his various studies, now in his father's possession, would do credit to a research fellow at Oxford or Harvard. For an adolescent it was a truly uncommon intellectual achievement, and one is at a loss to explain how a boy could have accomplished it — or, if he was so exceedingly bright, how he could have persisted in his conviction that he was going to become rich by recovering a fortune lost to the sea. But then he had a passion for that wreck, and nothing stimulates intelligence so much as passion, or so decisively prevents its application to commonsense considerations — which is why the most brilliant individuals, great experts or even geniuses, are no more sensible in their aims than the greatest fools.

When Mark finally brought a girl to his room, his father had no joy out of it.

They were living in London at the time, where Niven was playing in an American musical at Her Majesty's in the Haymarket. Although appearing only in the first half of the show, he was nonetheless expected to be present in the long line of players at the final curtain call, bowing to the applause intended for actors with bigger parts, and didn't get home to their Earl's Court flat until nearly midnight. Mark had the place to himself in the evenings, and Niven hoped something would come of this. Returning one night even later than usual, he heard a girlish laugh coming from Mark's room. He stopped in the hallway to enjoy the rippling sound and bowed deeply to the clothes-tree, just as at the final curtain call but this time without the sick feeling in his stomach — on the contrary! Unable to resist the impulse to take a look at them, to witness the aftermath of youthful passion, he knocked at Mark's door, turning the knob at the same time, and, finding the door unlocked, walked in.

He was met by two pairs of curious eyes, waiting for him to say something. "Good evening," he said.

"Hi, Dad. This is Jessica." Mark made a vague gesture to include the whole room, then dropped his arm slowly as if wondering whether he needed to explain Jessica any further. "Jessica McCombie," he added after a pause, then turned to inform the girl: "This is my father." His voice conveyed a certain detachment from family ties, as if to let her know that she didn't have to like him.

"Why, hello, Jessica — it's nice to meet you."

Relieved that Niven appeared to be friendly, Jessica responded with a quick smile, although her eyes remained grave and serious. A girl of about Mark's age and height, she had buck teeth which made her mouth protrude in an awkward way and her hair was mousy, but her large clear gray eyes and buoyant breasts overcame these disadvantages. She was sitting at Mark's table in pink panties and low-cut bra, with a stack of paper and a portable typewriter in front of her. On the rumpled bed Niven noticed a navy serge tunic with a large white button pinned to it, bearing the inscription TRY ME. 'No wonder Mark finally worked up his courage,' he thought. 'This girl's a psychologist.'

As he looked back at her, Jessica tugged at her bra to hide her nipples but then thought better of it and let them show, making it clear with a proud smile that she considered the human body sacred and nothing to be ashamed of.

"Where did the typewriter spring from?" Niven asked with studied casualness.

"It's Jessica's," Mark explained, unable to conceal his pleasure and satisfaction. "She's typing my notes."

Niven nodded, his tired midnight self again. "Well, I'm going to bed, enjoy yourselves."

He had just fallen asleep when the clatter of the typewriter made him sit bolt upright in bed. "Goddammit!" he shouted. "It's after midnight!"

The typewriter fell silent, but little sounds kept coming from Mark's room which made the actor smile and sent him off to sleep.

Jessica came around regularly after that, primly serious about her affair, her TRY ME button replaced by another bearing the chaste slogan SCRAP THE SYSTEM. She found in the dark-eyed, purposeful boy a lover who never tried to put her down; all Mark's ego was invested in finding the treasure, and it never occurred to him to hide how pleased he was with everything about her.

Niven couldn't attack his son in her hearing.

"You shouldn't keep on criticizing him like that, Mr. Niven," she said, her white buck teeth flashing and disappearing as she compressed her lips softly between sentences. "He's learning a lot and he's not doing anybody any harm. What would you rather have him do? Prepare himself for a stupid job in some corrupt business?"

Mark nodded approval. "I'm opting out of the system."

"The system you want to scrap is the gold system, my lad, and you're looking for gold. But as Jessica so aptly observed, you're not doing anybody any harm — and that's no way to become a millionaire. Just look at that!" Niven exclaimed bitterly, referring to a temporary eclipse of the sunlight as a dense cloud of exhaust fumes covered the window. "The guys who own those trucks won't have the exhaust pipes fixed because that would be capital expenditure with no return. They prefer to let their trucks roar around London spouting poisonous muck. You can bet your bottom dollar they never breathed the dust from old manuscripts. They make a killing by choking everybody else to death."

36

"But that's the story of my ship," protested Mark. "I know all that!"

"Then think about it! You kids know everything and think about nothing. People get rich by eating other people alive — God knows, that much ought to have rubbed off on you from the movie business. And you weren't born a cannibal, so forget it."

"I'll get rich without bothering anybody but the fish."

"My son, the innocent millionaire!"

"You don't have to be so sarcastic, Dad."

"You can be as innocent as you like with dream millions."

"If Mark finds the treasure ship," said Jessica, inspired, "he might get rid of all those poisonous lorries for you."

"How do you make that out?"

"He could set up factories to produce electric cars. Don't make faces, Mr. Niven, you'll be an old man soon if you close your mind to new ideas like that. I'm not talking about Utopia, I promise you. There are milk delivery vans and post office vans running on batteries right now. All we need is more powerful batteries and a new manufacturing company. The big automakers won't do anything, they're stuck in the old technology — Mark could change all that. And with electric cars people could live in cities and breathe the air."

The idea of his son setting up factories of any sort or description struck the actor as the most absurd thing he had ever heard. "You're talking of something that will never be, Jessica," he sighed, weary of adolescent nonsense. "Mark has no head for business."

"I'll help him, I'm sure I'll be able to help him," declared the future founder and president of British Solar Glass, a company producing windows to warm buildings in winter and cool them in summer. "He'll do useful things."

"Yes, why not!" said Mark, pleased that his girlfriend was so clever and he had one more reason to look for the wreck. "I'll find the *Flora* and then we'll clear the air!"

THERE had already been two expeditions looking for the *Flora* around Andros Island in the northwestern Bahamas — the first led by Jean-Pierre Simard in 1954 and the second by Bert Brownlee in 1962, both of them unsuccessful. Brownlee, a builder from Anna Maria Island, Florida, later wrote a book about the attempt made by himself and two friends, all experienced divers; his account of their nearly fatal search, *Never Again,* is perhaps the best document we have on the hardships and hazards of diving for treasure among dangerous coral formations and in shark-infested waters. Mark knew nothing of these earlier expeditions until his father, trying to make up for his disastrous present of Menéndez's old book, gave him a copy of Brownlee's new one. With the sharp eyes of an anxious parent Niven noticed it as soon as it appeared at Hatchard's in Piccadilly, where he usually stopped to browse on his way to the theater, and bought it at once. He read it backstage that same evening, terrified and reassured at the same time; *Never Again* was bound to scare Mark to his senses. Now that he was no longer afraid of girls, surely he must be afraid for his life.

"Did you know that a guy called Brownlee was looking for the *Flora*?" he asked as he entered Mark's room and threw the book on the bed.

"What, what Brownlee?" Mark leaped up from the table, overturning his chair, and stood waving his arms silently as if trying to fight his way out of a net. He wavered and might have fallen if his father hadn't grabbed him by the arm.

This spectacle, which resembled something between a silent tantrum and a heart attack, shocked Niven. 'That's what I've been afraid of,' he thought. 'When he realizes he'll never find the ship, he's going to kill himself!' Aloud, he managed to sound almost casual. "Imagine what you'll be like at thirty if you carry on like this. You're a bit young for fainting spells, don't you think?"

"I'm all right, stop preaching," Mark interrupted impatiently, recovering his senses through sheer annoyance. "Who is this Brownlee? Did he find anything?"

"No, he gave up. It can't be found," Niven declared triumphantly and with a tinge of malice, in spite of, or rather because of, his alarm for his son only a moment earlier.

Mark snatched the copy of *Never Again* from the bed, read a few lines, then looked up as if surprised to find his father still standing there. "I thought you said this was *my room*."

He stayed up half the night racing through the book. The recitation of disasters ate into his heart. What if he had no more luck than the people before him? Was he an idiot, just as his father said? Would he fail, too? Would he lose heart and give up? There was a moment when he did lose heart, but then he looked up at the photograph of the Madonna of Lima on the wall and decided to think of better things. Trying to picture how it would be when he found the *Flora,* he furnished his shabby room with treasures from the ship's hold: statues of the Madonna, cast in solid gold, stood in every corner, outshining the lamps. His father would come in, awkward and embarrassed, gaping and nodding in admiration. "Forgive me, Mark," the old man would say, edging forward contritely, "I was a mean son of a bitch, keeping at you all the time, driving you to despair. I didn't realize how I was wearing you down, adding to your troubles. I don't know how you stood up to it. I was a bad father, I had no faith, no vision, but thank God, you didn't listen to me! You knew what you were doing. You were right all along. Forgive me, son, forgive me. Will you forgive me?"

Mark forgave him.

NEXT morning Mark was humming the Beatles' "I Want to Hold Your Hand" as he served the scrambled eggs and coffee for the two of them.

"Don't tell me I bought that book for nothing!" growled Niven.

Mark fell silent and his eyes widened with incomprehension: it took him some time to remember that his father didn't believe in him. "No, no, the book's great," he finally said, recovering himself. "Thanks for getting it. Brownlee gives a lot of tips on what to look out for — it's really useful."

"What's so useful about it?"

"For one thing, they proved that it's crazy to go looking for a wreck without knowing where it is, so I'm right to do my research first. For another, Brownlee mentions a lot of expensive equipment that was no use, so I won't have to waste my money on it."

"What about when the shark ripped his partner's leg off? What useful tip did you glean from that?"

"The guy got scared too easily. You shouldn't start thrashing around when a shark's coming at you," Mark commented briskly, attacking his food.

Never Again became Mark's constant companion. He liked to read bits of it at random, to fortify himself.

The actor resolved to wash his hands of the whole business. The thing to do was to forget all about it. Ignore it! *"I will be the pattern of all patience; I will say nothing,"* he said to his mirror.

It was a brilliant solution; he was unconcerned for days.

But one afternoon, seeing his son beaming over a stack of photostats in the kitchen, he lost his head. Grabbing the boy by his shirt, Niven shook him and kept shaking him until the complacent expression drained from his face, then pushed him away. "At the most *hopeful* estimate, your chances are one in a billion."

"You're pathetic," Mark said coldly when he had stopped trembling. "At least I have a better chance of finding my ship than you have of making it as an actor!"

Niven threw his head back with an inward look — checking his memory, hoping that he hadn't heard what he thought he had heard. Having suffered the lordly disdain of directors, rejection and scant praise, the indifference of the public, the disillusionment of his wife, made him no less vulnerable to his son's insult. His lips turned white. "Well, you really mean business, don't you?" he said.

As always when he was upset, he started to pace the floor, gaping like a fish. He opened his mouth as wide as it would go, then closed and opened it, repeating his silent howl over and over again. Then he thrust his lower jaw forward and moved it up and down and sideways, slowly and laboriously, as if grinding his teeth. His eyes bulged and the cords stood out on his neck from the effort. These strenuous exercises of his jaw muscles were intended to make sure he would not develop a double chin, so that he would be ready to play romantic roles just in case the opportunity came his way.

The life of these two bachelors, each in the grip of his own obsession, each wise to the other's folly, dreaming and bickering, traveling without getting anywhere, could have been a worthy subject for the author of *Waiting for Godot*. Neither of them suspected that they were alike: the father's treasure ship was stardom, the son's stardom was the treasure ship — and this made all the difference in the world as far as they were concerned.

7

Help from the Dead

Posterity will bless our name.
NAPOLEON

EMPLOYERS have better than average opportunities to indulge their bad temper and spite, but no office manager would think of insulting his window cleaner just for the fun of it — the man could pick up his pail and go to wash windows somewhere else. There is always another job for most people, at least in times of general prosperity, and this puts some limit on the rudeness they can be subjected to. Employees are treated according to the amount of pride they can afford, and by this law of social relationships actors are spared nothing but the rack and the wheel, owing to the fact that ninety percent of them are out of work at the best of times. No doubt the proverbial viciousness of directors and producers derives from their license to be insolent with impunity to a great many luckless individuals who are helplessly dependent on them: this is how they acquire the habits of absolute monarchs, amusing themselves by toying with their subjects' self-respect or, better still, taking it away altogether to savor as a tidbit between meals. Another person's ego is the most exquisite of delicacies, kings' caviar — those who taste it can never resist it.

Still, the lot of the working actor is enviable in comparison with what he has to go through when he is looking for a part. During his periods of unemployment Dana Niven started out every morning by performing dozens of cheerfully confident expressions in front of the mirror to brace himself for the day's work of swallowing insults. He rarely knew ahead of time whom he would be able to see, but he could be absolutely certain that if he had the luck to meet anyone with the power to cast him in a film or a play, it would be an experience that would leave him writhing for hours. Despite his many years in the profession he could not reduce his pride to fit his circumstances; yet he sought out the people who would assure him that he was not young enough or old enough, that he was too short, too heavy or too lightweight, that they were looking for an actor with *real presence*. Nor was it easy to obtain the signal honor of being humiliated by one of these great men. They would bestow their insolence only on a favored few, as a sort of vague promise that they might remember the victim on some other occasion.

Just to be noticed by one of these demigods was a rare privilege and Niven would not have had the good fortune to attract the attention of Robert G. Madesko if he hadn't been worrying about Mark at the time. 'What's wrong with a kid having wild ideas?' he reflected as he walked along the Champs-Elysées in the rain, on his way to the Paramount Building, trying to convince himself that his son was all right. 'He might end up as a writer — he can imagine anything! He might do a script for me someday. I'd get a part without having to eat shit for it.' This possibility looked particularly attractive after hours of waiting in the Paramount reception room, hoping to talk to somebody important. 'But even if he goes to the Bahamas, what's so terrible about that? He could have a great time diving for treasure and working as a lifeguard. The air's clean there and the sun shines and when it rains it makes a change! I've got a nerve trying to reform him — I'm sure lifeguards in the Bahamas earn more than I do. I shouldn't fret — I'm turning into a cranky old woman.'

Noticing Madesko hurrying through the reception room, he called out: "If you ever make a drag film, Mr. Madesko, cast me as an old woman!"

Robert G. Madesko was a producer of moneymaking films. In his late forties by this time, he still looked like a college athlete, thanks to his habit of walking fast. At the beginning of his career, he walked fast to convince people that he was busy and successful, and by the time he was busy and successful enough not to need to draw attention to it, he had become keen to remind people that he was still young enough to be quick on his feet. But though he was always in a hurry he took the trouble to greet everyone he knew, or rather everyone who knew him, with a nod and a warm smile, which testified to the extraordinary fact that Robert G. Madesko, who no longer needed to notice anybody and could have walked through the world as though it wasn't there, still gave thought to people. As they used to say of Hollywood liberals, he believed in the equal worth of all human beings no matter how insignificant they might be.

From the way Niven tried to catch his eye Madesko remembered him as a face glimpsed once or twice on the screen, and he nodded and smiled as he rushed past; but then Niven's remark stopped him in his tracks. He turned around and gave the apparently heterosexual actor an appraising look, the look a shopper gives a bargain counter, which Niven could never have obtained from him but for his idiotic request. "So you want to play an old woman . . . I haven't heard that one for at least a week," he said, though he hadn't heard it for months. "Why an old woman?"

"Because I *am* one. It happens to many men, especially fathers."

"Let me see you in profile."

Niven turned his head.

Madesko pursed his lips to show that he was unimpressed. "I'm sorry, but you don't look like an old woman to me."

"How do I look to you?" the actor couldn't resist asking.

"Let's see — short, dark, heavyset, thin mouth, touch of madness in the eyes — yes, you look more like Napoleon to me. Who said you have nothing going for you?"

"Nobody, I hope."

"Well, people say a lot of things, but they're fools," the producer responded emphatically as if Niven had confirmed the calumny instead of denying it and he, Madesko, felt obliged to cheer him up. "And the worst fools pass through these offices. Hardly anybody in this business knows the first thing about it. You couldn't design tunnels if you had no idea of the problems of weight distribution, the resistance of various metals, the use of compressed air and steel liner plates . . ." and Madesko went on listing the rudiments of tunnel making, partly because he was aware that it was surprising how much he knew about the subject, and partly because he enjoyed watching his listener's brooding face, knowing for certain that Niven must be wondering whether there was anything for him at the end of the tunnel. "Or take medicine . . . !" he exclaimed.

Niven's face darkened.

"No, you're right, medicine is just like the movies," Madesko conceded with a sigh. "There's a general decline of competence — and that's how the world is coming to an end. But in the meantime!" Here he paused and gave a slight smile to indicate that he kept ticking over, thinking, *working,* even while chatting away — and indeed he was thinking that unknown actors cost next to nothing and he ought to pay more attention to them. "In the meantime, I think you might have a future."

"Thanks."

"No, no, I'm serious. I'll tell you what I'll do to prove I'm serious — I'm going to look foolish for you. I'm willing to undergo the embarrassing experience of confessing . . ." (he looked calmly at his watch to show that there was no question of his being embarrassed) "that I haven't the faintest idea what your name is, so I have to ask you for it. I wouldn't do that if I wasn't interested, would I?"

'He doesn't know who I am but he knows that people say I have nothing going for me,' Niven thought, wishing he could afford to hit the bastard. But he gave his name and the name and phone number of his agent.

"Ah, the unsuccessful Niven!" exclaimed Madesko, writing in his notebook with the sorrowful expression doctors assume when they are confronted with a dying patient but are not quite ready to give up. "Of course, of course I know you."

Niven managed eventually to forget the experience, or rather it became indistinguishable in his mind from other disagreeable encounters. But fourteen months later, while he was playing in the musical at Her Majesty's in London, he got a call from his agent: Madesko wanted him to test for the leading role in a film about the rise and fall of Napoleon. The screen tests were successful and Niven was offered the part for a fee of $42,500 — and a percentage of the profits which he knew perfectly well he would never collect.

"We're not paying you much," Madesko told him at the signing of the contract, "but we're giving you a break that's worth a fortune."

"I'll tell that to my bank manager."

"You'll be able to make the producer of your next picture pay for our stinginess," Madesko remarked with a self-mocking smile which was meant to indicate that he knew full well that he was taking advantage of Niven and had every sympathy for him. "Seriously, I feel terrible about your contract," he added in his serious voice, becoming a changed man as he bent a little to shoulder his sorrow. "I had better things in mind for you — but you know what the money situation is. The distributors are squeezing us dry — middlemen take all the profit these days — and artists are the first to suffer. I only wish we lived in a different world."

The actor replied in the bantering tone men use to speak their minds when they can't really afford to. "It's awfully good of you to feel sorry for the people you exploit."

"He has a big house, a big car and a big heart," quipped the agent.

Niven, playing the part for $42,500, wore costumes which cost $175,000. The fees of the leading actor and scriptwriter were the only costs on which Madesko economized. He flouted the current fashion for low-budget films and relied on publicity about all the money squandered on the production, so that if everything else failed he could still count on the public's curiosity to see what $8,000,000 (a huge sum in those days) could do. The film was a success, eventually grossing over $60,000,000, but this didn't please Madesko as much as the fact that the profit would have been half a million less if he had employed an established star instead of Niven.

"You've got to trust your instincts," he told his hangers-on. "Who else would have had the guts to risk eight million on an *absolute nobody?*"

To journalists he spoke of Dana Niven as "a neglected genius who finally came into his own".

There was some truth in this even if Madesko couldn't make up his mind whether he meant it or not. French critics allowed that Niven's was a convincing performance (for an American) and compared it favorably with Marlon Brando's portrayal of Napoleon in an earlier and misconceived film. If Brando had greater magnetism, Niven had more style and intellectual force; and in the scenes of defeat, particularly the burning of Moscow and his farewell to the Imperial Guard at Fontainebleau, he became the personification of profound, unstated despair, creating the kind of reverent hush that is not infrequent in the theater but is the rarest thing in movie houses.

"There isn't a thing I don't know about failure," was Niven's own sullen comment on his performance.

At no time did he feel so keenly the injustice of eighteen years of neglect as at the very moment when he proved that he hadn't deserved it. Unlike writers or painters or composers, actors cannot practice their art in isolation, in defiance of other people's poor opinion of their abilities, and Niven was maddened by the thought that with such an opportunity earlier in his career he could have spent his best years acting instead of worrying about the rent. Now famous if not rich, he was outraged by the general incredulity and amazement over the fact that he had anything in him, and his bitterness about all this spoiled much of his pleasure in his "sudden" rise to prominence.

Mark was inclined to credit no one so much as Napoleon himself for the dramatic change in their fortunes.

"Just think about it!" he exclaimed, walking to and fro with his head bent and his hands clasped behind his back, like his father in the film. "Listen! If Napoleon hadn't turned Europe upside down, there wouldn't have been a film about him and it wouldn't have helped you at all that you can look like him." It was about this time that Mark was struck by the realization that the past wasn't past at all, and what happened hundreds of years ago could be more important for him than what happened yesterday. He had already worked out Napoleon's connection with the *Flora:* if Napoleon hadn't occupied Spain in 1808, then Spain's grip on her overseas colonies might have remained firm enough to prevent or at least postpone the revolutions in South America — in which case San Martín would not have invaded Peru, there would have been no reason to load the *Flora* with the treasures of Lima, and he, Mark Niven, would not have been looking for them. He was delighted now to realize that his father's career had been influenced by the same emperor as his own. "I bet not even Napoleon could have imagined that one of the consequences of his campaigns was going to be that an actor from Rochester, New York, would make the big time in the movies!"

"I haven't got another job yet," Niven warned him dryly.

"But doesn't it leave you absolutely dumbfounded," Mark persisted, "doesn't it absolutely floor you, the way dead people, people who lived maybe hundreds of years ago, who could never have dreamed of our existence, are mixed up in our lives?"

"To coin a phrase, I know all that."

"Do you?" Mark asked soberly, taken aback. "It was news to me."

"Well, I suppose you're right, it's amazing when you think about it. Good old Napoleon . . . ! Still, you might eat your words and give me some credit too."

"Come off it, Dad, you *know* you're great," Mark protested. "Do you want me to flatter you?"

Niven burst out laughing. "Yes, why not! Do you realize that you may yet see your father paired with the greatest actor of the age? Olivier might produce my translation of *Robert Guiskard* at the Old Vic — if he can find the right one-acter to go with it — and he and I would play the leads!"

There seems to be such a thing as family luck. It was in the spring of the father's success that the son finally found what he was looking for: three lines in the logbook of an Italian merchant ship, the *Sant'Andrea* of Genoa, whose captain noted that she passed the *Flora* just after eight on the morning of September 27, 1820, some twenty minutes before the hurricane struck them. According to the captain's indications the English brig was *making for the northeast coast of Santa Catalina,* one of the small Out Islands of the Bahamas — the same coast where, only twelve days later, a Spanish frigate passed pieces of wreckage scattered on the reefs. (Sightings of unidentified wreckage were the sort of information, meaningless in itself, that Mark had diligently collected through the years in the hope that it might turn out to be useful.)

But the *Sant'Andrea* logbook was really the find of the librarian at the maritime archives in Genoa. This middle-aged lady, Signorina Angela Rognoni, had spent many hours collecting papers for Mark to scan, working for him even during the long intervals between his visits. While his father was attending the world première of *The Emperor* in Cannes Mark had another chance to go to Genoa, and the *Sant'Andrea* logbook was among the documents she had put aside for him.

Reading those three decisive lines was a moment for which Mark would gladly have given his right arm if he hadn't needed it for diving. His first impulse was to go and hug Signorina Rognoni for her help, but he managed to suppress it. This news was too big to be shared with strangers. What if she gossiped about his discovery? Taking a quick look around, he reached for his razor blade, cut out the page and buried it in his pocket. *Meno male!*

Carrying the documents back to Signorina Rognoni's desk, he convinced himself that the person he should be grateful to was the captain of the *Sant'Andrea,* who was so good at keeping records. This notion allowed him to face the signorina's questioning glance with a clear conscience. Though her hair was gray she had bright eyes and a childlike, expectant face, as if her whole life were still ahead of her, and she felt a sympathy for the young man which made her blush. When she asked him whether her work had been of any use, he had the strength of will and the meanness to deny it.

Signorina Rognoni was distressed and apologetic, as if she had failed him; but Mark maintained his dejected expression while all the time, crazed with joy, he was jumping up and down inside his head.

8

Hope Deferred

The gods had condemned him to keep rolling
a huge stone uphill which, when he had pushed it
to the top, always rolled back of its own accord.

CAMUS

MARK hitchhiked back to Cannes and found his father in the vast
marble bathroom of their suite at the Hotel Majestic; the victorious Napoleon of the film festival was having a shower, washing off
the sweat and dirt of a press conference. Shouting his all-but-incredible
news over the noise of the water, Mark asked for ten thousand dollars.

The actor turned off the taps and sought refuge in towels.

"All I need is my air fare and I can start in a couple of days," Mark
went on without stopping for breath. After four years of hard work which
his father and everybody else considered absolutely hopeless and pointless, he had succeeded in tracing the most famous treasure wreck in the
world, and he assumed that the rest was just a matter of detail. "I have
to buy a dive boat, metal detector, wet suit, a few things, and I'll need
something to live on till I find the wreck. I'm planning to get everything
I can secondhand, so I should be able to manage on ten–twelve thousand."

"Staying at a five-star hotel must have softened your brain," growled
Niven, dashing into the bedroom to dress. "All this luxury is on the
publicity budget, not us, kid — it's a one-week bash, remember?"

"Dad, you're not listening, we're rich!" exclaimed Mark, following
him. His dark eyes shone with such brilliance that they seemed to be
lighter in color. "Think — we can have a big bowl with eleven thousand two hundred and fifty-four pearls in it. You can put your hand in
the bowl and let them roll around your fingers! The manifest says most
of the pearls are flawless. Even if half of them got washed away, we
can still play marbles. And *you* said it couldn't be done!"

To Niven all this meant that he was going to have more trouble with his son than ever before. A trim and youthful forty-four, filled with the vigor of exercise, controlled appetite, fresh success, he nonetheless began to feel old. Though he still had only his trousers on, he stepped out to the balcony, turning his back on Mark's enthusiasm. The balcony had a grand view of the Bay of Cannes: it faced the statue of King Edward VII in the little park on the other side of the Croisette, and beyond the park, the beach and the long range of hills rolling far out into the sea to form the western rim of the bay. The turreted U.S. warship on the vast sheet of water looked like a toy boat, and the myriad blues of the hills, the sea, the sky were blinding.

"When the festival's over we'll be back on the Earl's Court Road breathing air full of lead," Niven said, heaving a deep sigh. "That doesn't sound very rich to me."

Mark followed his father out to the balcony and slapped his bare back. "Cheer up, Dad! We have seventeen tons of gold! We're on top of the world, and you're a star!"

"I'm an old man."

"You want me to leave the wreck lying there, when I'm the only person in the world who knows where to look for it?" asked Mark with bitter incomprehension.

Niven escaped back into the room. *"What* do you know? All you know is that it's somewhere around some island in the Bahamas. That sounds like a lot of sea to me."

"All it takes is time," argued Mark, still at his heels.

"Time and money."

"I'm only asking for ten thousand dollars, Dad." He pronounced *ten thousand dollars* in the deprecating tone of a man who was counting in millions.

"Only ten thousand! That's just about all we've got left from the movie since I paid off my overdraft! Only, only! How can you say *only?* Hell, I could have brought a girl here — we could have had a pretty good time watching those blue hills from the bed. But no, I bring my manic son for company, and by way of thanks he tries to rip the shirt off my back!" Niven was buttoning up his shirt as he said this, looking determined never to part from it.

"What are you talking about? Twelve thousand dollars couldn't make any difference to you. You're famous. Your film is a hit and you're going to do your Kleist play with Olivier!"

"You can't be sure of anything! Remember all those articles raving about my Monte Cristo, and they didn't even finish the film? Well, I'm not going to burn money this time. No new apartment on the Ile Saint-Louis, no custom-made shirts . . ."

"What have custom-made shirts got to do with it? You're the only one who wears custom-made shirts. All I'm asking —"

"No custom-made shirts for me and no big loans for you. And no fancy restaurants for either of us. Take-out food is as far as I'll go until I see money on a new contract."

"Poor Dad," Mark said, forgiving everything. "You were poor too long!"

"Yes, that's how you learn," replied Niven, frowning at the mirror as if it were an old poster. "I can be a giant on the billboards and still end up as a welfare case — and that's all there is to fame."

Hearing the fear in his father's voice, Mark was overcome by a joyful sense of being the stronger of the two. He put his arm around his old man's shoulder — they were now the same height — and shook him a little. "You have *no worries,* Dad. We'll stage plays, we'll produce films — you've got the talent, now you'll also have the money!" The prospect of providing his father with the missing part of his luck so moved Mark that he couldn't help embracing him, nuzzling his strong neck smelling of soap. They hadn't been so physically close for years and both were moved by a sudden, surprising sense of being of the same flesh and blood; they hugged each other with a passion of family feeling that brought tears to their eyes.

"Thanks for the generous thought," said Niven as they disengaged, "so long as you understand that we don't have ten thousand dollars for a treasure hunt."

"Sure, but now you're a name and you can borrow it!"

The suggestion that he should go into debt awoke so many anxieties in the actor that he lost his self-control. "And I was worried that you weren't rotten enough to be rich!" he groaned, hoarse with indignation. "You'd ruin me without a qualm! You're turning into a rotten bastard, you know that?"

Mark reddened. "You don't have to insult me."

"I'm your father, it's my job to insult you," Niven insisted, letting go of his temper in the way most parents do, by thinking that it is for the good of the child. "I haven't done a thing for the past eighteen years without considering how it would affect you. You were still in the womb when I started to worry about you. And now you're trying to shake me down for some crazy gamble without giving a thought to my welfare. Do you have a soul?"

"I told you we'll share!"

"Share what? You expect me to provide for you but you don't do anything for your keep — you hardly ever go to school and you don't take in a word I say. You'll never be any use to anybody."

Mark had never heard such abuse from his father; he was still at an age when words hurt more than anything and he was horribly shaken. But he hated back, putting all the violence of his soul into his voice to show that he wasn't beaten. "What are you so worked up about?" he shouted. "When I'm rich, I'll be useful! I'll finance oil-free cars, clear the air in Earl's Court for you."

"That's just something you heard from Jessica."

"What's wrong with listening to advice?"

"You mean you're ready to listen to advice?"

"I mean — You know what I mean."

The actor dismissed the subject with a look.

Muttering curses without moving his lips, Mark walked out. Leaving the Hotel Majestic, he ended up with the rest of the early evening strollers on the promenade by the beach, breathing sea air spiced with perfumes. He had planned to spend the evening with his father celebrating his triumphant breakthrough, and was bitterly conscious of being on his own. He was so agitated — his nerves stood on end — that he noticed girls more than at other times. He wished that one of them would run to him, embrace him, love him, live for him, knowing straight away that he was all right.

Most of the strollers were pretty girls who had converged on Cannes for the film festival and were showing off their legs and breasts on the Croisette — office girls, shop girls, divorcées, would-be actresses who made a point of spending their holidays in places frequented by the rich and famous, hoping that they would never have to go back to their jobs in Düsseldorf, Brussels, Birmingham or Melbourne. They paid no more attention to Mark than to the sailors from the U.S. warship in the bay; their eyes searched constantly for the unappealing. Looking blankly past handsome youngsters in or out of uniform, they scanned the crowd for aging unattractive men — preferably short, bald, fat, disfigured — any man with something revolting about him, something gross enough for him to know that he couldn't be loved solely for himself. Many of them looked sullen, realizing that it was no use: there were just not enough ugly rich men in the world.

The spectacle drove all amorous thoughts from Mark's blood, and he suddenly knew why he loved the women of Perugino. Remembering beautiful faces ennobled by the disinterested curiosity and serene self-possession that come to those who are not for sale, he watched the purposeful girls with growing aversion. How different, how hideous was self-abasement! A delicate brunette on the Croisette greeted him with a smile, then immediately and visibly forgot him as a white Rolls-Royce with a uniformed chauffeur rolled by. There was no passenger in the car, but she seemed to offer herself to the empty back seat, her face glowing with submissive, craven avidity.

'Well, he won't see me with that kind of please-give-me look,' thought Mark. 'He won't see me beg. I'm not going to him on my knees.' He longed to get away from people and pluck his fortune from the clear blue water.

Coming to a flight of steps leading from the promenade to the beach, he ran down to the sea to get his feet wet. He took off his sneakers, rolled up his jeans, and walked on the wet sand at the moving edge of the water shining with a dull glitter in the dark. The chill that ran through his body made him feel he was being charged with the strength of the earth and the sea, and for an instant he was intensely happy. But then his father's accusation that he didn't have a soul came back to bother him. What was so terrible about asking for a loan? Why, he planned to give away millions — millions! — to people in trouble. And whose picture hung on the wall of whatever little room he could call his own? Who was the man he admired more than anyone else? Why, General José de San Martín, who liberated half of South America from Spanish colonial rule and wanted nothing in return — the brilliant and incorruptible leader who was offered the kingdom of Chile and refused it! Mark was certain that only an honorable person could truly appreciate such a man. But then he remembered his library thefts, and thought of Signorina Rognoni's blushing face when he had told her that her help was no use. She must have spent a lot of time hunting through the archives to find the logbook of the *Sant'Andrea,* and by way of thanks he had made her miserable with a lie.

One moment he saw himself as a monster, the next moment he recalled all the good he planned to do with his wealth, all his sympathies and ideals, which proved conclusively that he was a decent human being.

DANA Niven, who had gone to bed early, was wakened by his son storming into the room.

"How could you say that I don't have a soul?" Mark demanded, pale with indignation.

"What . . . ?" asked the poor man miserably. "Do I talk in my sleep?"

"Do you know anyone who works as hard as I do? Whatever I find, I'll have worked years for it. I'm not a parasite. I don't want anything for nothing."

"Who said you did?"

Mark sat down on the edge of his father's bed. "I want to know what you really think of me!" he begged feverishly, biting his lips, ready to listen. Only he could not wait; he got up again to unleash a torrent of words refuting every single critical remark his father had ever made.

Having listened to Mark's self-justifying arguments till dawn, the actor suddenly remembered one of the consolations of leaving his youth behind. "Oh, God," he groaned, "I'd almost forgotten! What a relief it was when I stopped worrying about being good!"

52

THERE is a special torment fate reserves for ambitious and gifted people whose sound ideas and unsparing efforts bring them to the brink of great wealth only to see all their labor rendered null and void by *lack of capital*.

Mark tried everything.

If he couldn't get money from his father, he would earn it. He would work his way to the Bahamas as a cabin boy or deckhand, take a job on Santa Catalina Island to earn his keep and the cost of equipment, and search for the wreck on his days off.

As soon as they got back to London he went to the Office of the Commissioner for the Bahama Islands to ask about job opportunities. Since his father had always looked after their documents, he had no idea of the difficulties of settling in a foreign country and obtaining that awesome piece of paper, the *work permit*.

"Job opportunities?" The tall young consular official, recently transferred from the tourist office and as beautiful as the Queen of Sheba, had not yet learned the diplomatic art of hiding her feelings, and she laughed slowly and luxuriously, with the unhurried assurance of a woman who knew she had a mouth that drove men insane. "Job opportunities, you say? We have lots of our own people who would like to know about those!"

To obtain a work permit, she explained, he would have to find a local employer who was able to prove that no Bahamian could do the job intended for him. "We welcome tourists, of course," she added with a welcoming smile, "but you must have your return ticket on arrival and proof of sufficient funds for your stay."

"Are there no exceptions?"

"There are always exceptions. You're welcome to settle on any of the islands, if you don't have a criminal record and if you don't have to earn your living. All you need is a private income."

"A private income . . . I see," repeated Mark, straining to recover from the blow. "Please, could you tell me what sort of businesses are there on Santa Catalina? Maybe I can convince one of them that they need me."

The Queen of Sheba's huge bright eyes grew even brighter. "Santa Catalina? Say, you know people on the island?"

"No, not yet, but I can't wait to meet them."

She laughed as if Mark had said the funniest thing. "I'm afraid it's a very-very private place. Sir Henry Colville lives there."

"Who is Sir Henry Colville?" Mark hardly ever read the papers, and never bothered with the financial pages. He wanted a fortune, but he wasn't interested in the ins and outs of money.

"You don't know who Sir Henry is?" The Queen of Sheba looked down at him from her superior height. "Well, he's the sort of person who's very particular about his neighbors. Santa Catalina is more or less his private island and he shares it with only a few families, the kind of people he can mix with, if you know what I mean. People a few cuts above millionaires."

"And who might they be?"

She made an O with her gorgeous mouth. "People with hundreds of millions. There's a hotel, but that's very-very private too. If they have any job opening, I'm sure they have dozens of Bahamians waiting for it. Don't take it to heart," she added, letting him see the tip of her pink tongue. "You know what they say — if it's not possible, then it's *impossible.*"

What if the wreck got washed away or buried too deep in the sand before he could get to the island? As Mark listened to her throaty laugh, he understood the terrible truth that rules and regulations can kill.

His father was delighted, though he tried not to show it.

"I can tell you what you could do at that hotel," he suggested. "You could be an interpreter. They must get a lot of tourists from South America and Europe these days, and I don't suppose there are many multilingual Bahamians looking for a place on that godforsaken island, so you could qualify for a work permit. But you would have to be at least a grammar school graduate. You can't expect them to argue with Bahamian Immigration for a dumbbell who couldn't finish school."

"Who's a dumbbell?" Mark protested. He was desperate, but in the way the young and healthy are desperate; he despaired of the world, not of himself. "Come on, Dad, I know a lot and I'm intelligent."

"Intelligent!" The actor shook his head mournfully. "Intelligence is no recommendation. Most people haven't the faintest notion of intelligence — it could be tall, short, black or blue — if you want to get a good job, any kind of good job anywhere, you need some official proof that you have brains. It seems to me the most sensible thing you could do is to get top marks in your final exams. Study as if you wanted to go to Oxford. If your exam papers are good enough for a top university, they'll impress hotel keepers too."

"Hey, Dad, you've got something there," said Mark, grateful that his father was no longer opposing him.

'I'll get you to college yet,' thought Niven, learning the ways of parental deceit.

After further inquiries Mark wrote a letter to the president of North–South International in New York. Listing the English, Italian, French and Spanish schools he had attended, mentioning in addition his serviceable knowledge of Dutch and Portuguese, adding that he was now preparing for his final exams and studying German, he respectfully applied for a job as interpreter at the company's hotel on Santa Catalina.

54

He had, he said, "personal family reasons" for wishing to live on that particular island.

Determined to qualify for the hotel job, he threw himself into his studies, with as much superstition as intellectual prowess: he believed in every kind of exertion as Haitians believe in voodoo; work had a kind of magic in his eyes which would save him and bring him luck. But when two weeks had passed, he became anxious again and wrote to the president of North–South International reminding him that his application had not yet been answered. It was an oddly stern letter to the president of a multibillion-dollar conglomerate; on the other hand Mark spoke more languages than many top officials of the U.S. State Department and he only wanted to be a hotel clerk. In any case, he gave the man another week and then began to wait for the mail.

His father found him one morning in the hallway, sitting on the floor and staring at the letter slot with an angry face. He couldn't help being moved by the boy's unhappiness.

"Come on, don't take it so hard — I may be doing a play on Broadway. If we get to New York you can try to see this guy in person and ask him what's on his mind . . ."

Mark got up from the floor, his eyes burning with reproach. "If you'd lend me the ten thousand I wouldn't have all these problems. You're not a poor out-of-work actor now."

Niven raised his hands to ward off any misunderstanding. "I'll gladly support you as long as you're studying, but I'll never lend you ten thousand dollars to do idiotic things."

"I know, I know!" replied Mark, thinking, 'When it comes to money, I have no father!'

Next morning Niven found him flipping through bills and brochures which had come in the mail.

"Anything interesting?"

"That woman was right," said Mark, tears welling up in his eyes. "What I need is a private income."

Writing his exams offered him a few days' distraction, especially as he realized he was doing well, but then another morning without word from New York wiped out all his confidence. He had caught the sickness of helpless longing, the kind of deep frustration which wears one out even while one is asleep. And if he got up in the middle of the night to go to the bathroom, he stayed awake and composed another reminder or paced the floor uttering curses in a low voice so as not to wake his father.

Sometimes he went out to meet the mailman on the staircase and ask whether there was anything for him, but most days he stood or sat behind the door, dreading the moment when the familiar steps would pass by without stopping.

"Couldn't he or his secretary or somebody at least write a little note to say they're not interested?" he asked bitterly, as millions of job applicants ask every day. "Why don't they put me out of my misery? Do they enjoy tormenting people?"

He didn't know that America's efficiency experts had looked at the figures and decided that firms could save postage and secretarial time by ignoring inquiries which didn't interest them. No doubt eliminating politeness from society is a cost-effective way of hastening the day when people will bite each other in the street.

ONE night the actor was wakened by noise and talk and staggered to his door to see what was happening. Mark was stamping about the living room talking loudly to himself.

"What the hell are you doing?"

"Nothing."

"What's got into you? Are you sick?"

"I'm thinking."

"And what the hell are you thinking about?"

Mark stopped. He looked at his father with bloodshot eyes. "I wish I'd never gone to Genoa!"

9

Rumors of War

Governments were accustomed to seize upon
the bodies of citizens and deliver them over
by hundreds of thousands to death and mutilation.
EDWARD BELLAMY

YEARS earlier, when Mark was going to school in Rome, his enemy Luciano Galante had brought a copy of *Paese Sera* to class one morning, and after showing the newspaper to everybody, raised an accusing arm at Mark, shouting:

Loro fanno così!

'What have I done now?' Mark wondered, and walked over to the group around Luciano to see what they were looking at. There were pages of photographs of a Vietnamese village, the scene of a battle between Vietcong guerrillas and U.S. special forces which according to the captions had left only four of the villagers alive.

It was the first time that the Vietnam war meant anything to Mark, and he couldn't have been more horrified if he had foreseen that he himself would be drafted into the army to join in the killing. The photo that paralyzed him showed the corpse of a young Vietnamese woman with a dark bloody hole where one of her breasts should have been. For an instant he was that woman. He could feel nothing but her pain, her panic, her helpless terror: her death entered his heart.

It took him some time to hear the insults.

Americani — assassini!
Assassini — Americani!
Marco — assassino!
Mar-co — as-sas-si-no!
As-sas-si-no — as-sas-si-no!

Mark protested that he had never even been in the States, he was only born there, but since the gang kept chanting that he was a murderer, he jumped on Galante, though Galante was taller and played soccer. In the subsequent fight Mark got punched over his right eye, which immediately swelled up so that he couldn't see, but he managed to bite his enemy's nose.

His friends, the other foreign students, helping to wash his wounds afterward, assured him that he wasn't alone.

"I get blamed for Hitler, and he died years before I was born!" said one.

"That's nothing," said another. "I get blamed for killing Christ!"

Galante and Mark were both sent home from school.

Niven was so shocked when he saw his son hurt that he felt he ought to have more than one child. He hated the thought of Mark being involved in any fight, yet he also wanted him to stand up for himself. Putting a cold compress on the swollen eyelid, he told Mark to remind his classmates that the Communists had already killed more people than the Nazis, and mass murderers ought to be resisted. This was at the time when the first U.S. Marine battalions were landing on the beaches of Da Nang, and remembering the triumphs of World War II, Niven assumed that America could help to save Southeast Asia from communism just as it had helped to save Western Europe from fascism.

Perhaps to make up for not listening to him about the *Flora,* Mark accepted his father's opinions about politics without question. He tried to argue with Galante at school next day, but Galante, whose father was a member of the Central Committee of the Partito Comunista Italiano and president of an export-import firm doing business with Russia, kept boasting that he was going to bury all Americans, so they had another fight and were sent home from school again.

"Well, I can't tell you to turn the other cheek," sighed the actor, who had himself become involved in several arguments that nearly came to blows. Americans abroad are often taken to task for their President's policies even if they didn't vote for him.

When the Nivens left Rome for Paris, Mark had trouble in school there too.

At first he told everybody, as his father had told him, that America was in the right and would win. But as the war dragged on, it became increasingly obvious to anyone whose ego was not involved in the outcome that the people of the region, having suffered through decades of war against the Japanese and the French, preferred the Devil's peace to the steady rain of bombs, and whatever Washington was trying to accomplish there was doomed to failure. The kids in Rome and Paris knew this sooner than Mark, and Mark knew it sooner than his father, who needed another year of inconclusive news and an editorial in *Le Monde* castigating President Johnson before he got fed up.

"They say it's hopeless," Niven exclaimed, disgusted, and threw the paper on the floor. "They should know, they were there before us!"

From that morning he began cursing Johnson for persisting in a war which had already been lost by the French and told Mark that the whole "obscenely futile business" should teach him "how wicked it is to be stubborn". It was about this time that he decided to translate *Robert Guiskard*, Kleist's haunting dramatic fragment about the Norman conqueror of Sicily who rode in triumph to the gates of Constantinople, where he and his army perished of the plague.

Vietnam was Constantinople, Mark agreed with his father, but this did not always help him at school. Subjected to jeers and reproaches for the distant war he had nothing to do with and had grown to hate, the former Prince Marco Giovanni Lorenzo Alessandro Ippolito Borghese began to think of himself as a foreigner. A person unjustly accused. An American.

HE was an American against the war, yet he went to the States with his father a few days after he reached the age of compulsory military service. Maddened by months of waiting for a reply to his letters, Mark couldn't begin to worry about the draft. He was determined to see the president of North–South International and get that job in the Bahamas.

"I'm plotting to get him into Columbia," wrote the actor in one of his periodic reports to his former wife in Amsterdam.

> . . . I sent his exam results to old Walter (he's still registrar — I hope he remembers us). Why Columbia? Well, the Kleist play with Olivier fell through but Michael Langham is reviving *The Devil's Disciple* on Broadway and he wants me to star. Think of me at the Booth next fall, impersonating Shaw's hero of our revolution — now there was a good, sensible, winnable war, fought on home ground! . . . The present bloody foul-up in Vietnam fits in with my plot: once we're back in the States he's going to be hauled into the army unless he gets a student draft exemption. So it's university or the jungle for him . . .

The Nivens landed at Kennedy Airport at the end of August, arriving during the worst heat wave New Yorkers had to suffer in the 1960s. At long last Mark touched the ground of his native city, but he didn't allow the occasion to distract him. While his father was sleeping off the effects of the transatlantic flight and the first shock of the city's heat, humidity and foul temper at the Algonquin, Mark made his way to the

North–South Building, one of the swaying tower blocks of Lower Manhattan.

A receptionist guarding the entrance to the presidential suite of offices on the 56th floor sent him to the personnel department on the 64th floor and, after a long wait, he managed to see the vice-president for personnel, Mr. Anthony Heller — a most unusual executive whose office ignored as much mail as any other, but who made a point of being accessible to everybody in person. A portly, graying man with a small mustache and lively eyes, full of sympathetic curiosity, Mr. Heller came forward to meet Mark halfway across the great expanse of carpet, shook his hand, waved him toward a deep leather armchair, and offering him coffee and bonbons, invited him to talk about himself.

Mark was dazed by this royal treatment, but had enough diplomatic sense left to introduce himself as his father's son. As it happened, Heller had seen *The Emperor* and admired Niven's performance, and he spent over an hour chatting with the actor's son. It turned out that they shared a love of Italian art. Mr. Heller, who spent a month in Rome and Florence every spring doing nothing but walking about in the great churches and galleries, was delighted to find someone, a teenager at that, with whom he could discuss Donatello and Bernini and their unacknowledged superiority to Michelangelo.

"Bernini can carve character, he can carve movement, states of mind; Michelangelo's great only at sculpting repose and muscles," Mr. Heller said with a severe expression, as he had come by this observation on his own and felt very deeply about it.

"Right," replied Mark, delighted to be Mr. Heller's equal at this sort of thing. "Bernini's David's a real killer, Michelangelo's could be anybody who has reason to feel pleased with himself. And for that I'd prefer Cellini's Narcissus in the Bargello . . ."

No doubt Mr. Heller's colleagues would have found this conversation supremely ridiculous, but there is a deep bond between strangers who discover that they speak the same language. "I can go weeks without meeting anyone who's interested in what we're talking about," sighed Mr. Heller. "Tell me what you want me to do for you, young man, and *I'll do it.*"

The words of the genie!

Mark thought he was dreaming. He said what he wanted was a job as an interpreter at the Seven Seas Club hotel on Santa Catalina Island.

"I don't understand . . . why would you want to run away from the world?" asked Mr. Heller, taken aback. "I assumed you were going to ask me for a job in Rome or Paris."

Mark blushed. "I'd like to go some place I haven't been."

"But what made you think of Santa Catalina? I thought Sir Henry's private fiefdom was practically a secret."

Looking about him intently in the otherwise empty room, Mark lowered his voice. "I might as well tell you . . . I'm planning to dive for wrecks around the island," he admitted hesitantly but hopefully, encouraged by their friendly talk about art. "I think I might find something."

Frowning, Mr. Heller put a peppermint cream in his mouth and said nothing until it melted away. "You want to go on a *treasure hunt?*" he asked unhappily.

"I've done a lot of research into it."

"That's no occupation for an intelligent young man. At your age you're too old for play and too young for wasting your time. I must admit I don't see how I could wrangle with the Bahamian government for a thing like that. Nor do I think I would be doing you a favor. You're too bright for a hotel on a small island. You should go to college first."

Mark froze: not his father all over again! "I can learn a lot on my own," he said after a despairing pause, begging for mercy. "And I wouldn't want any big salary, I'd be satisfied with a part-time job. Actually a part-time job with a small salary might be better, it would give me time for diving. And I would work at anything. If there's no need for interpreters, I could —"

"Don't, please don't, don't!" cried Mr. Heller, standing up and shaking his head with embarrassment. "You don't need to recommend yourself. I'm most impressed, really most impressed. And you mustn't talk to me about small salaries, I'm not that much of a company man. I assure you, I'll do my best for a Berninist. Only you must come to me with something reasonable."

'A Berninist!' thought Mark bitterly, feeling sick as he dropped down to earth in the express elevator with the speed of a free-fall. 'What a phony, what a hypocrite!'

This was most unjust.

Past fifty and a bachelor, Heller had lost his ambition to rise higher in the world, and had no desire to appear anything but what he was. Having saved and invested enough to last for the rest of his days, he didn't even care particularly about keeping his job, and acted on the principle that people needed more consideration than the giant conglomerate he worked for. His chief amusement in life was to help spirited men and women who were too troublesome to get ahead without him. Such adventurous executives, given to generous impulses, who no longer seek their own advancement yet still retain the positions of power for which they fought in their days of servile zeal, keep the bureaucracies of business and state from becoming totally moribund. Heller wouldn't have minded breaking some rules for Mark, but wishing to be truly helpful to him, he sent him away with an apologetic handshake.

"I'm surprised that he'd see you at all," said Niven.

"Yeah, I'm getting all the breaks."

"That's right, you are. My agent found us a nice big apartment in Morningside Heights. Twentieth floor, you can see lots of trees from the windows. You can walk to Columbia, your parents' alma mater — and I strongly urge you to follow in our footsteps. I already had a chat with the registrar about you and he says you can get in."

"You did? When?"

"I just wanted us to be ready in case the hotel people let you down."

"You never believed I'd get to Santa Catalina, did you," said Mark, feeling betrayed.

The actor sighed. "Listen, kid, you've been spoiled, being a tourist all your life, with no government bugging you. But tourists are the only free people on earth, and you're not a tourist any more. Not here. This is your country, you're an American citizen, your government owns you. They can grab you any time they want you. There's a war on, remember? And when they make war they need all the kids. The only way you can escape their clutches is to go to college. Being a student is almost as good as being a tourist. You should go and talk to the registrar. Unless of course you're planning to visit Vietnam, see the jungles of the Orient."

"What's the difference!" Mark said bleakly. If he didn't have the ten thousand to go to Santa Catalina it didn't matter where he went.

Nothing was any use.

Only money could find money.

Next morning, trying not to think, he set out to explore the city, but didn't look at anything long enough to like it. He missed the chimney pots and garden squares of London; everything was strange. He walked the streets for days, prowling around Manhattan like a caged lion.

10

The Discovery of America by Christopher Columbus

They appeared to think
that we came from the sky.
COLUMBUS

'WHAT if there is a God and I'm being punished?' Mark asked himself as he walked past a Korean fruit store on upper Broadway. Without being aware of it he stopped to take a breath of air smelling of ripe grapes and melons, but his thoughts remained dark. 'There doesn't even have to be a God. Mr. Heller could have sensed that I have a mean streak in me, and that's why he didn't give me the job.'

He was bothered by the recurring memory of Signorina Rognoni's stricken face. He could still see the bruised look in her eyes, and her painful blush. How dark and deep her eyes were! He wished he had known her better. He wished he had hugged her and thanked her for finding him the logbook. Didn't he deserve his misery? He expected everybody to help him and how had he treated the only person who actually went out of her way to do him a good turn?

Decent people are often saved from the extremes of self-pity by pangs of bad conscience. Intensely ashamed of himself, he asked his way to the nearest post office, waited in line for twenty minutes and bought an air letter. Standing at the counter, he wrote to Signorina Rognoni, care of the archives in Genoa. He confessed that she had found the right logbook for him, the very thing he needed, the clue to the location of the wreck, and he hadn't thanked her because he was afraid of starting rumors about it. But that was no excuse and he now realized that he had been a rotten, ungrateful bastard, *un mascalzone!* He begged her to forgive him. He would never forget her kindness, and if he ever got away from New York and found the *Flora,* he was going to bring her *qualcosa veramente bellissima.*

Doing the right thing made his adrenalin flow: ready to start all over again, he felt his brain wake up. Walking south on Broadway, he decided to treat himself to some paintings, and went into Huntington Hartford's Gallery of Modern Art at Columbus Circle — a fine museum that New York would have for only eight years. (Where else could a *museum* have such a short life?) Mark liked most of the paintings, but one in particular, Salvador Dali's *Discovery of America by Christopher Columbus,* struck him with the force of revelation, reminding him that none of the natives of the Bahamas and Haiti had lived long after Columbus discovered them.

It was an amazing moment.

He found himself staring at a radiant vision of the Spaniards' landing in the New World, with the air cover of heavenly figures and crosses flying out of the clouds like missiles. Below, from a frothy white and blue sea teeming with lances and halberds, banners and crosses, came the Spaniards — half-naked, strong, handsome, pink — led by a tall, curly-haired, triumphant Columbus leaping ashore with Saint Gala floating off his banner. This Columbus was a young Saint Christopher, beautiful as flesh turned into myth — and yet what an ominous shadow he cast on the land!

This cunning masterpiece, derided by the art experts of the day, had been consigned to the stairwell, and as Mark backed away from it for a better look, he lost his balance — for an instant he had no idea what was happening — and fell down some steps. It was a typical episode in the life of this intelligent fool: he failed to do the easy thing, to look where he was going — yet he could think even while being surprised by fright and pain, which was quite an extraordinary accomplishment. By the time he got up, stretched his back, bent his legs, brushed off his trousers, he already knew how he was going to raise ten thousand dollars. Or twelve thousand. Or more.

ONCE they had moved into their apartment in Morningside Heights, Mark pinned up his pictures of the Madonna of Lima and General San Martín in his new room and went to see the registrar at Columbia.

"I've signed up for courses in Latin American history," he informed his father next morning at breakfast, their customary time for talking business. The more they moved about the more fixed they became in their habits. "They have a terrific Spanish Department — because of all the Puerto Ricans here, I guess."

"Wonderful," commented Niven, troubled by Mark's confident coolness.

"I knew you'd be pleased."

Spending his days in the library even before term started, moving about with stacks of books, full of energy and purpose, Mark appeared to be dedicated wholeheartedly to a student's life.

"You seem to be enjoying yourself," his father observed one morning, fishing for information.

"Yeah, I'm keeping busy," replied Mark mysteriously, with the air of knowing something he alone knew. "How is *The Devil's Disciple?*" he inquired in his turn. "How are rehearsals going?"

"Not badly. They haven't hanged me yet."

Mark laughed and laughed as though he couldn't stop. "Hey, Dad, that's funny!"

'What is he up to? Why is he so happy?' wondered Niven.

Parental curiosity knows no shame. Searching Mark's room one day when Mark was out, he discovered a pile of exercise books on the upper shelf in the clothes closet.

He should have guessed!

Mark was all set to finance one dream with another dream.

After leafing through the exercise books and then carefully replacing them on the shelf, Niven went back to his own room and, humming "The Battle Hymn of the Republic", a favorite tune of his childhood, sat down to write another report to Amsterdam:

Good news about our treasure hunter! He's saved. We can stop worrying about him. He has a new obsession, and it's going to keep him away from both the Vietcong and the sharks.

I know you won't believe this, but he's actually writing a book. What it's about will come as less of a surprise — he's trying to write a history of the conquest of Peru and what came after. I looked over his jottings (by stealth, of course, for God's sake don't give me away) and do you know, they're quite impressive. His earlier papers on trade routes and wind charts were beyond me, but his notes on Peru really tell you something. Of course it's all in aid of raising money for his treasure hunt — I gathered this from the equations on the margin of the manuscript. One of them reads "world rights = $12,000" — which is what he figures his expedition would cost him. . . . But it makes no difference why he thinks he's studying and taking notes — so long as he keeps at it. Eventually he is bound to find history more interesting than sunken wrecks. And sooner or later New York is going to grab him. Let's just hope he won't get mixed up with the "drug culture." (What do they mean, culture!) Who will be his friends? That's my only worry now . . .

Mark's first friend in New York was a bronze horseman. Walking along Central Park South one day he discovered that the equestrian statue he had already passed several times without bothering to take a second look was none other than General José Francisco de San Martín, the Liberator of Argentina, Chile and Peru. 'So here we are, both of us!' he thought with amazement. Suddenly the fact of his having been born in this strange city made sense.

It also made sense to the authorities. Though granted temporary draft exemption as a student, Mark received a summons to register for military service, a powerful reminder that his body didn't entirely belong to him. He was a citizen with the duties of citizenship and there was no way he could forget about them and mind his own business. Every glimpse of sunlight glittering on the Hudson made him think of the warm seas of the Bahamas, of gold and glory, but there was always someone to wake him.

"So you don't want to fight for your country?" remarked the superintendent of their apartment building, a lean and bald veteran of the Korean War, when he heard that Mark was going to college.

"I did fight for my country," replied Mark, without specifying that he had done so with his bare hands and teeth.

"No kidding? In what war?"

"Not in a war. I don't believe in killing."

"I see, you want the good life without paying for it."

Mark reddened. "I'll pay for the good life in my own way."

The superintendent made a long speech in body language: he rubbed his bald head, screwed up his pale thin face and sharp red nose, looked craftily away, then added aloud: "I don't blame you. Cowards live longest."

"I'm not a coward."

"Let's just say you know how to take care of yourself."

At first Mark felt that he had landed in the only true democracy in the world, where everybody had the right — and, it seemed, the duty — to insult everybody else.

One of his classmates at Columbia called him a square because he wasn't interested in drugs and threw up when he tried marijuana.

Another called him a fascist because, quoting his father, he said that Stalin had killed even more people than Hitler. And he was called stupid because he didn't go to an antiwar demonstration.

"Are you stupid enough to think you can ignore what's going on?" he was asked by a tall, beautiful girl with light brown hair and dark brown eyes. She pounced on him during a corridor discussion, calling him stupid without knowing anything about him.

"I may be stupid but you're a bossy bitch," retorted Mark bitterly, because he was impressed by her long, slender neck, her long slim legs, narrow hips and flat bottom, and her amazingly full breasts, which seemed to be the only part of her body that stuck out. Her manner was so scornful that he didn't realize she was criticizing him because she liked his dark look.

Vietnam meant abuse, arguments, exhortations, yet it was mainly because of the war that Mark began to feel at home in America.

A few years later, when President Nixon had abolished the draft to make students lose interest in what the government was doing, Mark would have gone through college without worrying his head about public issues, a tourist in his own country. But in 1967 the shared prospect of having to fight in the Vietnam War if it lasted long enough created a critical, spirited community that pulled in everyone. Discovering the thrill of belonging, Mark began to attend coffee-shop discussions and protest rallies, though less frequently than most students, for he was a studious person.

When they occupied the president's offices at Columbia, Mark helped to hoot out the security guards who made halfhearted attempts to evict them, and held the paint for two sociology students who were defacing the walls with slogans. Later generations of college students would make news by taking down their trousers on national television, by dragging their girls onto the football field and pouring beer over them, or by jumping in unison to one side of a passenger plane in flight "to see what would happen". In the 1960s and early 1970s young Americans made a nuisance of themselves to call attention to cruelty and injustice. And unlike the later fads for beer ball and nude wrestling in all-male fraternities, hell-raising inspired by notions of the common good brought the sexes together; for the rest of their lives many alumni of the 60s would feel a buzz in their blood when they thought of those days.

It was during the Columbia sit-in that Mark found the girl who had called him stupid. Her name was Martha Friedman and she was majoring in zoology at Barnard. They spent the night together, sitting beside each other on the floor, singing with the crowd, *We shall overcome . . .* She had brought along a little bag of raisins and nuts which she shared with him, and though the lights were on, he managed to slip his hand down the back of her jeans to massage the base of her spine and her small bottom.

In the morning when they were carried out by the cops and dropped on the pavement beside each other, he leaped to his feet and helped her to get up. She said she felt sleepy, so he suggested that they go to his place, which was nearer than hers, to have a nap before going to classes.

"A nap?" asked Martha. Her laugh came from deep down like a mating call and went on and on like a song.

That laugh carried them all the way to bed, and in the end they didn't sleep. As they were getting dressed to go out again, Mark confided his great secret to her. He was going to locate the most famous treasure wreck in the history of the seas, loaded with Inca gold and diamonds.

"Surely you can aim higher than *that!*" she exclaimed, raising her voice and stamping her foot, then brushing her long hair away from her face so that she could glare down at him with her honest brown eyes.

She was taller than he was, in every way. And it wasn't just her eyes and stern expression either. She hadn't buttoned her shirt yet and her white breasts were still showing, tempting and accusing him.

"You're mad at me because you didn't enjoy yourself," argued Mark defensively.

"I did so!" she protested, flushing. "I told you it was nice. Don't spoil it. And don't try to change the subject. It's your materialistic attitude I'm objecting to."

"Are you sure that's all you object to?" asked Mark dispiritedly, thinking that it was a mistake to make love when they had been up all night.

"You don't know how it is with girls," she said, exasperated. "It's quieter with us. Just because I don't writhe and moan all the time doesn't mean I don't enjoy it. Wasn't I moist?"

"Yeah, I guess so."

"Well, then, what more do you want? If I get moist it means I'm enjoying myself. A big, big orgasm is a once-in-a-blue-moon thing for women. You seem to think life is all about sex and money."

To defend himself, Mark made her sit down and read what he had written about Columbus, and she liked it so much that she gave him a strong kiss and told him she would drop by the next day.

Martha was the daughter of a prosperous and happy couple: both her parents were dentists, and dentists are the luckiest of all healers, since they are not confronted with mortal diseases and earn their living freeing people from pain, knowing for certain that there is less misery in the world because of them. The parents' rewarding profession made them kindly and benevolent, which must have contributed to their daughter's exacting idealism.

She often asked Mark to think what it would be like to be a victim of war or poverty, to be burned or starved; a strict vegetarian, she even urged him to make an effort and imagine how he would feel if he were a chicken — a chicken who was never allowed out into the barnyard to hop about in the sunshine, who had to spend his life squeezed into a space so small that he could move nothing but his head, who was hemmed in, pinned down from birth to death in a poultry hell called a battery farm.

Mark could not quite make the kind of creative leap that would have enabled him to see himself as a suffering chicken, but he could see himself as an Inca prince who had tried to resist the invaders and was dragged to the gallows in his own city, followed by the crowd of his heart-stricken subjects. Once when they were having a hard time in bed he told Martha the story of the betrayal of Atahualpa, and she pressed him to her as tight as she could and wouldn't let him go, and when they made love again she melted. Sometimes she had a frozen smile on her face whatever he did, and he found he could regain her affection only by telling her a story that moved her. To have stories to tell her, to have things to show her, gave him an extra reason to learn all he could about Peru.

His history of Peru was an over-ambitious project, born of inexperience: practically everyone who finds it easy to read a book assumes that it is easy to write one, and Mark was no exception. At first he planned a big thick volume which would include everything from the Incas to San Martín and Bolívar. Once he began to shape his notes into paragraphs, however, his whole concept changed: the shortness of the book was to be the very essence of it. Still, he kept at it, filling one exercise book after another and hiding them in his clothes closet.

"What I find most encouraging," Niven reported to Mark's mother, "is all the revising he does."

. . . He crosses out whole pages — I've seen a dozen versions of the same paragraph. He's evidently trying for the best way of saying things. And as we know only too well, he isn't a quitter.

Before he knows it, he'll have his Ph.D. and a job teaching at some university. By then the war will be over. Frankly, I think the treasure ship is going to fade from his mind, like all the big ideas of youth, once he's carved out a place for himself in the world . . .

Parents are only too keen to clutch at any straw of hope that might deliver them from fear for their children's future, but who is to say that Niven could not have turned out to be right? Certainly Mark's four-year odyssey through libraries and archives in search of clues to a fortune had prepared him for nothing so much as scholarly pursuits.

Besides, Martha wanted him to be a teacher. She thought they should stay in New York and try to get jobs teaching at the same school.

With lectures, his book, meetings and demonstrations, Martha, there were days when he didn't get around to thinking about the *Flora* at all.

Is it altogether inconceivable that he might have made a fresh start in life at the age of eighteen?

An Incident Involving an Apple

I will ease my heart,
albeit I make a hazard of my head.
HOTSPUR

THE demonstration in front of the Butler Library was above all a big
sound. The roar of several thousand strong young voices. They
drowned out the traffic noise and the helicopters; for once people sounded
mightier than machines.

Hell, no, we won't go!
Hell, no, we won't go!

Vice-President Hubert Horatio Humphrey was coming to Columbia
University to explain to the students — and to the nation via television
— why the war had to continue: he was carrying President Johnson's
message, and the students wanted to make sure that he carried their
message back to the President.

Hell, no, we won't go!
Hell, no, we won't go!

It was one of those battles without guns in which President Johnson
was beaten into retirement. The kids screamed no to his war. They were
high on the sense of their numbers, on the immense sound they could
produce, on outrage, on the horror of death, on compassion, on slogans;
some were high on dope or love for Ho Chi Minh or hatred for their
parents. But ultimately they screamed no to war because they did not
feel that America was in danger. It was a mystery at the time how one
half of a small backward country could fight the most powerful nation
on earth to a standstill, though it was precisely this disparity of power
which in the end defeated American arms. No nation, no democratic nation, can fight a war successfully unless its citizens feel personally
threatened, and there was no way Americans could conceive of Com-

munist Vietnam ever being powerful enough to burn their homes. To be sure, there were Asians who were said to need protection, and there were global considerations, but not many people want to kill or get killed for distant strangers or the balance of power.

"No President can conduct a prolonged war against a small country and expect to have the nation behind him," a liberal congressman said on television, commenting on the live broadcast of the demonstration. "The American people have no taste for clobbering the weak. Most of us still believe in fair fights."

Hell, no, we won't go!
Hell, no, we won't go!

It was a bright cold December day. Martha wore her big tartan scarf which covered her face up to her nose and reached below her knees; in her shoulder bag she carried biscuits and apples in case they got hungry. Milling about with the other kids, laughing and talking excitedly between their angry shouts, they felt their hearts beating together, which made them beat faster. Neither of them had ever been in such a big crowd before and there was surprise mixed with their pride that they were part of it and their voices were part of that roar which sounded as though it came from the bowels of the earth.

"Mark?" Martha said.

Mark stopped to listen.

"You know what?" she said, moving the scarf from her mouth.

"What?"

She leaned close to him to whisper. "Your face looks exactly the way it looks when you make love with me."

He took a deep breath, trying to get hold of himself and just look on, but the excitement was too great for him not to be caught up in it. The crowd thickened and began to heave about; someone stepped on Martha's scarf; she stepped on somebody's feet. But it made no difference: they were all held together by a profound, almost physical bond of brotherhood.

Hey, hey, LBJ,
how many kids did you kill today?

Mark yelled with Martha. Tossed about by people surging in various directions, separated from each other several times, having to run to avoid being trampled on, they were hoarse, sweating and out of breath by the time they found their way barred by a burly policeman making a stop sign with his oversized hand. They had ended up near the Vice-President's motorcade just as the cars were coming to a halt. There was a sudden stillness, a tense moment of waiting, but no one got out of the cars, the doors remained closed, giving the crowd a sense that the occupants were afraid to come out and face them. Then came a sudden explosion of hysteria: a group of students began to scream.

"Fucking coward!"

"No-o-o-o-o-o!"

"We won't go!"

"Chickenshit!"

"Cocksucker!"

There was a philosophy behind the obscenities, based on the belief that the men who were running the war were, as Norman Mailer put it in *Armies of the Night,* "capable of burning unseen women and children in the Vietnamese jungles, yet felt a large displeasure and fairly final disapproval at the generous use of obscenity in literature and in public." If they could feel revulsion and horror only at four-letter words, then let them feel revulsion and horror at something. Every *shit-fuck* was a challenge, an accusation. So you think words are shocking, and you're not shocked by napalm raining on children? You set fire to people, and you tell us we should have good manners? *Shit-fuck* meant: it isn't the words that are obscene, but the deeds!

"Fucking cowards!"

The cars with the people in them seemed to be petrified.

Mark took a McIntosh apple from Martha's shoulder bag (it felt as cold as ice) and kept munching it to steady his nerves. Eventually two Secret Service men sprang forward to open the passenger door of the vice-presidential limousine and Vice-President Humphrey emerged from safety into hostile daylight: a tall, stout and ruddy figure, clearly visible in spite of the ring of guards around him.

"Pig!"

"Fascist!"

"Asshole!"

"Murderer!"

"Motherfucker!"

The Vice-President stood and waved and smiled.

Was there a bullet for him in the crowd?

The Vice-President stood and waved and smiled.

Hubert Horatio Humphrey, often referred to in headlines as HHH, steeped in the compromises of a lifetime of politics, and now defending a war he was said not to believe in, still retained something of the valor of a man whose middle name honored a hero of the Roman Republic: Horatius Cocles held a bridge over the Tiber single-handed against an invading army in 507 B.C. A name, even a middle name, which recalls a brave act that has survived for twenty-five hundred years is bound to affect its bearer.

> *Alone stood brave Horatius,*
> *But constant still in mind . . .*

In Humphrey's youth, when Latin and the history of honor were on the curriculum, the poem about his ancient namesake was printed in all school readers, and it must have made a great impression on him.

> *Then out spake brave Horatius,*
> *The Captain of the Gate:*
> *'To every man upon this Earth*
> *Death cometh soon or late.*
> *And how can man die better*
> *Than facing fearful odds . . .'*

Macaulay's poetic style had grown as musty as the sentiments expressed, yet they fortified many generations. A few years later, dying of cancer, HHH still attended public functions and gave the smile of a happy man till his last hour. The demonstrators held no terrors for him, at any rate no terrors that showed. Most people watching the scene on television were impressed by his courage, even if they thought he was brave in a bad cause. From where the crowd stood, however, Humphrey's bravery looked like arrogance. The students around him were shouting themselves hoarse with hate words, fascist-asshole-pig-murderer, and all Mark could see was a fatty-faced politician who went on waving and smiling — smiling! — as if they were cheering him, as if the whole crowd meant nothing.

On a sudden impulse of self-assertion — not only for himself but for all the kids, just to say *we're here!* — Mark threw his half-eaten apple and hit the Vice-President of the United States of America right between the eyes.

The policeman with big hands, an ox in perfect physical condition picked for crowd control, didn't see whether it was an apple or a grenade — he only saw an object flying — and, maddened by the fear that he had been standing beside an assassin and failed to spot him, leaped on Mark with his whole body, knocked him to the ground, then kicked him hard to make him get up. Bleeding from the nose, with a roar inside his head louder than the crowd's, Mark staggered to his feet and was led — half carried — to a police car. His body felt so strange and painful that he longed to sink down and die.

A sergeant, worried about lawsuits and mindful of the death of Lee Harvey Oswald in police custody, grabbed him under the arms to hold him up. "Breathe deeply and tell us if it hurts."

By the time it was established that he had nothing broken or torn inside him and could stand on his own two feet without assistance, an order had come through the radio. At the request of the Vice-President, he was released and told that no charges would be brought.

They gave him back his library card and let him go.

Unluckily, his throw was caught by the television cameras for all the world to see, identifying him for the university authorities.

Losing his chance of a scholar's peaceful life took no more than a moment's blunder. Expelled from Columbia, forfeiting his draft deferment as a student, he became subject to the directive of General Hershey (now dead and forgotten, though Dana Niven still curses him) ordering protesters to be drafted ahead of everybody else to fight in the war they protested against, and promptly received his call-up papers.

As for Mark's history of Peru, it was never completed, or indeed properly started, but his notes on his reading, his drafts for various chapters and an introduction are among the papers his father has preserved. Written in the forthright style of his generation which so irritates the elderly in spirit, the introduction includes these extraordinary sentences:

> Columbus descended upon the Americas like an Angel of Death, widening the horizons of human rapacity and cruelty and the frontiers of the Spanish Empire. This celebrated criminal, who was himself responsible for the extermination of the native peoples of Haiti and the Bahamas, opened two continents to like-minded alchemists of the new age, who employed every conceivable method of turning human flesh into gold, achieving their most spectacular results in Peru.

No doubt Mark's refusal to grant any merit to Columbus was inspired by the radical spirit of the Vietnam War years, when most students viewed the whole of Western civilization as a kind of malignant force in history. Though he argued with Martha that Western civilization wasn't Auschwitz or the Spanish Inquisition but the Sermon on the Mount, Dante, Perugino, Bernini, Goya, the Declaration of Independence, he couldn't help being affected by the prevailing hostility to all authorities, alive or dead. He wanted

> . . . to make up for the lack of outrage in other treatments of the subject, which are so replete with solicitude for the hardships endured by the conquistadores in the course of enslaving, robbing and murdering the inhabitants of foreign lands where they had no business to be in the first place.

This is from his notes on the Spanish method of pearl fishing:

> The Spaniards had themselves rowed out to the oyster beds, threw the savages into the sea, pressed their heads under the water with the oars and wouldn't let them come up for air unless they had shells in their hands. The Indians either produced pearls or were drowned; none survived long.

There are two exercise books filled with his attempts to describe how the Spaniards kidnapped the Indians from their villages and drove them down into the silver and mercury mines.

These Indians, who had believed in their heathen days that they were the children of the sun, were kept underground for six days and nights at a time, and many fell to their death or were fatally poisoned on their first shift in the "infernal pits", robbed of light forever.

Mark's descriptions show many signs of his ability to put himself inside other people's skin — a rare gift which might have been his saving grace, for whether people are good or bad, useful or harmful, depends not on their moral principles or even their conscious aims, but on the strength of their imagination.

"He was half an actor. He couldn't play other people, but he could feel like them, if he put his mind to it," Dana Niven often says, still insisting bitterly that Mark had the makings of a good man and a good historian, if only he could have continued his studies.

But then the history of his own day caught up with him.

Touch and Go

What in the world is the meaning of this?
Why are you sitting here in such a frightful state?
Have you committed some crime?

APULEIUS

THE day began with a blizzard in New York. By late morning the
falling snow had melted to a drizzle and the wind slackened to a
breeze, but at Kennedy International Airport flights continued to be delayed for hours. With sixty or so passengers aboard, most of them pale
vacationers longing for a spell of summer, the BOAC jetliner scheduled
to take off at 11:30 A.M. hadn't yet moved from the ground at one o'clock.
Bored children roamed the aisle to stare critically at strangers, blocking
the path of the harassed stewardesses, who were busy trying to satisfy
the many urgent needs that seize people when they are locked up in a
plane that won't fly. Their restless din rose in waves against the endless,
even flow of piped music.

Mark, sitting by one of the windows, kept refusing the free drinks,
candies and magazines, waving the stewardesses away with brusque impatience. Later he just ignored them. His face was beset by changing
expressions of anger, helplessness, desperation, incredulity and, most
alarmingly, an occasional gleam of bliss.

The passenger in the aisle seat, having spoken to him several times
without eliciting the slightest response, reached out to shake his arm.
"Say, just between you and me," he inquired with conspiratorial condescension, "you tripping out on acid or something?"

Mark jumped when he was touched, as if he were about to spring to
his feet, but then settled back with studied casualness, though his lips
quivered involuntarily. "It's just that I hate waiting around," he said.
"It gets on my nerves."

"Your nerves are shot, all right," the older man agreed with unmistakable satisfaction, feeling rather unsettled himself. Earlier he had been
hard at work trying to squeeze his enormous behind into the narrow

economy-class seat, and eventually had hit upon the idea of pushing back the retractable armrest and spreading the fat of his body over the empty place in the middle; but then he had celebrated his hard-won comfort with a couple of bourbons too many. Though well dressed and apparently well off, he had a poor complexion, and his pallid, bloated face, his whole demeanor, suggested one of those busy traveling men who spend most of their life in hotels and bars, taking their share of alcohol and shoddy deals while they grow overweight, middle-aged and sour. He adopted an air of hostile familiarity toward the distraught stranger. "What do you know, a kid your age and already a nervous wreck. Where you from?"

Mark rubbed his nose with his fist in frustration. A casual *where are you from?* was never a simple question for him, but this time he missed a heartbeat. He had such a longing to be home, to be with Martha, with his father, to walk in the park with the kids, that he actually started to get out of his seat before he remembered where he was and why he was going. "I came from London. I was only born in the States," he declared bitterly. "I don't really belong here."

This mystifying outburst confirmed the fat man in his original impression. "Who said you did? I didn't say you did. I just asked you a simple question. You're in bad shape, son, you better watch it. You don't know whether you're coming or going."

"Well, we aren't doing either, are we!"

The fat man's small eyes almost disappeared under rising folds of excess flesh as his extremely thin lips, scarcely visible otherwise, twisted into a malicious smile of superiority. "Is it acid?"

"I don't even smoke!"

In truth Mark was drugged with fright, having no idea what was going to happen to him next. Once they took off he would be free, start his new life (there were moments when he was sure he would make it) but while they were on the ground he could be dragged off the plane at any time. He was now a draft dodger with a warrant out for his arrest; two FBI agents had already been looking for him at the apartment. Having felt the heavy hand of the law and at the same time knowing very little about it, he imagined that all the police in the country were after him. A novice lawbreaker, he saw himself as a dangerous criminal on the run with his picture on every Wanted list, and was certain that the police would check the passenger list during the plane's interminable delay. The thought kept him writhing in his seat.

The fat man on the aisle didn't miss a thing. "Yes," he said, nodding his head with spiteful satisfaction. "Yes — it's lysergic acid diethylamide, all right. That's what they call your trouble, LSD."

' Seized by the additional fear that his neighbor might denounce him as a narcotics user, Mark already saw himself being dragged off the plane, arrested on the wrong charge. "Not all kids are crazy, sir," he said, summoning up a deferential manner and combing his hair with his fingers to draw attention to the fact that it was short. Getting his shoulder-length hair cut had seemed to him the perfect disguise. "I wouldn't mess up my head with drugs."

"It's no use telling me stories," the inquisitive passenger announced, suddenly deciding to reveal his importance. "I'm an ex-police officer — Pittsburgh police force. Got my own agency in Chicago now. With some very big clients. I can see through people." This burst of self-praise put him in a more solicitous mood toward himself; he unzipped his fly halfway down to give his tightly pressed abdomen a rest and asked the stewardess for another free bourbon on the rocks before turning back to his companion. "It's just a question of what you're using, son. I can tell your type a mile off."

"Can you?" asked Mark with a sidelong look. He didn't think anybody knew him. Drugs were a case in point. As if there were no bigger thrills than grass and chemicals! He thought longingly of the company of Bernini's statues. "I don't need drugs," he said edgily. "When I want to expand my mind I just close my eyes and get high on *Saint Teresa in Ecstasy.*"

Who could have foreseen that the former policeman from Pittsburgh would react with anger to the mention of this legitimate work of art? But then he took every remark he didn't understand as a personal insult. Losing his grip on the conversation, he lapsed into the habits of his old days on the beat. "OK, what's your name?" he demanded in the raw, threatening voice of authority.

"Why do you want to know?"

The FASTEN YOUR SEAT BELT — NO SMOKING sign lit up, the jet engines shook the plane, and the aircraft began to move, rolling slowly away from the terminal building.

The fat man repeated his question in an ominous, show-me-your-driver's-license tone, ordering the offender to identify himself. "Come on, what's your name!"

Liberated by the movement of the plane, Mark let loose some pent-up hostility of his own. "Listen, you'd better stop pestering me. You're getting to be a bore — why don't you just leave me alone?"

The other's attitude altered abruptly. "My name's Howard Sypco-vich," he said in a weak voice, recoiling into his seat as he was hit by the memory of a hard punch he had received at a Chicago hotel a couple of months earlier. His lack of any sense of other people's privacy helped him in his work but also earned him many snubs and a few blows. "Here I am trying to make friendly conversation," he complained, elderly and paternal now, at once reproachful and forgiving, "and you jump down my throat. You kids are spaced out."

"With all that bourbon you drink, I'm surprised you have the nerve to talk about drugs. Do you know that alcohol is a bigger killer than heroin?"

Sypcovich was bewildered by the sudden transformation of his traveling companion, who now appeared tough, confident and hostile, with his wits very much about him. "What's got into you?"

"I don't like bullies."

Sypcovich couldn't help responding with a threatening posture; equally automatically, he veiled his threat in ambiguity — the threat wasn't made if it didn't work. "Take it easy, son, settle down," he advised grimly. "That kind of language gets people into trouble."

"Yeah. Cops from Pittsburgh kick them in the head."

The private investigator narrowed his eyes. "So . . . first it was Jack Daniel's, now it's the cops! Cops protect decent citizens from screwballs." He put special emphasis on *screwballs* to leave no doubt as to whom he had in mind.

There followed a brief exchange of heated political slogans. Identifying his neighbor with police brutality, Mark resented him not only on his own account but also on behalf of all those who suffered at the hands of the law. For his part, Sypcovich no longer had to bear the full burden of the youngster's hostility on his ego and could see himself as the representative of all right-thinking citizens. They could now despise each other as public enemies; personal antagonism was sublimated into righteous indignation, as each man used his bit of the truth to infuriate the other. Such are the unexpected benefits of troubled times, when social tensions create enough public acrimony to ensure that people do not have to hate and be hated in solitude.

Their argument was punctuated by a jolt, as the slow-moving aircraft came to a dead stop.

"That was a false alarm, ladies and gentlemen, boys and girls," the captain's cheery voice reported through the intercom. "It seems we still have a few big silver birds ahead of us on the runway." The captain's announcement was followed by the resumption of piped music and some groans and sarcastic comments about airline humor from the other passengers.

Mark had turned pale with disbelief. Would he spend the best years of his life in jail while someone else found the wreck? What maddened him most was the unfairness of it all. He had planned everything so carefully! He had taken the precaution of getting on a BOAC flight after ascertaining that the U.S. authorities had no power to recall a British plane once it left American airspace, and it galled him that he could still be arrested when he should already be out of their reach according to the airline's schedule.

"Well, well," Sypcovich remarked with the fearsome joviality of the shrewd interrogator he imagined himself to be. "Looks like we have sufficient time at our disposal to get acquainted."

Mark did not respond, and they passed some minutes in silence, while Sypcovich savored the spectacle of his insolent companion's dejection.

"I gather from our little chat you're some kind of a student — against everything, eh? You look pretty well-off, too. Cashmere sweater, hand-made boots, expensive watch. A spoiled kid, the world isn't good enough for him. I have an eye for these things, you know — I'm made that way. It's what they call innate. I could have a barrel of bourbon and I'd still spot your type a mile away."

"You just can't leave people alone, can you!" Mark said through clenched teeth, turning his head away to stare at the dark, wet day beyond the oval window.

"Some kind of a violent radical, maybe," mused Sypcovich, and his grinning lips straightened to a thin, mean line. "I wouldn't be surprised. Maybe you're up to something right now. Maybe I should have a talk with the captain. Get the cops to check you out. Wouldn't do any harm — what do you say?"

But the fugitive didn't answer. The aircraft was moving again. It gathered speed and suddenly lifted them above the earth; his troubles were falling away like the land of America. They climbed through the drizzle, swept above the clouds, and in a magic instant the dark, sludgy winter sky turned into limitless blue space filled with sunlight. Mark pushed his seat belt aside, stood up and plunged his hands into his pockets.

Sypcovich eyed him with the gravest apprehension, regretting that regulations had compelled him to leave his gun at home. "What's up, friend?" he inquired carefully. "You planning to hijack this plane to Cuba?"

"It's none of your business!" declared Mark, rejecting any further intrusions on his privacy.

Having found his ballpoint pen, he sat down again, lifted the airline publicity folder from the cloth pouch on the backrest of the seat in front of him, and removed the free postcard depicting a silver BOAC VC-10 jetliner in a bright turquoise sky. Using the folder as a writing pad, he addressed the card to Mevrouw Barbara van der Harst, in Amsterdam.

Dear Mum — how are you? They threw me out of Columbia and
I got drafted, so rather than get killed in a stupid war or rot in jail,
I decided to clear out and get rich after all. I guess it's fate. Love,
Mark.

He planned to mail the card as soon as they landed in Nassau, as he hadn't written to her for months.

13

Interesting Combinations

> . . . there were high chances of a meeting,
> but no definite appointment.
> BRIGID BROPHY

'I'M trailing a frigid bitch and I'm sitting next to a nut,' Sypcovich fumed to himself. 'What a world!' However, the effects of the bourbon and the steady, monotonous drone of the jet engines gradually dulled his sense of alarm and exasperation and, finishing his latest drink and securing his trousers, he trotted off to the toilet in a stoical mood, not caring much whether they landed in the Bahamas or Castro's Cuba.

The private investigator was bound for Santa Catalina Island, tailing Mrs. Kevin Hardwick. He was in the adultery business. On his way back from the toilet he walked to the front of the plane to peek into the first-class compartment and see whether she was talking to anybody. When he saw her his fat face puffed up with indignation; she was sitting by herself, reading a book. In his entire career of catching lovers off guard, she had proved to be his most frustrating assignment. She was also his most valuable quarry: Hardwick Chemical Industries, with its synthetic fabrics, plastics and environmental products divisions, was said to be worth over a billion dollars. HCI was a small concern compared to giants like Du Pont or Union Carbide, but her husband owned 70% of the shares.

Mrs. Hardwick and the children lived the year round on Santa Catalina, while Kevin Hardwick commuted to Chicago for a five-day week to run his business and live with his girlfriend, the famous Pauline Marshall. Although he was away from his wife most of the time he refused to break up his marriage because he feared she would commit suicide if he left her, and Sypcovich was employed by the skeptical girlfriend to spy on the wife in the hope that she was carrying on an adulterous affair, the proof of which would persuade Hardwick to overcome his scruples and get a divorce. And since Miss Marshall was determined to marry her extremely rich lover at the end of it all, Sypcovich was paid two hundred dollars a day plus expenses and had a contract guaranteeing him a fifty-thousand-dollar bonus if he produced conclusive evidence of Mrs. Hardwick's infidelity.

It was a perfect deal all around; the only hitch was that Mrs. Hardwick apparently didn't have a lover.

High hopes were raised by her shopping trip to New York, where Sypcovich trailed her tirelessly through department stores, bookstores and art galleries — to restaurants, theaters, concerts — but could observe nothing useful for his purposes. Although she wore the shortest mini-skirts he had ever seen and evidently enjoyed making men stare at her, Mrs. Hardwick either kept her own company or went about with women friends; the elderly gentleman who escorted her to the opera on two occasions turned out to be her husband's uncle. Now she was on her way home, with a book as her companion.

"With all that money, she reads!" Sypcovich muttered to himself. What would have been his disgust if he had known that she wasn't even reading a best-seller but an out-of-print book by a dead Australian about a dead Austrian composer whose name, according to a PBS survey, was unfamiliar to 87% of American college students before Hollywood made a movie about him. "She reads, the stupid bitch!" he complained aloud. He resented her as if she avoided men on purpose, to prevent him from collecting his bonus. She was *robbing* him of fifty thousand dollars. The thought that he might never get that money made him so mad that he nearly knocked over a stewardess on his way back to his seat.

It is a peculiarity of human nature that one cannot hate two people at the same time with equal intensity, and after they were served snacks and coffee, Sypcovich felt more kindly disposed toward the young man beside him, who had been harmless long enough to allay his anxiety about hijacking. "I gather you grew up outside the States," he remarked cordially, as though they had never exchanged an ill word.

Relaxed and mellowed by boredom, drained of all emotions, Mark answered Sypcovich's questions willingly enough.

"That must have been interesting. An actor's son, eh?"

"Well, he was just a glorified extra, really. He played bit parts in crummy Hollywood movies made in Europe — like those Roman epics they used to make with a lot of semi-nudes and mangy lions running around the Colosseum. The lions lapped him up before you noticed him. How he stood it for eighteen years I'll never know."

Sypcovich snickered quietly, with the merriment of a man who understood.

"It wasn't funny. My mother couldn't stand it — they ended up getting a divorce."

At that the investigator began to chuckle with his whole bloated body. "It's kind of funny he kept it up so long. Eighteen years. Being a glorified extra, like you say."

Mark took exception to his own phrase. "Don't get me wrong, he's always been a good actor. It's just that nobody would give him a chance."

"Don't let it get you down," Sypcovich said piously. "He had the guts to hang on for eighteen years, you got to admire that. Not everybody can be a winner. What's he up to now?"

"Oh, now he's a big star," replied Mark, exaggerating in a deliberately offhand manner, as if his father's greatness meant nothing to him.

Sypcovich acknowledged this piece of information with a grunt, letting go of his bulk as he unzipped his fly again.

"Dana Niven — you must have heard of Dana Niven. You probably saw him in *The Emperor* — it was a big hit last year."

"Never heard of it."

"Well, if you didn't see the film, you must have seen his picture in the papers. He made the cover of the *New York Times Magazine* last summer."

Sypcovich listened with growing sullenness and resentment. With the peculiar logic of the truly malicious, he took the sudden rush of confidences as a put-down, quite forgetting that he had prompted them. 'What a punk!' he thought. 'Just because his daddy's a dime-a-dozen movie star, I'm supposed to listen to all his troubles. What's it to me if his parents got a divorce? Why should I care if the guy got his picture in some magazine? The world is full of famous people!' He made a point of showing that he wasn't impressed by confining himself to the curt observation: "Yeah, there's a lot of divorces these days."

This taunt had the intended effect of silencing Mark, and Sypcovich ordered a glass of soda water to celebrate. However, he couldn't rest until he found another way to score off the young punk who had insulted him by flaunting his father's success. In a fit of vanity he was even ready to gossip about the Hardwicks and his assignment, to cut the actor's son down to size. "I'm on a big case right now," he remarked with an expansive show of casualness. "There are some big names involved. You know what I mean? *Important people.*" This was meant as an additional snub. "When I break it, there'll be quite a splash in the papers."

Sypcovich saw no reason why he shouldn't confide his professional secrets to a stranger who happened to be sitting next to him on a plane, heading for the crowded tourist trap of Nassau, or, just as probably, flying on to Montego Bay. As it happened, since Mark was on the way to Santa Catalina himself, he was quite likely to meet Mrs. Hardwick — and he did, that very day. But that was in the unknown region of the future, half an hour away.

Buoyed up by his ballooning ego, Sypcovich continued dropping hints to prompt his companion to ask him questions. "A private investigator isn't like a movie star, you know — you have to work for your money. But the job has plenty of excitement, I grant you that." He gave a tantalizingly mysterious smile. "There are some interesting combinations."

Chance presented Mark with the opportunity to be forewarned, and some experience of the world would have inclined him to listen with at least a show of curiosity. There is nothing so sacred to a man as the way he earns his living, and even if he despises his work he expects others to take it seriously; after all, he is spending his life at it. But Mark was bored and irritated in advance by anything that the 'fat slob' might want to say, and turned to face him with a painfully false expression of abject regret. "Forgive me, do you *mind?* I have a headache."

Accustomed as he was to giving and taking abuse, Sypcovich was so offended that he didn't say another word, not even good-bye as they landed and left the plane at Nassau Airport.

'What's bugging him?' Mark wondered as he walked toward the terminal building, intoxicated by the sudden summer around him. 'I only said I had a headache.' Just the same, it was one of the unluckiest remarks he ever made.

As Santa Catalina Island had only a single airstrip with no bureaucratic facilities, passengers going there were obliged to retrieve their luggage and submit to customs and immigration checks at Nassau Airport before boarding the small plane to the Out Islands. Mrs. Hardwick was spared such rigmarole as a matter of course. Her driver, John Fawkes, and a Bahamian customs officer were waiting on the tarmac to greet her as soon as her feet touched ground. The driver had flown in from Santa Catalina to relieve her of her coat and overnight case; the customs officer was there to welcome her back to the Bahamas and tell her that she could go directly to the other aircraft.

Like most officials of the first black Bahamian government, the customs officer was a young man, and he resented his orders to waive the rules for a rich white woman. "If you'll give me your baggage checks, I'll be only too glad to have your things transferred," he said in a hostile voice which contrasted oddly with his offer of assistance.

"Why, that's very kind of you!" she exclaimed with exaggerated gratitude to conceal her annoyance. Though she was used to her privileges she couldn't get used to the resentment they generated, and after a week of anonymity in New York, where people treated her as just another attractive blonde, the officer's tone cut her to the quick. "Very kind indeed," she repeated with an involuntarily pleading smile as she handed over the blue tickets. Through the years she had come to know most of the people working at the airport and prided herself on her ability to recognize them and greet them as old acquaintances, but she couldn't recall the cold eyes which looked through her as if she were thin air. "I don't think I know you, you must be new here."

"You don't have to know us, Mrs. Hardwick," the customs officer answered with steely politeness, ignoring the invitation to introduce himself. "It's enough that we know you."

'Well, fuck you!' she thought, but uttered only a ladylike "Oh, really?"

The customs officer, about to salute, changed his mind, dropped his arm, and, taking this small opportunity to defy the power of white money, walked away with a silent cheer for Frantz Fanon. Those were the days when the notion of getting rid of whites still held the promise of a better life.

"Well, I'm home," Mrs. Hardwick said wryly. "I can't wait to be back on the boat. How are the children, John?"

"Everything's fine, mistress," answered John Fawkes, to dispose of any further questions.

They could now go to the small Twin Otter plane of Out Island Airways ahead of all the other passengers, but found that it wasn't ready for boarding. Mrs. Hardwick soon tired of standing on the burning tarmac, inhaling the sickening fumes of planes and oil trucks, and started out toward the terminal, where the less privileged passengers who had paid their dues to officialdom were sipping iced drinks and listening to Blind Blake's Band playing goombay music, the welcome extended by the Ministry of Tourism.

"I'd be a whole lot better off if they would just leave me alone," she complained. "This whole business is so idiotic. I don't ask to be treated differently. Honestly, I think they do it out of spite. They hope I'll get a sunstroke."

"They just don't know no better, mistress," commented John Fawkes, his features composing themselves into a sorrowful expression. He had the unnerving knack of assuming instantaneous and heartfelt sympathy for all her grievances.

Fawkes's performance upset her no less than the customs officer's disdainful politeness. 'It serves me right,' she thought. 'I ask for it every time.' As her husband often said, she was "morbidly sensitive" and couldn't quite cope with her role as one of the enviable persons of this world. Three years earlier, seeing him fondling another woman at a party at their house in Chicago, she had made a public spectacle of herself by bursting into tears in front of everybody. This ridiculous behavior didn't fail to scandalize the guests, some of whom voiced their disapproval within her hearing. "What's *she* crying about? They have at least four hundred million!" exclaimed one matron, who had less than five million dollars to her name and thought that she herself had as much right as the poor to display grief whenever she felt like it.

Such experiences made Mrs. Hardwick keener to hide her feelings, but she had hoped she would not have to be so careful once she moved to Santa Catalina. Like many city dwellers she had the notion that islands were a better world. Living in isolation with only her two children and the household staff for company, she wanted to be friends with her Bahamian servants, and at the beginning she had a running argument with John Fawkes, objecting to his insincere solicitude and demanding that he behave naturally with her, express his *true feelings.* "I was hired to do my work," he protested. "I got no time to worry if my feelings pleases you." It wouldn't matter, Marianne argued, whether she was pleased or not. "It matters to me, mistress," he answered. "I wants to keep my job." In vain she tried to convince him that she wouldn't dismiss him for being outspoken; Fawkes couldn't overlook the fact that Mrs. Hardwick had the privilege of changing her mind about that. It was enough for him to do his job, he didn't want to take on the extra work of being sincere with her. "We has a right to our privacy, mistress," he would say, speaking in this matter for the whole staff.

Kevin Hardwick rebuked his wife for her naïveté. "You really should stop bugging the servants about their true feelings, darling. If they gave way to their true feelings they'd cut your throat, or take over the house and make you serve *them* breakfast in bed. At the very least, they'd stop working for you. You must get it into your pretty little head that they are here for the pay, not for the company. My father used to say that to have servants is to know that you can't buy affection. And that's truer now than it ever was — practically everybody who's poorer than you are thinks you're rich at his expense. You might as well learn to live with it. You have a good life, everything is done for you, so why shouldn't you be satisfied? The trouble with you is, you want to be loved!" And so she did, without much hope. She named her small yacht the *Hermit,* and often daydreamed about being rich without anybody knowing it.

As she entered the terminal building she assumed her public expression of serene indifference which she wore like a veil. The goombay band and most of the tourists were already leaving, spirited away by the buses of the British Colonial and Nassau Beach hotels. With John Fawkes in her wake, she walked through to the departure lounge. In sharp contrast to the glossy arrival area, the large, bare room for departing passengers looked shabby and dirty, with paper cups, cigarette butts, squashed cigarette packs strewn about the floor. Wooden fans hung from the ceiling like giant bats, stirring up the heat. These dismal surroundings did nothing to brighten her mood, and she responded with some relief to the admiring glance aimed at her.

Fawkes dropped into the background as soon as she and the dark-haired young man began eyeing each other.

In reporting their first impressions it is difficult not to feel some envy of the 19th-century novelist, who wrote at a time when skirts and conventions covered everything and it was possible to trace an intricate and subtle pattern of emotions, developing slowly from a shared enthusiasm for the Kreutzer Sonata, clever conversation and charitable works to an incidental acknowledgment of the flesh. Still, a storyteller must mirror his own age, and today people are no longer innocent of what they want: they think of making love at first sight.

For one thing, Mark was in the process of undressing on account of the heat. Having thrown his winter coat over a chair, he had taken off his pullover and was unbuttoning his shirt to wipe the sweat from his chest when he caught sight of her. For another thing (and this was of such extreme significance for Mark that he responded to it without reflection) she appeared to be shorter than he was. Having always been one of the shortest boys in the class at the various European schools where they were lined up according to height, he worried about not being tall enough. Once when he took Jessica to an X-rated film in London he was asked for proof of his age, and once when he tried to kiss a big girl who was wearing high heels he bumped his forehead against her chin. Such unhappy experiences had formed his affinities, and though with Martha he had come to feel that height didn't really matter, the fact that the slender blonde was not too tall was one of the most seductive things imaginable for him. Her straight, smooth, shining ash-blond hair reached down past her breasts, framing her oval face, which was not so much pretty as fascinating and might have seemed horsey but for its softness; no bones showed, the soft features were held together by reserve — not the aggressive constraint of "don't you dare touch me" but the reticence of pensive withdrawal, suggesting that this person lived far, far beyond her face, in seclusion. A woman of twenty-three and mother of two boys, she looked like a girl of seventeen; the difference had been erased by more than enough sleep (which the ancients equated with divine beauty), plenty of swimming and sailing, and just the right food. This was the unfair magic of money, which gave her the added grace of six invisible years.

But to tell the truth, Mark was drawn to her long before he took in her whole appearance. It was her elegant Italian walking shoes that first came into his field of vision, bringing along a pair of trim ankles, slender calves, smoothly rounded knees, and then deeply tanned thighs topped with a cream-colored wool skirt so brief that he felt he would need to lift it only ever so slightly in order to enter her — a swift thought, but then her legs were leading up to it!

Marianne Hardwick watched him just as intently, taken by his bright dark eyes. Mark's obsessive ambition had its physical side: he had the clear, powerful look of someone who knew what he was doing with his life. With his pullover slung over one shoulder, his striped shirt open at the neck, he cut a figure that appealed to both the girl and the mother in her. He had a handsome big head and surprisingly small hands and feet, a combination which made him appear both sturdy and vulnerable

— a young man who could protect yet needed looking after. His shirt was damp with sweat, which prompted her to imagine him in bed straining himself to please her.

They had an orgy looking at each other, in the free, open, unashamed spirit of idle fancy.

When Mark came over to her, spoiling her pleasure in their exchange of meaningful but safely distant glances, Marianne Hardwick's sea-green eyes grew blank. He was, after all, an absolute stranger.

"Are you waiting for the plane to Santa Catalina?" asked Mark.

"Yes, I am," she said with sufficient coldness to discourage any further familiarity.

Mark's joy deserted him in an instant. "Me too," he said mechanically, since that was what he had planned to say, but in his heart he gave up.

It was not often that Mrs. Hardwick had seen a man turn pale because she sounded annoyed — only Benjamin, her younger son, depended on her quite that much — and as Mark turned away, she became curious to find out who he was. "Are you on vacation?"

Her voice gave him back his self-possession. "No, I'm on the run," he confessed with ill-concealed pride.

He surprised her — that was in his favor. "Really? What have you done?"

'Why, her hair is longer than her skirt!' thought Mark. "I threw an apple at Vice-President Humphrey," he managed to say almost simultaneously.

"That makes you a fugitive?"

"Well, it was quite a big apple," said Mark, not wishing to minimize his offense.

Miss Marshall's private detective stood petrified at the snack bar, watching incredulously as Mrs. Hardwick succumbed to a conversation with the actor's son to whom he had nearly divulged the secret of his assignment.

14

The Weekend Marriage

My wife, poor wretch, is troubled by her lonely life.
PEPYS

MONEY was Mark Niven's great adventure, his faith and fate — there was money involved even when there was no money involved, even in the exchange of glances with a pretty blonde, in the responsive gleam of her sea-green eyes, dimmed by passing clouds of hesitancy.

Marianne Hardwick was timid and unadventurous, her vitality consumed by physical activity and longing, her intelligence by indecisiveness, but this had less to do with the innate characteristics of the *weaker sex* (as her father, Creighton Montgomery, called it) than with the enfeebling circumstances of her upbringing. Creighton Montgomery had enough money to mold his daughters according to his misconceptions: girls were not meant to fend for themselves, so he protected them from life. Which is to say that Marianne Montgomery grew up without making any vital choices for herself. Prevented from acquiring the habits of freedom and strength of character which grow from decision-making, very rich girls, whose parents have the means to protect them in such a crippling fashion, are the last representatives of Victorian womanhood. Though they may have the boldest manners and most up-to-date ideas, they share their great-grandmothers' humble dependence.

Most parents these days have to rely on their force of personality and whatever love and respect they can inspire to exert any influence over their children at all, but there is still an awful lot of parental authority that big money can buy. Multimillionaires have more of everything than ordinary mortals, including more parent power, and their sons and daughters have about as much opportunity to develop according to their own inclinations as they would have had in the age of absolute monarchy.

The rich still have families.

The great divide between the generations, which is so much taken for granted that no one remarks on it any longer, is the plight of the lower and middle classes, whose children begin to drift away as soon as they are old enough to go to school. The parents cannot control the school, and have even less say as to what company and ideas the child will be exposed to; nor can they isolate him from the public mood, the spirit of the age. It is an often-heard complaint of the middle-class mother, for instance, that she must let her children watch television for hours on end every day if she is to steal any time for herself. The rich have no such problems; they can keep their offspring busy from morning to night without being near them for a minute more than they choose to be, and can exercise almost total control over their environment. As for schooling, they can handpick tutors with *sound views* to come to the children, who may never leave the grounds their parents own, in town, in the country, by the sea, unless for an exceptionally secure boarding school or a well-chaperoned trip abroad. It would have been easier for little Marianne Montgomery to go to Cairo than to the nearest newsstand.

The rich of course wield an immense influence over their children's future, for they have the awesome power to disinherit. And strange as it may seem, they are seldom told that they are too old or stupid to understand things. It is ordinary parents who face the loss of respect for the older generation, as the child realizes that the family home is only a temporary refuge and they can do little to help or hinder him once he grows up.

There is a breathtaking difference between a young radical telling off a minor executive who has sold his principles for a lousy forty-thousand-a-year job from which he can be fired at any moment, and the same sort of young man listening to the ravings of a psychopathic chairman of the board who can bequeath him twenty million or leave it all to the Cancer Fund. The monster of corporate fraud who has amassed a fortune from the profits of jerry-built "luxurious suburban homes", where healthy and affectionate family life could not possibly flourish, is an ideal father: no children of *his* tell him that they reject his stinking material values. It is the parents who have mortgaged their life's earnings for one of his flimsy split-level houses with tubercular plumbing, which their young understandably cannot wait to leave, who are lectured on the evils of acquisition and have the door slammed in their tearful faces. "I don't want what you have!" is the cry of the middle-class child whose parents have very little.

Whatever their real complaints, in fact, middle-class children are the freest people on earth, free to develop according to their bent, to pick their own friends and their own ideas and to pursue their own follies, while the children of the rich live under a totalitarian regime the nature of which depends on the character of the dictator. True, the roles are reversed when they come of age: then the rich gain their liberty and the middle-class lose theirs as they become wage slaves. The poor, of course, suffer the oppression of scarcity from the cradle to the grave.

Marianne's father, though a steel man, saw himself as a sea captain who ran a *tight ship*. Once his children were old enough to be talked to, he never touched them; nor did they ever see him touch their mother. They might have been excused for assuming that they came into the world as the result of snippets of conversation exchanged over the whole length of the dining room table. He was determined to protect his household from *rot*. Television was for other people's servants. "If you want to see horses, go and ride," he told his children. He himself taught them riding and sailing, and his ideas about the world were to form the unchallengeable principles of their education. They learned from an early age, for instance, to be wary of politics. Politicians were dishonest — they never quite did what you paid them for.

The manner in which Creighton Montgomery put an end to the marriage plans of his older daughter, Claire, may sum up the spirit of his reign. Six years older than Marianne, Claire confessed at the age of twenty that she had a boyfriend, a young painter, whom she wanted to marry. The aspiring artist was placed under round-the-clock surveillance; men from the security department of the Montgomery steelworks even broke into his studio to install various listening devices. The painter had talent and a genuine fondness for Claire, who was pretty and adored his paintings, but he was naive enough not to realize that by courting Montgomery's daughter he was submitting himself to a more thorough security check than a prospective CIA agent. The fool allowed a former girlfriend to visit him in his studio, and when she wanted to make love, he begged off with the excuse that he was afraid of getting involved with her again, since it might jeopardize his chances of marrying millions. Confronted with the tape of his conversation, he claimed that it was just talk: he hadn't wanted to hurt the girl's feelings by admitting that he was in love with someone else. No one would ever know the exact truth about this, perhaps not even himself, but Claire cried for weeks and broke off their engagement.

What parent, faced with his daughter's unprepossessing suitor about whom he knows nothing, could fail to envy Creighton Montgomery for his power to check up on people? And what fourteen-year-old girl could fail to be impressed by the fact that her father had eyes and ears everywhere? Marianne was made to listen to the tape repeatedly to hear what boys were like and to learn to mistrust everybody.

"You're prettier, but she has money," said the voice on the tape.

A year later Marianne was allowed out into the world, a finishing school in Lausanne — a tentative sort of girl, wary of boys and uncertain of her thoughts. It was on an excursion to Geneva that she bought, with a sense of great daring, her first copy of that left-wing scandal sheet the

New York Times. Only when she got to Bryn Mawr, at seventeen, did she hear that the *New York Times* was in fact an out-and-out capitalist rag, brazenly slanting the news to protect the system. In her intellectual development she had to travel from the Dark Ages of her father's mind to the dazzling confusion of the modern world — is it any wonder that she didn't quite make it? Between the conflicting philosophies about newspapers, the social order and the purpose of life, she ended up having no firm opinion about anything and no notion of herself except as a girl who should marry and settle down.

SHE met Kevin Hardwick at a classmate's party shortly after she went up to Bryn Mawr. A few months later Hardwick's parents and only brother died in an air crash, on the maiden flight of their new family jet, and he became the youngest business giant in America; but when he met his future wife he was still a student. A graduate of the Harvard Business School, he was staying on to broaden his mind with courses in psychology and philosophy and to fulfill his personal ambition of bedding one hundred girls by the end of his college career. Purposefulness even in pleasure was very important for this businesslike young man, who had nothing but contempt for the idle rich and had nursed since childhood the ambition to double the worth of his father's companies. At twenty-three he was already an imposing figure, tall and fleshy, with a broad nose and a no-nonsense mouth, and when he strode across the dance floor to cut in on Marianne's escort (a classmate of her brother's from Groton), he fixed his light, unwavering eyes on her with the kind of deep attention that she found thrilling.

She was wearing a long chiffon dress which needed a lot of floor space, and as she had to bend to pull it from under the foot of another dancer who had stepped on the hem, Kevin asked her whether she didn't think it was too crowded. "Yes, it is, isn't it," she said, hoping that he would take her out to the balcony to kiss and neck. He scooped her up in his arms and wove his way deftly past the dancing couples, carrying her as if she were as light as a plate of biscuits, but took her no farther than the other side of the room, where he set her down on a window seat. And while she was still catching her breath, he asked her whether she had any idea how crowded the earth was.

Later on when the population explosion became an obsession with him, she would feel like screaming whenever the subject came up; at their first meeting, however, she was very impressed when he told her that people had copulated for *millions of years,* from the Stone Age to 1850, before they multiplied to one billion. And did she know how long it took them to reach the two billion mark? She didn't? Well, obviously not millions of years, not thousands of years — not even a century! They made it to two billion by 1930, in eighty years. And by 1961 they numbered three billion; a billion more people came into the world in only thirty-one years! "There'll be more than six billion people in our lifetime, think how crowded the dance floor will be then!" he said, stroking her thick blond hair with his firm hand, as if to reassure her that he would always be there to protect her. He spent the whole evening with her, talking about serious subjects. (Young Hardwick found serious subjects, with some reference to copulation as part of the general picture, the most potent aphrodisiacs for college girls.)

"I admire your father, but from what I've heard of him, he's too dogmatic about things," he told her in his slow, thoughtful drawl, which gave him an air of natural and unassuming authority. "I don't believe that anybody has a lowdown on the absolute truth. It all depends on your point of view, doesn't it?"

Marianne was flattered that he knew who she was and pleased that she could follow what he was saying. She felt safe with him: the Hardwicks were as rich as the Montgomerys, so she could be sure that he was interested in her for her own sake.

"What about antibiotics, for instance?" he asked. "Modern medicine's great — everybody's for it. It's the most beneficial, least controversial human activity, right? If it wasn't for medical science we'd still have plagues wiping out half the population every few decades, you'd stand a good chance of dying in childbirth, and most of the children you did have would die in infancy. But now even the dead can recover and multiply, and guess what? — we're hit by the population explosion, which is so bad that it's going to wipe out the whole human race, some experts say. I guess this is very funny in a way, but it makes you wonder whether there is anything that is all good or all bad . . ." He went on talking in this vein, in clear, declarative sentences accompanied by broken gestures of doubt: he would raise his arm for emphasis, then drop it helplessly in midsentence, smiling down on his own words; there were just too many pros and cons to everything.

Only later, only too late, did she wonder whether he was simply practicing on her even then, perfecting his technique of handling people. He cultivated his modesty and even temper as much as his air of authority; he had an innate sense of how these virtues enhanced each other. Like her brother Everett, young Hardwick had been brought up to rule, but according to more sophisticated principles than those old Montgomery could pass on.

"I may be wrong," he told her on the window seat, "but it seems to me that even the people who are agitating against pesticides might have something. It's the same story as with antibiotics, I guess — they're great from one angle and not so hot from another angle. My father does a thirty-million-a-year turnover in pesticides and herbicides, but we wouldn't knock the wildlife types. They're not all crazies. There's always room for argument.'' He mentioned Rachel Carson's *Silent Spring,* the first book to create widespread alarm about the use of chemicals in agriculture. Miss Carson was one-sided, of course, and certainly she exaggerated a lot, but he admired her concern. She said something worth thinking about, and he meant to give every opinion its due; he would always listen. And so he did, interjecting frequent questions to elicit comments from Marianne.

It can be imagined how this open-minded tolerance affected a college girl not yet eighteen, coming from a home ruled by a fanatic. The notion that everything was a bit right and a bit wrong seemed to relieve her from the strain of trying to sort things out for herself.

Kevin offered to drive her home, and as he was making passes, she explained that she didn't think she should lose her virginity just because everybody else did, and that she believed two people ought to know each other well before entering into a physical relationship. Again he listened intently, and even parked the car to give her his full attention, the steady gaze of his light, unwavering eyes. He was good at listening well and respectfully — a vital attribute for people who are prepared, if necessary, to ignore every opinion but their own, without wishing to cause too much resentment. He had also a profound understanding of the power of *point of view*. It was his favorite expression, replacing primitive words like *true* and *untrue, right* and *wrong* — words which could give his opponents a chance. If there was such a thing as right and wrong, they could be right and he could be wrong. *Point of view* took care of all that, for it goes without saying that there are as many viewpoints as there are people, and who is to decide that one person's opinion is better than another's? The method young Hardwick later used so effectively to screw his executives, his competitors and the public was tried and tested yet again in his seduction of the pretty Montgomery girl. He never became aggressive or argumentative: he appreciated her concern, her determination not to rush into a physical relationship; there was a lot in what she said and he respected her for it — but they ended up in his friend's apartment just the same.

Marianne fell in love with him, and seven months later, in a state of shock after the sudden death of his parents and brother, feeling lost without a family, he married her. Old Montgomery, reflecting on the advantages of the match for the grandchildren he hoped to have, reluctantly gave away his daughter, who was still a minor. During the preparations for the wedding he persuaded the bereaved young man that the family union should extend to their respective banking interests, which would give them great opportunitites to further each other's fortunes. Hardwick enjoyed only benefits from the shifting of shares and seats on the board, but he realized soon enough that Montgomery had acquired the power to cause him a great deal of trouble without giving him a corresponding opportunity to meddle in the Montgomery concerns. This fact was never far from Hardwick's mind when he contemplated the possibility of a divorce. The network of interlocking directorships among the ruling families is a far cry from the conspiracy against the public interest that some radicals claim it to be; it is simply the way in-laws and cousins hold guns at each other's heads, just in case.

The groom regretted his marriage even before his first son was born. As the tragedy of the plane crash receded into memory, he found old-fashioned domestic life an intolerable constraint. To be young, handsome, rich, powerful, and expected home early every evening by an anxious, adoring wife may not strike everyone as the worst misfortune in the world, but it was sufficient to drive Hardwick to despair. Besides, Marianne could not or would not share his enthusiasm for his work.

One incident among many may suggest the nature of his disappointment. On the publication of the first U.S. Surgeon General's report identifying cigarette smoking as a major cause of lung cancer, there was panic selling of tobacco shares, because investors feared that people would stop smoking, and prices fell accordingly. Hardwick was not much interested in playing the stock market, but this struck him as an opportunity not to be missed. "What's all the fuss about?" he asked his wife. "Have you heard of alcohol and fast cars going out of fashion?" Marianne said she hoped that people had more sense than he gave them credit for. However reluctant she was to judge things, it didn't seem right to her to speculate on human weakness. As if there was anything else to speculate on! Hardwick risked all the ready cash he could raise to buy tobacco shares at their next to lowest point and sold them at the moment when prices returned to normal, collecting a tidy profit of nearly two million dollars. And even then she wasn't pleased.

"It's like making money on poison," she said.

Refraining from reminding his wife that some HCI chemicals were poisons, Hardwick argued that tobacco helped to check population growth and improved the species by getting rid of inferior people. "Smokers are too stupid to realize that they're killing themselves. Or they haven't got the willpower to quit. Are you getting sentimental about addicts now? Considering that the earth can't hold everybody and his uncle, letting the weak and stupid finish themselves off is a step in the right direction. Your problem is that not enough people are smoking."

He tried to explain to her that she should be proud of him. "It isn't all that easy, you know, to make a couple of million on the market with one transaction. You need courage and psychology to do it. I risked a great deal on my judgment." But she was too sentimental to understand or appreciate his triumph; as far as she was concerned, the whole business was too depressing to think about.

By contrast, Pauline Marshall, a girl who had to make her own way in the world, who was beautiful enough to make the cover of *Vogue* four times, and smart and hardworking enough to put herself through college with her earnings as a model, was ecstatic.

"You're fantastic, incredible, I adore you!" she told Hardwick at her apartment, where he was as yet only an occasional visitor. "I know a couple of lovely lesbians, darling — you must let me fix you up a little orgy to celebrate. You'll be the richest man in the States soon. What am I saying — in the world, in the world!"

"I started out with too little for that," Hardwick demurred with a resigned shrug, pleased as he was with the compliment. It was certainly the sort of compliment he would never receive from his wife. He couldn't understand how he could have been so stupid as to marry a rich girl. With a tax-free annual income of a hundred and seventy-five thousand dollars of her own, Marianne had absolutely no interest in the art of making money.

And then she had the nerve to be jealous!

"I can't stand your scenes," he told her after the party at which she had burst into tears in front of their guests. He followed her to her bedroom, a small room adjoining the nursery, where she insisted on sleeping to be near her babies — a habit which he considered preposterous and had countered by moving to a separate bedroom. "I could understand it if you were happy with me, but you're not! You couldn't care less about our business, you don't like my friends, you go about with a long face, but let me touch another woman and you make us ridiculous by crying in front of everybody!" He tried to keep his voice down to avoid waking the children but it was one of the rare occasions when he nearly lost his temper, not knowing whether he should strangle her or dare to hope that she would decide to walk out on him.

Marianne stood by the bed, still in her evening dress, covering her chest with her hands to hide her modest décolletage.

'Is she trying to punish me by depriving me of the sight of a few inches of skin below her neck?' Hardwick wondered. 'The poor pathetic skinny bitch!'

Watching his hard face slacken to spiteful indifference, Marianne became so enraged that she felt capable of anything. "If you stop loving me," she said, narrowing her eyes to make herself look vicious, "I'm going to kill myself." She meant it as she said it. Beneath her jealousy, anxiety, disapproval, she had always had a deep sense of well-being in his presence, and she hated him now with all the wounded pride of a girl scorned by her first and only lover, with all the panicky fear of a twenty-year-old mother unwanted by the father of her children. "I'm going to kill myself," she hissed venomously, uttering the threat that was to bother him for years, "and you can explain it to your sons when they grow up. And to my father!"

Hardwick stared at her. "That's the most disgusting thing I've ever heard!"

"It depends on your point of view," she said pertly. Her threat had cheered her up. It made everything seem so simple; even if they had to part, she could make sure that he would never forget her. She no longer felt humiliated. Dropping her hands from her chest, she turned and walked into her dressing room with light steps.

Hardwick spent half the night walking in the roof garden. His valet, who had taken him up in the elevator and switched on the lights, stood by to await instructions, dozing off from time to time as he leaned against a huge stone urn.

"Never get married, Gianni!" Hardwick exclaimed with a heavy sigh, stopping in his stride when passing by the urn.

Gianni was a clever Italian from Reggio Calabria, trained at the Schweizerhof in Bern. As a rule, his dark, round face shone with the contentment and aplomb of a man fond of sweets, but now it was thrown into confusion: he had got married only a few months earlier, and Hardwick had given him one thousand dollars for the wedding and a two-room apartment in the house. His eyes, his eyebrows and his mouth kept shifting about, busy with the effort to wake the thinking part of his brain.

"You look like you need some sleep."

"Yes, sir," sighed Gianni with relief.

However, Hardwick was too agitated to think of actually telling the valet to go to bed, and continued his pacing along the gravel paths. If only he could love his wife and be content! Or better still, if only she would fall in love with someone else!

After all, she could go wherever she pleased and do whatever she wanted. But no, she was sticking it out. She would remain forever her father's creature. Old Montgomery had brought her up to be fit for nothing but the role of a good, unhappy little wife. Thinking of the unpleasant way she had narrowed her eyes at him, Hardwick concluded that she no longer loved him, or rather — out of timidity, indolence, sheer inability to think of anything better to do — loved only the idea of having him, and hung on to his neck with venomous passion. 'If she loved me for myself, I'd have a chance,' he reflected, 'but she loves me with all the strength of her limitations. That'll last forever.' Yet he had no heart to insist on a divorce. Whether she meant to commit suicide or not (and how many people killed themselves without quite meaning to?) there was no doubt that their marriage was her whole life, and he couldn't help feeling sorry for her. Nor could he help feeling sorry for himself. It is in such predicaments that couples murder each other.

Hardwick, however, had the means and opportunity for a less drastic solution. Noticing that the big waxen leaves of a spotlit rubber plant were covered with soot, although they were supposed to be washed every morning, he decided to persuade his wife that they had no right to bring up their sons in a dirty and violent city like Chicago.

"I don't want the garden hosed down for a few days," he told the valet as they stepped into the elevator. "Tell Miguel to leave it alone."

Gianni grimaced apologetically as he stifled a yawn. "Yes, sir."

Hardwick waited a week before taking his wife for a walk in the roof garden and feigned surprise at how black all the plants were. When they were back in their sitting room he began to wonder aloud whether they shouldn't move to a healthier place. The proposition that they should make their *real home* in the Bahamas had the hallmark of what Hardwick considered a truly successful move: he would have his way without asserting himself too much. Marianne, pale and subdued ever since her outburst, turned out to be surprisingly compliant.

"Will you be there on the weekends?" she asked him, turning her head aside as if wishing to take a good look at the wall.

"What do you mean, weekends?" Hardwick was the personification of hearty amazement, brushing aside her silly question with both hands. "I'll be there every minute I can spare — weekends, weekdays. That will be our *real home,* darling. I can't wait for us to find a place and build our house."

The impatience to put a distance between them which slipped into his voice made Marianne feel as if something had torn her entrails. She was flooded with shame that she had ever cared enough about him to be jealous. At that instant the girl turned into a woman and deception became mutual. Never again until the end of their marriage would a true word pass between them about their feelings for each other. "I think I'll get a sailboat," she said.

Her voice shook and her lips trembled but she didn't make a fuss, and Hardwick was overcome with an enormous sense of relief. She was a spunky little thing after all. Her extreme paleness, her air of being lost, set her off to advantage, like a becoming dress that turns an overfamiliar woman into a promising new girl. He couldn't fail to be moved and foresaw that he would become quite fond of her again, once she was out of the way.

THE prospect of regaining his freedom without complications kept Hardwick in a state of euphoria for weeks. He felt on top of the world, he could think faster than ever; his head became a gold mine of brilliant ideas. The poor are happy to no purpose, having nothing to show for it once despair regains lost ground, but if a man is rich enough his ebullient moods tend to be profitable.

For one thing, he bankrolled the magazine Pauline Marshall wanted to launch. (Within a year *Opulent Interiors* became America's most successful home-decorating magazine, earning HCI a 1.6-million-dollar profit after taxes; so even his girlfriend made money for him.)

When two of his research chemists held a press conference to announce their resignation from HCI, in order, as they said, to end their involvement in the production of defoliants used in the Vietnam War, and to draw attention to the deadly side-effects of even "peaceful" herbicides and pesticides used in the United States, the bad publicity inspired Hardwick to found yet another company.

"I hate to lose good men of integrity," he told the disloyal scientists, who had expected scathing recriminations when they were summoned to his office. "I have the greatest respect for your point of view, though of course I wish you had come to see me before talking to the media." This small complaint was tossed in lightly and he went on in a serious tone. "I assure you, I would like nothing better than to phase out all our controversial products, if it wouldn't mean simply giving a boost to our competitors." Waving away the problem which was beyond his power to solve, he continued briskly: "Anyway, our real business is peace and growth. I'm as concerned as you are about the harmful side-effects of our products — and, let's face it, most industrial products. And it seems to me that this is not just a matter for your personal conscience, it's something we can build on. Instead of walking out why don't you stay with us and create an enterprise more to your liking? I see a great future in the environment."

As a result of this parley, HCI Clean Earth Products for the treatment of industrial waste were to be the first on a fast-growing new market. To dispose of HCI's own toxic wastes which could not be treated, Hardwick overcame his reluctance to risk involvement with organized crime and accepted Chicago Mafia boss Vincenzo Baglione's offer to have them trucked away in the special containers of the Illinois Safe Transport Company.

The young industrialist was in that indescribably blissful state when nothing could go wrong for him. By way of rewarding himself he bought a Boeing 707, in spite of the vow he had made never to own a private plane. Not to lose time and energy traveling, he had the aircraft fitted out as a combination of office, apartment and health club. Bedrooms and showers were quite common on private jets but his was possibly the first to be equipped with a sauna and a massage parlor.

He actually had fun with Marianne, flying down to the islands, choosing a property, discussing plans with the architects — and she left him alone for days, too, going down to Florida on her own to watch her boat being built. Yet now and then he would be assailed by anxiety, finding it strange that she never once protested against the arrangement which would keep them apart most of the time. Was she only pretending to be reasonable, out of spite, planning to spring her suicide on him when he least expected it? He was bothered by news stories he kept reading about morbid characters who poured gasoline over their bodies and set fire to themselves by way of protesting against one thing or another. One day he sent out a memo to all his vice-presidents and section heads, promising HCI preferred stock to anyone who could explain what these self-immolators hoped to achieve by committing suicide. This query increased his reputation as a man with a sardonic sense of humor.

In retrospect the idea of suicide struck Marianne as so absurd that she couldn't imagine how she had ever thought of it; still less did she suspect that it had made an impression on her husband. Since the day it got through to her that Kevin no longer wanted to live with her, she had lived in a state of surprise, for she felt neither bitterness nor despair. And far from hating him or wishing to make him miserable, she could even think of an argument in his favor — at least he was taking the trouble to pretend for her sake. Much domestic peace depends on such efforts to look on the bright side of deception; if hypocrisy is the tribute vice pays to virtue, marital lies are the tribute indifference pays to love. There were moments when Marianne felt tempted to tell her husband that it wasn't necessary to act for her benefit, but then she thought, 'Why not? Let him sweat a little!'

Once they were settled on Santa Catalina, Hardwick more or less kept his promise and came down to the island almost every weekend. These visits were much less of a hardship than he liked to think; who wouldn't enjoy his family in moderation?

The sun and sea were a pleasant break from his routine, the boys were cute and kept growing and clambered around him with excited curiosity, and he didn't mind sailing and skin-diving with his wife. Their relationship, based as it now was on profound insincerity on both sides, became smoother and more pleasant. Hardwick ascribed this to the beneficial effects of island life; living close to nature had evidently done her a lot of good. There didn't seem to be any danger that she would do away with herself, at least not while he continued to come and see her. She stopped complaining and asking questions — a startling change which impressed him all the more as he assumed that she was still jealous of him, and took it for granted that she must realize that he couldn't possibly spend all his time alone in Chicago. And yet she didn't sulk, and she even quit pestering him about sex; he could put it off for as long as he liked. She evidently tried to make his stay as comfortable as possible. The poor girl was willing to take him on his terms after all, just to avoid losing him altogether.

The ultimate rationale for their weekend marriage was the health and safety of their children; the small well-protected island inhabited almost exclusively by millionaires seemed to be relatively free of pollution and crime.

"If you were the whirlwind type, always off somewhere instead of making a home for us here, these boys would have been knifed or kidnapped by now," Hardwick told his wife when it seemed to him that she was getting restless. "I wonder whether they'll ever understand or appreciate that they owe their lives to you in more ways than one."

"MARIANNE's an old-fashioned woman," he complained to his mistress when he got back to Chicago. "She might as well be living in the Victorian age."

"She never had a job, poor girl, she was never challenged to grow," Pauline Marshall sighed with the condescending sympathy of a successful magazine editor.

"Right. As far as she's concerned, marriage is marriage, her husband is her husband, she's a wife and mother, and that's all there is to life. Christ, I'm not even thirty yet, she must know I screw around, but she doesn't want to face it. Even a little thing like fucking the masseuse on the plane once in a while — you couldn't tell her, she'd drop dead from the tragedy of it all. How could you talk sense with a woman like that and split up like reasonable people? And considering how little it takes to keep her happy, I'd feel like a monster if I cut her off completely. I can't get rid of a sense of responsibility for the mother of my kids. Some guys can do it but I can't — I'm not made that way."

Pauline Marshall understood his attitude perfectly, and admired him for it.

His wife in fact knew about Miss Marshall, if not about the masseuse, and was quite able to face his sexual exploits; she was only reluctant to mention them, sensing that any discussion on the subject would lead to a divorce. This she didn't want, or rather she couldn't decide whether she wanted it or not. Hardwick had reasons to curse her inbred indolence and lack of enterprise; she lacked the confidence, the initiative, the spur of acute discomfort to change her life. Although she was becoming promiscuous in affairs of the eyes, she remained wary of new involvements, and the only certain consequence of divorce seemed to her the additional problem of coping with her children's bewilderment and her parents' disapproval. There was no way out for such a person except through the emotions which can lend strength even to the meek: ashamed as she was to admit it even to herself, she waited and longed for passionate love.

In this, Marianne Hardwick's story was the story of many wives. She could imagine running off with another man at a moment's notice, but saw no point in breaking up what was left of her marriage unless she had something to replace it.

15

Why Not?

My heart sometimes overflows with tenderness
— and at other times seems quite exhausted and
incapable of being warmly interested in anyone.
MARY WOLLSTONECRAFT

SHE turned out to be the most inquisitive person Mark had ever met. Despite the noisy surroundings of the departure lounge at Nassau Airport, and without quite knowing how it had come about, he was giving a thorough account of himself, telling her about his parents and all the places he had come from. She questioned him in a persistent and methodical way while retaining her distant manner — a combination which he found confusing.

In fact, he was making a better impression than he thought. At first she was troubled by his attack on the Vice-President and wondered whether he was prone to violence, though he couldn't have appeared more docile, staring her clothes off with humble eyes. Not quite knowing what to make of him, she found him fascinating — a student radical who talked about his favorite palaces. It came as something of a shock when he told her he was going to be a clerk at the Seven Seas Club on Santa Catalina.

"But couldn't you have done better somewhere else?" she asked him bluntly, abandoning her reserve. "What made you decide to come to our little out-of-the-way island?"

Suddenly on his guard, Mark answered with a question. "Why do you live on your little out-of-the-way island?"

She nearly said that it was safer for the children, but then changed her mind; a nervous flicker turned into a gesture as she pushed her hair behind her ears with both hands. "Oh, I'm an island person."

"The same with me — I just wanted to get away from it all." Glancing from one of her shoulders to the other, scanning her breasts in between, and now and then stealing a glance at her face, Mark had to admit to himself that he had never made love with a girl who was quite so beautiful. 'Could it make any difference?' he wondered.

Their flight was called and Mark, forgetting his winter coat which he had left on a chair, followed Marianne out to the plane. It wasn't until months later that he realized he had lost his coat, but he thought every day of her back as she walked up the steps ahead of him.

As they stood close to each other at the head of the aisle, a shade of regret on his face prompted her to ask him whether he would prefer to sit by the window.

She could read his thoughts! "I wanted to take a look at the island from the air," he confessed, lowering his voice involuntarily on account of the other passengers behind them.

The growing attraction of two strangers for each other is a touching sight, but there is no feeling in this world, no joy, no pain, that is not simply a question of money to somebody. Last to come aboard, Sypcovich watched their intent faces as they sorted out their seats; having got over his scare, he was beginning to consider the hopeful aspects of the situation. He leaned back into his seat in an expansive mood, resolving to invest his bonus in ITT shares, if anything should develop between the two. 'And why not?' he asked himself, kneading his flabby cheek fondly between his thumb and folded forefinger.

It was quiet inside the small plane even when they were flying, and Marianne and Mark, squeezed together in the narrow seats, were brought still closer by the necessity of talking in undertones in order not to disturb the others and not to be overheard. Such constraints in crowded places are responsible for a great many sudden intimacies; the most innocuous conversation becomes a conspiracy of whispers against the rest of the world. At one point their foreheads touched, and as they drew back they both smiled contentedly, their faces lit up by a kind of joyful insight of the senses. It was as if their bodies, in the collective wisdom of the cells, had decided that they fitted each other.

Though he wouldn't mention that he had anything definite in mind, he told her that he had come to search for sunken treasure.

"It's really funny," he added, bowing his head and staring at her knees as though they held the answer to the mystery of life. "I'd been thinking about it for years, but I didn't have the money and couldn't get a job in the Bahamas. My father was dead against it — you know what parents are like. But when I got drafted, he came around. He says it's a father's job to keep his son alive. Getting into trouble was my biggest break. He even borrowed twelve thousand dollars for me. And he actually said maybe I was meant to be a treasure hunter. That's weird, isn't it?" He raised his strong, bony face with an intent look. "Do you think there's such a thing as fate?"

Watching him, she forgot to answer.

"But it's just a hobby, really," Mark hastened to assure her in a deprecating tone, with the cunning of a lunatic who wishes to appear sane.

She gave him a coaxing smile and seemed to lean closer to him, though she didn't move. "Have you seen *Elvira Madigan*?"

The smile drew all his attention to her lips, soft and fresh without lipstick, and he could hardly manage to shake his head. "No, I haven't. What's it like?"

"I'm not going to tell you."

Her eyes were bright with promise, as if she were holding back the secret only for the sake of sharing it with him on a more intimate occasion. The film library in her house on the island stored prints of all her favorite films, but she screened Bo Widerberg's romantic masterpiece more frequently than all the others put together. Reenacting a true love story from the turn of the century, it never failed to move her to the depths of her whole being; it tempted her to become a different sort of person — naive, rash, trustful, daring and happy. None of her acquaintances liked the film or could sympathize with the central characters, the none-too-pretty tightrope walker and the none-too-bright officer who deserted from the army to run away with her; but Marianne felt a deep affinity with the fugitive lovers, who lived in the paradise of their passion until their money ran out and killed themselves before starvation could spoil their bliss. They often prompted her to daydream of an island inhabited by gallant, reckless, passionate people. If only there were such a place on the map! If only she could match the ropewalker's courage, instead of hedging her way through life!

And wasn't Mark a sort of deserter, after all?

"What will you do if you get rich?" she asked. "I mean if you really find something?" Maybe he had the answer.

"Nobody gets rich from sunken treasure." This was said all the more readily because he didn't think it was relevant to his own exceptional case.

She insisted.

"Well, first of all I'll have to borrow a fortune to salvage it." He pointed to the thick envelope in his shirt pocket. "And I'll have to pay my dad back his twelve thousand dollars."

It was a great deal of money at the time. None of the millionaires she knew would carry such a sum in their shirt pocket, let alone advertise the fact; she rather liked his careless disregard for actual cash. "All right, but what will you do with the rest?"

Unable to keep up his pretense, Mark answered in a firm and prompt manner which implied years of deliberation. "Everything!"

"So you don't know either." She was plainly disappointed. "Santa Catalina is full of rich people who don't know what to do. It's quite a problem, you know, deciding what you should do when there's nothing you *have* to do.''

"Well, I'm going to back electric cars," said Mark eagerly, afraid that she was losing interest in him. "And I'm going to write a history of the Indians and Spaniards in Peru. I've already started on it . . . I'm going to produce some films for my father . . .''

She listened, watching his eyes. "But who will be your friends when you're rich? Have you ever thought about that?"

"I don't see why being rich should make any difference to what friends you have."

"It does, though. People will either like you for your money or they'll resent you for having it. So you're stuck with a small group who are as rich as you are, and that doesn't give you much choice."

"I always thought I'd have more friends if I were rich!"

They were talking at cross-purposes. "I guess it's more difficult for girls," she ventured hesitantly. "For instance, I know a girl who fell in love with a struggling painter. They nearly got married, but her father found out that the man wanted her for her money. So now she's married to a rich man who doesn't need her money — he's impotent and wants her for show."

For the first time Mark began to wonder how she fitted into a millionaire's resort. "That couple you're talking about — do they live on the island?"

"Oh, no, they live in London. She's lucky in a way — she's quite a good lieder singer and has a busy, successful life."

"How come you know her?"

Marianne took a deep breath, deciding to give herself away but protect her sister. "She's a childhood friend. But rich girls without talent have only one dream, really. I remember when we were at school in Lausanne, that was all we ever talked about — boys falling in love with us without having the slightest idea who we were." She made a grimace to indicate that she realized it was silly, but her voice was wistful.

Mark kept nodding gravely as if to say he knew how difficult it was for rich girls, but noticing her watching him, he gave up pretending. "You're the first one I've ever seen!" he admitted.

They laughed, and the plane was just the right place to laugh about it. Having no first-class compartment, the Twin Otter was a kind of no-man's-land where everybody paid the same price and got the same ticket. Modern travel is Utopia: all passengers are equal, or nearly so. Big money was only money then — she didn't want it to matter, and he didn't think that it did. It was all colored for him by his hopes, its absence a mere postponement, the waiting period for the grand prize. He was beginning to see her as a good omen. He hadn't even arrived yet and already he had met a rich girl who liked him. She laughed with her lips so close to his that they almost kissed. Maybe she sensed that he was lucky. He might just find the *Flora* right away and marry her. Why not? He would be richer than she was.

"Actually, I'm not a girl," she said, drawing away. (Better to laugh it all off at one go.) "I have a husband and two sons."

Mark's face acquired the bleak look of a man who had taken a long journey only to find that he had come to the wrong place. "You must be pretty busy," he said glumly. "Being married, I mean."

She twisted her neck to ease herself. "My husband's busier."

"What does he do?" Mark asked dispiritedly.

"Oh, he runs his business."

Trying to think of rich Hardwicks, Mark remembered a leaflet he'd been handed on campus. "He isn't the Hardwick of Hardwick Chemicals, by any chance?"

"Uh-huh." She colored with the effort to sound matter-of-fact; she wasn't suggesting anything. "He works very hard — in Chicago — he's only home on weekends."

Still resenting the Dutch architect who had taken his mother away, Mark didn't think adultery was *fair,* and it took him something like a full minute to change his ideas on the subject. Why should he try to be fair to a man who made money from poisoning the world? "Do you love your husband?" he asked her abruptly, with the firmness of an inner struggle resolved.

She pushed her long hair behind her ears with her exquisite small hands. "What a question!"

Taking this as a rebuke, Mark turned his head to the window.

He seemed so put out that Marianne felt sorry for him, and as the plane began its shaky descent she made the impulsive decision of a procrastinating woman who had finally lost patience with herself. She could save him from a stupid job; they could look for wrecks together, live and sail together on the *Hermit* — and why not? What was there to hold her back? At that moment she felt ready to sue her husband for divorce. "By the way, Mark, won't you need a partner? Somebody with a boat who could also dive with you?"

Mark missed the point of the question; after years of careful planning, he was thinking so far ahead that he had no feel for the unexpected. "I'll buy my own boat," he said, watching the sea fill up with waves as the plane dropped again. "Hire a guy to keep an eye on the anchorline and jump in if I'm in trouble. That's all I need. Jacques Cousteau says if anyone is going to find sunken treasure it'll be a loner." Now he could make out the dun-colored coral formations; for all he knew, he was looking straight at the spot where the *Flora* lay. Here and there patches of the sea floor could be seen through the transparent water, and in his excitement he was trying to locate the long lost wreck from the air.

"A loner doesn't have much fun," she commented in what she thought was an unmistakably suggestive voice. "Wouldn't it be easier with a real partner?"

"Partnerships mean fights," he answered obtusely, holding on to his seat with both hands. "Anyway, a team attracts too much attention."

'Far be it from me to be a problem!' thought Marianne.

As the plane banked, Santa Catalina showed up in the window: a bright green mass of roughly trapezoid shape marked off from the many-colored sea by a pale pink ribbon of sand. Mark felt feverish, as if he had become drunk.

The airstrip, running right down to the sea, was flanked by a field of burned-out grass where small planes and cars, some of them taxis, were parked side by side; all the metal looked beaten and worn down by the sun. On the other side of the airstrip there were vegetable plots coming up to the edge of the runway and a cluster of small cement-block houses with corrugated tin roofs, beyond which towered the island's garbage dump. A group of black men and children ran over from the houses to see who was arriving. On this sunny green island of roughly twenty-seven square miles, rich and poor alike suffered the affliction of bore-dom.

It wasn't Mark's day for paying attention — or rather, he was trying to pay attention to everything at once, breathing in the bracing smell of salt and seaweed, nodding benignly at everyone, even at Sypcovich — and only later, in retrospect, did he attach any significance to Marianne's rather curt good-bye as Fawkes drove up her battered old station wagon.

She didn't like his confident parting grin. Disappointment made her suspect his motives. 'Well, he won't screw me once!' she resolved. Perhaps only other young, rich and beautiful women will hear without surprise that Marianne Montgomery Hardwick, who had everything in the world going for her, could be worried about such a possibility.

Past Crimes and a New Blunder

Of all the things that you can do in the world,
you can do more of them in the Bahamas.
BAHAMA ISLANDS TOURIST OFFICE

WHEN Columbus landed in the Bahamas, the islands were inhabited by the Lucayans, an extraordinarily gentle, playful people with no knowledge of weapons or tradition of warfare. The Spaniards marveled at their peaceable and trusting disposition, turned them into slaves and used up the whole race in less than two decades. Some were drowned for failing to bring up pearls from the sea; the rest were crammed into ships and carried off to the other islands, dying by the thousands on the way from suffocation, starvation and fever. For years navigators charted their course in the Caribbean by the corpses floating in the water. The captives who survived the voyage killed themselves or were worked to death in the mines and plantations of Hispaniola.

No traces of the Lucayans remain on Santa Catalina, but the Spaniards left a memento of their passing: the ruins of a fort built in the 16th century by Admiral Nuñez de Alvarado still stand on top of the island's only hill, a source of local pride.

After the brief Spanish presence Santa Catalina fell into disuse until the abolition of slavery in the Bahamas in 1834, when a few black families came over from New Providence to settle. These former slaves subsisted on fish and the few vegetables they could raise in the thin topsoil; most of the island remained a barren tract of scrub and salt marsh, a domain of mosquitoes.

The lush paradise that Mark saw from the air was Sir Henry Colville's creation. A longtime winter resident of the Bahamas, Sir Henry acquired Santa Catalina in 1938 on a ninety-nine-year lease from the British government, just in case it might come in handy. At the end of World War II, despairing of Britain, which had elected a Labour government and allowed it to *give away* India, he decided to retire to his own island. The blacks who were already there were bought out with an offer of one thousand pounds apiece for their smallholdings. To make the place fit to live in, as he said, he had the marshes drained and used his own tankers to bring in the best-quality soil and countless tons of sod and seedlings to keep it bound, along with the choicest shrubs, flowers and trees from all over the world. He also brought in a desalinating plant which produced eighty thousand gallons of fresh water daily from the sea, sufficient to keep the island blooming through the rainless summer months. *National Geographic* magazine called the result "one of the great landscaping achievements of the century". It also turned out to be a profitable real estate venture, though of a restricted kind, as Sir Henry didn't want to be crowded. Keeping the hill and surrounding area for himself, and reserving some land for common facilities, he divided the rest of the island into eleven lots, ten of which he sold to families from Britain, Canada and the United States. The remaining and largest property was purchased by North–South International, which built the Seven Seas Club hotel and a shopping center to provide the necessities and a few of the more expensive luxuries of life; people were expected to do most of their shopping in Nassau or New York. For the blacks who wished to stay on the island, Sir Henry built houses in the service area next to the airstrip. Just then capital was flowing the other way, into devastated Europe, and he dealt fairly with the islanders at 1947 prices, although if they had held on to their beachfront properties until the late 50s, they could have become rich. As it was, they went to work as servants at the private residences or the Club. Those who were left out continued to live by fishing and doing odd jobs. Charles Weaver, the manager of the Seven Seas Club, allowed some of the men to take turns driving the hotel taxis.

The young Bahamian who drove Mark from the plane lived in one of the cement-block shacks between the airstrip and the garbage dump, sharing two rooms with his mother, his sister and her four teenage children. He could have inherited a fortune in beach property if his father hadn't sold it to Sir Henry. This sort of disaster happens the world over as people sell their apparently worthless land cheaply, then watch it yield millions for its new owners through rezoning and development. However, the loss and bitterness are nowhere so great as on stagnant paradise islands where there are no opportunities for advancement and a person can acquire very little beyond what he was born to. The clever real estate deal which leaves the native-born in hopeless poverty is the most explosive social issue in Vacationland. Dispossessed Virgin Islanders and Hawaiians kill tourists in blind revenge; Bahamians are more peaceful, less American — though Mark's driver had hit his dying father when he realized that it was his last chance to pay him back for robbing him of the world. Driving the taxi from the airstrip, he could count on no more than Mark's tip and half the fare as his earnings for the day, and he was far from satisfied.

"Wanna blow some grass?" he asked as he started the taxi, watching his passenger hungrily from the rearview mirror. "This ain't no bad inferior grass, man, like they gives you in New York. Ain't no chemical shit in my grass, I raises it myself."

"No, thanks. I don't smoke."

"If you needs help," said the driver significantly, taking his hands off the wheel for extra emphasis, "any kind of help at all, you just say the word *Coco* — it's like sesame around here. That's the truth I'm tellin you, man, just say Coco." His hair was graying but the rearview mirror showed a thin, boyish face.

"Your name's Coco?"

"Walter Turnquest, that's my official name, but I prefers Coco, it's more colorful."

"Hi, I'm Mark, Mark Niven," said Mark, who didn't realize that it was possible to listen to someone introducing himself without giving his own name in return, and would be shocked to learn at the Club that one-sided introductions are the way of the world.

His passenger's out-of-place politeness prompted Coco to adopt a cheery and condescending tone. "Mark, eh? You want some woman, Mark? I has them really-truly young, fresh as the morning."

"No, thanks."

"They's to please everybody. Cunt, mouth, arsehole — they's easy, man. They's my nieces, I teached them myself."

'That's what life's like,' Mark thought. 'And I was worried that she was married!'

"Boys?"

"No, thanks."

"What you do for fuckin? You American?"

"I guess so."

"Hey, Mark, you ought to sponsor me, sign me an affidavit so I could go to the States."

"What for? To run the Mafia?"

"To get me a job."

As they drove on between rows of Australian pines, it dawned on Mark that Coco saw him as just another idle tourist. "I'm not on vacation, you know — I'm coming to work here."

"They ain't no work here. Ain't no work for us Bahamians. I ain't got no work and I was borned here!"

"I've got a work permit from the government."

"Now you talkin crazy, boy. They's a new law now, no more whites. We comes first."

"The company that owns the hotel asked them to make an exception in my case. You're getting a lot of tourists from Europe and South America these days and I'm going to interpret for them."

"And they's always exceptions for a white American boy," Coco commented grimly.

Mark felt compelled to explain that he was a victim of American imperialism himself, a fugitive from the U.S. Army.

Far from being impressed, Coco became so angry that he pulled over to the side of the road, stopped the car, and twisted around to glare his hatred at Mark. "You does make me mad, boy. You talkin like you's some big sufferer. And what happens when you get trouble? You don't know nothin about trouble, never. You's always one of the boss race, always. You just picks yourself a nice easy job in a black country, grabs it from some poor unemploy black bastard and cools your arse with air-condition. Where you think I go if I gets trouble here?"

"What do you want me to do?" asked Mark, feeling both guilty and indignant. "Go back and let them put me in prison?"

"Go somewheres else. Shit, boy, pick on some white country!"

"But I like diving," Mark ventured cautiously.

"Hey, I like skiing — maybe I go to Switzerland."

"I was planning to do some underwater photography."

"Pictures! What for, pictures! You comin an' takin up room in this poor-arse country, boy."

Mark hesitated. "Well . . . I also sort of thought I might look and see whether there are any old cannons or pieces of eight lying around."

Coco grinned approval and slapped the steering wheel with enthusiasm. "Pieces of eight? Hey, hey! That's different. They's better than pictures. Why you keep it a secret? I knows all about treasure divin. I knows all about them big black silver pieces!"

"It's only for fun, really," Mark replied hastily, alarmed. "I don't expect to find anything. I just thought I might take a look around while I'm here anyway. I'd appreciate it if you wouldn't talk about it."

"Good Jesus Christ, I's be silent like a fish. I wouldn't ask people to laugh at you." He looked as if he were about to laugh himself, then settled back with his elbow resting on the steering wheel, like a man who had all the time in the world. "Yuh, I knows all about them old Spanish silver pieces rollin in the night! When I was a kid I was gonna be a world-famous scientist *and* a diplomat at the Court of St. James's. *Sir* Walter Turnquest. When I was a kid — oh Lord, I was gonna be famous! I was already winning the blasted Nobel Prize for Peace and the Nobel Prize for Physics." The recollection which had cheered him at first suddenly made him angry again. "And now I low-rates myself with prostitutes, and all them tourists brings they wives."

"Would you be interested in running a boat for me?"

"*You* has a boat?"

"I'm going to get one, and I need somebody to sit in it and watch out for me while I'm diving. Jump in and help if anything goes wrong."

"I is your Savior!"

Mark hired Coco then and there, busy making progress while still on his way from the airstrip to the hotel. He had never been anything but prompt and efficient. Yet his father had good reason to worry that he didn't have the right sort of character to become rich: what millionaire would have been moved to hire a man because he was so poor that he pimped for his nieces and used to have big dreams?

Coco asked five dollars an hour, prepared to take half as much, but Mark thought that five dollars was only fair and agreed at once. Coco, who hadn't had much experience of fairness and had acquired none himself, took Mark's ready consent as proof that he was weak or stupid or both and couldn't possibly know what he was about.

An Island of the Very Rich

The word millionaire alone was to blame, not the millionaire himself,
but just the word alone; for quite apart from the moneybags, there is
something in the mere sound of the word which affects equally
people who are scoundrels, people who are neither one thing nor the other,
and good people; in short, it affects everyone.

GOGOL

The poverty of the rich.
GEORGE MIKES

MARK certainly had no idea of his standing in the world. Looking
on his job at the Seven Seas Club simply as a way to provide for
his room and board and Coco's pay while he searched for the wreck, he
did not expect that anyone would take him for a servant, and as soon as
he stepped out of the taxi he began to earn the acrimony meted out to
people who do not know their place.

Two porters brought a dolly to carry his bags to the staff house, while
a third led him inside the main building. He tipped them all, oblivious
of the offended looks they gave him as they pocketed the money. Did
he think he was a cut above the rest of them?

He did, and this ensured that his relatively easy job would be a hard
one, full of disagreeable surprises. He would come to hate the pleasant
grounds shaded by huge trees, the bright plaza formed by two crescent-
shaped shopping arcades leading up to the main building, an imitation
southern colonial mansion with Greek columns — the whole luxurious
mess — although he liked it well enough at first sight, especially the
gardens. The lobby was done up in Spanish style with leather, dark wood
and wrought iron; indeed, as he learned from the brochure which he picked
up while waiting to see the manager, all the rooms were furnished in
different styles ranging from Japanese to Jacobean, and the trees and
shrubs in the gardens were selected from five continents. The manage-
ment, it seemed, didn't want the guests to miss out on anything. The
chief offering of the establishment, however, was peace and quiet and

freedom from holiday crowds — in a word, exclusiveness. Mark didn't see a single guest in the lobby, only a silent army of clerks and porters.

Getting into conversation with one of the desk clerks, he learned that, besides the twenty-six bungalows renting for six hundred dollars a day, there were only a dozen suites in the main building, at four hundred dollars a day. At the time these were still fabulous sums for a day's comfort. Food was extra and expensive.

"Who could afford to stay here?" Mark exclaimed.

"A better class of people than you see in most hotels," answered the clerk stiffly, squaring his shoulders and twisting his fleshy nose for greater emphasis.

"What an obscene waste of money!"

"We have our own yacht harbor and a championship golf course. And we also have the only Spanish fort in the islands."

"There isn't much of it left," Mark commented, wondering whether he would ever identify that much with a place where he had to work.

"It's not your business to criticize," the clerk rebuked him, losing patience. "Look at yourself — you're even dressed impertinently!"

"What do you mean?" Mark looked down at himself; he was rather proud of his elegant striped shirt and cashmere pullover.

"The manager sees you without a jacket and tie and you'll be out of here on the next plane. Who do you think you are, some sort of a guest?"

Dashing to the staff house to change, Mark couldn't understand how he could have overlooked such a simple matter. Hadn't he stayed in hotels often enough? It was a stupid rule, though. Why should they care how he dressed as long as he was clean and presentable? And why couldn't he criticize things? By the time he was summoned to the manager's office he had worked himself up into a temper. 'So here's somebody who'd give me a hard time just for a lousy tie,' he thought, giving the man behind the desk a protesting look and introducing himself in a loud, firm voice.

Charles Weaver responded with a frown and a slight nod. A chubby, sandy-haired Englishman with a freckled face and the healthy appearance that goes with living in a semi-tropical climate, he had nothing about him to suggest that he merited more sympathy than resentment, but he was in fact a thrice-deserted husband. In his thirties he had conceived an irresistible passion for eighteen-year-old girls and in quick succession had married three of them, all of whom were evidently attracted only to an inexperienced notion of the married state and left him within months. Shy and diffident to begin with, Weaver was convinced by these fiascos that he was a dull and dislikable person, and became as withdrawn as his position allowed him to be. He would not impose himself on his staff beyond telling them what to do. With the new employee, however, there was a problem. He hadn't asked for anybody. Picking up the letter from the head office, signed by Mr. Anthony Heller, vice-president for personnel, he re-read it with a puzzled expression.

"I see you have no previous experience in the hotel business, and you're being employed part-time, for a four-day week."

"That's right," said Mark.

Taken aback by this unsolicited comment, Weaver raised his sandy eyebrows. "I imagine you're not the first member of your family with our organization."

"No, I'm the first."

"Perhaps you're related to Mr. Heller in some way?"

"Oh, no."

"He's an old friend of the family, then?"

"Mr. Heller? No, I only met him when I went to his office. He wouldn't give me a job at first, but when I got drafted I went back to see him, and he changed his mind. He said he felt he ought to help me in honor of his namesake who wrote *Catch-22* — you know, that great funny anti-war novel. Seeing that I was a draft dodger, I mean."

"What?"

"You know — we're both against the Vietnam War. Big countries should leave small countries alone, don't you think?"

Weaver held up his hands. "I don't want to hear about it!"

He felt the sort of bewilderment that plagued him about his former wives. Was the time coming when he would have to worry about bell-boys and waiters starting political arguments with the guests? "No hotel employee has views or opinions about anything," he said, staring down at his desk. "You left your opinions back in New York, is that clear?"

"Yes, sir," said Mark, swallowing.

"Only guests have opinions. And remember, when they complain they're always right, except possibly about the bill."

"Yes, sir." Mark shifted his feet, glancing at the two empty arm-chairs in front of the desk.

"You're expected to be at the reception desk whenever planes arrive or leave, but otherwise you're here to interpret between foreign guests and the staff. Mr. Heller writes that your father is an actor — perhaps you can be of some use to Miss Little, our social director. We have crab races on the beach every afternoon, and nightclub shows and films in the evening, but any additional entertainment ideas are welcome." For the first time Weaver looked searchingly at the handsome young man, then bent his head to study his fingernails. "I assume you know how to behave yourself."

Mark straightened his tie. "Yes, sir."

"You have three days off a week. What do you plan to do in your spare time?"

"I dive, sir."

"It's a dangerous sport."

"I've had a lot of practice — I've been diving for nearly six years, off and on."

"Right, we'll have a word with the waterfront director — maybe he'll have some use for you." Hoping that the new employee would be able to earn his keep after all, Weaver loosened up a little. "You've already seen something of the island. This place was nothing, you know, until Sir Henry Colville took it over. No doubt you've heard about Sir Henry. . . . Only vaguely? Dear me. He was a big man in Middle East oil. He's still alive, you know — he dines at the Club once or twice a year. Incidentally," he added in a changed tone, "you must not wander around outside the Club's property. Apart from the roads and the natives' compound, and the ruins of the fort, which Sir Henry keeps open to the public, everything here is private. And people value their privacy. I say 'value' not as a mere figure of speech — each of these estates cost between a million and a million and a half dollars just for the land. The dogs here are Alsatians, and they're trained to bite."

'And she was complaining how hard it is for the rich to have friends!' Mark thought. He had been planning to walk over and see Marianne one evening, but as he listened to Weaver, he remembered that she hadn't invited him.

"If you get sick," said Weaver, perhaps reminded of the subject by Mark's change of color, "you're entitled to go to the clinic on the island, as our employee. Sir Henry built it and they say it's one of the best in the world for its size. The doctor who heads it is paid three hundred thousand a year," he added for emphasis. Mr. Weaver was a man who believed that high salaries were proof of excellence.

"I'm not the type to get sick, sir."

Weaver raised his eyebrows again, troubled by so many unsolicited remarks. "I certainly hope not. I've arranged for you to be instructed in the way things are done here, and you'll have a couple of days to settle in. Tomorrow you'll go to our tailor in Nassau to be fitted with a uniform. One more thing. Even though I didn't hire you, I can fire you if it should become necessary," he concluded with a resigned air of authority. "Be guided in everything by the head clerk."

'So now I'm an employee, an absolute nobody,' Mark reflected bitterly as he left the manager's office. 'From now on I can only exist on my time off.' This thought drove every other idea from his mind. The clerk who had to instruct him in the daily routine thought he was stupid.

STILL distracted, Mark left the main building and took a turn around the crescent-shaped shopping arcades, seeing nothing. Only the shock of a collision woke him: hurrying along with his head bent, he nearly knocked over a tall man standing in front of a shop window.

There was a flash of mutual hostility and Mark suddenly found himself in the air.

The man had seized him with both hands and lifted him two feet off the ground. However, this considerable feat of weight-lifting had evidently exhausted his fit of temper, for he set him down again, somewhat more gently. "Sorry, my reflexes ran away with me," he said with a conciliatory grin. "I'm Ken Eshelby, I run the camera shop here. I was just admiring my new window display when you happened along."

Mark's first impulse was to hit the man, but by the time he had caught his breath he felt less violent and decided to shake Eshelby's outstretched hand instead — especially as he looked reassuringly unconventional, with a crimson scarf around his neck in place of a tie. Besides, there was a sense of affinity: they were both the kind of people who tended to blush for their ill feelings, and the prompt change of mood from belligerent to amiable marked them as members of the same civilized world. "Sorry I bumped into you like that," said Mark, apologizing in his turn. "I'm new here — this is my first day."

"Oh, well, that makes all the difference," conceded Eshelby with a benevolent nod. "You can't be expected not to knock people down on your first day."

Mark's ungrudging laugh at his own expense livened up their conversation and earned him an invitation into the shop. As they passed through the door under the Kodak sign, he thought for a moment that they had made a mistake: there were more books than flashbulbs inside. Seeing all the Penguins and Livres de Poche lining the shelves, he decided that Eshelby must be intelligent, and confessed to him that he didn't like their boss.

"The poor man! What has he done?"

"Well, for one thing, he made me stand all through the interview."

Eshelby gave him a wondering look. "This must be the first job you've ever had."

"Hey, that's right — how did you know?"

"Just guessing."

Mark liked Eshelby in spite of his mocking tone. "You're clever!" he complimented him.

"How kind of you to notice! But I musn't commit the same mistake as Mr. Weaver — have a seat." Evidently welcoming every opportunity to show off his strength, he picked up a heavy swivel chair with one hand and hoisted it effortlessly over the counter. "Tennis," he explained in response to Mark's amazed look. A tall, thin man in his early forties, with quick blue eyes, he had a supple body and an easy grace, gifts of form and style common to refined sportsmen and some homosexuals. He was both, but apart from tennis, his passions were talking and reading. ("Sex is too spasmodic to sustain passion," he said to Mark later on in relation to one of the bellboys.)

"I brought a camera with underwater casing, I hope to take some pictures of the seabed," Mark told him, wishing to establish himself as a worthwhile customer. "So you'll be getting a lot of color film to develop."

Eshelby promptly refused to have anything to do with it. "It would bore me and ruin you," he replied with an expression of mild disgust. "Why don't I just teach you how to develop film and let you use the darkroom in the evenings. Don't look so worried, I won't charge you for it." He had been a high-school teacher in Edmonton, Alberta, until it had come to light that he was cohabiting with another man, and his interest in shopkeeping was casual to say the least.

The former teacher and former student, both forcibly interrupted in their scholarly pursuits, got along very well, and as the cheer of sudden comradeship made Mark feel likable and important again, he wanted to talk about Marianne.

Summoning an offhand manner, he asked about the rich residents of the island. "Do you see them much around the Club?"

"No, you don't."

"How come?"

"That's the whole point, dear boy — they don't want to be seen. It may not have occurred to you, but nobody needs to lay out the kind of money they do, just to buy a bit of land and some beach. All those extra millions go to erect the *expense barrier* — to keep out the poor, God forbid, middle-class riffraff like you and me, and the not so terribly rich. Everybody, in fact. To keep out people, period."

"Come to think of it," Mark commented sullenly, "they don't even need the dogs, do they?"

"That's to protect the paintings. Dogs, nothing! Sir Henry has armed guards with submachine guns. You can never have enough protection in this vile world. It's tragic."

"They must have fantastic houses, though. I wouldn't mind looking around them."

"Well, they're not your Renaissance palaces, I can tell you that. In the old days the great ones of this world built with vision and marble — now it can be ready-mixed concrete for all they care. Sir Henry's the only exception — he built his whole vast house out of marble — the floors, the walls, the ceilings, the stairs. Not for the grandeur of it, mind you! It's just that marble is cool and he dislikes air-conditioning. As for the rest of the very rich, what shows who they are is the silence all around. Relative silence I should say. Not even the Queen of England can do anything about the planes."

"So I guess the thing to do is just leave them alone."

"Whatever gave you that idea?" asked Eshelby, enjoying his own amazement. "Actually, they're starved for company. They succeeded in

118

isolating themselves so perfectly, you see, that they get lonesome. Just *think* what eleven families can find to say to each other, year in, year out. It's easier on the men, they're reading Saul Kent's *Anti-Aging Revolution* and breathing condensed oxygen at the clinic every day — keeping alive keeps them busy. But the women — dear God, the women!''

"What about them?''

Eshelby seated himself on the counter and leaned forward toward Mark, visibly eager to explain it all. Although it was eight years since he had given up teaching, he still retained his authoritative classroom manner and his zest for enlightening the young. "This is an old man's island — apart from Kevin Hardwick, our chemical overlord, who comes and goes — but the wives are mostly on the young side. After all, what would money be worth if it couldn't even buy you fresh, juicy flesh? You should read Balzac on the subject!'' he exclaimed, casting a searching glance at Mark to see whether the name meant anything to him. "But of course in Balzac's time it was different — old men were stuck with their old wives, and girls could milk them for fortunes, clean them out and leave them. Now there is divorce with alimony and the old men pay off the old wives and marry the girls, and the deal is 'you get nothing now but when I die you'll get everything.' Only they don't die. And they expect to be looked after properly. They've spent their lives making people jump and they're not about to lose the habit now. The toast must be just *so* crisp and just *so* hot. And they want to be kept warm in bed, too. Those poor girls could all quote Eugene McCarthy — *Stubbornness and penicillin hold the aged above me.*''

He made a grimace to show sympathy for the deceived wives and slid off the counter to pace the floor. "So the darlings end up like maids, and by the time they catch on, their youth is gone. Their waistline. Worse — their jawline. They wear diamonds in the evening, but who is to admire them? They have no visitors to speak of — anybody who is young and rich has better things to do than come to Santa Catalina. So every new face — every new white face, I should say — is a sensation. That's how I passed. Actually, even our poor manager had his chances, but he was found wanting. Just couldn't manage to be amusing, I'm afraid. If you like, I'll take you along the next time one of them thinks of me.''

"I'm not amusing either,'' Mark retorted with the belligerent pride the young take in their deficiencies.

"You're handsome, that makes you already half entertaining. For the rest, you'll simply have to make a valiant try.''

"What's the point? I'll just be a hotel clerk in one of those idiotic red jackets with gold dolphins on the lapels.''

"Why, you change for the evening. You'll be fine, just don't mention submarines.''

"What submarines?''

Eshelby raised his index finger. "Imagine, you spend millions to get away from the world — from bad weather, muggers, people with germs, pollution — and then you find you're right next to the path of the Russian submarines cruising back and forth with their missiles and releasing God knows how much radioactive waste into the sea where you take your morning dip. Mentioning submarines to our billionaires is like telling them that money isn't all it's cracked up to be. They know it, they know it only too well, but they don't like to be reminded of it."

"They'd still think I don't count for anything."

"What an extraordinary idea!"

"That's how they look at you, isn't it? You are what you've got, that's all you amount to."

"If that were the case, they wouldn't invite me. Anyway, you could pick up some tips for the stock market, and then you'd amount to more. I haven't done badly."

Mark shook his head. "I'm not interested in making money that way — profiting from other people's work."

"Heavens, dear boy, you're hard to please!"

Mark got up from his chair to examine a revolving rack of color slides. "But Mrs. Hardwick couldn't have married for money. She was a rich girl herself, wasn't she?"

"Ah! I was *wondering* what all this was about! So you know her?"

"Not really," replied Mark. His voice betrayed a deep sense of dissatisfaction.

"Where did you meet?"

"On the plane coming here."

"You're right, Mrs. Hardwick is in a class by herself. You don't need to worry about her — she's incontestably perfect, a steel princess in her own right."

This light remark elicited a morose frown. "Lucky for her. If she didn't marry Hardwick for his money, she must love him."

Eshelby raised his hands to disclaim any special knowledge. "I couldn't tell you otherwise."

Mark turned from the color slides and scanned the rows of paperbacks with a desolate air, as if he meant to take up reading. "They must get along."

"Oh, well, I guess there is something I can tell you," Eshelby relented. "If you're so keen on her." His liking for his new friend had an undercurrent of physical attraction, but in spite of this, or perhaps for this very reason, he was fascinated by the possibility of an affair between the two.

"What is it?" Mark asked, coming back to life.

"She has a lot of time on her hands."

Mark's face fell. "What do you mean?"

"What do you mean, what do I mean? I mean that to have time on your hands is to be half in love with anybody who wants you. The would-be widows aren't much fun for her, as I'm sure you can imagine, and Hardwick's only here on weekends. He commutes from Chicago in his Boeing 707."

Mark looked positively aghast. "You mean he has his own private Boeing 707?"

Eshelby spread his arms to open wide the doors of understanding. "He has his very own private Boeing 707 the same way as I have my very own private bicycle. Mind you, he has more problems with his plane than I have with my bicycle," he added not without satisfaction. "The Boeing's too grand to land on our little airstrip, so he has to come down in Nassau and take an air taxi from there. Come to think of it, with all his flying about, Marianne Hardwick has a better chance of becoming a widow than the other wives around here. But what I envy is her sloop, the *Hermit*. That's a splendid boat."

"A Boeing 707!" muttered Mark uncomprehendingly. Much as he had dreamed of having his own jet, he had never thought of getting himself such a huge one. His head was becoming crowded with platitudes about the gap between the rich and the poor — he felt the distance growing in his heart.

LONGING to throw away his uniform even before putting it on, Mark used his trip to the Club's tailor in Nassau to buy everything he needed to become rich himself. At the Pilot House Diving Shop, he managed to get a three-stage fourteen-cubic-foot air compressor, four cascade tanks, fittings, a cesium magnetometer and weight belt secondhand; the rest he bought new. From Pilot House he was sent to Brown's boatyard, where he picked out a fifteen-foot fiberglass boat with a diving platform, inboard motor (a must for navigating among coral reefs, which are death to outboards) and decked-over stowage cabin for his gear. Mainly, though, he chose it for its white canvas awning supported by four thin steel poles, which reminded him of the canopy over his parents' bed in the apartment on the quai d'Orléans. While he was getting his boat registered, Mr. Brown's man painted the name *Ile Saint-Louis* on it for him, and he drove it himself to Santa Catalina that same afternoon, spending four difficult hours learning how to navigate on his own out on the open sea.

Mark knew the charts of the region by heart, but seeing the wilderness of corals for the first time he had a sickening feeling that he would grow old among them. It was a terrifying prospect for a nineteen-year-old. He had to drive his boat fifteen miles out of his way to get around what the charts called the Long Reef; the wreck of the *Flora* could have been lying either side of it. Farther south, nearer to the island, he came to the Santa Catalina atolls — large rings of coral forming lagoons so shallow in places that the seaweed rising above the surface made them look like submerged fields (which is what they were, having submerged at the end of the last Ice Age some forty thousand years ago). A hurricane could have driven the *Flora* through the gaps in the reefs into any of the lagoons, which covered, with the sea in between, more than thirty square miles. Still farther south, less than a mile from shore, running right along the Atlantic side of the island, lay the fringe reefs.

Deciding to begin with the fringe reefs, Mark went diving on his first day off. Neither books nor color films nor diving in the Seine had given him any inkling of the beauty of the world he descended into. Even when his depth gauge showed that he was down at forty-two feet, the water was as sunny and transparent as the air above. He could see the shadows of the fish on the sand. The Bahama Islands have no rivers to muddy their sea and Bahamian waters, sheltered by reefs, are the clearest in the world. And more alive with plants and animals than the thickest jungle. Everything Mark saw bloomed in unimaginably bright colors. The pink, red, yellow corals were like bushes, cacti, giant leaves, leafless branches, ruined towers, pillars, leaning trees; the sand of the seabed was dotted with pink conches, purple starfish and red fire sponges; trailing vines of green, yellow and brown seaweed swayed back and forth with the currents. This whole shimmering world was teeming with blue, orange, yellow, silver, bloodred, blackest-black fish. And fish that were of every color at once. The poisonous puffers puffed themselves up when they saw him.

He was glad he was wearing his heavy black rubber wet suit when he found himself entangled in the stinging tentacles of that deadly bright blue bubble, a Portuguese man-of-war, and he hoped that his rubber covering would protect him also from stinging coral and anemones. He was just getting used to moving about carefully when his cesium magnetometer signaled the presence of metal under a mound of sand, only about twenty feet below the surface. With Coco minding the motorboat and filling his empty tanks, he spent hours moving the sand, and at the end of his labors unearthed a rusty oil drum. Every day he went diving his magnetometer located some garbage on the seabed. That was all he found. Whenever he got sick of being fooled by the metal detector and took down his camera instead, the pictures showed that the things he missed with the naked eye were garbage too. He had to get used to being a hotel clerk who rushed to any guest who beckoned.

One day the director of Sir Henry's clinic, Dr. Attila Feyer, who often lunched at the Club, summoned the young interpreter to his table, demanding to know *vy* he didn't speak Hungarian. In an English which lacked the sounds of *wh* and *th*, stressed the first syllable of every word and was indifferent to gender (he referred to Mr. Weaver as *she* and to his own wife as *him*), he assured Mark, as Hungarians tend to assure every stranger, that Hungarian was a language worth learning because of its poetry. A tall, fat man with an enormous face which ended in a triple chin trembling all by itself, the doctor reminded Mark of a brooding emperor penguin he had once seen in Regent's Park Zoo. Formerly on the staff of Columbia Presbyterian Medical Center in New York and now a consulting surgeon with the University of Miami Veterans' Administration Hospital, Dr. Feyer spent three or four days a week on Santa Catalina, to be at hand in case Sir Henry broke a bone or was shot by a terrorist. (These were Sir Henry's chief worries.) The director of the clinic was a nephew of Imre Nagy, the former prime minister of Hungary, who liberalized the communist regime during the brief thaw of 1953 and headed the revolutionary government in 1956, trying to free the country from Russian occupation. The Russians executed Imre Nagy but they left his nephew alone and Dr. Feyer prospered as surgeon in chief of the hospital of the University of Budapest. However, he did not wish to live in a country where his uncle could be hanged for believing in national independence. He was a man of decent feelings — he treated poor people as devotedly as millionaires and never sanctioned unnecessary tests or operations just because the patient could pay for them — yet he was quite insane about money. There was a void where his native places used to be, and his unease and anger at finding himself a foreigner who couldn't even speak properly turned into pathological greed. A surgeon of international reputation who could have had a full and active professional life on the mainland, he agreed to bury himself on Santa Catalina for days every week simply for the money Sir Henry was paying him. He also hoped to get into some rich men's wills. Suffering immense boredom for his greed, he kept two sports cars on the island, a Mercedes and a Ferrari, to speed along the only road, which with all its twists and turns measured no more than seventeen miles in length. He complained to Mark that he was wasting his skills; neither of them could have dreamed that one day he would describe Mark as *de first patient vorty of me on dis island!*

The new clerk's intelligent eyes earned him many confidences. Still, most of the guests were content to give him orders, or simply looked through him as if he weren't there. Like all wage slaves, he had two crosses to bear: the people he worked for and the people he worked with.

The way the guests were ignoring him and ordering him about at one and the same time made him so miserable that it took him weeks to comprehend that his fellow employees treated him like dirt because they envied him. They could not abide the part-time interpreter who didn't quite share their common lot and was rich enough to buy a motorboat and even pay a Bahamian to help him. Ignorant of beaten men's sensitivity, Mark committed all the blunders of inexperience. His diving boat was viewed as a deliberate affront, a willful reminder that he was better off than they were. It was one of those small craft which Bahamians and Floridians call inter-island bumboats — and to yachtsmen it was just a *stinkpot* because it burned oil — but it was new and shiny and looked even more expensive than the $3500 he had paid for it. And to add insult to injury, he had given it a fancy foreign name!

"It's something French," said the barman at lunch in the staff canteen, casting a glance at Mark sitting at the next table, just to show that he didn't mind being overheard. "Mr. Smart-Ass doesn't want you to forget that he's the interpreter around here."

"That's not it at all!" protested Mark, still hoping to reason things out. "It's just the name of the island where we used to live in Paris when I was a kid."

"See? He wants to tell us that he used to live in Paris!"

"On an *island* in Paris," a doorman corrected him.

"Paris is a city. There's no islands in Paris."

"There are two big ones in the river that runs through it," Mark explained.

"Don't argue with him, he has to know everything better. We're just ignorant bums."

"I didn't say that!"

"He says we're ignorant bums, but you got to be a nut to search for treasure."

"He tips the porters but he don't take tips himself."

"Why should he? He's a big man — he owns an ocean liner."

"How's your ocean liner?" they kept asking him.

It is possible to fill the simplest question with such derision that it will leave a man shaking for hours, and Mark learned the hard way that he should have bought a serviceable secondhand diving boat and complained incessantly how much it cost. His good looks, his lively eyes, also told against him: bright and attractive people are discriminated against like all minorities.

"They say knowing languages is no good for your mental intelligence," a gray-haired bellboy remarked to him one day with a mixture of diffidence and disdain. "Do you think that's a fact?"

Mark pretended not to hear, deciding to play deaf and dumb.

"You're thinking again," Weaver admonished him, passing through the lobby. "You're forgetting to smile."

But to smile and do as he was told, to stand about for hours on end, ready to jump at the wave of a hand, was by no means as light a task as he had imagined, and there was hardly an evening when his joints didn't ache and his pride wasn't bruised. He often thought of Marianne Hardwick, but made no attempt to see her. The would-be prince, historian and millionaire was brought low with a bout of identity crisis, a malady that robbed him of the courage to love. He spent his free days diving and his evenings in Eshelby's darkroom, abandoning himself to his search for the wreck with the single-minded dedication of a young man whom the first shock of earning his living had taught that money could buy more than marble halls: it could buy back the freedom of his adolescence.

18

The Twists and Turns of Falling in Love

Believe me, Madame, cold tranquillity, the soul's sleep,
the imitation of death, does not lead to happiness;
only the active passions can lead to it.

LACLOS

STENDHAL, who summed up his life with the initials of twelve women, argues in his treatise *On Love* that love has very little to do with the beloved person and everything to do with the lover's imagination. Nothing is so seductive as our own thoughts; the passion that sweeps us off our feet is our own. At any rate, there seems to be no other way to account for the fact that Marianne Hardwick fell in love with Mark long before they saw each other again.

First she became lively and energetic.

Like most people with slightly low blood pressure and nothing urgent to do, she was a late sleeper and a slow starter, spending the first hours of the day in a lazy haze, but the morning after meeting Mark she woke early and was wide awake the instant she opened her eyes — she felt fizzy, as if her blood had turned to champagne. Jumping out of bed, she ran to the window to draw the curtains. The sea was gray and choppy; the night breeze wasn't spent yet, though the sun already signaled its coming by lighting the clouds from below the horizon. She put on a bikini and went downstairs, listening to the silence in the house. 'I've got a head start on everybody today,' she thought with the elation of a racer breaking a record. The wolfhounds sprang from the flagstones of the terrace and bounded ahead of her through the garden and down to the wide sandy beach — only to back away as they got their paws wet, growling and whining to excuse themselves.

Marianne felt as if she could make love with the sea. She stretched out on the water, let the cold penetrate her, then started to move with eyes closed, rising and sinking with the waves. By the time she felt warm enough to open her eyes again the sun was high in the sky, the clouds had disappeared, the wind had gone, and the sea had subsided to a slow, heavy roll. Taking a deep breath to make herself float, she let the waves pull her forward and toss her back, stroking her breasts, her limbs, her groin. As a strand of seaweed grazed her belly, she contracted with a spasm of pleasure, flooded by an inner wave — then swam out for nearly a mile.

As she headed in to shore, breakfast was already set on the round stone table at the edge of the garden and the boys were hopping up and down on the beach, waving to her to hurry, setting their blond hair flying with each jump.

"Say, you ought to go to New York every week, Marianne!" commented Joyce, the children's nanny, handing her a big fleecy towel. "It teaches you how to start the day right."

Marianne took off her bikini to dry herself, first with the towel, then with the sun, opening and closing her thighs to catch the warm rays between her legs.

Joyce couldn't resist the opportunity to flatter and tease her at the same time. "Look at your mother, boys! Hasn't she got a lovely body?" She reached out impulsively and pinched Marianne's slender waist.

Laughing with embarrassment, Marianne jumped back. "Ouch!"

The smaller boy, Benjamin, suddenly went wild and began running around and around and around his mother, then threw himself upon her and tried to bite her thigh with great passion. His excitement kept them laughing until he complained that they were making fun of him and started to cry convulsively as if he meant to choke himself. She picked him up, hugged and kissed him, sniffing his neck, breathing in his lovely smell, still as fresh as a baby's, and as his tears dried up and he started to chuckle quietly in his deep voice, her own eyes filled with tears of wonder. It was only when she put Benjamin down and he ran off to dig sand that she became unnerved by the thought that she might be so keyed up because of her meeting with Mark.

The day ceased to be perfect.

Remembering his confident parting grin, she hid her naked body in a dry robe. 'And even if he makes me feel sexy, it's nothing personal,' she reflected, trying to regain her peace of mind, the safe comfort of indifference. 'I live in such an emotional stupor, it's no wonder a little flirting shakes me up. A new song, a good novel or film could have done that much for me.' The better she reasoned, the duller she felt.

"Joyce — aren't you bored with us here?" she asked as they all sat down to breakfast.

"Why? You want to send me away?" Joyce laughed uneasily, wishing she hadn't touched her employer. A slim, small-boned girl with big breasts, a beauty of contrasts, combining Arab and Negroid features, she had a delicate fragile face, an aquiline nose and large, thick lips. Just turned eighteen, she was full of life and ambition, keen to learn everything and to save every penny she earned, hoping eventually to open a small hotel on one of the islands with a loan from the Hardwicks. "I'm not bored, no, not me, never," she protested vehemently. "I like it here."

"I'm growing stupid — I can feel it!" exclaimed Marianne with a sudden upsurge of unhappiness. "There's nothing to think about here. I read the papers every day when I'm in New York — here I don't even get around to reading Art Buchwald! My brain's running down. All that sun and sea make you think that nothing happens beyond the horizon. We might as well be a family of monkeys!"

This uncharacteristic outburst inspired Joyce to guess her trouble, but as the boys were watching them with intent curiosity, she commented silently, drawing a circle in the air over Marianne's heart. This pantomime dispelled Marianne's bad temper, and she replied with a tentative grimace. Joyce giggled. They both giggled. Their non-verbal camaraderie led to a decisive exchange of confidences which prompted Marianne to resolve that she would make love with Mark as soon as he asked her.

"You met a man," Joyce declared, once the boys had left the table and run off with the wolfhounds, their bodyguards. "Yes-yes, somebody you like!" she added hastily, to forestall any belated denial. "I'm really-truly glad, because I can tell it to you now!" She was so glad, so relieved, she pressed her hands to her cheeks to contain her emotions. "You won't mind none of that now."

"Come on, what *is* it?"

"Mr. Hardwick, he done a thing last October. Yessir. When your sister come visiting, you know, and I looked after her rooms in the guest cottage. Mr. Hardwick came after me there and grabbed me. He pushed me down on the green couch. You were here all the time, right down here at this table having breakfast, you and your sister."

Marianne still had the illusion that she could satisfy her husband at least for the weekends, and at first she could only stare.

"Take off your pants is all he says, and then he just done it." Joyce swayed her breasts as if by way of proof. "I'm telling you no lies."

"I believe you."

"But ever since," added Joyce, making no attempt to hide the bitterness of her humiliation, "he don't do me the favor of a single smile. No sir, never once. He looks at me — he looks at me like he don't remember."

"He's a shit."

"Amen!" echoed Joyce.

From that time the two women became fast friends with shared secrets. Marianne, perhaps wishing to show that she wasn't bothered by Joyce's news, told her about Mark, and they agreed that he was bound to call.

But he didn't.

Keyed up and let down, she seduced her husband the following weekend, giving him nights that left him numb with swollen vanity and incomprehension. As these nights changed nothing, she began to hate both Hardwick and Mark for her predicament. Not even the little hands of her children could calm her. She spent her time sailing with them, crisscrossing the same few miles of water, not knowing where to turn.

Camped in the cool shade of the Spanish ruins on top of the hill, Sypcovich was mildly stirred when she walked on the deck topless, trapped in the circles of his powerful navy binoculars. Mostly, though, the deck of the *Hermit* presented him with a boring domestic scene. Mrs. Hardwick left the ropes and canvas to her Bahamian servants only to play games with her children or sunbathe on a wide mattress built into the deck. The forty-eight-foot sloop, built at the famous Bertram Yards in Florida to race the winds and make the most of the slightest breeze, covered a great deal of water but never came too near Mark's *Ile Saint-Louis*.

SYPCOVICH wished that Mrs. Hardwick and the actor's son would ram each other's boats and sink. They gave him a headache, a painful hangover of misplaced optimism. He couldn't understand why they didn't get together, when they could hardly keep an inch between them on the plane. 'What's wrong with that kid?' he fumed to himself. 'With all the little virgins screwing around these days, he's probably never had a married woman. What a world!' His fifty-thousand-dollar bonus was turning out to be a curse; he hadn't got it yet, but he had already lost it many times.

On days when Mark was working at the Seven Seas Club, Sypcovich didn't bother climbing up the hill to the fort but kept an eye on him at the hotel, just in case Mrs. Hardwick turned up. "You're too busy," he told Mark one morning with a friendly and paternal smile, catching the interpreter by the sleeve of his uniform as he walked through the Sand Bar. "We haven't had a good talk since our plane ride."

Mark inclined his head but freed his arm. "Sir?"

"You work too hard — why don't you take it easy now and then? Look around for a bit of fun."

"That's the privilege of the guests, sir." Mark bowed and walked off, playing the role of the humble but hard-pressed servant.

"That's what you think," said Sypcovich grimly into his glass, trying to absorb this new snub.

'Are private detectives millionaires?' wondered Mark. 'He's been here for over a month — how can he possibly afford it?' However, he disliked the man too much to keep thinking about him.

Sypcovich's long stay at the Club was expensive but as far as Miss

Marshall was concerned, the private detective was welcome to stay at the Seven Seas Club for months on end: *Opulent Interiors* was paying for it all.

In his rare good moods Sypcovich regarded his visits to the island as the world's best-paid luxury vacations, but he had too much professional pride to be content with anything but *results,* and no amount of free sunshine and bourbon could compensate him for his lack of progress and constant disappointments. The same day that he tried to talk sense to Mark in the Sand Bar, he saw Coco hanging about the taxi rank in front of the main building and motioned him aside for a walk in the garden. They were old acquaintances; Coco occasionally brought one of his nieces to Sypcovich's suite by way of the service elevator.

"I bet you could use five hundred bucks," Sypcovich said with his thin smile as they reached an empty stretch of gravel path.

At the mention of five hundred dollars Coco assumed the pious expression of a man who understands that sex for the fat and aging is no laughing matter. "You wants something special, boss? My girls is to please, they waxes their ass for you if you wants them to."

Sypcovich gave a busy man's impatient grunt to dismiss the frivolous suggestion. "I'm going away and I want you keep an eye on Mrs. Hardwick and that punk you work for."

"Mrs. Hardwick?" Coco was amazed. "He knows Mrs. Hardwick?"

"Yeah. And I want to know if he screws her."

Coco thought this was as unlikely as a snowfall, but he looked down at the ground to fill himself with humility, then looked up again, a faithful dog ready to do his master's bidding. "OK, boss, it's a deal. You gives me a hundred now and I keeps my eyes and ears open."

"Listen," Sypcovich snapped, "I used to book guys like you. You'll get paid if and when you earn it. Here's ten to pay for the telegram if you come up with anything."

'Fancy that, a police!' thought Coco, pocketing the envelope with Sypcovich's address and the ten dollars. Having failed to trick him into paying an advance, he made up his mind that Sypcovich was a clever, tough bastard who was worth taking seriously. As he didn't take Mark seriously, he felt no obligation toward him.

Miss Marshall, Sypcovich, and now Coco had an unwitting ally in Eshelby. "Why don't you call her, for heaven's sake?" he asked Mark as they were having lunch together in the staff canteen.

"Why should I?" replied Mark bitterly. "She might look like a girl who doesn't know where bank-notes come from, but I bet she's as cold and hard as the rest of them. You can't tell me they aren't cold and hard. You'd wonder how they can restrain themselves from doing something to help the few dozen Bahamians who live right here on their own island in those appalling tin-roofed shacks. Right by the garbage dump. Naturally.''

"What do you want her to do? Ask Sir Henry to move the garbage to her garden? I'm sure the dear girl gives a lot away. Nobody can help everybody.''

"That's a good excuse to do nothing.''

"Well, she's on the board of the Chicago Lyric Opera. There was a little girl with a great voice right here by the garbage dump and she's footing all the bills for her to study in Milan. She says the world needs more than one Sandra Browne. Another kid is studying at Juilliard at her expense. She's a patron of the Canadian Opera Company too. And she must be signing lots of checks we don't know about.''

"And what could I be a patron of?'' Mark said gloomily.

How simple everything had seemed when he first caught sight of her legs! Alone at night in his small room in the staff house he masturbated thinking about her, but he thought of her as the Hindu beggar would think of the Maharajah's daughter — as the girl to meet once he was reborn in a higher form of existence, once he found the wreck.

SYPCOVICH flew back to Chicago swearing never to set foot on the island again unless he heard from Coco. He was so sick of the whole case that he saw nothing for it but to advise his client to give up on Mrs. Hardwick altogether. Back at his office, making up his final account, he reflected that he was about to terminate a lucrative assignment of his own volition, and was so impressed by his professional integrity that he felt it was only fair to reward himself by adding some more fictitious expenses to his bill. It is with such combinations of rectitude and fraud that crooks in all ranks of society bolster their self-respect while advancing their fortunes.

"I could lead you on,'' he assured Miss Marshall, presenting himself at her office after a haircut and a manicure. "I could keep you sending me down there and fattening my bank account, but I don't want to waste any more of your money.''

Miss Marshall could hardly stand the sight of Sypcovich's bloated face and piggish eyes, his sickly flesh, suggesting unpleasant smells behind the cloud of lotions. She found him repulsive in the extreme, and now that he was advising her to give up, she began to wonder whether he had ever had a chance to find out anything about women. "She'll slip up sooner or later,'' she said in her lazy, throaty voice, which could send tingles down Hardwick's spine or envelop him all over like a warm bath. "She'll melt for the right man.''

Sypcovich snorted and heaved himself to his feet. Did she think he didn't know what he was talking about? "Miss Marshall," he asked, pulling in his belly and trying to hold it in, an effort which lent his face a solemn expression, "did you ever hear of that Queen Elizabeth of England who never had an intimate relationship with a man? The one they call the Virgin Queen? She had all those old castles at her disposal, full of nooks and crannies — hundreds of bedrooms — and all those knights and lords at her beck and call. But oh, no, she wouldn't lower herself! Nobody was good enough for her royal you-know-what. Well, the same goes for your Mrs. Hardwick."

The editor of *Opulent Interiors* was unimpressed. "Good Queen Bess must have had more nooks than you think. But tell me more about that actor's son."

"What is there to say about him!" exploded Sypcovich, letting go of his belly and his exasperation. "I told you, he doesn't even give her a try. Her money isn't good enough for him, he wants his own. They're impossible people."

"Why, Mr. Sypcovich — you're not quitting, you're getting emotionally involved!"

PERHAPS nothing would have come of the ill-fated romance if it hadn't been for the Hardwick children. As they were getting bored and restless on deck one day, Fawkes pointed out the *Ile Saint-Louis* in the distance and told them about the diver who was supposed to be looking for old coins. Although Creighton was only four and Benjamin not quite three, both little boys had their own flippers, masks and snorkels and were almost as much at home in the water as on land, and, inspired by Fawkes's stories about sunken ships, they announced that they were going to join the treasure hunt.

But their mother wouldn't hear of it.

"Why?" Creighton demanded in the bullying tone of his Grandfather Montgomery.

"Because there are sharks and barracuda out here, that's why."

"Just baby sharks, I bet," replied Creighton, kicking his younger brother and giving him a commanding look to make him nag her too.

"Just baby barracuda," Benjamin chimed in obediently.

"Oh, boy, we'll never hear the end of this," Marianne sighed, bracing herself for a long struggle.

Every time the boys spotted the *Ile Saint-Louis* they started an argument to wear down their mother, and while trying to get it into their heads that the sea could be dangerous, she began to worry about Mark. How could he risk diving alone? Wasn't there anybody at the Club to warn him? Only six months earlier a yachtsman who went diving among the reefs on his own had disappeared without a trace, and the most intensive search had failed to turn up so much as his aqualung. This incident preyed on her mind, and she got into the habit of watching Mark's diving boat with her binoculars. (Long-distance observation was very much part of their story.) The sight of Coco sitting at the stern, rolling a speargun between his palms, did nothing to allay her anxiety. What use would he be if Mark was ever attacked by a shark? He couldn't even get into the water in time.

Fawkes, wishing to help his mistress persuade the children that they shouldn't think of diving, now talked of nothing but sharks, and keeping a lookout for them, noticed one day a fast-moving fin and tail cutting the water some thirty feet off the stern. Although the *Hermit* was flying before the wind under full sail, the fin and tail were gaining on them.

"That there's a mako," said Fawkes. "They's the fastest."

As the sharp-nosed mackerel shark shot past the boat, it leaped into the air: a slim projectile, cobalt blue on top and snow-white below, with dead eyes and open mouth. It was in the air for only a few seconds before it splashed down and disappeared, but nobody on the *Hermit* said a word for quite some time afterward.

In the end Fawkes said, "All right, Creighton, you want to go and swim with that one?"

Creighton shrugged. "I don't know."

"Them beasts not only eats you, they kills you even if you eats *them!* Does you know that shark liver is the most poisonest thing? It makes your muscles freeze until you is dead!"

That night Marianne had a nightmare about Mark. They were meeting at Nassau Airport again, except that the airport was at the bottom of the sea and Mark was looking at her through water filled with floating fish heads and entrails. He cried for help with his eyes and she swam toward him but didn't get any closer. As he kept jerking his head to avoid the slimy debris, his eyes came out of their sockets, leaving two dark holes under his forehead. Looking away, she saw that his chest was torn open and small fish were picking the flesh from his ribs. Then he disappeared in a cloud of blood and she woke up trying to scream. Damp with sweat and shivering, stiff with horror, still in the sort of daze that made her prone to belief in premonitions and forebodings, she felt she must do something to save him.

Next morning, to make an early start, she had her little crew breakfast on the sloop, and still under the influence of her nightmare, told Fawkes to sail around the island while she searched the sea with her binoculars. When she spotted the *Ile Saint-Louis* the first thing she saw was Coco asleep in the shade under the canvas roof. There was no sign of Mark; evidently he was somewhere underwater. "All right," she told the children in an unsteady voice, trying to control her rising panic. "We'll take a closer look, see what they're doing there."

Fawkes tacked briskly toward the motorboat.

She felt that something terrible was happening. Her heart froze and all the sounds changed. The flapping of the sails grew harder and firmer; the waves broke against the bow with an ominous thud. After a while the sight of Coco continuing to sleep with a blissfully carefree expression while Mark was in danger so enraged her that she found the strength to move — she ran for the storm gun which was kept in the cockpit, raised it with both hands, aimed it into the air over Coco's head and fired. Roused by the loud report of the exploding rocket, Coco sat up with a start and looked around. Seeing the *Hermit,* he began waving enthusiastically.

"He should be in the water instead of waving!" cried Marianne. "Get closer, John! We've got to find the diver!"

"Can't tell how high the reefs is over there, mistress," replied Fawkes. "Can't get no closer."

The *Ile Saint-Louis* was anchored about a mile off the northeast shore of the island, at the edge of the fringe reefs, by two long strips of mountainous star coral which rose like boulders here and there above the water, and in many places the submerged coral growth was no more than a foot below the surface.

"Never mind the reefs, go ahead! Children, Joyce, watch for the diver! See if the water is red, quick!" She waved them to both sides of the deck, oblivious of the heavy storm gun in her hand.

"There he is!" Creighton shouted, pointing to a figure in the transparent water.

"Where?"

"There!"

With a bewildered look, as if she no longer knew whether or not she could trust her senses, Marianne stared down at the masked and gloved black-suited figure with tanks on its back and flippers on its feet, kicking its way toward the surface. "Good," she finally said, annoyed with herself for taking fright. "He won't need us."

The boys, who had an unerring instinct about when to leave their mother alone, were quiet; Fawkes and Joyce exchanged knowing looks.

"I don't understand Mr. Niven, why he hire that pimp for his helper," Fawkes commented as they left Coco behind. "He thinks they's no honest Bahamians round here?"

"Yes, I'm afraid he isn't very bright," Marianne said grimly. She assumed that she hadn't heard from Mark on account of some pretty waitress at the Club; it didn't occur to her that anyone brave enough to dive alone among sharks could be afraid to call her for lack of an invitation. The whole incident had taken only a few minutes, but she had been so scared that she had no strength left. She dropped the storm gun over the side and told Fawkes to head for shore.

"Oh Lord, you is slow!" complained Coco as Mark's head and shoulders emerged from the water.

Mark took out his mouthpiece, pushed up his mask, handed up his cesium magnetometer, then climbed into the boat, moving slowly like a man who came from a different world.

"You just missed good company!" Coco went on, lifting off Mark's aqualung.

Too tired to be curious, Mark unzipped his wet suit and stretched out on his back to fill his lungs with fresh air. He gave himself twenty minutes' rest, often a short nap, between dives. "I don't want to get friendly with anybody out here," he said when he had caught his breath. "Next thing you know they want to dive with you."

Coco looked at him with disgust. "You think *she* wants your rusty oil drums? That there's Mrs. Hardwick's boat."

Mark sat up to look, but the sloop had gone — a white streak dissolving into the blue of the sea and the sky.

"She don't need to watch crazy fools — she got real wide-screen movies at her house that makes her laugh. You don't know 'bout that?"

"No."

"*She* don't need your empty beer cans."

"I know."

"She don't need nothing from you."

"I know, I *know!*" Mark shouted to be heard above the noise of a small plane flying over them.

"But you's acquainted with her, isn't you?"

"I met her once."

"You like to tell me lil bit about it?" suggested Coco, in the voice of a friend who only wants to know what he can do to help. "I's be silent like a fish."

"There's nothing to tell. We just chatted on the plane."

WHAT a thing is memory! The human brain retains every image, every sound, every sensation that has ever reached it; everyone carries in his head a minute-by-minute recording of his whole life — but to retrieve any of it is another matter. Most of what our minds hold remains forever unknown to us; the memory cells tend to play back only what is called forth by random new impressions. During the six weeks since their meeting Mark had often mulled over his conversation with Marianne, yet he had not once remembered what she said as they were descending toward the island. But now the noise of the small plane and the last flash of white sail on the horizon brought back her voice asking whether he needed a partner. "Somebody with a boat who could also dive with you?" He could hear her in his head quite distinctly, and it hit him that she must have meant herself. They could have been together at this very moment if he had paid attention.

Whether it was the change in the sun's position or his devastating sense of loss, Mark suddenly found the light too strong. The sea was turning into a vast mirror blazing with a white metallic light. "I'm going back down," he told Coco, moving quickly to get ready.

"Doesn't you stay and nap a lil bit?" asked Coco, who wanted to talk.

"I've napped more than enough."

Trying to get away from himself, Mark swam back into the channel between two strips of star coral which he had been exploring since early morning. The channel, packed with fish glittering in the sunlight, was only about twenty feet wide and quite shallow; close to the sand at the bottom, his depth gauge was indicating twelve to fourteen feet. He swam midway between the rocky reefs, moving his cesium magnetometer left to right, right to left, mechanically, from force of habit.

Why hadn't he listened to her? A barracuda knocked its nose against his face mask, but he hardly noticed. He forgot that he didn't want partners, didn't want to share with anybody: he suddenly knew with absolute certainty that if she were with him he would be happy. Why had he looked away from her?

She liked him then, she was ready to live with him, to dive with him, and he had brushed her off. Was he insane? Did he have to be his own worst enemy? She must despise him now — she must have forgotten him!

Mark was in no mood to trust his luck. Overcome by that peculiar feeling of despair and self-loathing which accompanies the realization that one has done something irretrievably stupid, he did another stupid thing: he failed to attach any significance to the fact that it was the sudden movement of the metal-detecting needle on his cesium magnetometer that drew his attention to the big sea anemone sitting on top of a mound of sand. The mound was oblong in shape, strangely symmetrical — but in his agitated state, it was the shape of living things that caught his eye. The sea anemone looked like a striped earthenware vase filled with gracefully waving green fronds. A squirrelfish, swimming past Mark's mask, tried to snatch a clownfish through the waving fronds, but once it got within reach, the fronds turned into hungry tentacles, seized the squirrelfish and sucked it in. The tentacles disappeared with their prey and the vase-shaped anemone collapsed into a bulging gray lump.

Fascinated by the demise of the squirrelfish, so well suited to his gloomy thoughts, Mark pushed ahead half-heartedly, kicking his flippers and scanning the sea floor out of habit, without observing anything, and soon gave up. What was the point?

136

However, the morning was not a total loss. The near-encounter of the would-be lovers by the two strips of mountainous star coral marked a decisive turn in their relationship. Now they both hated themselves on each other's account; something had to happen.

19

The Twists and Turns of Falling in Love
(Cont'd)

Nothing is so interesting as passion,
because in passion everything is unexpected.
STENDHAL

AFTER mooring the *Ile Saint-Louis* and paying Coco, Mark went to
the staff canteen and took a seat at the counter with his back to the
people at the tables — mainly waiters and busboys having their last cup
of coffee before serving lunch to the guests. "Hey, Doris, better serve
his soup in a *gold dish!*" one of them shouted to the waitress at the
counter. A ripple of laughter swept the room. Since the joke about his
ocean liner had exhausted its power to amuse, they baited him with sarcastic references to sunken treasure.

In principle, Mark didn't mind being laughed at. As long as no one
took him seriously, no one would go to the trouble of tracking his
movements at sea or notice his interest in the northeast reefs. The sarcastic smiles and jeering remarks covered his purpose with a smoke-
screen of derision, and so he had learned to tolerate them. Great ambitions numb the pain of ridicule.

This time, however, the stings of communal malevolence went deeper
than on other days, and as he heard someone mention *gold doubloons*,
he swung around with a murderous glare.

"What's the matter? Can't you take a joke?"

A multitude of white and black faces grinned at him with the familiarity of contempt.

"Yeah, sure, I can take a joke," Mark replied, and turned back to
his soup. But he was too agitated, too depressed, too unhappy with himself to take the long-term view and pick up his spoon. He jumped up
instead, to go for the man with the widest grin. Soon they were rolling

on the floor, knocking over tables and chairs, fighting to the sound of flying cutlery and breaking glass. Mark's violent reaction had taken everybody by surprise, and two full minutes passed before the fighters were separated.

It was while she was watching the fight that it occurred to Sarah Little, the social director of the Club, that the interesting young interpreter was very much on his own and needed a friend. As he took his place back at the counter, making a point of not retreating from the scene, she sat down beside him to see if he was all right.

"Did he hurt you?" she asked.

"He'll limp for a few days," replied Mark, taking a deep breath. Then he took another deep breath, and forgot Marianne. Sarah smelled like fresh bread. Occasionally he had helped her with the crab races on the beach, but he had never sat so close to her before. A plump, rosy brunette with deep dimples, she was brimming with libido — a twenty-year-old Earth Mother. She had such force of gravity, he felt his head drawn down to her breasts.

"Are you sure you're all right?" she asked with a look that said "I like you too".

"I'm a little dizzy."

"You should have your lunch."

"I don't feel like eating."

"You should have your lunch and then go and lie down," Sarah advised him, blushing.

Mark forced himself to eat and she tried to reassure him that the others didn't really mean to hurt his feelings. They were just being silly. Sarah's blind faith in people's good intentions, her willingness to see a world of good in everybody, had made Mark shy away from her up to then, suspecting that she wasn't very bright. But there is nothing like a kick in the stomach to make a man appreciate goodwill, and the heat of Sarah's body, the look in her wide gray eyes, *melted his heart* — that is to say, produced a melting sensation in his chest which spread upward into his head and lingered there. He agreed with her that they didn't mean any harm.

"It's rotten coming to a strange place, though, isn't it? Not knowing anybody yet . . ."

"I hate it."

"I know the feeling myself," she lied to make him feel better; Sarah was at home everywhere.

"How long have you been here?"

"A year ago this time I was wearing woolen knickers in Manchester," she said, as a thrill of nostalgia slipped into her voice along with the cadence of her native Lancashire. She looked at him, then looked away. "Which reminds me, I have to go back to the house to change."

"I'll go too," said Mark hurriedly, afraid that she would leave him behind. "I guess I'll take your advice and lie down for a while."

As they walked back to the staff house together, Mark steeled himself to ask her to visit him. He had never had the moral courage to suggest anything more direct to a girl. He knew what he wanted, all right, but just when he would have had to suggest it he became less certain whether he could give a girl what she wanted. He was still at the stage when young men worry whether their penis is the right size.

"I'd love to see what you've done with your room," said Sarah.

"You're my first guest," he confessed as he opened the door for her and stood aside.

It would have been difficult to do much with the tiny cubicle filled to capacity with a single bed, a chest of drawers and a washbasin. There was nowhere to sit except on the bed, but they were saved from embarrassment by the framed photographs of the Madonna of Lima and General San Martín which Mark had hung on the wall; they could stand in front of them and stare as if they were at an exhibition.

"He has a good face," Sarah said, pointing to San Martín. "Who is he?"

"He was a great Argentinian general who tried to help his fellow men but gave up in disgust," explained Mark, very much identifying with his hero. Since he had put aside his history of Peru and decided not to concern himself with the affairs of the world, and especially since his troubles with his fellow employees, he felt that he understood San Martín better than ever before.

"He doesn't look disgusted to me."

Mark grinned. "Well, he was very fond of young girls."

"You don't seem to have many friends here," said Sarah, sitting down on the bed.

"I get along with Eshelby," answered Mark, sitting down beside her. "We have good talks."

As they discussed Eshelby they kept twisting about restlessly, bumping against each other, and the sensation of these collisions brought forth bursts of smiles on their tense faces.

"We're both blushers!" Sarah exclaimed with delight, changing color all the way down to her plump little breasts. Averting her eyes from Mark, she glanced at the picture of the Madonna of Lima on the wall. "Are you religious?"

"I pray sometimes," he replied wistfully, feeling his penis ready to jump out of his trousers.

Sarah drew back to look at him. There was a moment's doubt in her eyes, but Mark's beseeching expression settled it, and she took his head between her dimpled hands and kissed him lightly on the forehead. Then she sprang to her feet, chubby yet light as a feather, very much in her element organizing pleasurable social activities, getting lonely guests involved in their own entertainment. "You lock the door, I'll draw the curtains and turn down the bedspread," she said, dividing the tasks between them. What women learn in the workplace is often very helpful to them in the bedroom.

Shutting out the world, they undressed, lay down on the bed, and began running their hands over each other to get acquainted. They felt stronger and wilder with every touch.

"I thought you didn't like fat girls," she said as he squeezed her thighs and kissed her neck.

"I do now."

She offered him her salty nipples, and not wishing to hold back anything, confided in a firm voice: "I believe in sharing, sex and the stars."

The stars didn't sound far-fetched from the lips of this extraordinary girl, who welcomed him with earthquake and flood, giving him a sense of the Creation and an immense confidence in his power to cause joy.

"It's so nice when you're in the mood, isn't it?" she said when she had rested a little.

"Great. I have no marrow left in my bones. I feel like an empty jug."

"I love first times," she sighed, tasting his shoulder as though he were whipped cream. "The first time is the best. Do you feel more at home now?"

"I'll say . . ." said Mark, but then, feeling the cold wall against his skin, he frowned, wishing they were in a big bedroom in a Palladian villa in the Veneto. "But I hate small rooms."

"You have a nice big window, though. And a super view of the garden."

"Oh, well, I'm not really complaining!" He hadn't moved a muscle since his great moment of accomplishment.

They lay quietly for a while, until she began shifting gently under him. "I don't want to let you go, Mark," she said with a funny-remorseful grimace, "but I must get up. I have to run, I'm on duty."

As she dressed Mark watched her from the bed in an exhilarated mood, feeling convinced that Marianne Hardwick would be wild about him if they ever made love. It seemed to him that he had never stopped thinking about Marianne and he attributed his sense of well-being to the thought of her. Such is the ingratitude of those already possessed by longing.

No sooner had Sarah waved good-bye to him from the door than he jumped out of bed. About half an hour later he rang the bell at the gate in the wall surrounding the Hardwicks' garden, setting off what sounded like the barking of a whole pack of ferocious dogs. Mark remembered

Weaver telling him that the dogs on the island were trained to bite, but he didn't care. 'I love her and she'll love me,' he thought. He felt omnipotent.

MARIANNE was lying on her bed thinking of him when he rang the bell at the gate.

She had been lying there ever since she got back to shore. After her hysterical attempt to save Mark when he wasn't in any danger she felt so foolish, so humiliated, so exhausted, that she let Joyce take charge of the children and lay down to sleep, to sleep and forget everything. She slept restlessly, tossing about, and woke herself hitting her hand against the edge of the night table. It hurt, and it made the hurt of waking alone more painful. Shivering for an instant in spite of the heat, she hugged herself and rubbed her arms. The sleep had done her no good; she was as tense and unhappy as before. She wished Mark were there; together they could be cozy and safe. She put her hands under her T-shirt and began playing with her nipples to feel better, but that only made her long for Mark. She wanted his body on top of her; she wanted his weight to hold her down, so that she could just breathe and relax. Why wasn't he there? Her right hand went down inside her shorts. She tried to imagine that it was Mark's hand. Then she thought of nothing. Growing hot and moist inside, she concentrated on her pleasure. But as she was about to contract, pleasure turned into disgust and she withdrew her hand: she didn't want to come alone. She was wishing she could just fall asleep again when she heard the dogs barking, and then Joyce came in to announce the visitor.

"I left him in the guest cottage looking at the pictures. I took him there so you will have a whole house to your own two selves — no children, no servants," said Joyce, all excitement and hurry. "You're still dreaming. Don't think — don't wash the sleep off your face, it makes you look sexier — get up and run! I told Ruby to send over a tray with a big bowl of strawberries and a dish of clotted cream to dip them in. A real *lovers' tray*. All waiting for you by the time you get there."

"What *are* you talking about?"

Joyce raised her arms like the Baptist preacher of her childhood in Governor's Harbour. "Vengeance is mine, saith the Lord!"

Mark was walking around the living room of the guest cottage, studying the Libby Hague lithographs and the Dufy racing and regatta scenes on the walls, trying desperately to think of some witty remark to bridge the void of six weeks between them, when Marianne came in, flushed from running and excitement.

"Here you are — alive and well!" she said, seizing both his hands.

There was so much genuine feeling in this simple remark that the maid who overheard it as she brought in the tray felt a pang of jealousy, wondering what the young man must have done to inspire it.

The next morning, when Mark didn't show up at the *Ile Saint-Louis,* Coco went to look for him but couldn't find him anywhere. He asked around, and later in the day sent a telegram to Howard Sypcovich in Chicago.

Second Chance

Is it not time to join our best days,
Our kindest selves, our most sacred moods?
GEORGE JONAS

SEX is a mixed blessing. This news is old enough, yet it is every day's news. Men and women are not made for mutual satisfaction. Women cannot always flow, and even when they do, they well up slowly, while men are quick as torrents — they are primed by nature to burst forth at different times.

True, there are occasions when lovers are swept away on the same wave, but this only serves to confuse them, giving credence to the resentful suspicion that the world is full of passionate women and loving men who can go to bed and meet each other halfway with ease — and every time — and that *this is in the nature of things*. It would be difficult to conceive of another notion that could afflict so many perfectly normal human beings with such a bitter sense of inadequacy. They take the blame for nature's fault and torment themselves with the imagined perfection of their neighbors, and so a common plight remains a private shame.

Mark and Marianne were too young to feel bitter, but they were not very perceptive observers of their sexual experiences, and their pleasures and letdowns were mysteries to them. Mark was afraid that he was too small or too quick, Marianne was afraid that she was too slow; it wasn't often that either of them had crossed the twenty-minute gap, the abyss between the sexes.

But when they made love with each other, there was no gap between them — he let her go ahead of him. Wrestling for what is best in life, they bathed in her joy three times over before he spent his forces. Experienced lovers — experienced in frustrations and disappointments — will know what a strong bond such a beginning was bound to be.

It left them lying stunned on top of the white quilted bedspread in the white bedroom of the guest cottage, with thin shafts of sunlight filtering through the louvered shutters to cast a glow on the deep wool carpet, as white and fluffy as fresh snow. She smelled like milk, they both smelled like pine, and they only moved their hands to make their fingers happy.

"I like your room," Mark finally said, when he had gathered enough strength to prop himself up on his elbow and look around.

"It isn't mine — it's new to me too. It's better that way, don't you think?" It is a rich woman's luxury not to be tied to the marital bedroom even at home. Could new love blossom on the same old bed between the same old walls? Marianne didn't even want to stay on the same old island. "Let's go away, let's leave this terrible place," she said, breathing the words on Mark's chest as if wishing to talk directly to his heart.

Immensely proud as he was of himself, Mark couldn't believe her. "Would you go away with me?"

"Tomorrow. Today."

"What about your husband?"

"He's through . . . finished." Her face glowed, her voice had the firmness of her contentment. She smoothed his eyebrows with her forefinger. "You finished him off — he is no more."

LATER as they were soaping each other in the shower and Mark was washing her vagina with one hand and her anus and small round buttocks with the other, mad with joy, he was moved to confess his encounter with Sarah Little earlier in the day.

She pushed him away and told him to leave. "How could you come to see me right after being with another girl? It's sordid."

"I didn't plan it," Mark pleaded, meaning to apologize but smiling against his will. "Nothing like that ever happened to me before."

She gave him another push, and he slipped on the wet tiles. Worried that he might have hurt himself, she helped him up and almost forgave him. "Did you have a shower afterward, at least?"

"I was in too much of a hurry. I was too impatient to see you."

She attacked him with a bar of soap, trying to wash away all traces of the other woman, even if it was too late. "And did you make love with her for half an hour?" she asked, squeezing his penis mercilessly.

"Hey!"

"Did you or didn't you?"

"Not nearly that long."

Her hands grew softer, helping him to harden. "How long?"

"I don't know." Not too keen on the subject, Mark busied himself with her bouncy breasts which, slippery from the foam, seemed to have a life of their own. "Three-four minutes, I guess. The same as usual."

"You like her better, then." She turned on the shower, the cold-water tap, to punish him.

"Why? What do you mean?"

They were drying themselves (separately, she wouldn't let him touch her) before she gave him an answer.

"You took longer with me, that means you didn't want me as much."

"I wanted you more, but I wasn't bursting."

Their eyes met in a flash of sudden understanding. Happy lovers are not born, they learn to outwit nature in some roundabout way.

They were sitting side by side on the edge of the bed eating strawberries with clotted cream when they were surprised by the children's voices. Marianne put her hand over Mark's mouth and they listened quietly in the half-light.

"She shouldn't have goed to Nassau without telling me!" protested Creighton. "She brings us presents!" Benjamin replied. Though he was the younger, he had a deep, husky voice which made him sound older than his brother.

"Let's have a race, let's see who can run fastest!" said Joyce. "One, two, three, go!" The boys allowed Joyce to hurry them past the cottage, which looked locked up from the outside. The windows were open but the shutters of all five rooms were closed.

Mark gave Marianne a searching look, trying to imagine this long-haired teenager as a mother.

'Now he thinks I'm old!' she thought. Mark kissed the frown from her face, but she could no longer stay put. What if he didn't like the children? What if the children didn't like him? She asked Mark whether he was hungry enough for a real meal.

"I didn't even finish my lunch!" he exclaimed.

"All right, let's have dinner with Creighton and Ben," she said in an oddly severe voice.

They walked over to the main house across the freshly sprinkled lawn. With dusk came the no-see-ems, invisible sand-flies which jabbed Mark like needles; Marianne no longer felt them, but his skin hadn't yet got used to the bugs of the semi-tropics.

"Who shall I be?" he asked with the uneasiness of a man who had faced one trial too many that day.

She pressed his hand. "Just be yourself."

The boys were in their playroom, and when they saw their mother they demanded their presents.

"I brought you a friend for a present," she said, pushing Mark forward. "You know this man — he's the one you saw diving for coins!" She turned to Mark. "They want to know all about sunken ships."

"No, we don't," said Creighton, throwing a rubber truck against the wall. "My pony has a sore foot."

Mark stood silent. It was only then, when he actually saw the two small boys with their mother's oval face and ash-blond hair, that he began to appreciate that he had become involved not with a girl but with a family. Could they sense that he had made love with their mother? The younger boy, Benjamin, came up to him and stared at him with big, watchful eyes. Mark nearly broke and ran.

"I'm almost three," Benjamin said solemnly.

"That's great!"

"And mines hasn't!" Benjamin went on.

"What hasn't?" asked his mother unhappily. "You must speak in complete sentences, darling, otherwise people won't understand you."

"My pony hasn't have a sore foot!" Benjamin shouted triumphantly, scoring over his brother for the first time in his life.

"So you have ponies!" Mark exclaimed with wistful amazement.

"Just little Shetland ponies, they're quite safe," Marianne hastened to assure him.

But the boys did not misunderstand, and they were quite pleased to meet someone who envied them.

"I give you my peacock for a present," Benjamin told him magnanimously. "I don't want him any more."

"Mummy, you didn't tell us you went away!" Creighton said accusingly.

"I'm sorry, darling."

Creighton shook his finger and glared at her. "Don't you ever do that again!"

"All right, I won't," Marianne said, relieved to see Mark laughing. She could already picture them as a new family. "Let's eat in the kitchen," she proposed.

The vast, bright kitchen was full of people. Mark was introduced to John Fawkes, whom he had seen at the airport; Joyce, who had taken him to the guest cottage earlier in the day; the maid who had brought the strawberries; the cook, the gardener and his wife. He bowed and said hello to each of them and tried to escape from their mutual embarrassment by admiring the rows of copper pots and earthenware bowls and the long chains of purple onions hanging from the wooden beams.

Creighton wanted to show him the cellar. There are no basements on coral islands, everything has to be built above ground, and the Hardwicks' wine cellar was a windowless, air-conditioned room right off the kitchen. Mark was surprised to see only a few racks of French wines and thousands of bottles of French water. As they sat down to dinner and the cook emptied several bottles of *eau de source naturelle* into a kettle, Joyce explained that they used imported spring water for everything. The elderly cook, who was in the habit of starting to look for the teapot only after the water came to the boil, left the hissing kettle on the stove as she began her unhurried search, and Mark watched the clouds of expensive steam with such an anxious expression that the others started laughing. Realizing that they were laughing at him, he laughed too, which made everybody like him.

Marianne reached across the table to seize his hand and hold it; there was an electric silence, and she smiled at the servants as if to say "this is my man!"

Shocked and joyful, Mark gathered the moral courage to look Fawkes straight in the eye. If Hardwick had been there, he would have been ready to fight a duel with him. The silence was broken by the children, who both wanted to hold their mother's hand.

After she had put Creighton and Benjamin to bed, telling them that she was going to Nassau again, Marianne took Mark to her screening room to see *Elvira Madigan*. Cuddled up on the sofa, they held on to each other in tears as they watched the doomed couple for whom love was everything. Seeing the tears in Mark's eyes, Marianne remembered that Kevin had fallen asleep during the film. 'Mark isn't like him!' she thought triumphantly. 'He's capable of being moved by something besides money.'

However, when they went back to the cottage and were lying on top of the bed, still dressed, Mark told her the story of the *Flora*; now that he believed in his luck again, he wanted them to start looking for the ship together the next morning.

As she listened Marianne lost her glow, her soft features grew hard and grim and her face acquired a pitifully horsey look; she could think of nothing but the torn body she had seen in her dream, and fear made her ugly.

"What's wrong?" asked Mark, worried.

"I thought we agreed that we'd leave the island!"

"We will, we will . . . we'll leave as soon as we find the ship. I mean as soon as we've salvaged it."

"And when will that be?"

"Why, we could find it tomorrow."

Marianne's eyes widened. "Tomorrow? You really think you're going to find that thing tomorrow?"

"It's right out there among the reefs — you must sail past it every other day," sighed Mark. "It's just a question of luck — we have as good a chance of coming across it right away as after years of searching."

"But you're talking about some thirty square miles of reefs."

"Forty-five square miles," Mark corrected her tersely.

"Well?"

"What's the difference. It could still be next week, next month, next year — or tomorrow!"

"Or never."

Mark turned away.

"I want you alive!" she said, drawing him back to her and kissing his eyes, the palm of his hand. She told him about her nightmare, confessing that she believed in it. Not exactly believed in it, but felt uneasy about it. Yes, when they first met she had thought they could dive together, but since she had dreamed about fish feeding on his ribs she wouldn't let him dive for all the treasures of the world. She described in horrifying detail the wounds inflicted by sea wasps, killer clams, stingrays, moray eels, venomous catfish, scorpion-fish. His wet suit would often protect him, but not always. She told him about the yachtsman who went diving on his own and disappeared without a trace: the sharks must have swallowed even his aqualung. She did her best to scare him, to make him see the mangled corpse that she had seen.

'How awful she can look!' Mark thought, overcome by a new kind of protective love for her. 'She must really care about me if it can spoil her beautiful face.' Longing to comfort her, to cheer her up, he tried to swallow his impatience. "All right, I won't go diving for a while."

She continued to stare at him with an ugly face. "What good would that do?"

"All right, I won't go diving at all, ever." He lied in a humble voice, hoping that the effect of her nightmare would wear off in a day or two. "Forget the whole thing, I'll give it up."

"You don't mean that. Men don't give up anything for women."

Mark turned pale, then met her fearful eyes with a defiant look. As his lie wasn't believed, he began to believe it himself. If she could picture him dying in some horrible disaster, he could see himself as the man who renounced the riches of Lima for a woman's smile. They were both in that state of vibrant exhaustion in which anything seems possible. "I'll quit," he said.

"You promise?"

"I want you to be happy."

"Good!"

Marianne became bright and beautiful again, as she began to have a sense of her power over him. It was a clear, calm night with a radiant moon, and she proposed that they move onto the *Hermit*. They went back to the main house, moving quietly so as not to wake anybody; she collected things, and they ran down through the garden, under the sea grape and silk-cotton trees, past the palmettos and big-leaved crotons colored eerily purple by the moonlight, with the dogs whining restlessly at their heels, confused by the nocturnal activities of their mistress. On the boat, Mark watched Marianne rig the sails, holding what she told him to hold. He seemed confused too, so she tried to cheer him with Edward Lear.

> *The Owl and the Pussycat went to sea,*
> *In a beautiful pea-green boat.*
> *They took some honey, and plenty of money*
> *Wrapped up in a five-pound note —*
> *They sailed away for a year and a day . . .*

"What a beautiful Pussy you are, you are!" Mark chimed in, kissing the back of her neck as he passed on the compliment paid to him long ago by his mother. No man loves unless he feels he is a child again.

They sailed out of sight and dropped anchor at the edge of the round silver lake in the sea. It was the end of April, warm enough for sleeping out; they lay down on the mattress built into the deck, holding hands and looking up at the sky. The atmosphere was so clear that the stars seemed round and almost tangible. Suddenly Marianne sprang up and ran down to the cabin, and a minute later Mark could hear the music of the film they had just seen coming through the speakers on deck.

Though he had liked the tune in the film, hearing it again hurt. He put two and two together. She was a member of the board of the Lyric Opera of Chicago and he knew nothing about music. He couldn't understand what such a clever, educated, beautiful rich woman saw in him. She knew everybody! If she was sick of her husband, she could run off with a world-famous singer or conductor. 'She must think that I'm just an ignorant kid,' Mark thought, hating her. 'She's bound to get bored with me.' He wished he were back with Sarah.

Marianne came running back and lay down, lifted his arm, put it under her neck and placed his hand on her breast; Mark was careful not to move, not to press her, convinced that she didn't need him.

To make matters worse, she was quoting from a book he hadn't read. Happy with her lover, with the night, with the stars, so brilliantly close that she felt the sound of Géza Anda's piano must reach them, she remembered Turner's definition of art in his book about Mozart. "It stuck in my mind," she said, poking Mark in the ribs. "Turner says art is the expression of the relationship between the individual and the universe. That's true, isn't it?" She wouldn't have mentioned it if she hadn't wanted to share the thought with him. But Mark tried not to listen. And did Mark know that when Mozart was a little boy, he would put his hands over his ears and cry if he heard the sound of a trumpet? His father punished him by blowing a trumpet if he misbehaved. He always wanted to make music with the adults, and wasn't content with any subordinate role either. "*Anybody* can play the second violin!" he protested when he was only four years old, the same age as Creighton. "Creighton and Ben won't be great musicians," she added mournfully. "They would already have shown some sign of it."

Thinking of her sons, she became aware of the stiffness of Mark's body and of his silence, and fell silent herself, listening to his heart. After a while she asked him who was his favorite painter. There was no response. "You know a lot about painting, sculpture, architecture, and I know about music," she coaxed him. "We'll swap!"

Mark stretched himself, and as she began breathing kisses on his chest, he felt the ridiculousness of his vanity measured against the vastness of the world above them. What was he so touchy about? He began to listen to the concerto, because he knew she wanted him to, and the music of love and sadness made him feel keenly how defenseless they both were unless they held each other. He had never seen the night sky so blue.

"Remember, you promised," she said.

"I remember. I'll quit," said Mark, glad to say anything that pleased her.

She knew that he only half meant it, but it was good enough for a start. She had time, she could wait.

She was patient about everything. "Don't mind me," she told him when he ran ahead of her in the morning. "I'll wait for the second coming!"

They spent most of the day on the *Hermit* — lovers are hermits too — eating, making love, sleeping, listening to music. They were naked all the time, though Marianne always looked half dressed with her long hair. She made him tell her everything he knew about Peru.

"My father says that for a woman to love a man and think he's a genius is one and the same thing," she told him. "But I'm sure I'm objective about you. I knew you were brilliant as soon as we started talking at the airport. You must go back to college and finish your book — in Peru or in Spain or in England or wherever you like. And I can support us while you study. There's nothing demeaning about that — lots of rich girls marry medical students, and it works out even in the end."

Mark couldn't help sighing. "It'd be simpler if we were both rich!"

'He doesn't mention his ship,' Marianne noted with satisfaction. 'That treasure-hunting business was a lucky thing after all. If he didn't have to give up anything for me, how could I tell whether he really loved me?'

She offered him many consolations; for the first time in his life Mark was having a holiday.

Listening to *Così fan tutte* down in the cabin, they sat in armchairs with their feet on a pouf and their toes touching, and every so often sprang to their feet, screwed up their faces and acted and sang the magnificent double-bluff from the opera —

Siete così contenti?
Contentissimi!

They parted the next day, Friday. She was expecting her husband for the weekend and Mark was due back at the Seven Seas Club. She drove him to the hotel in her old station wagon, and as they said good-bye in front of the staff house she drew his head down to kiss him, unperturbed by the presence of several onlookers and the passing figure of Mr. Weaver, who greeted them with an animated bow. Noticing two bellboys ogling her as she walked back to her car, Mark wished that she wouldn't wear such short skirts.

MRS. Hardwick's public declaration of their affair was soon known all over the island and made a great impression. The residents who came over to the Club for lunch, especially the wives, eyed the handsome young interpreter with thoughtful looks. Sarah passed him with a pale smile, and Eshelby saluted him with a V-for-Victory sign. The clerks, porters and bellboys who had never tired of baiting him treated him with respect amounting to reverence.

'Who would think more of her because of me?' he brooded, standing by the reception desk in his uniform with his legs apart and his hands behind his back — a posture common to clerks and soldiers, who have to stay on their feet for hours. 'I'm still a nobody.' He was overwhelmed by remorse for his indolence. 'If I keep this up, I'll never amount to anything. She loves me and she's kind and brave — not many wives would have the courage to kiss their lovers in public, let alone think of giving up their marriage for a man they hardly know. Just the same, it's the grand style of a woman who doesn't need to worry about alimony. Whatever people may say or do, it makes no difference to her way of life. She can live as she pleases — nothing she does has any material consequences. She doesn't understand what it is to be poor!'

But how could he explain it to her?

"We could sleep together every night," she had told him before they parted. "From tomorrow you could come and live here. Kevin's coming home for the weekend, but I'm going to send him on his way again. There's no reason why we shouldn't be able to agree to a quick and friendly divorce. I'll urge him to marry his model. I'll tell him I don't blame him for anything. I see now that I was never in love with him, and under the circumstances it was only natural that he should play around, looking for real affection. That ought to set him free, don't you think?"

Unluckily, Hardwick decided at the last minute to go skiing in the Laurentians with Miss Marshall, and he phoned his wife on Friday afternoon to say that he was too busy to fly home. He was there the following weekend, but by then Marianne had nothing to tell him about divorce or love.

A Monstrous Remark

The feminine conception of happiness suffers the fate
of all feminine conceptions: it does not interest men.
MONTHERLANT

HAVING listened to her husband explaining that he was too busy to
fly home, Marianne joyfully put down the phone, ran to her car
and drove back to the Club to fetch Mark: they had been apart for six
hours and she didn't want to spend any more time without him. Mark,
who was on duty in the lobby when she arrived, went to the manager's
office to request a week's leave from the part-time job which he had
held for less than two months. If the young man had only had the backing of Mr. Heller at head office, Weaver might have fired him; if he had
only been a friend of Mrs. Kevin Hardwick, Weaver might still have
fired him; but he didn't feel up to creating problems with both head office and the island's greatest lady. With a startled blink and an unhappy
smile, he granted Mark a week's leave without pay.

Mark and Marianne were gone by the time the day's guests, fresh from
the plane, crowded into the lobby. Sypcovich, one of the new arrivals,
was pleased to note Mark's absence, though he continued to act with
caution, carefully ignoring the conspicuous figure ahead of him at the
reception desk.

This conspicuous figure — a pale, thin, bearded man in his thirties,
bedecked with cameras and silver chains — had just made out his reg-
istration card, giving his name as Anthony Edward Masterson and his
occupation as film director, and was magnifying his impact by loudly
ordering the desk clerk to cut short "the bureaucratic shit". Mollified
by the clerk's inquiry whether he wished to occupy the Louis Quinze,
Old West or Hokusai suite, he opted for the Old West.

Later he could be seen in the Club's gardens with four cameras around
his neck, taking pictures of the yellow paradise trees and the flame trees

with their fiery red flowers in bloom, and then walking down to the beach to photograph "the light". As he explained to some inquisitive guests and bellboys who gathered around, he was "scouting locations", trying to decide whether he should film his next picture in the Out Islands.

In spite of — or perhaps because of — his uncouth manner, Masterson played the part of a film director very convincingly. An expectant would-be artist, he believed that one day he would be as famous as his idols, Hitchcock, Fellini and John Huston. Having already acquired several expensive cameras, had his sharp nose reshaped by plastic surgery and rounded out his absurdly pointed chin by growing a beard, he imagined that he was progressing toward his goal with giant steps. While waiting to become a great film director, by transmutation as it were, he earned what he called "a reasonable income" with blackmail, especially in small towns where reputations were still worth something. He worked mostly with his beloved Apollo 220, a hand-held 16-millimeter cine-camera with telescopic lenses which he named his "spin-off baby" because it owed its existence to the technical innovations in aerial photography developed in the U.S. space program. With the Apollo 220 he could film couples behind closed windows or at a distance of several miles. Fascinated by Masterson's stories about people who refused to be blackmailed with compromising still photos but would pay far beyond their means for the same thing as a motion picture, Sypcovich liked to provide his clients, if they could afford it, with this most up-to-date kind of evidence, and occasionally took Masterson away from his criminal activities to do some "honest work" on divorce cases. The two men had got to know each other when Sypcovich was hired by a worried businessman whom Masterson was blackmailing and collected sufficient evidence against Masterson to have him put away for life; blackmailing the blackmailer, he saved his client and also provided himself with a cameraman who would always do what he was told. Sypcovich may have been only a small independent operator but he chose his associate according to the same sagacious principle that allowed President Lyndon Johnson to dismiss warnings about the unreliability of a political ally with the historic phrase: *I trust him — I have his balls in my pocket.*

The private detective and his cameraman pretended to get acquainted and strike up a friendship at the Club's bar on the evening of their arrival.

The following morning Coco, five hundred dollars richer, drove them up to the private detective's favorite haunt, the ruins of the Spanish fort on top of the hill. It was a romantic spot: tall grasses and low wild trees grew out of the limestone rock; the crumbling thick stone walls, as high as six feet in places, were covered with vines trumpeting green and purple, and flowers grew out of every crevice, for — in the words of Earle Birney's poem —

Flowers live here as easily as air
. . . they grow on light
A scalloped leaflet lying on a stair
will puff pink buds and root itself in stone —

A constant gentle breeze blew from the sea, and the birds, bright as flying flowers, sounded all their notes. At 264 feet above sea level, the hilltop was also an excellent observation post, giving a panoramic view of the Hardwicks' garden and beach as well as the surrounding waters.

Coco drove back down to the Club and the two men from Chicago spread their straw mats in the shade of the ruins. They had to wait only about an hour before the lovers, walking hand in hand on the beach, came into the range of the binoculars and the Apollo 220. Masterson had been standing up filming the couple intently for some minutes when he felt something cold on his bare toes. He looked down and — a city man not used to any living thing touching him — let out an unearthly scream that silenced the birds. The lizard froze and turned as pale as Masterson's skin.

"What if they heard you?" hissed Sypcovich.

"It looks like a crocodile!" Masterson cried out, kicking himself free, when he could speak and move again. "The place is full of them!" Trying to get rid of his fear, he put down his camera, picked up a stick, and began to chase lizards among the ruins, bent on destroying some of nature's loveliest and most useful creatures, which flicker about like lightning, change color most amusingly, eat evil insects, and all this without making a sound: unlike their loud and clammy relatives, the frogs, they are cool and dry and don't feel the need to croak about all the good they do. If the hilltop wasn't swarming with biting flies and mosquitoes, it was thanks to those lizards the blackmailer tried in vain to kill.

"You missed them kissing," said Sypcovich, who had kept his binoculars trained on the beach. "Get back to work!"

"What for?" asked Masterson, who wanted to get away from the place. "We got them holding hands. That ought to be enough for the dumbest husband."

"I want hardcore evidence!"

Masterson grinned, and moving his fingers briskly, scratched his beard on both sides: he thought he understood. "That's smart . . . you won't give these films to Miss Marshall, you'll sell them to Mrs. Hardwick. She'll pay us more! Good."

The private detective, who had been observing Mark and Marianne from a sitting position, resting his back against an old wall, lowered his binoculars and looked up. His small eyes glittered between the folds of fat; he hadn't thought of the possibility of blackmail. "Nobody's paying *us,*" he grunted. "I'm employing you on a flat-fee basis."

"I already earned my flat fee."

By the time they stopped arguing the lovers had gone into one of the cottages.

Next day Masterson managed to film them on the *Hermit:* Mrs. Hardwick walked about the deck topless, and several times the actor's son had one arm around her with his hand tipping her breast.

"Now we can get back to the pool," Masterson declared. "I got miles of film here showing them half-naked on the boat — and I need a swim!" He packed away his "spin-off baby" and began wiping the sweat from his armpits.

Sypcovich just shook his head, feeling too hot to speak. It was one of those May afternoons that turn into burning summer at the 20th parallel.

"Well then, you watch them and tell me if there's anything new," said Masterson peevishly. "I'm going to sit down and rest." The shade had moved and he moved his straw mat over to it. After casting a searching look at the ground, he lay down on the mat and fell asleep, but was promptly wakened to film Mrs. Hardwick and the young punk lying on the deck mattress. Not that it amounted to much: they were only talking.

Sypcovich got his hardcore evidence on the seventh morning. "Didn't I tell you we should start early!" he exclaimed triumphantly, focusing his binoculars on the *Hermit* anchored less than three miles away; he could see them clearly.

Masterson could see them too. "I got them in close-up," he said hoarsely, not wishing to appear affected; he always became agitated when he saw a woman making too much fuss over a man. A lizard ran across his feet, but he didn't feel it. "Listen, Howie, she must have her own money," he went on in a careful voice, so that he wouldn't jolt the camera and blur the picture. "If she's the big Montgomery's daughter like you say. You get me? It's your show, I'm not trying to take it over — but there's more in this than a fee on a divorce case. You ought to give her a chance to buy the picture for fifty grand."

"Paying money means nothing to her, but you show this film in court during the divorce proceedings and she'll never live it down!" Sypcovich exulted, flapping his open shirt with his left hand to make the most of the breeze. "She'll never be able to come back to Chicago." He was a great local patriot, and not being able to live in his adopted city seemed to him a real misfortune.

"That's what I mean, Howie. She'll be glad to pay fifty, seventy-five thousand."

"They'll take her children away from her, and she'll blame that young punk for it!"

"She'd *appreciate* this movie, Howie, she would want to keep it — you'd be doing her a favor."

The private detective shook his heavy shoulders as if wishing to shake off some oppressive feeling. He wanted to savor the joy of vengeance, and Masterson was spoiling it for him. "These people are not interested in what you can do for them," he sputtered. "You go to that young punk, you talk to him just to be friendly, just to establish contact, like one human being to another, and he'll tell you he has a headache! That's right. And why is she mixed up with him? Because his daddy's some two-bit movie star —"

"Listen, we could split seventy-five big ones, Howard! She's a lady, she would pay that much just out of shyness."

Sypcovich gave a violent scratch to his belly, as swollen as a pregnant woman's and as furry as a monkey's. "I have my professional ethics. I don't double-cross a client."

"Pamper your client or make a packet. It's that simple." As far as Masterson was concerned, not to double-cross people was to pamper them.

"I'm telling you, she'll lose her children and he'll lose her. They'll both have a headache then. It won't be easy for him to find another woman with a yacht."

"Lay off them, why don't you," said Masterson. "So long as she pays, who gives a shit?"

"Look!" Sypcovich snorted, disgusted. "They're shameless. Nothing's sacred to people like that."

THE "shameless" lovers on the *Hermit* were still in that state of sweet obsession with each other's bodies that springs from youth, health and the thrill of discovery, but — there *is* a difference between the sexes — Mark needed more and more rest while Marianne needed less and less. That morning she had been awake for hours, sitting beside him on the deck mattress with her knees drawn up against her chest and her arms folded over her shins, watching him sleep, until the rising sun made her feel warm and she decided to wake him.

This was what Masterson filmed and what Sypcovich hoped would be grounds to part her from her children, though it is a natural and common way for lovers to say hello: she lifted Mark's penis with her tongue and put it in her mouth. Until she had fallen in love with him she herself had considered such closeness an unclean thing and had never done it for her husband, but during the last few days it had become a ritual; this was the way she started her lovemaking with Mark every morning. She wanted him in her mouth first, to cure him of impatience, to get her *second chance,* to have him move inside her for a long, long time, so that she could come and come until she was near death. Moist with expectation, she fondled him with her lips, and when Mark was awake he drew her to him and they made love the way lovers do when they want to drink each other.

Masterson had it all on film — not that anything that mattered about it could be filmed.

What medium could communicate sexual ecstasy, the singing of all the senses?

Afterward they were quiet for a while as if still listening.

Mark, stretched out on his stomach, was gazing at the water, or rather, at the shadow of the *Hermit*'s mast on the yellow sand some sixteen feet below, while Marianne leaned against him, her head resting on his shoulder. Her body exuded that singular freshness that some women share with fruits and flowers when exposed to sun, wind and water.

Only one thing was wrong.

There was a clock ticking inside Mark's head, striking every hour, marking all the time that he failed to spend looking for the *Flora*. With Marianne beside him he managed to ignore it, trying to adapt to the quiet, slow rhythm of the waves. But then she got up and went down to the galley to see about breakfast. As soon as he began to feel her absence, he was overwhelmed by an intense feeling of guilt and anxiety.

What was he doing vacationing on a luxury yacht, when nothing about his future was settled?

He hadn't looked for his ship for six whole days!

Was he a beach bum?

A gigolo?

Marianne had never returned to the subject of their going away so that he could finish his studies and write his history of Peru; she didn't want him to do anything. He couldn't depend on anybody, not even on her. He remembered his mother trying to jump out of the window in Madrid because nobody gave a damn what happened to them; he remembered his hunger, and suddenly felt certain that one day he would starve. All the harsh truths of life crowded in on him when Marianne left him alone. He decided to have a serious talk with her, explain to her that she must stop being a spoiled rich woman bossing him around. (He could be very critical of her when she wasn't there.) He swore he would make her understand that there was more to life than making love and listening to music, that he didn't want to be kept by anybody, that he had to find his ship if they were ever to be each other's equals, that sharks weren't all that dangerous if one was careful . . . But when she came back, her eyes laughing, he thought of her ugly look and said nothing. Love made him a coward every time: he didn't have the courage to upset her.

She was carrying a jar of orange juice with two straws in it (having never lived without servants, this was how she cooked when they were on their own). Noticing that he looked morose, she took this to mean that he had missed her and pressed herself close to him, offering him one of the straws. "If Kevin comes tomorrow I won't let him stay the night," she said. "Let him sleep at the Club! Soon we'll be able to get married if you want to."

As they put their heads together to sip the orange juice, Mark couldn't help thinking that if they had been looking for the wreck all this time they might already have found it. And then there would be no conflict between them.

"What are you thinking about?" she asked him, thinking of making love again.

"I was just thinking how time goes," he sighed. "We've wasted six whole days!"

Surprise made the insult all the worse. She still had the taste of his sperm in her mouth, mixed with the orange juice. "What do you mean, *wasted?*" she asked, pulling away and staring at him with disbelief.

He tried to explain.

They argued, drifting farther apart.

"I despise people who think of nothing but money," she hissed with tears in her eyes.

"Marianne, please!" Mark begged, unshaken in his monomania. "Once we've found the *Flora* we'll have our whole lives to enjoy ourselves!"

She looked at him as if he had turned into a stranger. "No, thanks. I already have a husband who puts first things first."

It was all over.

THE two men watched from the hilltop as Mark tried to get hold of her arm. She freed herself, ran below deck, and when she returned she was dressed.

"They had a fight," observed Sypcovich, putting his binoculars in their case. Not bothering to bend for his straw mat, he started down the hill.

"If they break up, she'll want my movie as a memento," said Masterson, following him. "Seventy-five, maybe a hundred big ones, Howard, a hundred big ones!"

"That's right, a hundred thousand!" Sypcovich snorted, as if his nose were stuffed with all those bills. Staggering under his own weight, he breathed harder with every unsteady step. "They're costing me a fortune. I don't do favors to people like that."

By the time they reached the Club, Coco was waiting for them in front of the main building to report that Mark was back, looking gloomy and holed up in his room in the staff house.

"Tomorrow is Friday, the husband's coming home and she doesn't want trouble," said Masterson with a meaningful glance.

Leaving them without a word, Sypcovich went up to his suite and collapsed into an armchair. When Masterson came in an hour later he found him sitting there motionless, staring into space.

"Do me a favor, Howie," said Masterson, "Do yourself a favor!"

Sypcovich glared at his tormentor. "What is this? Are you trying to get me involved in the crime of blackmail?"

"If you don't want to get involved, I'll go and see her myself. We can split afterward."

"You wouldn't be trying to interfere in my business?" asked Sypcovich in his thickest voice.

"I'm only making a suggestion, don't be so touchy!" pleaded Masterson. He couldn't have been more desperate or persuasive if he had been pleading for his life. "I thought that was what you had in mind all along. Come on, Howard, I've known you for years. What's got into you, for Christ's sake? Talk to me. What's happened to you? Why the agony, why the pain? Have you lost your faith? Don't you believe in money any more?"

Sypcovich heaved a deep sigh. He could picture himself calling on Mrs. Hardwick and scaring her with a few well-chosen words. He was convinced that he would get more out of her than Masterson could ever dream of.

And why not?

What was there besides money?

Had he succumbed to temptation — and he himself was convinced that he should, he must — the reels of film of Mrs. Hardwick and her lover might have been destroyed. But to his own intense surprise and bewilderment, there was something in him stronger than greed: he could hate, no matter what the cost. It was his finest hour.

BACK on duty in the lobby when the two men were checking out, Mark was surprised to see the familiar bloated figure among the departing guests. It didn't look as though the private detective had come back for the sunshine: his face was as pallid as ever. 'Is the old gumshoe on a job?' wondered Mark. 'Whom could he be spying on here?'

He could hardly have conceived that the old gumshoe was spying on him. Marianne had never hidden their affair from anybody; she had kissed him in front of half a dozen people; there was nothing to find out about them. In any case, it was all over: she had thrown him out without giving him time to collect his toothbrush. Besides, Mark's life, as he saw it, was about finding or not finding the *Flora,* not about the errands of private detectives. He took it for granted, without really thinking about it, that everything important that would ever happen to him would be connected with his ambition. He didn't share Marianne's fears that he would be torn apart by sharks while looking for the wreck, but he accepted it as one of the hazards of treasure hunting. Life was logical. Although he was devastated by his breakup with Marianne, it made sense that they should break up over the *Flora*. Adept as he was at making the most far-fetched connections — he understood how Napoleon had helped his father's career, how General San Martín and the wars of independence in South America had led him to Santa Catalina — he could never have seen himself as the missing link in a divorce plot. What could Sypcovich or the phony with the cameras have to do with Captain Parry's ship?

"Who's that?" he asked a bellboy, pointing with his eyes toward Masterson.

"A big movie director from the States," replied the bellboy.

"You're kidding."

"Look at his equipment!" rejoined the bellboy, surprised that Mark should doubt the word of a guest. Anyone who could pay his bills at the Seven Seas Club was above suspicion; and besides, the bellboy liked Masterson, who wasn't too proud to chat with the staff. "He's been going around the island filming . . . what were you filming, Mr. Masterson?"

Masterson stopped in passing and nodded to Mark as if they had already met. "Hi. Oh, just scouting locations. Using up a few reels to get the feel of the place."

"What did you decide? Are you going to make a movie here, Mr. Masterson?" asked the bellboy.

Masterson made a little dance with his head and his hands.

"I can't promise anything, but it's a possibility. I mean, just pray for your colors, hey? If the colors come out right, I'll be back with Paul Newman and my whole crew. We'll take over the hotel — you'll have to send all the other guests away. It's a possibility!"

Nothing came of the picture with Paul Newman; a few months later an unmarked truck which had been following Masterson's car for some time sideswiped it on an overpass, sending it flying over the guard rail onto another Illinois state highway twenty feet below. The blackmail photographer was still alive when the ambulance arrived but his spine was broken and his spleen ruptured, and he didn't make it to the hospital.

A Successful Woman

Love, power, riches, success, a good marriage, exciting sex, fulfillment, are not impossible dreams. They can be yours if you want them.
DR. JOYCE BROTHERS

The only means of advancement are talent and calculation.
BURCKHARDT

DOCTORS, dentists, lawyers hang their various diplomas on their office walls; Pauline Marshall's office at *Opulent Interiors* was decorated with giant framed photographs of the magazine covers on which she had appeared. The earlier covers showed her for her beautiful face and figure, for the clothes she was modeling, but the last few displayed her for her triumphs as THE WOMAN WHO CARES ABOUT THE DECOR OF YOUR HOME, A SUPERACHIEVER WITH STYLE and AMERICA'S MOST GLAMOROUS WORKING WOMAN UNDER THIRTY.

"I'm not very bright, but I'm practical," she told interviewers, with the disarming modesty which is an absolute must for the ambitious.

She was practical about everything. Marianne Hardwick's ideas about equal commitment in love which Hardwick had complained about explained perfectly to her why the marriage had failed; and no doubt she would have found it preposterous, if she had known about it, that Marianne had broken with Mark because he wanted things his own way. Pauline Marshall never expected any man to be fair or considerate; she never dreamed of equal love and respect, give and take, hurt for hurt. Her relationship with Hardwick was based on something far more substantial.

"The way to enslave a man is to be his slave," she advised a trusted friend, an advertising executive, who came to her office to discuss business and find out, while she was there, the secret of catching and holding a rich man who was also young, handsome and brilliant into the bargain. "Let him be the boss."

"Pauline, nobody would believe me if I quoted the editor of America's fastest-growing magazine saying that."

"Well, then, don't quote me."

"Come on, darling — you a slave?"

"I've always tried to be a complete woman," replied the former model, smiling contentedly.

"And how am I to become a slave?"

"Get on your knees. Give him everything he wants."

"Oh, Pauline," cried the friend despairingly. "How can you tell what a man really wants!"

America's Most Glamorous Working Woman under Thirty raised her dark, perfectly arched eyebrows. "Have you ever seen a pig at a trough?"

"Not everyone had the privilege of growing up on a farm, dear."

"You can learn a lot growing up on a farm. You find out it's no use trying to improve the character of any living thing."

"Meaning?"

Pauline sighed, feeling alone in her wisdom. She understood everything better than anybody else she knew. "Men don't want this kind of woman or that kind of woman, they want all women. And they don't want you to nag them about it."

"You're telling me to give up my man as soon as I've got him?"

"All I'm telling you is, don't be hard on him . . . don't be jealous . . . don't turn your body into a prison for him," replied Pauline with the unhurried complacency of a woman who had legs and breasts to stun the world and eyes as moist as her lips, visible proofs that there was nothing hard or dry about her and she had nothing to fear from competition.

NOT that she would tell her friend everything. She herself went one better than not being jealous. When she first met Hardwick she realized immediately that the last thing the restless young husband needed was another commitment to a one-to-one-relationship, and had the happy inspiration of arranging an orgy for him.

He had relied on her ever since.

At parties she was quick to notice if Hardwick's glance lingered on a pretty face, and would make friends with the women who attracted him, invite them to lunch and gossip about the details of her sex life, turning their heads with her confidences. There is no way a man can seduce a woman as easily as through another woman. Pauline Marshall helped to seduce women for Hardwick and then helped to keep them away; she served him a bachelor's dreams, just as another girlfriend might have cooked rich, spicy dishes to keep him happy. She would even be jealous, a little — just so he would know she cared, but not enough to be tiresome. Mistress, procuress, hostess of occasional orgies starring Hardwick as the one and only male, she absolutely refused, however, to allow herself to be touched by anyone but him — even though he urged her sometimes to try a threesome, assuring her that he wouldn't resent a girl.

That was the one thing she wouldn't do for him.

"You belong to all women, but I belong only to you," she would whisper into Hardwick's ear, locking him into her arms.

Never wanting to give him cause for jealousy, she hired only women and bald or gray-haired men to work on the magazine — the kind of seasoned professionals who knew everything about the business and were used to running things themselves but who, having lost their executive positions, found it difficult to get any job at all because of their age. It was their wealth of experience that made *Opulent Interiors* such a success, though of course they wouldn't have had the opportunity without Ms. Marshall's concern for Hardwick's peace of mind.

Satisfying her lover's lust, his vanity, earning money for him with the magazine, she was convinced that she was the only woman for him, and was fond of him chiefly for that reason. His money was the least of it. He made her happy. By responding to her manipulative skills as she expected him to, he was the living proof of her intelligence, her sophistication, her knowledge of human nature. Besides, they had a future. It was a settled thing in her mind that they would get married, she would hand over *Opulent Interiors* to one of her bald assistants, move up to the post of executive vice-president of HCI, and have a baby.

Still, there was his wife!

His wife. His maddening, vain compassion for her. His maddening fear of his father-in-law. In all the publicity about *Opulent Interiors* and Chicago's superwoman, Pauline had to pretend that she was still looking for Mr. Right; she had to keep her own apartment and although she was occupying the wife's rooms in the Hardwick house, she couldn't change the décor. There was always some little thing to remind her that their relationship wasn't legitimate. The weekend they went skiing in the Laurentians, for instance, she would have preferred to go to Aspen, where the Hardwicks had a ski lodge, but because the Montgomerys had a place there as well, Kevin took her to Mont Tremblant instead.

The worst of it was the waiting. True to her philosophy, she didn't argue, didn't complain, didn't tell him what she was thinking; she let him have his way in everything — she didn't want to press him to break with his wife — yet she was growing more and more impatient, especially since her gynecologist had told her that the incidence of breast cancer was lower among women who breast-fed an infant before they were thirty.

When they got back from Mont Tremblant and Sypcovich called to report that he had a film for her, her joy was indescribable. She was glad to see Hardwick go off to Santa Catalina the following weekend, leaving her free to arrange her surprise for him. The certified check for $62,500 which she handed Sypcovich to cover his $50,000 bonus and final expenses left only a few thousand dollars in her account, but she felt she had made a good investment.

By the time Hardwick got back to Chicago on Sunday evening, she had the projector and screen already set up in the library to show Masterson's movie. And not a moment too soon.

"Marianne wants to move back here," Hardwick told her gloomily as she settled him with a drink in his grandfather's worn green leather armchair in what had been the smoking room when the solid old mansion on Chicago's Near North Side was still a new building. "I don't understand what's got into her!" he confessed with a puzzled frown. "When I called her a week ago — remember? — she sounded great on the phone, everything was fine, she didn't even mind I wasn't coming to see her. Now she's all woe. She misses the city and she wants to come back, she wants to get involved in politics, campaign with Gene McCarthy against the war, agitate for women's rights — God knows what else. I'd die of boredom. It'll have to be a divorce if she insists on coming home. That's where I draw the line."

"What did you tell her?" asked Pauline, sitting on the armrest of his chair and massaging the back of his neck, his comfort her only concern.

"I sympathized with her, of course," sighed Hardwick, stretching his legs. "I took her point. I only wondered whether it wouldn't be unfair to the children. We'll think about it, I said. We left it at that." He drew a line on the carpet with the heel of his shoe. "To give her her due, she didn't try sex on me. She spent the whole weekend curled up — thank God for that much. All the same, she's a clinger, and I'm tired of it."

"She knows you feel sorry for her, so she takes advantage of you," said Pauline in her lazy voice, as soft and strong as her fingers.

"Correct. I must have burned up half a million gallons of jet fuel by now, going down there to see her. Wait, that's not quite right — I should deduct two-thirds on account of the kids. But that still leaves us with a hell of a lot of energy burned up in the name of human kindness."

"Relax, relax, unwind, darling, your neck is getting tense."

"I certainly won't let her spoil things," said Hardwick, reaching back to pat Pauline's arm.

She rewarded him with a lick behind his ear, thinking that they would be married within six to eight months, and she would have a child before she was twenty-nine. However, she saved her news until after dinner. She wouldn't have dreamed of telling anything important to a man until his stomach was full.

"You still look worried," she said when they were having their after-dinner coffee and were once again free of the servants. "Don't let her upset you. My guess is that she only thought of coming back because she had a tiff with her lover. For all you know, they've made up by now and she's happy to stay where she is."

"Yeah, wouldn't that be great!" Hardwick exclaimed fervently. "I wish to God she *would* get a lover. Then I could leave her without having to worry what she would do to herself."

"I wouldn't say anything, darling, but she's making *you* feel guilty! I don't want you to be too mad at her — after all, she's the mother of those two beautiful boys. But on the other hand, if she gives you nothing but trouble and then makes a fool of you — that's not fair."

"If she would just find herself another man, I could get a divorce and not even her crazy father could object."

She jumped up and stood in front of him, clapping her hands to get his attention. "But darling, that's just what I'm trying to tell you, you're not listening!" she chided him, laughing, turning around on her toes, abandoning all restraint. "She does have somebody!"

"No such luck!" replied the obstinate husband. It was an old tune — *la mia Dorabella capace non è!*

Pauline tugged at his wrists to pull him to his feet. "Let me show you something, it's in the library. You can leave her, divorce her and she won't be able to blame you — it's all her doing."

Hardwick's ruddy face grew pale. "That sounds too good to be true."

'Everyone's a nudist these days, it doesn't necessarily mean anything,' he thought as he sat in the library and watched his wife walk about topless on the deck of the *Hermit,* with a strange young man beside her.

When the young man put his arm around her and lifted her breast with his fingertip, Pauline switched off the projector. "See what I mean? She's having the time of her life, and when you go all the way down there to see her, she nags you!"

"Keep it rolling, let's go over the whole thing from A to Z," Hardwick insisted in the dry voice of a corporation executive who wanted to know all the details. "By the way, how did you get this stuff?"

"I bought it," she said proudly, looking him straight in the eye. "I paid sixty-two thousand five hundred dollars for it. I would have paid anything to stop her making a fool of you. Aren't you pleased with me?"

"I must pay you back," Hardwick replied evenly.

She switched on the projector, and his wife and the stranger came to life again.

"Well, it's certainly a weight off my chest," Hardwick commented a little too loudly. "Good luck to them. . . . The only thing that bothers me is the ramifications. . . . They're lying on that mattress — they aren't doing anything, but that creep touched her tits when they were walking around. My cousins could use this to try to prove that Creighton and Ben aren't my kids. They might disinherit them, if anything happened to me. I'll need to have every copy of the film destroyed. . . . Otherwise, of course, this is a wholly positive development.''

Talking made the watching easier, at least until he saw his wife lean over the stranger (and the stranger disgusted him, so he saw her lean over a *disgusting* stranger) and take this disgusting stranger's revolting prick into her mouth.

It was obscene.

The 16mm uncut footage, at times blurred and out of focus, projected on the portable screen, looked cheap. But even if it had looked expensive it would have been obscene, because it was false. Like all sex films, it was as grotesque as a film of a concert without the music, showing the members of the orchestra bobbing their heads, screwing up their lips, puffing out their cheeks, moving silent bows across silent strings, going through all sorts of contortions — what a vile falsehood such a spectacle would be, passed off as a Beethoven symphony! The movements of the lovers' bodies told nothing about the beating of their hearts, the acrobatics of copulation communicated nothing of what they felt; what lived inside was shown as something outside. Hardwick didn't reflect on the falseness of the film, but he felt it; it made the whole performance even more deeply offensive, and when he remembered, in a lucid moment, that she was doing for that disgusting stranger what she had always refused to do for him, for her husband, for the father of her children, he couldn't contain himself: he grabbed the projector, ripping the cord from its socket, and hurled the thing against the wall.

"I'll kill him!" he screamed over the din of banging metal and breaking glass. But then, instantly recovering that iron self-control so characteristic of men of power, he added quite calmly, "I'll have him killed."

Pauline Marshall stood there aghast and unbelieving.

Shaken in her judgment of the man whose weaknesses she thought she understood, she made the mistake of answering all his questions about the stranger on the *Hermit,* her detective, the cameraman.

"I don't hold back, I tell you everything, I'm the only person you can count on," she cajoled him desperately, too upset to realize that she was telling him that he could be fooled by everybody else. "You need a woman you can trust!"

When she had told him everything she knew, Hardwick dialed the housekeeper and informed her that Miss Marshall and her maid were leaving and would need help with their packing.

"You can keep your job at the magazine as long as no one hears about this," he said to his former mistress.

"But Kevin, you're *bored* with your wife," Pauline said, crying, laughing, begging. "She hangs around your neck and weighs you down

— now you can shake her off, and she's the one who's responsible! Don't you understand? It's just what you wanted. You're the injured party! You can be rid of her and she can't even complain. Don't you see? You're free and it's all her fault!''

Hardwick looked at her with hatred. "If you had loved me, you would never have shown me this.''

The Triangle

He is so quiet that he seems to sleep
The tempest out, as dormice do in winter:
Those houses that are haunted are most still
Till the devil be up.

WEBSTER

To be jealous of a woman one doesn't love is the most ridiculous form of vanity, but Hardwick, surrounded by people whose livelihood depended on him, had no idea that he could be ridiculous. He descended upon his island home without warning in the middle of the week, hoping to surprise the lovers together, and caught a surprised expression on everybody's face. Even the children were taken aback by his unexpected arrival. There was no sign of the young man from the Seven Seas Club.

"I've been working too hard and I missed you all," Hardwick said jovially, putting his arm around his wife. "Any news?"

"I'm sick," replied Marianne.

Claiming menstrual cramps, she retired to her bedroom.

Was the affair over, Hardwick wondered. For a while he followed the children and the cook around, waiting for somebody to tell him something.

No one did.

He invited Fawkes to have a beer with him in the garden. "Hey, man," he said, attempting to sound black, "how's things? You know I'm looking to you to be the boss around here when I'm away."

"Everything's shipshape, sir," replied Fawkes. "Mrs. Hardwick, she looks after us all."

"Well, you know, man, I want you to be happy with us. I've been meaning to ask you, are you satisfied with your pay?"

"More's welcome," said Fawkes with a half-laugh.

"I want you to feel you can always tell me if anything's worrying you," Hardwick suggested.

Fawkes kept his eye on the beer bottle, almost as if he had been waiting for the question. "Yes, sir. . . . The gardens needs more topsoil from Florida, I think."

"Fine. You can go ahead and order some. Anything else, man? Don't hesitate to come to me if there's anything you can't handle on your own."

"Yes, well . . . they's been oil lumps on the beach lately, sir. They's too many motorboats and cruise ships round the island."

'I'll fire you one of these days, without severance pay!' Hardwick thought, nodding glumly.

Later, remembering the children's nursemaid, he went to look for her and caught her by the arm when he found her alone. She was too quiet, he said, he wished he could hear her lovely voice more often. "What could I talk about?" Joyce asked pertly and shook herself free, feeling secure in her mistress's friendship. "The only news I have is old news, and I'd be telling it to Mrs. Hardwick."

Hardwick didn't question Creighton or Benjamin — he didn't want to remind them of whatever it was they knew — but when his wife finally showed up in the living room before dinner and the boys ran to her the way they never ran to him, he couldn't resist taking Creighton away from her. Lifting him up, he swung him back and forth in the air, making him chortle with laughter, then set him on his knee and coaxed him to tell his dad all about their activities. Did they have any friends?

Creighton pulled away, scowling. "Everybody's my friend!"

"I mean new friends," Hardwick corrected himself. "Do you ever get together with the neighbors? Don't their grandchildren ever come and visit you? Ride your ponies? Daddy just wants to know what you've been doing."

His father's questions made the boy, usually so boisterous and talkative, oddly quiet. He looked at his mother.

Marianne hadn't warned her sons not to speak about Mark; she didn't want to teach them to lie or pretend. So now she sat playing with Ben's hair, sniffing his warm head, thinking that she would leave it all up to them. If they spoke, she would ask Kevin for a divorce, she would beat him to it. If the children didn't speak, she would wait and see. She felt quite thrilled about it: she had never gambled before.

"Tell Daddy what you've been doing," she told Creighton.

"My pony had a sore foot," declared Creighton, turning to face his father confidently. "But he's better now."

"His pony had a sore foot," echoed Ben in his deep voice.

'So you all think that you can make a fool of me!' Hardwick screamed in his heart.

How two boys under five could know about protecting their mother's secret is a mystery of love and intuition formed in the womb. Perhaps they were taking their cue from the fact that lately neither their mother nor Joyce nor anybody else around them had referred to their new friend.

Their father didn't give away anything either. He was the lord and master of his face: he smiled and joked and was charming to everybody. The president and principal stockholder of HCI couldn't have run his conglomerate if he hadn't learned that freedom of action is knowing and not telling.

The following day when Hardwick's 707 flew back to the States it carried not only Hardwick but also his wife, the two children, their nanny and a lot of extra luggage.

Having come to loathe the island, Marianne had decided to move back to Chicago. Sick of love, sick of men, she had fallen in love with the idea of being her own person, and had a great desire to do things which had nothing to do with being a woman.

HARDWICK planned to screw his wife as soon as her period — or sham period — was over: he wanted to get even in every way. But by the time he got back from the office on the first evening, Marianne was gone from the house. "She'll only be away for a few days," Joyce told him. Hardwick did not comment; he thought that Marianne was gone for good, and was greatly relieved to hear the unmistakable sound of the boys' feet running past the door of his study.

This was the spring of the dramatic presidential primaries of 1968, and Marianne volunteered as a campaign worker for Eugene J. Mc-Carthy, the poet and junior senator from Minnesota, whose near-victory over President Johnson in the New Hampshire primary had shocked the President into quitting the race for re-election and established for the first time that most Americans wanted an end to the war in Vietnam and didn't care who won it. It was one of those historic moments, rare even in democracies, when the rulers of the country seemed about to be overruled by the people, and hundreds of thousands of Americans, inspired by Eugene McCarthy's example, entered politics with no other motive than the satisfaction of helping their country. Hardwick was convinced that his wife got involved simply as a way of avoiding him, but he acted the part of an understanding husband, making sarcastic remarks only behind her back. "I'm letting her grow, I'm letting her *extend her horizons*," he would say when asked about her by other men.

The marriage was now a series of long-distance calls: Marianne phoned every day to talk with Creighton and Ben, and sometimes she also talked with her husband, discussing the latest developments in the primaries. When Senator Robert Kennedy entered the race for the Democratic nomination, she remained loyal to McCarthy but tried to persuade her husband to join her in financing a committee which would work to unite voters behind whichever reformist anti-war candidate generated the most popular support.

Without reminding her that it was a long-standing tradition in both their families to make substantial campaign contributions to all viable president candidates, he agreed to give money to her committee whenever she said the word. While making up his mind about his next move, he didn't want to give her any grounds for complaint.

Hardwick was thirsting for revenge but he had too many things to do. Running a huge conglomerate of any kind would have been work enough, but running a chemical conglomerate was the most thankless job in the world.

His problems could perhaps be best described in terms of his products and by-products, such as dioxin 2,3,7,8 TCDD, three ounces of which are sufficient to kill a million people. HCI was plagued with six hundred pounds of the stuff every year from the manufacture of trichlorophenol, used to make the herbicide 2,4,5-T and the disinfectant hexachlorophene. Since these two fast-selling items alone netted HCI over eighteen million a year, it was inconceivable to discontinue their production, even if they generated troublesome waste. At one point the manager of one of Hardwick's plants tried to dispose of TCDD by simply burning it and sending it up the smokestack, but this led to claims for miscarriages, birth deformities, leukemia cases, still unsettled lawsuits — and dioxin was just one of Hardwick's many headaches.

Hardwick manufactured only 124 of the 35,000 registered insecticides and herbicides marketed in the United States, but they were all trouble — and so were insulating materials, plastics, paints, paint removers, dyes, lacquers, adhesives, solvents, cleaning fluids, carpet shampoos. Even fertilizers and livestock feed supplements turned out to be poisonous. Gone were the good old days when all they had to worry about was selling the stuff and only emotional idealists bothered him with after-sale problems!

Often wishing that he had inherited a chain of flower shops, Hardwick was forced to listen to his scientists lecturing him with increasing frequency about the biological effects of chlorinated hydrocarbon, organic phosphorus and carbamate compounds — chlordane, lindane, benzenes, phenols, PCBs, urethane, CIPC, and so on.

What could Hardwick do?

He banned all aerosol sprays, detergents and cleaning fluids from his homes, told his servants to use soap for everything, ordered the manager of the old family farm in southern Illinois to go organic, put all his households on bottled spring water, and tried to get rid of HCI's toxic residues, liquid and solid, as best he could. But there was always something. While his wife was running around the country campaigning and burning money, a health official in Florida issued a report blaming the local HCI phosphate chemicals plant, and its open-air storage ponds filled with acid wastes and emitting fluorides and radon gas, for the higher-than-average incidence of miscarriages and birth defects in his district. The ponds had been dug in the 40s, in Hardwick's father's time; Hardwick didn't even know they existed until his legal department told him about the fuss in Florida. Thanks to the Vietnam War and the dramatic presidential primaries, the problem of the ponds received little national publicity, but all the same there was the danger of damage suits against the company. There were endless meetings on the subject, and Hardwick had to fly down to Tallahassee and make personal campaign contributions to several key committee members of the state legislature before he could get the author of the alarmist report transferred and replaced by a medical officer who understood that his job was to reassure the public, not to make them sick with worry.

Just to neutralize one meddling bureaucrat cost Hardwick more than a week's work; what with one thing and another, there were days when he felt that his wife's duplicity was the least of his problems.

DOWN in the Bahamas, people had a lot of time for Mrs. Hardwick's love life.

The fishing boats, small cargo vessels and pleasure craft that plow the waters between the Bahama Islands constitute a community not unlike a village, where everyone in sight is the subject of constant scrutiny and intense gossip. The skippers, who hail hearty greetings when they pass each other, are as likely as not to stop for a chat, exchanging information about local boats or ships in trouble as far away as the North Sea or the South Pacific; they discuss the weather forecasts, some rare fish or record catch, the curse of big cruise ships and oil tankers; there is chatter over the radio transmitters, more talk in the harbor bars in the evenings, about the relative merits of sex and liquor, the art of living and the affairs of acquaintances and strangers. Among these people, whose characters had been formed by the solitude of the sea and the togetherness of a close-knit group, the mysteries of the Hardwick marriage and Mrs. Hardwick's brief affair remained a general topic of conversation for quite some time. Did her husband know? What a comedown for the snobbish member of the board of the Chicago Lyric Opera, to fall for a hotel clerk!

Mark didn't have much of a reputation before the affair: his aimless meanderings among the coral reefs had been noted along with the fact that, apart from a hired hand who guarded his boat, he was on his own. Since it was the agreed wisdom of the time that everything worthwhile was done by a team, no one took his solitary diving seriously; it only showed that he wasn't very bright. But what did Marianne Hardwick see in him, if anything, apart from his body?

For a while Mark enjoyed a status conferred by curiosity that a handsome young man intent on having a good time or making connections would have found easy to exploit. Elderly multimillionaires, prompted by their wives, came up to him in the lobby of the Seven Seas Club to invite him to dinner or sent invitations through Ken Eshelby. Whenever he was on the *Ile Saint-Louis,* catching his breath between dives, some yachtsman always pulled up beside him, trying to engage him in conversation and asking him over for a drink and a chat. Having nothing of the social climber in him, Mark said "no thanks" to all invitations, preferring to argue with Marianne in his head.

What was so terrible about saying that they had wasted six whole days? It didn't mean he didn't love her. Didn't *she* ever say anything stupid? Why, she even believed in dreams! And how could she fail to see that it was demeaning to be a rich woman's poor lover? But whatever he thought of telling her, she wasn't there to hear it. There were times when he couldn't even recall the length of her long ash-blond hair, or the shade of green of her blue-green eyes, and these lapses of memory made her absence intolerable. He had a great longing to remember her exactly, and couldn't forgive himself for not taking pictures of her while he had the chance. But was it really all over? The Hardwick estate wasn't up for sale; Fawkes, the cook, the maids, the gardeners, the grooms, the peacocks and Shetland ponies were still there . . . Besides, didn't she have tears in her eyes when she sent him away? At moments when his heart was dead to all hopeful sentiments he thought they were tears of rage, the tears of an infuriated spoiled woman; at other times he felt that she had cried because she was hurt, and she was hurt because she loved him.

One evening, overwhelmed by remorseful longing, he walked over to the Hardwick house to ask John Fawkes for help. "Don't forget, I didn't give you nothing," Fawkes said, handing over a note with the address of the Hardwick mansion on Bellevue Place in Chicago and Mrs. Hardwick's private telephone number.

Mark called Marianne that same night from a deserted alcove in the lobby of the Club. It was Joyce who picked up the receiver in Chicago: "I'm really-truly glad to hear from you, Mr. Niven!" Marianne was in Los Angeles campaigning about Vietnam, she explained. "I swear you have something to do with it," she said, anxious to make peace between them. "You being a draft dodger and all. That might have given her the idea. Really-truly! She wasn't interested in politics at all before she met you. I'll give you her phone number in Los Angeles." Mark thanked her even more profusely than he had thanked Fawkes, moved almost to tears that the people around Marianne didn't despise him.

Wasn't that a good omen?

THE suave male voice answering the phone in Marianne's hotel suite in Los Angeles asked Mark's name three times and wanted to know why he was calling.

"It's personal," answered Mark, seeing the world grow dark in front of his eyes. He had to wait a long while for Marianne to come to the phone, and in the meantime he kept himself from going mad by listening to the voices in the background: at least she wasn't alone with the man!

The suave voice belonged to a lecturer in political science at Stanford named David Roman, a dark, attractive and amiable bachelor of twenty-eight. Ever since they met in New Hampshire he had been telling Marianne — in a teasing manner, without getting overbearing about it — that she was a poor rich girl interested only in amusing herself, and that she was amusing herself with politics only because she was full of inhibitions about sex. Finally Marianne decided that she would never have another man if she waited till she fell in love again, and so she had gone to bed with David just three nights earlier. At the end they assured each other that it was wonderful. He thanked her and she thanked him. "We must do it again," David told her, and they did it every night and they thanked each other every morning. It was wonderful, but it wasn't the real thing.

The news that Mark was on the phone made her heart jump into her throat. She felt her face burn and she began to tremble. She detested David for his raised eyebrows and sardonic smile as he told her about the caller and then stayed to watch her reaction, leaning forward and staring calmly into her face with the confidence of a man who had given her an orgasm three nights in a row. 'What gives him the right to watch me like that?' she thought. She got up and went to the bedroom, telling her friend Millie Rowland to put down the receiver when she picked it up on the extension.

"Hi, Mark!" she said, flustered and trying to sound offhand. "Why are you calling? Have you found that wreck you were looking for? Or have you decided to stop wasting your time?"

Shaken that she could sound so flippant, Mark didn't even have the presence of mind to say hello.

The silence on the line made her unhappy: he missed her, he was miserable, she could feel it. "Are you there, Mark?"

"When are you coming back?" Mark asked hoarsely. "I would like to take you up on that offer you made me on the plane when we first met. You know, we could look for the *Flora* together and split what we find."

It wasn't the answer she wanted to hear and yet she was glad. Her heart was pounding so hard she wondered whether he could hear it down there on Santa Catalina. If he had been there she would have thrown her arms around him, but he was far away. Trying to regain her self-possession, she spoke in a cold, hostile voice, directed more at herself than at Mark: she wanted to stop her heart from pounding. "I'm not going anywhere. There's an election about the war, I can't leave now."

How many lives are ruined on the phone! The eyes, the hands cannot have their say, there are only the words.

"I see you're still mad at me."

"I'm not mad at you, but we want young Americans like you back in the States instead of running around the world like fugitives."

"I don't mind being a fugitive, I just mind you not being here."

"Don't you care about the war? Is it all right with you if it goes on forever?" Arguing with Mark, who sounded indeed like just another apathetic non-voter, she was telling him the arguments she was using when canvassing on doorsteps and with these arguments, on which so many lives depended, she recovered her sense of elation that came from being involved in something bigger than herself. "I don't think I could live on an island again," she tried to explain hurriedly, to keep her voice from shaking. "There are a lot of people on this campaign who think I'm just a rich bitch interested in having a good time. Some of them even say so. That was true when you knew me, but I'm not like that any more."

"You certainly sound different!" exclaimed Mark bitterly.

"We shouldn't even be talking on the phone. You should come back here and help."

"How could I come back, Bozzie?" he asked, appealing to her with her family nickname which they had always used in their best moments. "You just said I'm a fugitive. If I go back, they'll put me in jail. If we found the ship we could finance the whole campaign."

"How I wish you'd grow up!" she sighed.

"Well, I'm sorry I disturbed you." Not trusting his voice any further, Mark put down the receiver.

HE decided to forget her, but a few nights later he dreamed that she was lying beside him. He felt such joy that he woke up. Realizing that he was alone, he started shivering. Unable to go back to sleep, he got out of bed, put on swimming trunks, a pullover and sneakers, and slipped out of the staff house, down to the yacht harbor. By the light of an almost full moon he untied his boat and, keeping the motor at a low throttle, made a wide circle away from land and then back in toward the Hardwicks' dock. As he drew near he cut the motor and glided silently in to shore. What would he do if he was caught? He would say he was drunk, he decided. As he was tying up his boat, one of the wolfhounds came loping down to the dock but gave only one short bark and then sat down to watch him. "Good boy," Mark murmured. "You have a better memory than your mistress."

Stealthily he boarded the *Hermit* and, using his diving knife, forced open the door to the gangway leading below. He was hoping to find a photograph of Marianne somewhere but had forgotten to bring a flashlight and had to spend a long time prowling and peering around the saloon and cabins in the dim light that came through the portholes. He couldn't find any photographs, but on her dresser there was a tortoise-shell comb with two long, glittering strands of her silver-blond hair caught in it. And in a drawer he found a pair of white silk panties; he buried his face in them and imagined he could smell her coming.

Tormented by the memory of her cool voice on the phone, he couldn't muster the courage to call her again. But when he heard she was back in Chicago he wrote to her to confess that he had stolen her comb and a pair of her white silk panties.

. . . I often wake up at night thinking of you and imagine you're awake too, thinking of me . . . I can't really believe that you've gone back to your husband. You said you didn't love him. You said I'd *finished him off,* don't you remember? How can you stand living with a man you despise? You promised you'd leave him! Is it possible that you've fallen in love with him again? At least tell me if you're in love with him! You must come back! Please. I hate myself without you.

24

Love and Deceit

. . . since you would save none of me, I bury some of you.
JOHN DONNE

L IKE millions of liberal-minded Americans of her generation who got
involved in the 1968 election campaign with high hopes of changing the world for the better, only to see Martin Luther King murdered,
Robert Kennedy murdered, Eugene McCarthy defeated in the conven-
tion, Hubert Humphrey defeated in the election and Richard Nixon elected,
Marianne felt like an absolute idiot for ever having concerned herself
with politics and vowed she would never read a newspaper again.

And she wished she hadn't had an affair with David Roman in Los
Angeles. What bothered her most was the way David had played with
her long hair, combing it with his fingers and covering her breasts with
it, just as Mark had always done. Whenever she remembered Mark
dressing her body in her hair, winding it around her nipples when they
stood up, she couldn't help remembering David too, and that was death.
The thought of the unloved lover spoiled her best memories. She felt so
remorseful and so disgusted with herself, she decided to have her hair
cut. It belonged to Mark. She didn't want anyone else to play with it.
Not even Ben.

The hairdresser did his job under protest and when, at the end of the
operation, she studied her new head in the mirror, she was shocked to
see how much smaller she had become. 'Well, my love, I made myself
ugly for you,' she thought, trying to see herself with Mark's eyes. While
driving back to the house, she half believed in telepathy. She thought of
Mark in his boat, sitting up, looking around disturbed, not knowing why
he suddenly missed her — she loved his puzzled look. Did he remember
her hair? ''I decided I won't let it grow until we're together,'' she said
aloud.''That's a promise. So why don't you call me, why don't you drop
me a line?''

178

And what if he could hear her? What if he could sense her thoughts somehow?

"Good Lord, what did you do with your hair?" Joyce cried out when Marianne got back to the house.

"Is there any message for me?" Marianne asked impatiently.

WEEKS earlier, when Mark's first letter had been delivered to Bellevue Place, Marianne had been up in her room asleep. Hardwick, breakfasting alone as usual, noticed the Bahamian stamp on her letter in the mail tray and slipped it into his pocket to read in the office.

Even though he had seen the film, Hardwick was shocked. A love letter to his wife confessing to breaking and entering and stealing her underwear, and reminding her that she didn't care for her husband and had promised to leave him! And what was this about finishing him off? Hardwick got into such a rage that he tore the paper into little bits before he knew what he was doing.

However, once the insulted husband got over what he dismissed as *an emotional reaction, a useless waste of energy,* he was quite prepared to look at the incident from another point of view and decided that it was a wholly positive development, forewarning him of the need to censor his wife's mail.

In more peaceful times this might have been quite a difficult task, considering that the house was full of unreliable servants whose loyalty was to her rather than to him. But these were not peaceful times. Some weeks earlier a chemical company executive had been assassinated in Venice by the Red Brigades, and this murder, bringing into focus the increasing hostility and violence against people connected with the chemical industry, made it quite natural for Hardwick to have all mail addressed to his home redirected to the security department in the HCI Building to be checked for explosive devices. The letters were then brought to his top-floor office, where he sifted through them before passing them on to his secretary for delivery by company courier to the house on Bellevue Place. Of course, the mail was *also* checked for explosive devices. Hardwick was the master of arrangements which served more than one purpose; he had the gift of making things play in several ways at once.

Mark wrote to Marianne every day, little suspecting that he was asking to be murdered. Though he knew that Hardwick was a rich and powerful man, he had heard too much about the equality of human beings to appreciate that powerful men must be feared. He assumed that Hardwick was no more of a man than himself; if anything he was a lesser man because Marianne didn't love him. (Most of the time he managed to convince himself that she still detested her husband.) Besides, she had said that Hardwick was in love with another woman, had all kinds of other girls as well, and didn't care for her. Mark was not vain himself and never imagined that Hardwick might become his deadly enemy out of sheer vanity; few people, and even fewer nineteen-year-olds, suspect qualities in others that they themselves don't possess. Mark wondered sometimes, as he wasn't getting any reply, whether his letters could have fallen into the wrong hands, but he always rejected the idea. He was certain that if Marianne's husband caught any of the letters he would make a row, but, as he wasn't in love with his wife, would bow to the inevitable and withdraw. In his most desperate moods he even wanted Hardwick to find out everything and get mad. Marianne would come back if her marriage broke up. So he kept writing to her, begging her to remember that she loved him.

"What is it with this guy?' Hardwick wondered. He tore up twenty-three letters before they stopped coming.

Marianne never imagined that anyone but a bomb-disposal expert had tampered with her mail. If anything, she was grateful to Kevin for protecting them all — it was proof that he was a caring person in his own way — and she always thought of this when asking herself why she stayed with him.

Still, a couple of weeks after Nixon was elected President, Marianne declared that she wanted to go back to Santa Catalina.

"Great idea!" exclaimed Hardwick with hearty animation. "Let's all go down for the weekend!" She couldn't leave her husband behind, but she insisted that he take her to lunch at the Seven Seas Club.

She hoped that Mark would be there and they would see each other: she would seduce him back with a look.

MARK was standing in the lobby in his hated uniform and had just caught a depressing glimpse of himself in a mirror, when he saw Marianne enter with her husband. Overwhelmed by a profound sense of his insignificance, he backed into a corridor, ran out of the building, through the garden and into the staff house, all the way to his room, locked the door and fell on his bed. So she was back, the proud heartless rich bitch who hadn't deigned to reply to his letters! How mean and severe she looked! She had cut her hair, her beautiful long, silver-blond hair which he had loved to wind around her nipples; she had got rid of it to spite him. How she must look down on him, thinking that he would never amount to anything. He couldn't decide whether she had noticed him in the lobby or not, but if she had he hoped she could see how he hated her.

Someone was knocking at his door. What if it was Marianne? He imagined her coming in and looking around disdainfully at his terrible little room. "So this is how far you've got since you stopped wasting your time with me!" she said with a malicious smile. "And where's my comb? What did you do with my panties?"

He was burning with shame. Yet *why* should he be ashamed? He hadn't killed anybody! What was there to be ashamed of?

The knocking was getting louder; he finally had to open the door. In the corridor stood his old enemy, the gray-haired bellboy, telling him with a sneer that Mr. Weaver wanted him back at the desk immediately. Mark told him to say that he was sick. The man would have been happy to report that Mark was lying, but could see that he was telling the truth: his face was gray and his teeth were chattering. Once alone, Mark locked the door again and fell back on the bed.

It was too late.

Hardwick's theft of the letters had made Mark and Marianne despair of each other. How else could Mark have assumed that she had cut her hair to spite him?

When he saw her walk into the Club, all he could think was that she despised him for being a nobody who hadn't accomplished anything (Marianne, who didn't know the meaning of the word *ambition!*), and when she caught his bitter look, she felt she had lost all her charm for him. 'So he can't stand the sight of me,' she decided.

Neither of them gave a thought to her husband, who didn't seem to notice anything.

On Monday Hardwick went back to the States alone, leaving his wife on the island. She waited, she didn't know why — she waited for some greater certainty. She waited for him to call. When she heard, a few days later, that Mark was having an affair with the social director at the Club, she flew back to Chicago.

"It's all for the best," she told Joyce on the plane. "I was right to get mad at him in the first place. Obviously he wasn't serious, he really *did* think that he was wasting time with me. If he didn't, he would have tried to get in touch with me again. It can't be that easy to discourage somebody who cares for you!"

"You got mad at him for nothing!"

Marianne raised her hands to her burning cheeks and looked at Joyce intently, thinking about her remark. "You're right." She nodded severely. "I didn't behave like a woman who was in love. We probably didn't really fit each other. So even if I had gone back when he phoned me, it wouldn't have worked out."

"And your marriage is really-truly working out," Joyce commented with restrained sarcasm.

"Well, Kevin's changed," Marianne replied defensively. "He's different, he's nicer."

"Maybe he heard something. There's a lot of big mouths on the island and everybody knew about it. He heard something and he's trying to win you back!"

"You think he *knows* and he's jealous?" asked Marianne incredulously.

They discussed the pros and cons very thoroughly. Millions are like this: they spend hours with friends trying to figure out what their husbands, wives, lovers know or think.

"If Kevin knew anything, and if he cared, he would either have it out with me or try to make love with me," Marianne finally said. "And he doesn't."

This argument seemed to be conclusive for both women.

"No, he's changed because his big romance with the model is over. He must have a sex life with somebody, but he evidently regards us as his family . . ."

To convince herself, Marianne tried to convince Joyce that there was a great deal to be said for her marriage. "He plays with the children, he worries about what we eat and drink, he always sends the plane for us, he looks after our safety — that's more than many wives can say for their husbands. He's not as heartless and cynical as he pretends to be."

Joyce rolled her eyes. "If you say so."

"My father says Kevin's doing more for pollution control than any other chemical manufacturer. They use HCI scrubbers now in the smokestacks at the steel plants."

"I know, you don't have to tell me," Joyce said, offended. "I know he got a medal for them." It didn't seem right to her that there should be anything good about the man who raped her and then looked through her without interest or guilt.

"And he's the father of Creighton and Ben," Marianne sighed. "I must never forget that. It's a marriage of friendship. We don't have any conflict. At least we're friends."

Kevin was at the airport to meet them, arms outstretched, smiling. When she saw his tall, imposing figure, his welcoming smile, Marianne steeled her heart and smiled back, saying to herself, 'Yes, at least we're friends.'

"Wonderful to see you all!" Hardwick exclaimed. While they were apart, he had made up his mind that the bastard who screwed his wife and the men who filmed them doing it would have to be done away with by Baglione. As for his wife, he was more or less satisfied with seeing her unhappy.

Business Associates

You must give great men leave to take their times.
WEBSTER

IT could not be said often enough that HCI manufactured, sold and *used* some of the best available technology for detoxification, filtering, recycling and high-temperature incineration. However, out of the more than 77 billion pounds of toxic chemical waste produced in the United States every year, HCI was responsible for approximately 600 million pounds, and whatever Hardwick could do, within reasonable budget limits, he was still left with a great deal of lethal garbage, which made Chicago crime boss Vincenzo Baglione one of his most important business associates. Not that Baglione could take care of everything. Hardwick was presiding over too many time bombs, such as the Florida ponds, to go through a week without some crisis. Even so, his life had unquestionably become easier since Baglione's Illinois Safe Transport Company, fronted by people without police records, took over the disposal of HCI's untreated residues for a very reasonable yearly payment.

In the course of doing business, Hardwick sold Baglione a 20% share in the new HCI plant in Cubatao, Brazil (known locally as the *Vale de Morte*), where there were no government regulations to hinder industrial growth. They met regularly, every three months or so, usually somewhere far from Chicago, preferably outside the United States. Business was business, though not unnaturally, the more Hardwick had to do with the man, the more he despised him.

Imagining that the waste-shipping operation of the Illinois Safe Transport Company was part of the Mafia's general move into legitimate business which he kept reading about in the papers, Hardwick at first believed Baglione's assurances that the truckers were hauling the waste to approved dump sites up in Canada. It was supposed to be a clean operation, but eventually Baglione, who really preferred to have the young industrialist as his willing accomplice, confided that licensed dump sites were prohibitively expensive and so the trucks moved at night with open valves, dripping their contents along the highway, or unloaded them in ditches, quarries, gravel pits, streams and rivers long before they reached the Manitoba border.

Like most businessmen who get involved with criminals in the pious hope that they are helping them onto the path of legitimate enterprise, Hardwick found that it was the other way around: Baglione was dragging him into the world of crime. It wasn't so much the random dumping of poisons that bothered him — something had to happen to reduce the population, if anybody was to survive. What he found unconscionable was that Baglione was trying to involve him in indictable offenses.

A few murders more or less would mean nothing to a man like that, Hardwick thought.

And they would be child's play compared with the murder of a President.

Hardwick had no patience with conspiracy theories; he didn't think that John F. Kennedy was killed by the Cubans or the CIA or the Russians. He was convinced that the assassination was organized by the Mafia. Of course he knew that a lot of fools thought the same, but he had his reasons: some odd remarks Baglione had made when they first met, at a fund-raising dinner, a few weeks before America's dark day in Dallas. "JFK's all right," Baglione had told him, "but with a publicity seeker like that Bobby for a brother, the poor guy has no future." Hardwick was amused by Baglione's way of putting down Robert Kennedy, the first U.S. attorney general to seek publicity by trying to rid his country of organized crime, but he couldn't figure why Baglione would call the President of the United States a *poor guy*. John Kennedy was a popular young President serving his first term; to say that he had no future sounded preposterous at the time — though when the President was dead and his brother no longer ran the Justice Department, it made perfect sense.

Especially on the night of June 5, 1968, when he was wakened by a hysterical call from Marianne in Los Angeles: Robert Kennedy had just been assassinated in the Ambassador Hotel, only hours after his victory in the California primary. It was then, while listening to the sound of her shrill voice — a voice he had never heard before and found most irritating in the middle of the night — that Hardwick began to think seriously about asking his mafioso associate for a favor. The second Kennedy assassination, which robbed Americans of their chance to elect an anti-Mafia President, confirmed his belief that Baglione could arrange anything for him.

THE next time they got together was at Recife airport, where the Chicago crime boss boarded Hardwick's plane for the flight to Cubatao.

Playing the gracious host, Hardwick offered the old man all the amenities of the 707, and Baglione had a shower and was rubbed down by the quiet and thorough masseuse before the two men sat down to dinner. Still full of life in his late sixties, Baglione could hardly contain his satisfaction with the girl: there were flickers of joy among his wrinkles. However, as soon as Hardwick began to complain that his wife had been having an affair with a hotel clerk on Santa Catalina, all feelings died on Baglione's face. He wiped the air in front of his nose as if brushing away a fly.

Hardwick, who didn't understand Sicilian body language, went on talking. He wasn't prepared to overlook adultery.

"You mean you want a divorce?"

"I'd be punishing my sons. I'm a family man, I don't have to explain this to an Italian, do I? It's her boyfriend I'm talking about."

Baglione nodded with sympathetic understanding. "Sue him."

"What?"

"You oughta sue him," repeated the Chicago crime boss. A wizened little man who looked as though he had never had enough to eat, he reminded Hardwick of a sad sparrow, but when he smiled, his predatory nose became his most prominent feature: it was the beak of a vulture. And he had the same rapacious eyes. "You oughta sue him for alienation of affections."

Hardwick shook his head in silence until he got over the old hoodlum's insolence. "Vincenzo, I wouldn't be telling you this if I wanted a lawyer."

Baglione put down his knife and fork and folded his arms to signify that he didn't want to be involved. "I appreciate your problem, Kevin, but what do you expect me to do about a kid?"

"I though you might have some ideas about how to get rid of troublesome people who don't know their place. Listen, this guy's writing me love letters."

Baglione raised his head, sniffing the air. "He's writing you love letters? My friend!"

"Well, to my wife — it's the same thing. I'm expecting another note from him any day."

Baglione's shriveled face grew thinner and sadder. "You want him roughed up?"

"No," came the firm, pitiless reply.

The old mafioso closed his eyes as if wishing to commune with himself in private. "A man's life is a sacred thing," he finally said in the most solemn voice.

Hardwick drew himself up in his chair. "I beg your pardon?"

The sharp tone of the question shocked Baglione. This spoiled rich fool dared to assume that he didn't value human life? What did he take him for? An animal who went around killing people, who would shed blood just because Hardwick didn't know how to look after his wife? Baglione was insulted. He was used to being treated with respect. And by everybody. Some years later, when he died of natural causes, the *New York Times* paid tribute to him as "the pre-eminent figure in organized crime in the United States." In a country where a vicious thug could be called pre-eminent by the newspaper which set the moral tone for the nation, Baglione had had no difficulty in scaling the summits of crime with his self-respect intact. He was a success in his chosen field, and he didn't take kindly to anyone casting aspersions on his honor.

"A man's life is a sacred thing," he repeated stiffly.

Hardwick didn't like the idea of a common criminal giving himself airs in his presence. "And it isn't just a question of the boyfriend either," he went on briskly, ignoring Baglione's sullen expression. "There's a photographer called Masterson."

Baglione kept nodding. "I appreciate your feelings. But feelings can change."

"This Masterson works with telescopic lenses. He filmed my wife with that hotel clerk — the son of a famous actor actually," Hardwick hastened to add. He wanted the bastard dead, but he didn't wish to make it appear that his wife slept with a nobody. "The two of them are starring in a dirty movie. For all I know, Masterson's busy making copies and he'll be selling them to sex shops in Chicago."

"You've got a problem there."

"It could be quite embarrassing for the whole family. I'm thinking mainly of my kids."

"I can send someone to talk to this guy, make sure he gets out of the movie business."

"I don't like half measures."

Baglione bent his birdlike head sideways with a mournful look. "Kevin, why go to extremes?"

Hardwick raised his eyebrows. He stretched himself, smiled broadly, leaned back, leaned forward, smiled again, playing for time like an overgrown schoolboy who had been asked a question by the teacher and didn't know what to say. He had given no thought to justifying his request. He wouldn't have killed the actor's son and the men who made the film if he had to do it himself — but why should he put up with them if he didn't have to? What was the point of doing business with somebody like Baglione if he didn't make maximum use of the relationship? He wanted to go to extremes because he knew Baglione and because Baglione made too much money with him to refuse him a favor. "There's also a private eye involved in this," he said coolly.

"I'm going to help you, Kevin, it's my nature to help people — *sono nato così!* But I say to you what I say to my own hotheads. This isn't

186

Sicily, this isn't the nineteenth century. And you're not even an Italian, my friend. You northerners are supposed to keep yourselves under control. Do you really believe in drastic solutions?"

"I'm under control," replied the jealous husband with a terse laugh. "I just want to protect my privacy."

"People want everybody dead when they get mad, but then they change their minds. You can't be hasty about these things."

Hardwick's face flushed, then froze. "I thought you might want to help out a friend, but it's not important. Let's drop it."

They sulked and talked in the sky over Brazil with mutual incomprehension. Hardwick thought he was talking to a professional killer, but Baglione didn't see himself as a killer. Starting from the premise that it was right and proper to remove people if they stood in his way, and having the power to kill anyone he wanted to, he considered himself an upright and compassionate man of extraordinary restraint. He never thought about the nine men he had gunned down in his youth, the two he had blown up, the one he had strangled and dismembered with his own hands, the scores of others whose executions he had ordered — he thought of the hundreds he had *spared*. But then, how many people judge themselves by what they have done? The good conscience of the wicked rests on all the villainies they refrain from committing.

The two men, both deeply offended, picked at their smoked salmon and filet mignon in silence, fighting with whatever hostility their bodies could generate. Even sitting down, the tall and fleshy Anglo-Saxon was almost twice as big as the little Italian, yet the fight was a standoff until the masseuse, doubling as serving maid, came in to pour their after-dinner coffee. Her fleeting presence, the perfume she left in the air, had a calming effect.

"I heard of Masterson, that's not his real name, he's an animal," recalled the pre-eminent heroin dealer, beginning to see the possibility of a compromise.

"We're only talking about three men, and two of them are nobodies," Hardwick said emphatically. He wasn't asking for much.

Deciding that the industrialist was raving mad in spite of his imperious manner and wouldn't leave him alone until he promised to kill everybody who failed to show sufficient regard for his better feelings as a husband and father, Baglione raised his hands from the table palms upward as if to show that he had nothing but good in them. "I don't know how to say no to a friend."

Visibly relieved, Hardwick reached across to another table for a folder and took from it an enlarged photograph, a frame of Masterson's film, showing the lovers walking on the beach. When Baglione had looked at the photo, Hardwick tore it in half, pocketed his wife's picture and handed over Mark's. "I guess your people will need this."

Baglione found Mrs. Hardwick quite good-looking and had no intention of harming a young man for making love to a good-looking woman whose husband didn't look after her. Especially not an actor's son. Baglione was fond of actors and singers; he liked show business people. But having figured out how to trick his associate, he became most compliant and agreeable.

"How can I say no if it makes you happy," he said, putting the picture of Mark into his briefcase.

"I don't have pictures of the other two," apologized Hardwick. "I have their addresses."

"We'll find them, don't worry." Baglione wasn't planning to do anything about the private detective either, but Masterson was a different matter. There were too many complaints about the animal; he was ruining too many marriages, too many reputations. In the spirit of a judge condemning a criminal, Baglione had resolved to rid the world of the blackmail photographer and to use this one murder as a means of delaying the other two until Hardwick calmed down and came to terms with his horns. "I'll take care of them for you, but I can't take care of them all at once. It'll take time, my friend."

Having got his way, Hardwick became deferential toward the older man. "If you say you'll take care of them, Vincenzo," he said, bending from the waist and spreading his long arms, "I know you'll take care of them."

Baglione never looked more honest and dignified than when he was lying. He assumed a grave expression, stared at Hardwick in a meaningful and straightforward manner, then closed his eyes and slowly nodded his head to confirm that the people they were talking about would pass away. "You can forget about it."

Protected by a gangster's sense of honor and decency, Mark was left free to do his worst to himself.

Moment of Truth

Ah, when to the heart of man
Was it ever less than a treason
To go with the drift of things,
To yield with a grace to reason,
And bow and accept the end
Of a love or a season?

ROBERT FROST

WORKING four days a week at the Seven Seas Club as a desk clerk
and translator, Mark spent all his free days diving and his evenings in Eshelby's darkroom developing film or in his room poring over
his pictures of the seabed and charts of the reefs, marking off the areas
he had already explored.

"I believe he feels guilty about sleeping," Eshelby told Sarah Little.

They were his only friends. He left people alone, they left him alone.
Even his fellow servants stopped teasing him about sunken treasure. He
had reached the bottom of the social scale: he was found boring.

He was idle only during tropical storms and on days of high seas when
Coco refused to get into the boat with him, and for months his social
life consisted of having tea and cookies at Eshelby's place in bad weather.

Eshelby, whose apartment in the staff house was furnished mostly with
books, spilling all over the place, even into the kitchen cupboards, tried
to make a reader out of his sullen young friend. The former teacher,
very much missing his classroom, gave Mark paperbacks of Stendhal
and Balzac, whom he called the Mozart and Beethoven of literature, and
did his best to convince him that it was silly to look for treasure when
it was possible to lead a rich life on practically no money by the simple
expedient of reading great novels. "And don't bother to read them once,
my dear boy," he warned him.

"Why not?" Mark wished Eshelby would talk about Marianne, but
starved for the company of anyone who gave a damn about what he did,
he was glad to listen to whatever Eshelby had to say.

"You get very little from a novel at first reading — just as little as from a symphony at first hearing. A great novel gets richer every time you go back to it. . . . That's the secret of happiness, my dear boy — don't read, re-read!" These admonitions were interspersed with patient pauses. The teacher and the tennis player were equally manifest in Eshelby's way of talking: he took care not to get too far ahead of his listener but he always talked on his feet, serving every idea with a tossing gesture as if it were a tennis ball. "If you keep re-reading the right books," he tempted Mark, "you will be as wise in a couple of years as most people are at sixty. Wisdom isn't much use to the old, but to be young and wise, that's what I would call striking it rich!"

Mark promised to read whenever he had the time.

"Make time, my dear boy!"

"I can't just put up my feet and amuse myself, I haven't accomplished anything yet."

Eshelby quoted an old Persian proverb for him to mull over. "A good book is a rose garden in your pocket."

"A rose garden in your pocket — that's beautiful!" However, the very idea of relaxation made Mark restless. Whatever roses he meant to pick were to be rewards for finding the *Flora;* he had got into the habit of postponing everything but his ambition. "When I get rich, I can spend the rest of my life reading," he assured his friend. "I'll have big libraries in all my houses."

"Have some more cookies," sighed his host. "I'm a short-distance arguer."

Sarah Little was another of Eshelby's pupils, receiving books and advice. When she ran into Mark at his apartment one day during a storm, Eshelby (a born matchmaker, like many homosexuals) claimed he wanted to be alone, and the onetime lovers left his place together. With gale-force winds shaking the windows, they ended up under the same blanket in Mark's room. This break in his solitary life made Mark voluble. Listing all the things he loved about Sarah, he blurted out — his brain softened by pleasure — that he was also grateful to her for Marianne. "If it wasn't for you, if you hadn't given me confidence," he said, "I wouldn't even have had those few days with her."

Sarah pinched him as hard as she could, and wouldn't speak to him for weeks.

'Every woman gets fed up with me,' Mark thought. 'I've no talent, I'm not even good company. I'm just one of those nothing sons of famous fathers. And if I'm wrong about the *Flora,* I'm also an idiot!'

Driven by despair as much as by ambition, he set himself the murderous task of diving seven hours every time he went out. Sometimes when he felt that he was about to dissolve in the sunlit sea, he would pause to watch the shimmering, sparkling crowds of tiny tropicals, the clouds of plankton lifting suddenly to reveal a coral spire, the wide-mouthed grouper passing by in their silver armor, staring with their motionless eyes as if they didn't see him, but observing him well enough to swerve away or swim right under his belly. Submerged in this teeming world, where to exist was a full-time occupation, he would envy the phlegmatic disposition of the fish, recalling Marianne's insistence that life was too short, too precious to be spent searching for *things*. The sharks were fast-moving, distant shadows, like gray lightning.

Since he was young and healthy, a good diver, it took months before he began to feel the effects of spending too much time at depth. He began to have dizzy spells and violent headaches, and once he came up too quickly and got the "itchy bends" — nitrogen bubbles under his skin which drove him mad for days. Which is to say that a man cannot turn himself into a fish even with the help of modern technology.

"If you carry on like this," Eshelby told him, "you'll be either dead or demented at twenty. I don't know which is worse."

Mark was always confident when opposed. 'But when I have my ship,' he was saying to himself, while appearing to listen attentively, 'I can tell Marianne, Look, *this* is what I had to find — it was worth a bit of wear and tear, wasn't it?'

On his twentieth birthday Mark had to endure a visit from his father. *The Devil's Disciple* had ended its Broadway run, and Niven, lured by the chance of working with James Garner, had signed for a series of guest appearances in a television series. Before leaving for Los Angeles he flew down to the Bahamas. A loving father, he felt guilty that he hadn't given his son a better start in life, and he was full of suggestions.

Mark couldn't return to Columbia, but didn't he want to continue his studies back in England? "I'd send you over and support you until you get your degree," he told Mark. "You might try for Oxford. What about the Sorbonne? You have the languages, you could go practically anywhere. How about Bologna? You want to go to Rome? You can study in Rome and I can send you a check every month. Your dad is almost a star, making pots of money. For God's sake, take advantage of me while I'm in demand!"

"I wish you would stop worrying about me," Mark kept saying. "It's my life, you can't live it for me."

"A few more years on this island and you'll never amount to anything but a hotel clerk. Do you want to say *yessir* all your life? I wouldn't mind, but will you be content with that?"

"Please, Dad, I don't like to see you upsetting yourself."

"This friend of yours, Eshelby — he's quite a bright fellow, he seems to know what he's talking about — he says you will go bald if you're always in the water."

"I'll find my ship long before that." Mark was careful to say nothing about his headaches and dizzy spells and to keep his shirt buttoned so that his father wouldn't get hysterical about his patchy skin.

"What scares me most," his father told him at the airstrip before boarding the small plane for Nassau, "is that you'll realize yourself that this is stupid, but you'll carry on just out of stubbornness. Don't get trapped by your pride."

Up to that time Mark had been diving in the shallow waters around the atolls and fringe reefs, but after his father's visit he decided to try his luck where there was the greatest danger — on the Atlantic side of the Long Reef. Risking more, he felt he might gain more.

He had been diving there without success but without trouble for weeks when he was caught one afternoon by a sudden powerful swell, one of those immense deep waves which are set off by tremors of the sea floor and crisscross the oceans at the speed of express trains. The swell hurled him away from the reefs, spun him around, and flung him over an underwater precipice. Totally disoriented, he only knew that he went below fifty feet, because the pressure of the water above him slapped his wet suit to his body as tightly as his own skin. Floating upside down without knowing it, he made a desperate lunge toward what he thought was the surface, and dived farther down into the depths. The shock of the darkness and cold made him frantic, and still not knowing what he was doing, he plunged deeper, as if he meant to come up at the other end of the world. Luckily, a stab of sobering pain made him turn around. From dark, cold night he kicked his way back into the daylight: after a while he could see fish. Steering himself in the direction where there seemed to be more of them, he could soon make out the vague outlines of coral hillocks, as if the time was just before dawn. Farther up it was midday, the coral sparkled in sharp colors of bluish white and dark red, and then he saw the sandy plateau where his boat was anchored. He had a surge of joy as he felt that the water was warm again, but he had come up too quickly, and he passed out.

He was out for minutes or seconds, he would never know how long, until an inner panic, a belated sense of danger, brought him back into consciousness. At first he thought the trouble was the pain in his hands; he was still clutching the underwater casing of his camera with a convulsive grip. While he flexed his fingers, he realized what was bothering him. All the fish were gone. The scintillating, bustling crowd had disappeared, sent fleeing by some distant vibration, some current of alarm: the sea was empty.

In this eerie stillness, two wide, flat heads emerged from the murk, heads nearly three feet wide, with rows of spikes as sharp as needles in their gaping mouths, and no eyes at all. Only as they moved closer, flapping their huge masses left and right (bodies at least twelve feet long, movements as quick and easy as a man snapping his fingers) did he see that there were eyes like knobs at the ends of the grotesque head lobes — worse, the eyes were seeing him.

The two hammerheads sailed past.

Paralyzed by fear, Mark needed time to loosen his muscles and turn around to look for the anchorline again. When he finally turned, one of the sharks reappeared and came straight toward him. At a couple of yards' distance it came to a sudden stop, settling into a state of total immobility, characteristic of hammerheads before they attack their prey.

In an automatic gesture of self-protection, just to put something between himself and the shark's hideous mouth, Mark thrust his camera straight at the rows of horrifying teeth and froze with his arms outstretched. 'You won't get me!' was his first thought, the stubbornness which had kept him going still intact.

There is nothing in the world as vile and loathsome as a hammerhead shark. Mud-colored and misshapen, it looked as if it was sweating shit and piss through its skin — a huge piece of floating excrement. Mark thought he smelled the stench, even though he was breathing through his tank. The hammerhead was putrefied, yet it was alive and powerful, with a curved mouth made for shredding flesh: it was as if death had a mouth.

The horror changed Mark in an instant. He understood what he had never understood before: he had to yield, there had to be an end.

He had messed up his life, but it no longer mattered. His wishful thoughts about the treasure and Marianne's return were sheer madness. She had forgotten him. This had hurt him, but no more — he let her go.

He knew instinctively that when the hammerhead attacked he was bound to be dead within sixty seconds, within ninety seconds at the most, and it came to him with the force of revelation that he could stand any pain for that long. It would be quick and it would solve everything. This certainty filled him with a peculiarly blissful sense of relief such as he had never before experienced.

Only a few seconds passed before the hammerhead moved again, but Mark still had time to wish that he could go back and tell people, go on television and tell everybody, that dying was easy, it was glorious, it was like getting out of a jam! He had never known such a sense of well-being. It was as if some enormous burden had been lifted from every inch of his body, and only now that he was free of it did he realize what a crushing load it had been. He was so conscious of this sudden freedom from weight, he couldn't get over it.

'So that was the burden of life!' he thought.

Friends

. . . without whom
this world would smell like what it is, a tomb.
SHELLEY

M ARK wasn't aware that he was still holding his camera in his outstretched hands, but when the shark moved, it bumped against
the plastic casing. Then it tilted its enormous head and glided off; the
swell in its wake hit Mark in the stomach.

Disgusted with his Calypso-Nikonos touched by the hammerhead, Mark
threw it away and watched it drift down and settle into the seaweed on
the bottom. In a state of shock, dying one minute, living the next, he
felt more alive than ever before — it seemed to him that even his vision
had improved. He thought he could make out the waving branches of
seaweed some thirty feet below. Almost hypnotized by the waving motion of everything around him and below him, he had to make a painful
effort of will to turn and let himself float up to his boat.

"You seen the sharks?" Coco asked as he lifted the oxygen tank from
Mark's shoulders. "I started the motor to make some disturbance."

Becoming aware of the sound of the idling engine, Mark unfastened
his weight belt in a slow, deliberate manner, but then flung his arms
around Coco and kissed him passionately on both cheeks. "You saved
my life!"

"Hey, you crazy? You is wet!"

Grabbing Coco by the shoulders, Mark began shaking him.

"Sit down, crazy man!"

"We must love one another, Coco," Mark begged him urgently. It
had to be done right away.

"You's turning over the boat! Sit down!"

Deflated by Coco's harsh voice, Mark dropped his arms, unzipped his
wet suit halfway down his chest, and lay down in the bottom of the boat.

Then he sat up again abruptly. "Coco, you can't imagine — that thing down there — we mustn't be too hard on each other."

"I's not hard, I saved your life! I's easy, man."

Mark laughed. "No, you're not easy, but that's all right. You're always talking as if you were mad at me, and you don't hide how stupid you think I am, but I don't mind. I know you lost a lot of beach land, and that's terrible. You've had a hard time and you've got a bad temper — you need somebody to abuse. I can take it."

"Say, what happen down there?" asked Coco, getting curious.

Mark answered by shaking his head. He looked at the sea around him the way a soldier looks at a battlefield after the shooting stops, then began to shiver.

"What happened?"

"One of them bumped its nose against my camera."

"Hey, you should have took a picture of it!"

"Yeah."

"Where's your camera?"

Shrugging, Mark turned from the sea. As he was getting out of his wet suit, he noticed his diving knife, which he wore in a sheath strapped to his leg, so that he could cut himself free if he got entangled in seaweed or coral. "I forgot about my knife!" he cried out. "I could have used it if I'd remembered I had it on me!"

"You's lucky you didn't. Knives makes sharks really-truly mad."

It was still morning, but Coco saw there would be no more diving that day and headed for shore.

"My God, what's wrong?" asked Eshelby, alarmed, when Mark burst into the camera shop, wild-eyed, pale under his tan and shaking all over. "You look like you nearly drowned."

Mark gaped. "How did you know? That's fantastic. I'd completely forgotten about it. You're right, I nearly drowned too!"

"What do you mean, *too*? What else?"

"I looked into a hammerhead's mouth."

Eshelby lifted a chair over the counter for him. Ignoring the chair, Mark kept walking about and shaking his head in amazement. "It's brilliant of you to guess about the drowning. You have these uncanny insights. That's why I like our conversations. Actually, that's why I dropped by — I wanted to tell you how much I appreciate our talks, even if I don't show it. A good talk means a lot to me. And you probably don't think so, but I remember what you say." He sat down, but his eyes kept jumping. "Oh, yes, I nearly forgot, I've been meaning to tell you — you should read about San Martín, he founded the National Library of Peru, you know. And he wasn't a republican like Bolívar!" he added, straining his forehead, determined to carry on a serious conversation the way a drunken man is determined to walk straight. "I used to think that a man who rebelled against the Spanish crown would be a republican, but no, he was for constitutional monarchy. He argued that people need somebody they can identify with and look up to all the time — but that person shouldn't have any power because he's bound to abuse it. They used to tell us the same thing in school in England, but I thought that was just because they have a queen."

"My dear boy, you're worn out. *Really-truly* exhausted. You should have a nice long rest, and then sell your diving gear." .

Mark looked at Eshelby, tears welling up in his eyes. "You're the only person who cares what happens to me. You and Sarah. I didn't want to mention it — I didn't know how touchy you might be about it — but you're the first homosexual I ever really knew, and you're great."

Eshelby laughed and put his hand on Mark's shoulder for a moment — the maximum physical contact he allowed himself with his hetero-sexual young friend. "Well, I must pay you a compliment too. When I think of all the people who are willing to risk everybody else's life at the drop of a hat, it's quite something that you're so hell-bent on risking your own. Except that I can't figure out why. You tell me you don't even know whether a ship ever sank around here."

"I was lying," Mark confessed. "But I was lying in self-defense. If the word gets around, people will keep tabs on me, and as soon as I find my sunken ship they'll go and dive where I've been diving. They'll pick the wreck clean before I can even organize the salvaging." He raised his hand in warning. "So don't say anything to anybody. Please. Seventeen tons of gold bullion are no joke. A lot of people were murdered for what I'm looking for."

Eshelby recoiled in mock horror. "Heavens! I wish you hadn't told me, then!"

"Hey, listen!" Mark exclaimed, forgetting whatever else was on his mind. "Did you ever hear any of the songs about San Martín? You know, they have songs about him all over South America — and even poor Indian laborers who can't read or write know them. I'll sing you one, listen —

> *Nuestra Señora de Cuyo*
> *Contempló la cruzada de los Andes*
> *Y bendijo el General San Martín*
> *El más grande entre los grandes . . ."*

He interrupted himself, cutting the air with his arm. "By the way, I know it's over between me and Marianne."

"Yes, it's a pity she never comes to the island anymore," Eshelby sighed in sympathy. "That's the trouble with rich people — they don't have to go to a place just because they own it."

"I didn't make any impression on her. If she liked me she would have understood me. It's over," he repeated, shaking his head. "I'm not going to force myself on anybody."

"Look here, I don't believe in running to doctors for every little thing, but you should consider yourself sick. If I were you I'd go right home to bed and stay there. You're a brave lad, but we're going to the desk now, get you a tranquilizer, and you're going to your room to sleep."

Next morning, having slept nearly twenty hours and feeling completely rested, Mark set out again with Coco for the Long Reef. They anchored the *Ile Saint-Louis* on the Atlantic side of the reef, and Mark got into his gear. He was just about to let himself fall backward from the diving platform into the sea when he changed his mind, straightened himself up and flapped his way over to the ladder. He couldn't get down the steps in his flippers, so he flapped back over to the diving platform and tumbled into the water. But instead of going down he swam around to the ladder and clung to it, shaking violently.

Coco watched him with a wary look, waiting for him to stop shaking. "Hey, what is it?" he finally asked.

Mark took out his mouthpiece. "It's my muscles."

"Shit, you is scairt."

"I'm scared out of my mind."

"You don't want to be no coward, Mark. If you scares now, you's always scairt to go down."

"They have rows of teeth like a shredding machine. They slice you up, Coco. You haven't seen them."

"Hell, you got me here!" said Coco in a cheery voice, beginning to worry about his five dollars an hour. "If I sees sharks I jus' starts the motor again. It scairt them away yesterday."

"What if it doesn't work today?"

"You's takin risks every day, isn't you?" asked Coco.

"That's true."

Still shaking, Mark put in his mouthpiece and made another attempt to lower himself into the sea, but could not let go of the ladder. In the end he removed one of his hands but only to take out his mouthpiece again. He held on to the ladder, in the sea up to his shoulders, at a loss what to do.

Coco watched him mournfully. "Listen, man, you doesn't want your camera back? You always says it was expensive."

"There's a lot of drifting sand there, Coco . . ."

"You doesn't remember where you dropped it? It's still there if the sharks didn't eat it. Try an remember where you dropped it!"

"Listen, I just remembered," Mark said at last, "it's the thirteenth today. I'd better not push my luck."

Coco was getting angry. "Hey, wait, you tellin me I is out of a job now? You ain't give me no notice!"

Mark climbed back into the boat and sat down, trying to steady his breathing. "I'll just skip today. I'll be back diving tomorrow."

"You is a man of your word?"

"Sure."

"You don't scare on me again? You is makin a promise?"

"Tomorrow."

Coco looked straight into Mark's eyes and spoke slowly, trying to hypnotize him. "OK, you knows it, I takes you out divin tomorrow. Tomorrow. You doesn't want to be no coward."

WALKING back to the staff house, exhausted by fear and hoping to recover his nerve with another long sleep, Mark passed Sarah in the garden. She thought he looked so depressed that she went to his room during her lunch hour to see him.

He was lying on top of his bed with his hands folded behind his neck, staring at the ceiling. She sat down beside him.

"What's wrong, luv?"

Mark took her hand and held it, but remained on his back and didn't answer.

"What happened? Are you still thinking of that hammerhead shark?"

"No," said Mark, continuing to stare at the ceiling as if staring at a different kind of death, futility. What if he couldn't go back into the sea? Was it all for nothing?

"You're still upset about yesterday. Let's talk about it, it'll help." She tried to start a conversation, asked him to tell her more about the shark, how he had lost his camera, but Mark was so unresponsive that she finally got up to leave.

This seemed to rouse him: he would not let go of her hand.

"I don't want you to go," he begged her. "I'd probably go mad if you left." He spoke with such conviction, his eyes burned with such a desperate flame, that she sat down again. "I'm a different person than I used to be. I understand how important friends are. You're a lovable, loving girl — please stay. You've always been good and generous to me — I couldn't have survived without you, I know it."

"Yes, friends are everything," Sarah agreed without false modesty.

With her free hand she began to unbutton her blouse, thinking of cheering him up in the best way she knew. As he helped her to undress they talked about the value of friendship, though Mark continued to look

198

depressed even when she had nothing on. She tucked up beside him, turned him over, placed his head on her breasts; she waited until she felt him growing against her belly, then lifted his chin to see how he felt. He had the same old sad look in his dark eyes.

She nearly lost heart — but he smiled when he entered her.

"There, you see!" she cried as she flung her legs apart and raised them triumphantly skyward. "Friends perk you up!" The acrobatics themselves were an act of consideration: she stretched her legs high and wide because her thighs were thick and she wanted to give him all the room he needed to go in deep and move around.

Mark was still inside her when it all came back to him — the day he first made love with Sarah and Marianne. He remembered his black mood that morning as he watched the waving fronds of the sea anemone seizing the squirrelfish on top of the oblong mound of sand. He remembered everything. The leap of the needle on his cesium magnetometer signaling metal — the sunlit channel between the two strips of star coral at the northern end of the fringe reefs, no more than a mile from the island. He even remembered paying no attention to the magnetometer needle or to the shape of the mound. It was shaped like a box, like a trunk. A chest. He felt as though he had two hearts, one on each side, pounding simultaneously.

As he fell back on the bed Sarah thought there was something wrong with him. She begged him to start taking care of himself, to grow up, to quit this childish game of treasure hunting. It was silly, dangerous, pointless.

"You're right," said Mark contritely, certain now of his triumph. "It's time for me to see reason!"

He walked Sarah to the lobby, then ran down to the harbor.

"Are you taking your boat out?" asked the harbor master. "Coco says you had a scare yesterday and you'll never dive again."

"Maybe not," said Mark philosophically. "It's really scary up there at the Long Reef." He wanted everybody to remember where he had been diving every day for the past few weeks; once the word got out that he had found a treasure ship, he wanted would-be raiders to look for it in the wrong place. "But I might take up boating. It's too hot."

"Yes, our August heat is the worst," said the harbor master. He was a jovial, husky Orkney man who prided himself on his rare O blood-type, which he said proved that he was descended from the ancient Atlantic people. "Hammerhead, was it? Coco says he chased it away for you. I had a run-in with a hammerhead myself once . . ."

"Think I'll go out and catch some breeze," Mark said as soon as he could get away without seeming to be in a hurry.

He headed his boat northward, and only when he could no longer be seen from the harbor did he make a wide turn south again. The detour took him half an hour. Was he covering his tracks for nothing? Was he going around in circles for another oil drum?

There was no oblong-shaped mound of sand in the sunlit channel formed by the two strips of star coral. The sea floor had changed many times in sixteen months, with the tides and currents shifting the sand. Mark could see no sea anemones or mounds of any kind. What he saw was a ship's bell, a broken spar and a completely uncovered ancient sea chest. There was no wreck in sight, so he swam through an opening in the coral wall and descended into a rocky valley, and there he saw the hulk — or rather, the wreck of a wreck, propped against the steep slope of a coral hill, its prow half buried in the sand. The shape of the vessel was discernible only from stem to midship, where she had broken in two; the rest had fallen away, and the fragments were wedged between large coral rocks of various heights, overgrown with tall weeds. Mark rose to the surface to check where he was in relation to his boat, and looking down at the wreck site from above, could make out only a dark hollow among the rocks and thick vegetation. The coral hill rose right to the top in jagged peaks which would have ripped open even a small boat; the wreck was protected not only from the currents but also from human curiosity. Diving down again, he checked his depth gauge. It was only sixty-seven feet at the bottom and he could still see, though not well enough. It was simpler to take a look first at the chest that lay in the shallower and sunnier channel.

Mark dislodged the chest easily enough, using his knife as a lever, and carried it over to the shadow that his boat cast on the sand. On the bottom the chest felt as it it weighed nothing, but as he floated upward it grew heavy and he had to kick his way to the top. He could hardly edge it over the lowest rung of the ladder, though this was still under-water, and when he tried to lift it one step higher it slipped from his grasp, right back down to the bottom. Back on the boat he took off his weight belt and tanks, drew a long, deep breath of real air, and dived down to snatch up the chest and bring it up at one go. This time he succeeded in propping his burden against the third rung of the ladder and panted there for a few moments, his head above water, before giving the chest another shove that toppled it over the gunwale. As it crashed into the bottom of the boat it fell apart. Mark climbed back into the boat, sat down and watched his arms and legs shaking by themselves. 'Here I am, shaking again,' he thought.

When he could move he began to clear away the debris, gathering up the pieces of crumbling wood encrusted with shells and coral and throw-ing them over the side. He picked up a blackened metal object that hadn't yet rusted away completely and looked at it carefully from every angle — was it the lock from the chest? — trying to postpone the terrible moment of letdown. Finally he grabbed an oddly shaped slab of soot and began rubbing away the sludge. When he raised the thing to look at it, he held in his hand a gold filigree cross flashing with emeralds. He counted them and then counted them again: there were seven. Some smaller black lumps became jewels and gold reales, as fresh and bright as when they were minted in Spain in the reign of Carlos IV. A long solid mass, washed clean and wiped with the deck cloth, turned into a spotless gold replica of the Madonna in the Cathedral of Lima.

Intense joy has the same effect on the body as intense pain — expecting to be happy, Mark was overcome with nausea. His nerves, his glands, his bowels could not tell what sort of news it was that put them under such unbearable pressure: he was shaken up in the same way as if he had just learned that he was about to be hanged, drawn and quartered. He leaned over the side of the boat and vomited.

When he raised his head again he stared at the sky as if it hadn't been there before, remembering the sky over Toledo the day he saw the city floating in the haze, the day he vowed to himself that he would find the *Flora*. Thinking of all the things that could have gone wrong over the years but had not, he marveled at the strange way everything had turned out for the best. He thought fondly of Vice-President Humphrey, of the university officials who had expelled him from Columbia, of General Hershey, who had drafted him into the army. Hadn't they all helped to set him on the right path? His heart filled with humble gratitude. As soon as he got to Nassau he would send cables to his father and mother, the same message to them both: THANK YOU FOR BRINGING ME INTO THE WORLD — THE COUNT OF MONTE CRISTO. The cable to Marianne would read: PLEASE COME BACK — HAVE GIVEN UP TREASURE HUNTING FOR GOOD — WILL NEVER AGAIN LOOK FOR ANYTHING BUT YOU — MARK.

But this was later in the day.

He sat in his boat for a long, long time, unable to rouse himself from his blissful stupor, staring at the gold Madonna.

Those who are familiar with the original, or have seen one of the gold replicas from the *Flora* which enrich most of the great museums of the world today, will know that the Madonna of Lima is an Indian child-bride, with a small, defenseless face and a trusting smile. Mark smiled back at her. There was a God after all, and He was a friend.

A Very Expensive Lecture

How wonderful life is! Lending
substance to airy nothings, it brings
our childhood dreams to pass.

                    THOMAS MANN

"BELIEVE me, Mr. Niven, if you knew anything about taxation you would consider yourself lucky to be taxed in the Bahamas," said the Chief Valuation Officer of the Ministry of Finance, Nassau's top she-bureaucrat reigning in a top-floor office of the new Treasury Building. "We're nothing if not fair, ask any of our white people. We have tax refugees here from all over the world. Naturally, you can't expect to keep everything. The state must have its share, Mr. Niven, but once you satisfy me I won't ask for more." She flashed a smile at him across her desk to suggest that such a handsome young man had no reason to give way to suicidal despair. Having earned her bachelor's degree at the University of South Florida, her master's degree at the University of Toronto and her doctorate at the London School of Economics, Dr. Mavis Rolle had the playful authority of a pretty woman with the right qualifications and a big job; she could crush a man and flirt with him at the same time.

Mark sat between his lawyer and his bank manager, staring at Dr. Rolle with a fixed look. He was too stunned to protest, while the lawyer and bank manager knew better than to start arguing too soon with the Chief Valuation Officer of the Ministry of Finance.

"I'm being truly generous to you, Mr. Niven," she assured him in that soft, warm, lilting voice which is the best music of the Bahama Islands. "You'd fare far worse in any of the overdeveloped countries." Her eyes glittered and her fingers floated in the air as she pronounced the words *overdeveloped countries*. Dr. Rolle wore no jewels but she liked to display her gems of wit. "Most people in this world have to contend with more taxes than you could count! And that's people on the poverty line — salesgirls, bus drivers, poor people. Income tax right off their wages, then taxes on everything they buy or use. Sales tax, excise taxes, entertainment tax, road tax, property taxes, local taxes — they're taxed at work, they're taxed at home, and they're taxed when they go out to have some fun. People who are too poor to pay income tax at all pay at least as much as forty percent of their welfare checks back to the state in indirect taxes. I understand you grew up in Europe, Mr. Niven, so you know about the European Economic Community — they put what they call a value-added tax on top of every other tax. You not only pay that yourself, you also have to collect it from everybody who does business with you. If you fail to collect it, they put you in jail. You work as a tax collector for the government, free of charge, or they lock you up. That's not even taxation, Mr. Niven, that's forced labor. Now you do fare better with us, don't you?''

"Dr. Rolle, what does it matter how they tax in other countries?'' pleaded Mark's Bahamian lawyer, Franklin Darville, a handsome, lively, fat man in his thirties, stretching out both his arms in a theatrical gesture of supplication. "Leave that kind of argument to us lawyers. We can justify anything by comparing it to something worse. You're too fine a person to stoop to that sort of trick. The most atrocious crimes — and I mean the most atrocious crimes — can be made examples of shining virtue *by comparison.''* He dropped his arms, overwhelmed by his own eloquence, then drew himself up and lowered his voice to express the depth of his indignation. "Our own Abandoned Wreck Act of 1964 allotted only twenty-five percent to the Treasury.''

"We couldn't take the 1964 Act as our guide in this particular case.''

"Why not in this particular case?''

"There's too much involved,'' she explained with the calm air of authority which makes brazen remarks sound reasonable.

Thomas Murray, manager of the Nassau branch of the Royal Bank, entered the argument in an almost apologetic manner. "It appears that the salvaging of the wreck will have to be quite a serious undertaking,'' he sighed. "You might perhaps take this into consideration when setting the levy.'' A tall, bony Scottish Canadian with a narrow head and a commanding nose, Mr. Murray had the tentative, self-effacing manner of a man who managed billions of dollars and knew how touchy people were about money. "Mr. Niven has all but concluded the leasing of a special barge which is going to cost him, crew and all, sixty thousand dollars a week. He'll need professional divers, expensive equipment — the insurance alone I'm afraid could be in the region of four hundred thousand . . .''

"There will be bank charges, legal costs . . .'' interjected the lawyer, as much to warn his client as to argue on his behalf.

All the fun left Dr. Rolle's face as she listened. With professionals she was professional: she concentrated on looking unimpressed. "I don't see how you gentlemen can raise the question of expenses at all," she said dryly, tapping the files with her fingertips for emphasis. "Your own people at the bank, Mr. Murray, estimate that the cross Mr. Niven has already recovered is worth seven hundred and fifty thousand dollars! All the newspapers I read say that the cargo of that ship is worth at least three hundred million. And it's all there, according to Mr. Niven. There are several fortunes here — plenty for everybody. So what are we arguing about? Surely, gentlemen, you don't wish to dispute that I'm leaving Mr. Niven more than enough?"

"Just as you say, Dr. Rolle," exclaimed the lawyer. "There are several fortunes here, several fortunes, but Mr. Niven found them all!"

"What point are you trying to make, Mr. Darville?" Dr. Rolle asked with a hint of exasperation. The clearest things were obscure to her if they didn't prove her right.

Mark was petrified. He wanted to speak but he couldn't move his tongue. What did she mean, she would leave him more than enough? If he had been interested in enough, he would never have started to look for the *Flora* in the first place. And how could *she* leave him any part of *his* ship? A possessive husband advised not to worry about the number of lovers his wife had because they left him more than enough of her could not have been more insulted or bewildered.

"Of course, what Dr. Rolle says is perfectly true," Thomas Murray ventured to argue by way of partial agreement, "Mr. Niven would be taxed more frequently elsewhere. If he sold his find and invested the money, he would have to pay capital gains tax, investment tax — I wouldn't dispute that. Some European countries are talking about adopting an annual wealth tax as well, which could add up to quite a bit in Mr. Niven's case, considering how young he is. And there would be an inheritance tax, eventually. On the other hand, we don't know what's going to happen to Bahamian tax laws either, so it might not be altogether unreasonable to argue that the initial tax perhaps ought not to be quite so high."

The Chief Valuation Officer saw no merit in all this. She wasn't in the habit of conceding anything. She was two women: she had a slim face, graceful neck, small breasts, slender arms, long delicate fingers, but she was heavy below the waist, spreading out monstrously, no doubt from sitting at her desk all day, broadening her power base. As a vulgar but possibly true saying has it, big shots have big asses, and Dr. Rolle sat on hers immovably.

She softened only when she switched back to Mark with a sympathetic smile to show him whose side she was on. "Believe me, Mr. Niven, most governments would keep at you until you were destitute. And if you were so clever that somehow you managed to hold on to something

. . . Good Lord, they would take that something away from you when you died, so you couldn't pass it on to your children. Here you pay a levy and that's the end of it. What you're left with is yours to keep. It's *yours*. It will always remain yours. We don't have income tax, capital gains tax, investment tax, inheritance tax. Our local taxes are the lowest in the world. There's only one government you have to live with, and it's a small one. We go easy on you while you live, and we leave you alone when you die." She gave Mark a mischievous look which had nothing to do with death or taxes. Her quick glances, her smiles, her warm lilting voice carried the conviction that black was beautiful, sex was beautiful, intelligence was beautiful, and power was the most beautiful thing of all. "Truly, Mr. Niven, if you think about it a little bit, you won't find a sixty percent levy so vexing!"

She raised her long delicate fingers from the files to demonstrate that a sixty percent levy had no weight.

THE lawyer and the bank manager kept raising objections, and Dr. Rolle dwelled on her own points; they argued at their leisure, discussing every aspect of the problem, repeating themselves, voicing every idea that came into their heads, as people do at conferences, chatting on time well paid. In the end, however, Mark's bleak silence began to slow down the conversation. He sat hunched over in his chair as if he felt the heavy hand of the Treasury on his shoulder.

Darville put his arm around his rigid client to involve him, introducing his very flesh and blood in evidence. "Look, Dr. Rolle — a while back Mr. Niven had a really-truly close look at some sharks. Now nobody from the Treasury was there to be scared with him, were they? So how could the Treasury profit more from his troubles than he does himself? I'm saying what you could be saying, Dr. Rolle — Mr. Niven enriched the world with these treasures, and he did it all without the help of our beloved government! If it hadn't been for his work, his perseverance, his bravery, there would be nothing for you to tax away, nothing to put your levy on!"

Dr. Rolle heard him out with an expression of moral rectitude; she knew that the lawyer was bound to make more out of this than she would, unless being firm about the levy got her a cabinet post. "You talk as if Mr. Niven had risked his life just for the money," she commented, assuming the patronizing sanctimoniousness so characteristic of public officials regardless of nationality, race, color, creed or sex. "Unlike you gentlemen, I don't believe that Mr. Niven is motivated by greed, I can tell that he isn't the sort of person who would want to keep all this wealth to himself. I'm sure he appreciates that the wreck lies in Bahamian waters and is the property of the Bahamian government. He wouldn't want to deprive the Bahamian people of their heritage."

Unaware of the horror she inspired, she tried to revive Mark with another quick smile. "I can tell, gentlemen, that in his heart of hearts, Mr. Niven believes in social justice. He's more sensible than you make him out to be. He doesn't strike me as a parasitic personality."

Her last remarks stung Mark to life — he raised his head and stared at her with burning eyes. They all turned toward him expectantly.

"It's not fair, it's not fair, it's too high," prompted Darville.

"Why only sixty percent?" Mark asked hoarsely. "Why not more? Why don't you take it all?"

The Chief Valuation Officer locked up her smiles. If Mr. Niven didn't want a license on terms acceptable to the Treasury, she would have no choice but to impound the gold statuette and the emerald cross in view of the fact that Mr. Niven had removed these treasures from Bahamian waters without a license. And to make sure that Mr. Niven would not take anything further from the wreck, she would propose to her colleagues that he be deported from the Bahamas as an undesirable alien.

These threats did not have their desired effect; Mark was too deeply offended to give in. "I'll leave it with the fish," he shouted. "The Treasury can have it all. The whole hundred percent! All you have to do is find it. And you never will. If I can't have it, you won't have it either."

"I guess here is where I should move for an adjournment," interrupted Darville. "We need some time to consider our position."

Dr. Rolle brushed the air with her fingers. "As you wish . . . I understand that there are a lot of divers around the reefs where Mr. Niven was diving. Since I have issued no salvaging license to anyone, they have a perfect right to claim whatever they find. If Mr. Niven doesn't want a license on terms acceptable to the Treasury, I'm quite content to grant one to whoever comes next. Once those divers pinpoint the site and get a license, the wreck will be all theirs."

"You mean forty percent of it," Mark corrected her, with the flicker of a malicious smile.

"Why, of course, Mr. Niven," she shot back with triumphant politeness. "Each one of us owes something to society. No man is an island — life is not just take, take, take!"

"DID you hear about the Miss Secretary contest we had here a few months ago?" asked Darville as the three men left the Treasury Building and were making their way back to Thomas Murray's office at the Royal Bank. "I know it's no news to you, Tom, but I thought I'd tell Mr. Niven about it — it might give him a bit of a laugh." The air had cooled a bit while they were at the Treasury, and the lawyer was happy: he could still smell the rain and he had a tale to tell that he was thinking of submitting to *Playboy* magazine.

They were walking along Bay Street, the main street of the Bahama Islands, where investment banks of all nations are flanked by fish markets, twenty-four-hour nightclubs and souvenir shops festooned with straw baskets. There was a constant flow of humanity in shorts and business suits; in Nassau even the most important people go about their business on foot.

"What has social justice got to do with it?" asked Mark, arguing with Dr. Rolle in his head.

"The first meeting with Treasury people is always difficult," replied the bank manager, bending his imposingly tall figure to make his reassuring observation from a less forbidding height.

"Believe it or not," continued Darville, persisting in his efforts to change the subject, "I was a member of the lucky jury which picked Miss Secretary of the Bahama Islands. At one point each of the finalists was asked what she thought was the most important quality of a good secretary. They all said something like punctuality, neatness, tact, knowing how to keep intruders away from the boss — you know the kind of thing. Then came this lovely girl, secretary to a minister, about twenty, twenty-two, very pretty, very shy — very shy and soft-spoken, you could hardly hear her. She ducked her head, kind of hid behind her long, thick eyelashes, then let us in on the secret: 'The most important quality of a good secretary,' she whispered, 'is *being passionate!*' "

"I always thought that depriving people of the fruits of their labor was exploitation, not social justice!" said Mark.

"I would have given the crown to Miss Passionate, but the other judges voted for an efficient old hag instead," the lawyer went on somewhat stiffly; he had never told the story before without getting a laugh. "All the best secretaries are old hags — mine is a great old hag."

"Up north, male secretaries seem to be the fashion," commented Murray. "I wonder what is the most important quality of a male secretary."

"Staying power," quipped Darville. "The male's pull is staying power."

Mark stopped abruptly in the middle of the sidewalk as if struck by mental lightning. "You mean that girl was secretary to a member of the Bahamian government? Whom does she work for? The Minister of Finance?"

"Now, Mr Niven, no lawyer in the world would be foolish enough to answer such a question!"

"So that's what I owe to society, financing government sex!" Mark exclaimed, oblivious of the stares of passers-by. "No man is an island, ministers must have company, life is not just take, take, take — life is screw, screw, screw!''

"Listen, that's the least harmful thing they can do with your money," Darville said almost angrily, offended by Mark's outburst, which he took for a racial slur. "White governments take your money and use it to screw *you!* Who builds all those nuclear submarines pissing heavy water into the sea right around these islands? So don't you go and begrudge Miss Passionate to an old man!''

"I thought you said anything can be justified by comparison!''

Thomas Murray was greatly relieved when he had them inside his private office at the bank, out of everyone else's hearing. He suggested the possibility of compromise.

Mark seemed to want to try out each chair in the office, which in deference to local handicrafts was fitted out with rattan furniture. Sitting down, standing up, he was intractable. Darville's harmless little story had incensed him beyond reason. What maddened him most was the thought that he had lost Marianne — there was no response to his cable — and all because he was in a hurry to contribute to an aging politician's sex budget! He had told the loveliest woman on earth that they had *wasted six whole days* — the happiest days of his life — and now all he had to look forward to was the happiness of the Minister of Finance! He couldn't accept it. His lawyer and banker argued in vain the necessity of a prompt agreement with the Treasury, the danger of others finding the wreck; Mark treated them to bizarre arguments which had no bearing on his predicament. "Why should I give in?" he asked. "The United States was born out of a revolution against taxes!''

"If you didn't know it, you could never guess it," Murray remarked, attempting some light humor of his own.

"Mr. Niven," protested the lawyer, fed up with all the nonsense, "in the whole history of the world, I doubt that there was a single instance of anybody refusing tons of gold and sackfuls of diamonds.''

"Do you think so?" asked Mark, taken aback for a moment. "Yes, I suppose you must be right, I'd be the first!" he added with flashing eyes, inflamed by the idea of doing something no one else had ever done in human history.

"You'd really-truly regret it," Darville assured him.

"My luck will hold!" said Mark, willing himself to hope. "No one else is going to find the wreck, and you'll see, Dr. Rolle will realize that they can't get any of it without me. They'll come down, they have no choice, they'll be reasonable!''

Darville shook his head. "Heaven's sakes, Mr. Niven, I hate to disappoint you, but when there is a dispute between an individual and the government, it's the individual who has no choice. We'll try to get the levy down a few points, but don't get your hopes high.''

208

Mark shrugged defiantly. "As long as no one else can touch my ship, I'll be happy."

"You mean to say forty percent is worse than nothing?" Darville asked, no longer bothering to check his exasperation. "Do you have a special way of counting?"

"I went through hell, I won't let myself be robbed!" Mark vowed, and sensing tears in his eyes, turned toward the window. "I won't let them cut me up!"

The lawyer made a courtroom show of astonishment, amazement, incredulity. "Who's cutting you up? I didn't see any knives at the Treasury — you're not bleeding. Nobody's touching you, Mr. Niven. We're not even talking about you. You're a person, a human being — we're discussing the disposition of inanimate objects lying at the bottom of the sea, miles and miles from here. So who is cutting you up?"

"I haven't risked my life for forty percent of anything!"

"Look, we'll do our best for you," Darville said threateningly, "but just between ourselves, speaking as your lawyer, I'm bound to advise you that even if *worst comes to worst* and you end up with only forty percent of three hundred million dollars, you'd better not complain out loud, because somebody might cut your throat! There — that's how you might find yourself cut up!"

THE signing of the salvaging agreement by the Bahamian Minister of Finance and Mark Alan Niven, resident of Santa Catalina, took place in the conference room of the Treasury Building eight days later. It was a ceremonial occasion attended by the Prime Minister and his entire cabinet, by high-ranking bureaucrats, bankers, lawyers, journalists, photographers, friends and other spectators. As Franklin Darville remarked, it was like the signing of a treaty on television. Miss Passionate was there, wearing a flowing Nina Ricci dress of pale apricot silk.

The ceremony was the culmination of a flurry of diplomatic activity. Darville had been negotiating with a political aide who offered to reduce the levy by five percent in return for a mere hundred thousand dollars' payment into a private account in New York. If the deal had gone through, a hundred thousand would have produced what was in effect a sixteen-million-dollar tax concession; a little bit of private money buys a lot of public money in most parts of the world. For his part, Thomas Murray had been meeting with the Minister of Finance, using the unconventional method of honest persuasion. But before these negotiations could come to anything, Prime Minister Bethel intervened to settle the matter personally. Prompted by a mysterious well-wisher, he ordered the Treasury to reduce the levy to fifty percent. According to the agreement, the licensee Mark Alan Niven had the right to salvage objects from the seabed within a 500-meter radius of a central point to be disclosed by the licensee at the commencement of salvaging. (Mark still refused to tell the authorities where the wreck lay.)

The government had *the right of first choice of any and all objects recovered up to fifty percent of their total dollar value.* This value was *to be determined by a committee of appraisers mutually agreed upon.*

There was also a clause stating: *the division of salvaging costs between the parties shall be a matter for further negotiation.*

"Remember, all this is only about things, inanimate objects!" Darville reminded his client in a warning tone at the signing ceremony.

"I know, I know."

Mark, wearing a suit and tie for the occasion, appeared carefree and content with his lot, carrying himself like a man who was counting his blessings, his fifty percent. While they were waiting for the arrival of the Prime Minister, he chatted with his lawyer and Eshelby. "Of course we all hate to be robbed, dear boy, but we must make an exception in the case of the government," Eshelby told him. Mark laughed heartily, in a good enough mood to appreciate a witty remark. Later, walking up to the dignitaries assembled around the long table covered with a green baize cloth, he listened respectfully to Prime Minister Bethel and chatted with everyone, even with Dr. Rolle.

"I don't blame you for our little argument, Mr. Niven," she told him sweetly. "Our problem was your inexperience. You're young, and diving was a happy-go-lucky occupation. You were a loner, an outsider, you didn't need to know much about anything. But it's different now, isn't it? A rich man is very much an insider, he's involved, he learns the rules — he has too much at stake."

"Yes, I'm learning fast," replied Mark with a determined air.

However, after signing the documents and watching Darville witness his signature, he walked away from the table with unsteady steps, and nodding to a reporter with a wan smile, collapsed unconscious on the floor.

"Good Lord, what on earth could be wrong with him?" Thomas Murray asked Darville as several people rushed to Mark's aid. "I trust it isn't possible for a twenty-year-old to have a heart attack."

"In his place I would die," replied the lawyer, who was to be the first to inflict on Mark the violence of a large bill, charging $241,204 for his services concerning the levy. "That ship is still at the bottom of the sea, and he's already lost half of it!"

Fame

Go where glory awaits thee!
And while fame elates thee,
Oh, still remember me!
THOMAS MOORE

THE cable Mark sent to Marianne the day he found the *Flora* was intercepted just like his twenty-three letters and ended up on her husband's desk.

Just then Kevin Hardwick was wasting very little time thinking about Mark. He was satisfied that he had found the right solution to his marital problem and it required no further action on his part. His wife had had a brief affair with a beach bum; they had made a fool of him, but he was getting his own back: she was unhappy. She was unhappy, and Vincenzo Baglione had promised to take care of the boyfriend. Hardwick's jealousy was like a dormant disease in those days: he had his bad moments, but on the whole he felt fine. He laid many women who crossed his path and mostly dined with his wife.

The obscene film lay half forgotten in an air-cooled safe concealed in the wall beside his desk. On the few occasions when he felt tempted to look at it again, he remembered how annoyed it had made him the first time and abandoned the idea. Why upset himself?

The only question was whether Baglione would keep his promise. By and large, he was inclined to trust him. The old mafioso seemed to be on the level: at another meeting in the sky, he announced the news of Masterson's fatal car accident and handed over the negative of the film, reporting that no copies had been found in Masterson's apartment or photo lab. When Hardwick had locked the negative in the safe with the only copy and crossed one of the three names off the list, he thought he could begin to forget the whole distasteful episode. At that time the anxieties produced by threats to his business were of far greater intensity than his anxieties concerning his personal life.

The environmental movement boosted the sales of his own waste-treatment systems, but neither the sixty-million-dollar-plus yearly turnover in HCI Clean Earth Products nor his nimbus as the enemy of acid rain could protect him from the public hysteria about pollution. Every week someone somewhere proposed a new law or regulation which would have forced him to wipe out HCI's profits simply to mollify people who seemed to think that if it weren't for chemicals they would live forever.

"We're up against crazies," he told a closed meeting of his top executives, urging them to pay more attention to public relations. "You can't be too careful with the kind of people who want it both ways. They want houses that won't burn, but they don't want asbestos. They want everything industry can produce, but they want it out of mother's milk. I'm not about to dismantle a worldwide company to please them, but we have to humor them somehow. Talk a lot about research. Much more research is needed before we can begin to judge whether anything is harmful or not . . ."

Such plain talk was of course for insiders only; in public Hardwick was far more circumspect than his competitors. He had never joined the militant faction of the Chemical Manufacturers Association whose spokesmen were making intemperate attacks on "meddlesome environmentalists", "the scare tactics of self-serving minorities", "exploitative, emotional TV commentators", etc. Hardwick belonged to that select group of company heads who preferred thinking to sounding off. In their creative inner life such men have more in common with philosophers, film producers or novelists than with accountants scanning balance sheets: they contemplate human nature and then gamble on their psychological insights.

When the World Health Organization published its report blaming between seventy and eighty percent of all cancers on man-made substances in the environment and a syndicated columnist used WHO's assertions to argue that cancer was "a problem of prevention, a political problem rather than a medical one", Hardwick decided to hit back not with a speech but with a $500,000 donation to the American Cancer Society. He was quite proud of the idea, hoping that it would buy HCI at least a million dollars' worth of peace, but still, it was a gamble. He donated the money on the condition that it be used to solicit further donations from the public with the advertisement HELP US FIND A CURE FOR CANCER! He reasoned that such advertisements might persuade people to worry less about minuscule quantities of this-and-that in their food and drink and start blaming cancer deaths on the failure of medicine to come up with a cure — and that any move in this direction made HCI's position stronger. Was he right? Did he judge the effect of the advertisements correctly? Or had he wasted $500,000? He would never be able to say for certain; he knew what he knew about the workings of the human mind and had to guess the rest.

Then there were all the legal problems, all the lobbying in Washington to attend to, all the university biologists whose research projects had to be funded if they were to produce useful results, all the executives he had to keep an eye on, all the people he had to fire and hire . . . how could a busy man be jealous?

He assumed — as it was the simplest thing to do, requiring the least of his time — that the beach bum would never be heard of again and that Marianne had forgotten all about her affair.

"Out of sight, out of mind," he found occasion to remark one evening, when the children had to be prodded into remembering their Grandfather Montgomery's birthday. "Absence kills all emotions."

"Too true!" seconded Marianne quite cheerfully, to his immense satisfaction.

Marianne was so certain that Mark had forgotten her that she stopped thinking she was beautiful. She still missed him, but whenever she became conscious of a deadly void in herself she thought of it as *maturity*. At twenty-four she felt her youth was all behind her, and she was relieved that Kevin showed no interest in her sexually. Mark was her last love; after her brief fling with politics, all that was left for her was to bring up her children and raise money for the Lyric Opera and the Chicago Symphony. Yet however mature she felt, her heart was still alive; it needed to express affection, love, passion. Ben could take all the love in the world, but Creighton began to complain that she hugged him too much and squeezed him too hard. She also developed a second crush on her big sister Claire and spent a lot of time talking with her on the phone.

THE cable arrived on Hardwick's desk the day before the discovery of the *Flora* became news, and Hardwick couldn't understand it. It was like a message from beyond the grave.

PLEASE COME BACK — HAVE GIVEN UP TREASURE HUNTING FOR GOOD — WILL NEVER AGAIN LOOK FOR ANYTHING BUT YOU — MARK

"How come he's still around, Vincenzo?" he muttered aloud. And how did the crazed, insolent nobody dare to assume that she would remember him after all this time? What made him so conceited?

Hardwick had a bad day and spent a restless night at home, alone in the house except for the servants.

The morning was worse. The story on the front page of the *Tribune* bothered him even more than the cable. He couldn't think of a multimillionaire as a beach bum. The actor's son was now a junior member of his own class. (Like most Americans, he thought of upper class as middle class with money.) Nor was it simply a question of money. Hardwick had to deal with too many vague and ineffectual employees not to appreciate performance. He liked doers, especially doers who knew what they were doing — people who delivered — achievers. This young Niven had to be good. 'So it wasn't a lie,' thought the jealous husband, remembering the first letter claiming that his rival had *finished him off* and his wife had promised to leave him. He read the papers at breakfast; the worst thought didn't hit him until he was in the car on his way to the office. The diver who found a treasure ship worth over three hundred million dollars was going to be famous! He was going to be on the news, on chat shows! He could turn Marianne's head even if they had never met before. Half the women in America were in love with guys they had seen on television. The thought that his rival could enter their bedroom at night and he couldn't even hit him, smash his face in, kick him in the balls, nearly drove Hardwick out of his mind.

It was a good thing Marianne was in London visiting her sister. He hoped she wouldn't come back for a while.

The security men at the executive entrance to the HCI Building were surprised that the boss, as a rule very friendly, didn't return their greeting.

'How will that bastard come across on TV?' he was asking himself. What did he look like? Hardwick had no clear recollection of him. He had to take another look at the record, study the facts. Passing all business on to his deputy, he locked the door to his office, took the film from the wall safe, and went into the screening room, where he latched the reel onto the projector and sat down to watch.

It was the beginning of madness.

There she was, his wife, walking about on the deck of the *Hermit,* with her lover beside her. Hardwick had expected the actor's son to look as he remembered him, a disgusting beach bum, but now the young man on the screen appeared handsome, intelligent, strong, athletic. Watching him, Hardwick involuntarily pinched his stomach with both hands to measure the fat. He was past thirty!

The handsome young man cupped Marianne's breast in his hand and she liked it. She smiled. She loved it.

Hardwick watched them walking, talking, laughing, touching, kissing, resting. They didn't seem to have a care in the world. They were rocked by the sea, warmed by the sun, cooled by the breeze; they were relaxed and happy. They slept like babes on the mattress. They weren't worrying about meeting a ten-million monthly payroll.

Then there was a cut and Hardwick saw his wife sitting naked on the mattress beside her sleeping lover, with her knees drawn up against her chest and her arms folded over her shins. After a while she turned around and bent over the handsome young man and lifted his limp prick with her tongue. Hardwick watched him grow in her mouth, watched them licking and fondling each other, watched the pleasure on their faces, and conceived an angry desire for his wife.

He wanted her right away, even if she was in London. After locking the film in the safe again, he picked up the phone and gave orders for the plane to be readied and his driver to come and take him to the airport.

He didn't let the masseuse touch him during the long flight across the Atlantic; he wanted his wife. He wanted her total submission. He wanted her to take his prick into her mouth and suck him off, and he wanted her to enjoy it.

MARIANNE'S sister Claire had left her nice but impotent husband and bought herself an Edwardian mansion on the Little Boltons, the kind of house a famous, well-paid singer could afford if she was also born rich, and had invited her sister to come over to London with the children and Joyce to "warm up the place" for her. Marianne was glad to go and to offer Claire moral support in starting her new life, but as it turned out, Claire Montgomery, who had sounded so depressed on the phone while she was married, now needed very little support, moral or otherwise. A buxom, florid, brown-haired beauty with the big chest of a singer, she stood firmly on her long slender legs and was absolutely delighted with her freedom, her concert at the Queen Elizabeth Hall and her unexpected affair with a visiting Italian tenor. She had also developed a peculiar kind of meanness which seems to be a side effect of happiness: she felt that everybody should be strong enough to take the truth and people were always better off knowing how things stood.

"You missed your chance, Bozzie," she told Marianne when they settled down for an all-night talk in the kitchen, drinking tea and discussing the news of Mark's find. "I mean your chance of helping him to do what he wanted to do. No man would ever forgive you for that."

"He certainly hates me," Marianne agreed bleakly. "The last time I saw him he looked at me as if he wanted to kill me."

"And now it's worse, he managed to succeed without you!"

Marianne's eyes turned red. "Yes. He didn't really need me, you know. He's strong, he knows his own mind, he's brave, he went diving among sharks on his own. He isn't just a handsome man with lovely skin."

"Oh, Bozzie, what possessed you to leave somebody like that! I don't have much experience in this, but I'm told that men who risk their lives are the best lovers. And to leave him for your husband . . . !"

"Kevin can't hurt me."

"And what about Mark? Did he beat you?"

"Mark could hurt me."

"Oh, Bozzie, don't be so *feeble!*" Claire pleaded in her deep contralto voice, taking her little sister's hand. "If another brave man comes along, grab him and hang on to him!"

"Yes, I let him down, and now it's too late to do anything about it," said Marianne, hoping Claire would contradict her.

"Well, I can't argue with you there, you were apart too long." Claire sighed regretfully. "If you'd broken up a couple of months ago, I'd say go and see him, board the next plane. But if you haven't heard from him for eighteen months, he's got over you. I don't want you to barge in on him and humiliate yourself for nothing. He must have had half a dozen girls by now. And after this . . . ! The sky's the limit. Listen, dear heart, I'm a romantic, I believe in falling in love, but I don't believe any man can fall in love with the same woman twice."

"You're not telling me anything I don't know," Marianne said dully.

IMAGINING Mark surrounded by young and beautiful women who had never told him to go to hell, Marianne fantasized herself into such a depressed state of mind that she was pleased as well as surprised when Kevin arrived and told her that he had come over to London on the spur of the moment because he missed her. With apologies to his sister-in-law, he took his wife out alone: to the Royal Ballet at Covent Garden and then to supper at Annabel's, a favorite haunt of the young royals of the day. And though they talked about a lot of things, neither of them mentioned the news of a treasure find near their island.

'She must have read about it,' Hardwick decided when he noticed that she had fallen silent and was staring moodily into her glass. "I've been wondering if we should do something different this winter," he suggested. "How about renting a farm in Kenya? The boys would love it."

"Marvelous!" exclaimed Marianne, brightening at the prospect of going somewhere far away. "How did you know I felt like a change?"

"I'm your husband," he said, with a grin that reminded her of Creighton.

"I guess that's true," she giggled. He was tall, impressive, easily the best-looking man in the room.

"This is how we first met, remember?" he murmured in her ear as he picked her up and carried her to the dance floor. "And you're still as light as a feather."

'What happened that you're noticing me again?' she thought of asking him, but didn't. Why spoil the evening? They danced close, he was feeling her breasts, and she began to think that maybe she wasn't altogether past it.

216

Kevin took her to his rooms at the Connaught, where she found free-sias and lily of the valley, her favorite flowers, in bowls and vases on all the tables. She let him seduce her, and tried to recapture with him the good times they had before the children were born. But it was no use: after a while everything died in her.

He had planned to wait until she had her orgasm, but sensing her growing dry, he pulled out and moved forward to kneel above her head. "Take it," he coaxed.

"Kevin, I can't breathe."

"Try. You should be nice to me, you'll miss me when you're in Kenya."

"I can't."

Hardwick got off, went to the bathroom and came back. "I washed it," he said, trying to take care of her next possible objection. He sounded like a man on the verge of murder.

By a great effort of will she submitted to his demands, and the grand romantic evening ended for her in a fit of coughing and choking.

She was ready for Africa.

A Loving Couple

. . . life in New York had removed
all his remaining scruples in matters of morality.
BALZAC

O N a wet October evening in New York, the millionaire art dealer
John Vallantine went to bed early with his wife to watch television, and catching a CBS interview with the finder of the *Flora,* decided to become seriously rich.

"I suppose he thinks he's done something special!" protested Shirley
Vallantine in the sharp voice of a thin woman with more nerves than
flesh; she had been irritated by one thing or another for over fifty years.
"It shouldn't be that easy to get rich. It's an insult to the poor!"

"Ssssshhh . . . !"

"People slave all their lives for nothing!"

"Sssshhhh . . . !"

"He's too young, he doesn't deserve it."

"He's all right," her husband said indulgently. "I'll act as agent for
him."

Fame brought Mark no more formidable adversary — Vallantine had
stolen his first million while still in his twenties. At the time he was
working as a graphic designer for a firm of stock promoters in his native
city of Montreal, and he hit upon an idea which turned out to be a gold
mine: he invented a gold mine in Nova Scotia and sold shares in it. A
born master of long-distance crime — the most difficult sort of crime to
detect or prosecute — he contrived to have his Cape Breton Gold shares
listed on the Montreal Stock Exchange for months, but promoted them,
through a few agents and a magnificent brochure, exclusively in Florida
and California. After this successful fraud, which wiped out the savings
of thousands of retired people, hastening their deaths, Vallantine rented
a yacht with a crew and took his wife on a cruise around the Greek islands, to get away from it all. On the trip chance brought him together

with a group engaged in looting temple ruins and burial sites in Greece and Asia Minor. They were just about to extend their operation to unguarded Italian churches, planning to cover up the theft of old paintings, statues, carvings and candlesticks by leaving behind clever copies, and Vallantine decided to get involved. Soon afterward he opened his gallery on 57th Street just east of Fifth Avenue. He referred to his past, if he had to, with the remark that like most New Yorkers, he came from somewhere else. An art dealer of excellent reputation, he was a pitiless thief and a receiver of stolen goods, but the goods were stolen on the other side of the Atlantic and were bought by the very best clients — museums, famous private collectors — and his gallery was often mentioned on the arts pages of newspapers, enhancing his good name. Moreover, he had an irreproachable attorney, William T. MacArthur — a former judge of the Supreme Court of the State of New York, former chairman of the judicial committee of the state Democratic Party and former vice-president of the New York Bar Association. This paragon of probity preferred to defend innocent men; few of his clients had ever been found guilty of anything in New York. He could provide Vallantine with the full protection of the law.

"I think I'll ask him for a six percent agency commission," said Vallantine as the program was interrupted by commercials.

"But we've never handled gold or diamonds," Shirley Vallantine objected, forgetting to take off her glasses, so that she looked at her husband with magnified eyes and magnified anxiety.

Vallantine played at being offended, raising and lowering his bushy gray eyebrows. "What do you mean, we've never handled gold?"

"That was different."

"And how!" the elderly and overweight art dealer exclaimed wistfully, heaving a deep sigh. "I'll never be that young again! I was just a kid, sowing my wild oats."

Now Vallantine made all sorts of deals, even some honest ones. In his best year he sold, among other things, a legitimately acquired Cycladic fertility idol; an ancient stone lion, lifted in the dead of night from Apollo's pride on the island of Delos, where it had been crouching in the high grass poised to leap for nearly two thousand five hundred years; Ghirlandaio's Saint John the Baptist taken from a little out-of-the-way church in Tuscany; two recently manufactured but supposedly ancient Mesopotamian oil lamps.

Pressed by the growing demand for everything old in an age when the present was being continually destroyed, Vallantine had been mixing, judiciously, some fakes with the genuine stolen goods. The Ghirlandaio was sold for one and a half million, the stone lion for $800,000, but he gave away the oil lamps at the low price of $5000 each. His crimes made him not only richer but also less vulnerable to suspicion. Most otherwise discerning museum curators were not alert enough to suspect that John Vallantine, whose business was worth several million dollars, and who was an educated and intelligent man besides, would run the risk of offering them fake odds and ends for the sake of five thousand taxable dollars which he manifestly did not need. It was the age of liberalism when people were taught to trust rich crooks by such foolish maxims as *the cause of crime is poverty*. Some of Vallantine's victims might have known better, but it did not make them any less vulnerable. There are ideas which color our thinking even though we know them to be untrue; so many falsehoods are drilled into us daily that it is impossible to remain uninfluenced by them. Those who kept hearing about the social causes of crime could not help expecting criminals to be poor devils or adventurers on the make — people who did not already have what they were after. No one would have suspected the president of the Vallantine Gallery of committing petty crimes — nor, for that matter, did anyone suspect him when he unloaded the stolen Ghirlandaio on an Arizona museum. 'Why should a millionaire run the danger of being caught and branded a thief, for any amount of money?' was the way his victims reasoned, if at all, failing to realize that the greed of practical men is as irrational as any other passion, and most financial crimes are committed for the same reason as the follies of love — for the inner satisfaction they bring.

Of course there was no possibility of getting caught, let alone being branded a thief. The copy of the stolen lion put in place of the original on Delos was well made, and the theft is yet to be discovered. The copy of the Ghirlandaio didn't turn out to be very convincing, but when the Italian government began to make inquiries in New York, the Vallantine Gallery had faultlessly forged documents to prove that they bought the painting from an untraceable Swiss agent. In case the trustees of the Arizona museum decided to give the painting back to the Italians, MacArthur offered on his client's behalf to partially compensate the museum for the loss of their $1,500,000 purchase price by handing over the $200,000 profit the Gallery had made as innocent middleman in this unfortunate affair. The good museum trustees, taking civic pride in Arizona's artistic riches, were not able to bring themselves to part with their Ghirlandaio, so Vallantine didn't actually have to give up any part of his $1,000,000 real profit on the stolen masterpiece, but the offer to return $200,000 was the sort of gesture which commands respect, confidence, the benefit of the doubt — or, at the very least, gains time.

In short, Vallantine's standing in the world was as good as any honest dealer's — better, for he was better off than most — and he had the right credentials and connections to show a professional interest in historic treasures. He had seen the headlines but hadn't paid much attention; it was only while watching the television interview that he learned the momentous news that the owner of all that wealth was young and on his own.

The Aberdeen terrier, Daisy, had been sleeping beside the bed, but as her master got up, she began to run around in circles, barking. The art dealer turned up the sound so that he wouldn't miss a word and shuffled over to his study for a memo pad to jot down a few reminders —

> *he always knew*
> *father — great actor*
> *favorite music — Mozart operas*
> *Così fan tutte*

After returning to bed and making a few more notes, Vallantine stretched out his arm across the space between the twin beds to offer the memo pad to his wife, who reached out for it with an impatient gesture. Taking a pen from the bedside table, she drew three large question marks on the pad and handed it back to him. The couple had slept in separate beds for well over a decade, but they were bound together by incessant discussions. Shirley Vallantine worked as her husband's assistant, and if they weren't talking, they were exchanging little notes.

"I don't like young men," she said as soon as there was another station break. "They don't want to be bothered with anybody over twenty-five. They think there's something wrong with you if you're middle-aged. Your hair is gray, and you're losing it too."

Vallantine rubbed the bald spot over his forehead, trying to stir up his brain. "Didn't you hear him say that his father is a great actor? He loves his dad, and his dad can't be much younger than we are — I can use that . . . I can use that in many ways!"

"But what about our lawsuits?" asked his wife, always loyal, always worried.

"We'll fly d . . . down there and I'll present him with a c . . . c . . . c . . . contract which will make us exclusive agents," replied Vallantine, something of his childhood stammer slipping back into his speech at the thought of his murderously expensive lawsuits.

"We'll waste a lot of time going down there, and then somebody will tell him that we're being sued by the Italian government because we took their precious painting, as if it was any use to anybody in a dark church, and then he'll call the whole thing off."

"You always say we ttt . . . took it," Vallantine chastised her good-naturedly, twisting his thick neck. "They *claim* we took it."

"I don't want you to put your heart into this."

"It's only a c . . . claim, an allegation."

"I know how you are. You'll go to a lot of trouble and expense, wear yourself out, and then he won't sign and you'll be depressed for months. You've already got your stammer back.''

"If they can't prove it in court, it didn't h . . . happen. That's our English heritage. If they don't prove you guilty, you're innocent by law."

"He's not a lawyer, he won't understand these distinctions."

"I'll explain them to him."

"If he'll listen to you!"

"Why shouldn't he listen? There's no harm in listening."

"That's true," she conceded, smoothing down her blanket. "But if we're going to give it a try, I don't see why you'd ask for only six percent commission. You should explain to him that if he was a painter, no reputable gallery would take less than forty-fifty percent for selling his paintings. It's the same in New York, Paris, London; fifty to the painter, fifty to the dealer, that's how they do it in every civilized country. And a painter *paints* his pictures, he doesn't just *find* them! Six is far too low, you should ask for forty percent at least."

Vallantine spread his hands with a knowing, rueful grimace that would have done credit to the great Molière actor Walter Matthau. "What's the difference?"

She took off her glasses to stare at him. "Are you going to take everything?"

"Heavens, no! We'll leave him . . . sssssomething."

His wife thought about this for a while, wondering whether it was right. "Well, it isn't as if he needed emeralds for food and shelter," she argued with herself aloud during the next lot of commercials. "He's young and healthy, he can work. He's quite good-looking too — I'm sure there are girls who would be glad to look after him. He'd never lack for necessities. And he's getting all this publicity — being on television must mean a lot to a boy like that." Shirley Vallantine would never have approved of taking anything from anybody which might have been of *real value* to the person. "If it's money he wants, he can make scads of money endorsing diving equipment."

The art dealer kept clearing his throat to gather his reflections on the matter. "He has his whole life ahead of him," he concurred gravely.

They felt the same about this, agreeing that the young man could do very well without the treasures. Thieves are judges and philosophers: they summon the victim to the bar of their conscience and find that he doesn't really need what they want to steal from him. They, too, believe in the Marxist imperative "to each according to his needs". What could be fairer and more philosophical? Or more convincing? People tend to perceive others as having more than they need and see themselves as lacking a great many things, so that *to each according to his needs* translates psychologically into *less to others and more to us!* It is simply a matter of natural justice.

THE CBS interview had been videotaped at the Seven Seas Club, where Mark was staying as a paying guest while waiting for the arrival of his salvaging barge from Galveston, Texas. The talk was mixed with shots of the 40-kilo solid gold statue of the Madonna of Lima and the Cross of the Seven Emeralds to give the viewers some idea of what the lucky young man had found. However, he was far less pleased with his luck than CBS's Caroline Adams had expected him to be. He was even unhappy about all the attention he was getting. "The more famous I get, the more people try to rob me," he said curtly. He couldn't have been more wary if he had been watching the Vallantines from the box as they were watching him.

"Come, now, you must have some consolations. I heard that you have an unlimited credit account with one of the Nassau banks. You must have bought yourself lots of wonderful things."

"Yes, I bought myself an M60 automatic rifle."

"Good heavens, why?" Ms. Adams asked with mock fright.

Sensing that she was putting him down, Mark gave her a withering look. "It's easy to see that you don't know what it's like to be rich."

"You're absolutely right! That's why I'm here, interviewing you."

Mark rubbed the scars on his knuckles. "Being rich," he said with great conviction, "is like having a flask of water in the desert in the middle of a crowd dying of thirst."

Caroline Adams, who as the leading woman interviewer on television took every occasion to display her faith in the public, wondered aloud whether the young millionaire wasn't too suspicious of his fellow men.

"You should be interviewing Pizarro or Philip the Fair!" replied Mark, alarming her by mentioning names that some of her viewers might not recognize.

"But what about all the nice things that must be happening to you?" she asked him quickly to change the subject. "I hear that you're receiving a sackful of mail every day — people write to you from all over the world. Doesn't that please you?"

"Today I got a letter saying, I need two thousand dollars very badly, no checks, send cash please!"

"I wonder what the writer needed the money for."

"He didn't say. People who go to the trouble of telling you why they want the money usually ask for a lot more than two thousand."

"That's fascinating. Tell us more."

"Well, someone wants me to pay for bumper stickers saying *taxation — castration*. I don't know, I might spend money on that."

"Oh, please," Ms. Adams begged in a mocking tone, "you're not going to be one of those boring rich men who are always complaining about taxes!"

"Is it only the rich who are complaining?"

"And anybody who tries to steal from you will get shot."

Mark bit his lip, then raised his head, looked straight into the camera, and answered loud and clear, wishing to be heard by all concerned: "Right."

"He's a raving maniac!" exclaimed Shirley Vallantine at the end of the program. "John, forget about it. And who was this Philip the Fair anyway? What was that all about?"

"He was referring to the Knights Templars," said Vallantine, who enjoyed telling little stories to his wife. "They were sort of fighting monks in the Middle Ages. They owned a lot of gold and a lot of land and castles in France, and the French king Philip the Fair owed them a lot of money. So Philip had the Templars rounded up all over France and had them tortured until they confessed to committing buggery, riding on broomsticks, kissing the Devil's asshole, that sort of thing — crimes for which you got burned at the stake, with everything you owned passing to the king. So the monks all died, the king's debts were wiped out and he was rich again! What do you think of that? And today people complain about . . . mmmmoving a painting!"

Shirley Vallantine had stopped listening to this as soon as she realized it was complicated. "He's an impossible person, John, he hates people," she said impatiently. "We've been warned, we should stay away from him. It's not worth the aggravation."

"Aahhh, he's just a spoiled kid, you'll see. An actor's son — the product of a liberal home. I'll bet anything no one ever hit him. When he wants to tell you how horrible people are, all he can talk about is what he's read in books. Anyway, we need a vacation someplace where it's warm."

"But before we go, we should try to find out more about his father's career. You could call your friend at Warner's — maybe he could arrange a screening of that movie about Napoleon. What magazine did he say had a cover story on his father — the *Times,* was it? I'll go to the library."

"A beautiful idea!" said her husband, glad to praise her. "We'll get to know him on a friendly basis. We'll be friends, you can trust me." He added the word *taxes* to his list on the memo pad.

"But what if he won't trust you, dear?"

Vallantine combed his bushy eyebrows with his fingers, then began twirling them the way other men twirl their mustaches, as his mind homed in on the principal weakness of his adversary. "He will, he trusts his luck!"

"How do you know?"

"He said he *always knew* that he would find the wreck."

His wife was struck by a new anxiety. "But we aren't the only people who saw this program!" she cried aloud.

"Don't you worry," he said, proud that he could be a tower of strength to her. "Just trust me."

It was a peaceful family scene. The dog was asleep again. The couple were sitting up in bed, fortified by pillows, a fretful wife and an indulgent husband, paragons of domestic harmony, watching television and sharing their thoughts, discussing the ins and outs of robbing their prospective friend.

THEIR loving closeness made them conspicuous at the Seven Seas Club, where they checked in three days later. They were sitting by the pool, warming their aging bones in the sun, with their Aberdeen terrier at their feet, when Charles Weaver pointed them out to Mark. Weaver, who looked up all new guests in *Who's Who*, expecting to find them there (and who was still worried about not finding Masterson in any edition), mentioned that Mr. Vallantine was one of the most prominent art dealers in America, but Mark was less impressed by Vallantine's social standing than by his successful marriage: this was the first time that he had seen a rich old man with an old wife. On another occasion he caught sight of them walking along a gravel path in the garden, with their square-nosed, wiry-haired little dog trotting ahead of them on its short legs. A squat, shambling figure, Vallantine, too, had short legs, and he was almost running to keep pace with his tall, rangy wife.

Such signs of lasting affection made a deep impression on the child of a broken marriage who still wished that his parents had stayed together. Mark had never heard of the white wolves of the Arctic who hunt the caribou in monogamous pairs and are known for their extraordinary devotion to each other.

'They must be nice people,' he thought. 'And they don't want to meet me — they're happy by themselves.'

"We're close because we w . . . work together," Vallantine explained to Mark later on when they did meet. "Being partners in work — work you really care about, mmmmmind you — is the only basis for a g . . . good marriage."

Kindred Spirits

It is a miserable state of mind to have
few things to desire and many things to fear.
FRANCIS BACON

I am unhappy
and therefore have a right to his aid.
PETER WEISS

STILL only a prospective millionaire living on credit from the Royal
Bank, Mark often insisted that he hadn't changed, but he was acquiring a rich man's notion of economy: the prices at the Seven Seas
Club no longer horrified him. In the old days he had thought that staying
at such an expensive place was obscenely wasteful; now it was more
expensive than ever, yet, having moved into the $500-a-day Florentine
suite instead of taking one of the $800-a-day bungalows, he imagined
that he was *saving money*.

He signed checks for tens of thousands of dollars in down payment
for goods and services in connection with the salvaging, but the walk-
in closets of his suite contained only his old clothes and the M60 automatic rifle. One of the island's octogenarian residents offered him a
Chagall — Moses with his long hair standing on end as he stares at the
Ten Commandments with terrified disbelief — and Mark was thinking
of buying the painting, even though it cost a fortune. But for the time
being he was content to adorn the walls with his old pictures of the Madonna and San Martín and his collection of framed telegrams.

ALL YOU HAVE TO DO IS LISTEN TO YOUR FATHER AND YOU WILL
BE ALL RIGHT — LOVE — DAD

MONTE CRISTO IS RICH ENOUGH TO COME AND SEE HIS MOTHER I
WANT MY SON NOT DIAMONDS — LOVE — MUM

226

YOU DID IT YOU DID IT HURRAH DONT FORGET ABOUT ELECTRIC
CARS HUGS AND CHEERS — JESSICA

GLAD FOR A BERNINIST — HELLER

FELICITAZIONI E SALUTI AFFETTUOSI — ANGELA ROGNONI

The rest of his mail was less gratifying. He looked through all of the
cables and letters, but none was from Marianne — which made him feel
all the more keenly that there was only one thing about him that interested people. Just for fun, Eshelby added up the figures: Mark was asked
to donate more than two billion dollars to the first thousand people who
thought of writing to him. What alarmed him about these demands was
the fact that they caught up with him at the Seven Seas Club on Santa
Catalina, even though they were addressed to

Mr. Mark Niven
The Bahamas

or simply to

Treasure Finder
Nassau

All requests for money reach the famously rich.

Mark's days were full of alarms. While waiting for the salvaging barge
from Galveston, he was cornered every day by some promoter, investment counselor or plain swindler offering to dispose of his treasures for
him. "Let me salvage them first," was his invariable reply. He didn't
even enjoy the sudden glow of pretty women. Some of the waitresses,
some of the young wives of the island's old millionaires who lunched
or dined at the Club, began eyeing him with avid looks and submissive
smiles — some whispered hot words into his ears — but they only reminded him of the girls hunting for ugly old producers in Cannes. He
ran from everybody.

And every day there were more boats anchored at the barrier reef where
he had been diving for weeks before he went to Nassau to report his
find. They were a safe eight miles' distance from the wreck site, but
what if they moved on and started looking for his ship around the strips
of star coral? Having lost half his fortune to the government, he had
become twice as anxious about the rest.

"To be rich is to be at war with the world," he told Eshelby, the only
person whom he could relax with, since Sarah wasn't speaking to him
again.

"And when do you think you might start enjoying yourself?" asked
Eshelby.

"Not just yet," Mark said mournfully. "I have to keep thinking about all the things that could go wrong."

Terrified of overlooking some danger, he was even preparing himself against armed robbery at sea during the salvaging. Every morning, accompanied by Coco, he took his M6o rifle and drove the *Ile Saint-Louis* to one of the uninhabited keys where he had had a rifle range built for himself by a firm from Miami. He practiced shooting until his shoulder got numb.

"You might as well try to collar a nervous cat," Shirley Vallantine complained to her husband.

"We'll have to fff . . . find an intermediary."

Since it was impossible to approach the young man with any hope of success, they were as nice as they could be to the staff, the people who had worked with him in the past. They were especially friendly with the Seven Seas Club's social director, Sarah Little, who became their natural if unwitting ally.

SARAH felt that Mark had betrayed their friendship. She was convinced that the last time they were together, just before he went off to Nassau, he must have already found the *Flora,* yet he hadn't said anything to her — he let her try to talk him out of treasure hunting, he even pretended to agree with her! She burned with anger and humiliation whenever she remembered Mark's contrite face, his humble voice telling her that she was right to advise him to give up, it was time for him to see reason! He had made fun of her concern for him, he had made a fool of her! They had just made love, and she wasn't close enough for him to whisper his secret into her ear? Did she have to hear about it on the radio like everybody else? Was he afraid that she would rob him? This loving and trusting girl, who believed the best of everyone, who imagined that even wicked people would be all right if they were treated with love and consideration, could not think of anything meaner than mistrusting a friend. Mark had insulted both her feelings and beliefs; she promised herself never to let him inside her again. She didn't go to Nassau to the signing ceremony, though he asked her twice, and she would not talk to him at the Club.

"You won't rest until you kill somebody, will you!" she called out to him angrily one day, unable to restrain herself any longer, when she saw him walking through the lobby with his gun.

The hostility in her voice cut Mark to the quick; he stopped short and took a deep breath, then suddenly smiled. "I'd rather have you scold me than not talk to me at all!"

Sarah wouldn't let him near her as long as he was holding the gun, so he handed it to a bellboy; she wouldn't go to his room, so he invited her to come and sit with him in the Terrace Café.

"It seems that every time we get together and I cheer you up, you just go and disappear," she said when he finally cajoled her into speaking.

Mark sighed, unable to think of anything to say in his defense.

Just then a tall blond man came to their table and, without waiting to be invited, drew up a chair to join them. "I've been wanting to talk to you for days, Mr. Niven," he said with a big smile.

"Please go away," said Mark. "Get lost."

"But you're dying to hear what I have to tell you!" the man rejoined with undaunted hearty confidence, his fair skin bright red from the sun, not from embarrassment. "You see —"

"I don't talk to strangers. Buzz off."

"I don't believe it," Sarah said when the stranger finally gave up. "Why were you so rude to that poor man?"

"I hate people who don't hear *no,* I'm sure he was a crook."

Sarah shook her head. "I don't think I like you anymore." Shy of her own hurt, she took offense on the stranger's behalf. "I can't get over how rude you were to that man. What's the use of being rich if you have to run from people? Why do you have to be so suspicious? You're afraid of everybody."

"Just to be on the safe side," replied Mark with a nervous grin, but meaning it. "Don't you want another milkshake?"

"If I were you, I'd listen to people, I'd help them, I'd let myself go! Why should you be so tense?"

Mark gave her an intense look. "I could go mad with hubris and ruin myself in no time."

He spent his soul on prudence, he suspected even himself — but he overlooked the danger of a friend's lingering resentment.

She lectured him at length, in the hope of annoying him and the half-hope of reforming him. "Do you want to be a lonely miser?" she asked. "The worst human being is worth more than anything you can find at the bottom of the sea. If there's so much interest in you, you should count yourself lucky to have the chance of meeting a lot of people . . ." Much of what she said may even have been true, but it was not the sort of truth Mark should have been listening to before meeting the Vallantines.

The Vallantines, who had been doing a great deal of walking in and around the Club to find an opportunity for just such an accidental encounter, walked into the Terrace Café, followed by their Aberdeen terrier. They nodded and smiled at Sarah in a tactful way; it was a kind of half greeting, demanding no response, but Sarah, who had grown fond of the nice, unassuming couple — and was pleased with the idea of forcing company on Mark — jumped up from her chair and waved them over to the table.

"But are you shhh . . . sure?"

Mark stood up to greet Sarah's friends, pulling out a chair for Mrs. Vallantine. His undeclared enemy's behavior put him off his guard, made him forget his unease about strangers. Meeting strangers was evidently an agonizing experience for the abnormally shy and awkward art dealer, who blushed furiously and hit his knee against the white wrought-iron chair when they shook hands, as if he was about to get a heart attack out of sheer embarrassment over his speech defect, his shapeless figure, his funny eyebrows, his balding head. There are predators who strike terror in their victims to numb them for the kill, but terror is not the only weapon: Vallantine struck pity in Mark's heart, which was just as effective in keeping him from running away. He felt safe with a man he felt sorry for.

As they sat around the table, Shirley Vallantine started talking about the difficulties of traveling with a dog. She would have much preferred to leave Daisy at home in New York with the maid, but John couldn't stand the thought of the poor little thing rushing about the apartment, pining for them. They never went any place where the dog couldn't go. She loved London but they couldn't go there any more, because the British wouldn't let Daisy in; they put cats and dogs in quarantine for months. John wouldn't stand for it. The best restaurants in New York were barred to them; John wouldn't patronize any place where Daisy wasn't welcome.

Vallantine listened to his wife's half-serious complaints with an apologetic air. Genuinely timid and awkward, he made the most of his disabilities, as if to demonstrate that he was easy to get along with. There was a touch of the henpecked husband about him, as he sat there scratching Daisy's neck — a slave to his wife and dog. The weaker member of any kind of alliance. He reddened at a glance! How could Mark have guessed that there was nothing in the world he would be ashamed to do to him? The art dealer got rid of the hovering waiter by ordering, with a blush, tea for two.

Mark made it a rule not to listen to anybody who so much as mentioned the *Flora,* but Vallantine brought up the subject only because he had heard from Sarah that at one point Mark was ready to leave the whole ship at the bottom of the sea rather than give half of it to the government. He wished that Mark had stuck to his guns. "There are already more than enough treasures in the world — what we are desperately short of is exemplary acts of defiance against the taxing powers of the state," he said with such conviction that he didn't stumble over a single word.

"It isn't that I'm against all taxes," Mark demurred. "I'm not against helping the poor."

"Nobody's against that, it's a g . . . gold mine." The art dealer laughed a little, blushing at his own merriment, and cast a sidelong glance at his wife, who smiled back at him appreciatively.

This little interplay at the mention of a gold mine struck Sarah and Mark as a further proof that the couple still loved each other in spite of their age. To the youngsters people in their fifties seemed incredibly old, and the sign of elderly affection impressed them both.

"I still remember the days when p . . . people got rich by exploiting people," continued Vallantine in his quavering voice, hovering over consonants even when managing to negotiate them. "Today you grab money and power by helping the less fortunate. Who is better off than a director of social services? High salary, the pleasure of giving advice, indexed pension — he has nothing to worry about except other people's problems, and they're a light burden. The best thing all these p . . . parasites could do for the poor would be to disappear. Their whole lordly existence is taxed out of the poor." He paused to peer reproachfully at Mark over his half-moon glasses. "Yes, to renounce a great fortune rather than let a government grab half of it — it would have been a magnificent gesture, it would have stirred the hearts of mmmmm . . . millions!"

"Everybody thought I was a fool."

The art dealer shifted in his chair with a sigh. He was painfully afraid of offending, but it wasn't in him to flatter anybody. "To be ttt . . . totally honest with you, to be b . . . brutally frank with you," he quavered, "you *were* a fool."

"John, really! You didn't have to say that!" exclaimed his wife. "You're so tactless."

Vallantine bowed his head with a sheepish grin as if to say that she was the boss.

If he had been poor he might have been ridiculous. As he happened to be a rich and important art dealer, renting one of the $800-a-day bungalows, his meek gestures were proofs of integrity: he was not impressed by his success, he had no sense of his own importance. Yet he would not let his afflictions or his wife's disapproval defeat him either. "It was as fff . . . foolish as looking for treasure in the first place. There's no getting around it, Shirley, he was born a foolish person."

"Please forgive my husband," his wife pleaded. "He's like a child — if he thinks of something, he blurts it out."

"He is completely unreasonable," Vallantine persisted. "But it's all right, *it's all right!*" he added, holding up his hands defensively and surprising them with another delighted little laugh. "The world needs fools." He turned to Sarah and Mark to explain. "I know that because my father, who was quite a good actor in his time — before *your* time, I should say — played John Tanner in *Man and Superman*. He toured all over the States and Canada with it and we used to travel with him when I was a little fellow — I heard him give that speech dozens of times! Let's see, how does it go? Can I remember it after all these years? *The reasonable man adapts himself to the world: the unreasonable man ppp . . . persists in trying to adapt the world to himself. So all progress depends on the unreasonable man.*" The lie, like truth in fiction, was tossed in as something incidental to what appeared to be the main point. It was one of Vallantine's maxims that a direct assertion might be doubted but an explanatory aside hardly ever. And indeed, it never occurred to Mark to doubt that Vallantine was an actor's son.

"My father's an actor too!" said Mark, unaware of the full extent of his own fame. (He himself had not seen Caroline Adams's interview with him on television.)

"Really? You don't mean it!" exclaimed Mrs. Vallantine with delighted surprise. "Is he one of the famous Nivens?"

"Which one, Dana or D . . . David? Now that you mention it, I can see a distinct resemblance to Dana Niven. Am I right?"

"Right! Good for you!" exclaimed Sarah, pleased that they were all getting along so well.

Mrs. Vallantine especially admired Dana Niven in *The Emperor,* while her husband preferred him in *The Devil's Disciple*. But they didn't overdo it.

CHANGING the subject, Vallantine remarked on a terrible crime he had read about in the *Times*. Had Sarah or Mark read about the three-year-old boy in Baltimore who was killed by his mother's lover? The mother was still at work and the man was drinking beer and watching a football game on television. The little fellow, who had been left alone all day, wanted someone to play with him and kept running back and forth in front of the television set to draw attention to himself.

"Oh, John, please don't remind me of it, it's too terrible," Shirley Vallantine begged, hiding her face in her hands.

"Yes, it's ttt . . . terrible," her husband agreed, and paused, contemplating some unseen horror. "The man kept telling him to get out of the way, but the poor little fellow, h . . . happy to be noticed, maybe thinking it was some kind of game, only got more excited and ran fff . . . faster and faster, back and forth, blocking the man's view of the television screen. So the man went berserk and kkk . . . kicked and punched the child to death."

"Oh, no, it can't be true!" gasped Sarah.

Mark sat silent, horrified.

The dog alone carried on as before, sniffing their legs.

"And that monster got three years. For manslaughter!" Shirley Vallantine said angrily. "That's treating it like an accident — practically nothing at all. I don't understand, do you? How can you call the murder of a little boy manslaughter? A three-year-old is not a *man!* Killing children should be called *childslaughter* — and if they execute people for anything, it should be for that."

"She's right, you know!" sighed Vallantine, letting his outraged feelings get the better of him: he looked so ashen, he made Mark ashamed of himself for not being a more caring person.

"It came out at the trial," Vallantine went on after a while, "that the boy had been admitted to hospital some months earlier with a broken arm and bbb . . . bruises, and the parents were listed as suspected child abusers. The social worker looking into the case made a mistake: she decided to let the child stay with them."

"I don't think the child's grandparents would have made that mistake, do you?" interjected his wife. "They wouldn't have overlooked a broken arm!"

"But they lived in another city and were too ppp . . . poor to travel," said Vallantine, stammering his way back to the curse of taxation. "Leaving aside the very rich, how many parents," he asked, "can afford to help their children buy a house or start a business? How many people can give a helping h . . . hand to their grandchildren? How many youngsters can go to their aunts or uncles for money when they need it? Politicians talk about the family, but they're doing more than anybody to break it up. Families are falling apart not because of this or that, drugs or the decline of religion or whatever, but because rappp . . . rapacious taxation is destroying the economic bonds between the generations . . ."

Sarah argued good-naturedly in defense of social workers, but Mark had ears only for Vallantine. He was beginning to think of the art dealer as a man whose chief interest in life was ideas, a man whose mind dwelled on the common good.

"All bureaucracies rest on the base ppp . . . pretense that people will spend all their money on themselves rather than help their own relatives but b . . . bureaucrats can be relied on to spend their budgets on absolute strangers instead of pushing for salary increases or trips abroad. Why, if only ten percent of all taxes collected by g . . . governments were spent on the poor and needy, every poor person on earth would be a mmmm . . . millionaire."

"Government ministers hire themselves beautiful secretaries, I know that!" exclaimed Mark, still bothered by Miss Passionate. "They have no problem spending money."

"Nnnnn . . . none whatever. You must let me tell you some day about my theory of *overhead profit.* Public money is always spent in the w . . . way which produces the maximum overhead."

"I know, I know!" echoed Mark.

The art dealer nodded with an appreciative look, joyful to find someone who *knew.* The levy on the *Flora,* he observed, was a tragedy for the poor Bahamians. The gold would be used to set up a huge bureaucracy and then people would be taxed to support the bureaucrats after the gold was gone.

"I should have told that to Dr. Rolle!"

"Bureaucrats are ddd . . . driven by the overhead profit motive."

"I know, I know!"

Everything Vallantine said suited Mark's own bitter feelings on the subject so perfectly that he imagined he had really known it all along. Though there is a manifest lack of connection between a man's character and his opinions, even if sincerely held, this is one of those well-known facts which are rarely called to mind, and people tend to identify with those who share their way of thinking. As he listened, Mark's sympathy for the eloquently stammering art dealer grew with the force of the faulty deduction: *he thinks like me, he is like me, he is a friend.*

Besides, the art dealer wanted nothing from him!

It seemed to Mark that they had hardly begun talking when Vallantine signaled to his wife; the couple got up and said good-bye, explaining that they always had a nap in the afternoon.

"They haven't got any children, isn't that sad?" Sarah said when they were out of earshot. "Mrs. Vallantine told me that she lost a baby in childbirth and then couldn't have any more. I guess that's why they were so upset about that poor little boy. Now aren't you glad you met some strangers? They're nice, aren't they?"

Mark agreed.

Neither of them had any idea how vile the nicest people can be.

THE couple were quite pleased with themselves for not mentioning business at the first meeting — but not for long. Their quarry flew away on a helicopter for the rest of the day, and the following morning they were wakened by the loud horn of a bright orange barge which, with its cranes and busy deck, brought an aura of northern industry to the sleepy blue bay. Hurrying down to the beach with other curious onlookers, they arrived just in time to see Mark board the *Mississippi* with a group of Bahamians. A bellboy told them that Mr. Niven had checked out.

Had they missed their chance?

In the following days Vallantine suffered so much anxiety that he came to feel that he had earned the treasures of the *Flora* many times over.

Every day at noon and every afternoon around four o'clock he watched two helicopters accompanied by a police helicopter gunship fly over the Club, carrying treasure from the salvaging barge to the vaults of the Royal Bank in Nassau. The best the unhappy man could do was to work on Sarah.

"I'm worried about your friend, Miss Little," he told her. "It would be so easy for him to do something fff . . . foolish."

What could have been truer? Sarah of course was concerned, and the art dealer managed to get her worried that Mark could lose millions by selling his treasures to the first comers. Needless to say, there was a solution: an exhibition. An exhibition would make money and at the same time attract numerous offers, allowing Mark to sell to the highest bidders.

It was a sound plan. Sarah, always keen to help in any way she could, saw nothing wrong with interfering, and one day when the water was too rough for salvaging and Mark hopped over in a helicopter to have lunch with her and Eshelby, she mentioned the idea to him. Mark just shook his head. Afterward, though, as they were having coffee with the Vallantines in the Terrace Café, she brought up the subject again.

Mark didn't like the idea any better the second time around. "An exhibition would tempt thieves."

"We show priceless works of art all the time, dear, and nothing has ever been stolen from us," Shirley Vallantine commented soothingly. "And of course you have insurance."

"At least let Mr. Vallantine explain it to you," Sarah urged him. "There's no harm in listening!"

Mark shook his head coldly. "Right now all I want to worry about is getting everything safely into the bank. There are a lot of people snooping around the reefs."

"Those ttt . . . treasures are not just gold and jewels," said Vallantine, unable to pretend any longer that he wished Mark had left them at the bottom of the sea. "From what I hear many of them are unique artifacts, and all of them are important to students of history — you can't lock them up and hide them from the world."

"Yes, the whole world has a claim to them," replied Mark bitterly, and stood up, anxious to get back to the wreck site.

"YOU could do it, John, you could talk rings around the smartest people, but you can't cope with the insane," Shirley Vallantine told her husband during their evening conference in their adjoining beds. "Please, John, I beg you, let's go home."

"There's that ivory jewel box with nineteen uncut emeralds," sighed

Vallantine, tossing and turning. "And what about the 743,050 gold doubloons?" (He, too, knew the *Flora*'s last manifest by heart.) "I wouldn't mind having half of them."

"Don't be childish, John, you're just tormenting yourself."

"But he likes us!"

"He may like you, but what good does that do? He's going to bury his treasure and sit on top of it. It'll make no difference how nice you are to him. He won't budge."

"Nnn . . . nothing worthwhile is easy."

The very next day they heard that Mark had fired at a small plane which flew past the barge; according to rumor the plane had been shot down and the pilot killed. Mrs. Vallantine started to pack, but her husband refused to leave.

"We'll never have another ch . . . chance like this, Shirley. He's afraid to make any move right now, but there must be a lot of confidence in him somewhere. We just have to wait for it to come out. Don't forget, he *always knew* he would find the wreck. He carried on for years against ttt . . . terrible odds, always sure he would get his heart's desire. Now what does that tell you? He's a dreamer, he believes that life will work out for him! I couldn't give up on a young man like that."

And indeed he could not. The dream of a crook is a man with a dream.

Paranoia

HURRICANES and tropical storms missed the Bahamas that autumn; with the exception of a few rough mornings, the weather stayed calm enough for salvaging. Each day yielded several fortunes. It was not uncommon for divers to bring up dozens of gold bars in a single morning, along with gold statues, candelabra, altar vessels and the odd blackened silver box filled with precious stones. Heavy objects were lifted out of the water with cranes. Sand blowers swept the sea floor around the wreck and underwater vacuum cleaners, connected by hoses to compressor engines on deck, sucked up thousands of gold doubloons.

Security was tight. A gunboat of the Royal Bahamian Naval Police, commanded by Lieutenant Dunsmore, lay at anchor right alongside the barge. Not content with police protection, Mark had hired six guards of his own from a security firm in Miami and equipped them with hand-held rocket launchers capable of ripping open a warship. No one but Mark was allowed to leave the barge. Captain Wellbeloved, the crew and the Customs and Excise officers were housed in a two-storey edifice under the bridge, while Mark and his divers, packers and guards, as well as the operators of the cranes and pumps, lived in prefab huts on deck. In the evening the men sang songs or played poker or served their turn at the round-the-clock watch. Mark had searchlights trained on the wreck all night; the lights in the shallow water attracted a great many octopuses, barracuda and other discouraging creatures.

The *Mississippi* was long and wide — with all its extra equipment and prefab buildings it still had room for the helicopters to land — but during the day when there was treasure on board, the slightest sound seemed to travel the length and breadth of the vast deck. A crowd gathered whenever a crumbling wooden chest spilled its contents, and everybody stopped and listened when a coin was rolling. The Customs and

Excise officers watched the divers, the packers, the barge's crew, Mark's guards and Mark himself, just in case any of them tried to steal anything before the Treasury could exercise its right of first choice. Mark in turn patrolled the deck, keeping an eye on the crew, his guards, his divers, the packers, the pump and crane operators, and the Customs and Excise officers. Or he stood on the bridge watching the sea and sky.

Whenever a boat strayed within a hundred yards of the barge, Mark got his automatic rifle and fired over the heads of the intruders until they veered away.

"I'll be held responsible!" groaned Lieutenant Dunsmore on the gunboat every time he saw Mark with the rifle. Lieutenant Dunsmore was convinced that the new millionaire would harm some curious tourist sooner or later and requested his superiors in Nassau to withdraw Mark's firearm permit, but by then Mark enjoyed the special consideration due to a man who, however young and reckless, contributed solid gold to the Treasury, and the request was ignored.

All the Lieutenant could do was to pay friendly visits to the barge, usually for supper at the Captain's table.

"Why don't you go and see the world, Mr. Niven?"

"Yes, indeed. Mr. Niven's rich enough to go around the world and then start all over again!" said Captain Wellbeloved cheerfully, glad to second sound advice.

"Thank you, I'm quite happy right here."

"You're not really needed," persisted Lieutenant Dunsmore.

"That's not how I feel about it."

"Everything that comes up is entered into the books and shipped to the bank. Nothing is overlooked. And we look after security for you."

"And let strange boats run all over the place!"

"Nobody ever listens," sighed the Lieutenant. "You might kill somebody with that rifle, you know." A tall, light-colored man, the son of a black woman from Eleuthera and a Scottish police officer from Stirling who had served with the Bahamian police in colonial days, Dunsmore had the sadness of two races in him. "Things can go wrong so easily," he brooded aloud.

"True, true," commented Captain Wellbeloved.

"You could be enjoying yourself in some great city!" said Lieutenant Dunsmore. People who live on remote islands long for great cities just as people in great cities long for remote islands.

"I've been in great cities."

"Have you ever stood on the Calton Hill in Edinburgh?"

Lieutenant Dunsmore talked eloquently about the New Town, the Old Town, the Castle Rock, Arthur's Seat, Holyrood, Princes Street, and as Mark tried to listen, it struck him that he hadn't thought of Marianne for days. 'And even now that I'm thinking of her, I don't feel anything,' he reflected, surprised. He had often made up his mind that their affair was over, but now he felt cured. It was as clear to him as the air above the glittering sea that he would never again search frantically through his mail looking for a message from her. Wasn't it ridiculous, the way he had avoided saying things just because he was terrified of making her unhappy and ugly-looking? Well, he would never be afraid of her again.

Lieutenant Dunsmore was pleased to see that he was making an impression on the young man, who seemed to have become more relaxed; and indeed, all the talk about Edinburgh had reminded Mark of his own Scottish ancestry. Weren't the Scots supposed to be miserly, in love with their strongboxes? So, fine, evidently he was a hardheaded Scot. Not the sort of person to whom women would ever mean very much. She had forgotten him and he had forgotten her. 'Nothing could be better,' he thought. 'I'll always have a few friends, and I'll be rich.'

He was quite calm and happy for a while, but then, free from the distractions of love, he relapsed into worrying about his fortune. Although he was becoming richer by millions every day, he became only more apprehensive.

And the call from Darville made him wild.

"THERE's a call for you from Nassau, Mr. Niven," said the *Mississippi*'s radio operator, a Californian in his forties who seemed to be always smiling and enjoying life in spite of his bald head and bulbous nose.

Mark was talking with a diver, still dripping, who had just brought up a goblet of beaten gold inlaid with gems. The helicopters had left with the morning's haul only about half an hour earlier; the goblet was the first catch of the afternoon. Mark thought it had to be the famous cup inlaid with bezoar which was supposed to change color if there was poison in the drink. He was turning it around in his hands when the radio operator came up to him to report the call. Handing the cup to the watchful Customs and Excise officer who materialized beside him, he followed the operator back to the radio room under the bridge.

Franklin Darville was phoning to report on his talk with Dr. Rolle about the division of the salvaging costs between his client and the Treasury. Darville had argued that they should be split the same way as the find, fifty-fifty, but in view of the reduction of the levy from sixty to fifty percent, the Treasury had ruled that Mark was to bear all expenses, which already amounted to over five million dollars. Mark, who had hoped that the Treasury would pay half, had to absorb a $2,500,000 loss from one minute to the next. He left the radio room, picked up his M60 rifle, and walked up to the bridge with a frozen face.

Only a few minutes later a small low-flying seaplane came near enough to cast a shadow on the deck: Mark lifted his rifle, aimed and fired. The little plane turned and fled, shuddering from too much speed and the hole in its wing.

Appalled, Lieutenant Dunsmore raced across the gangplank from the gunboat, then slowed down and walked with measured steps up to the bridge where the young madman was standing. "I imagine you'll have to reimburse the pilot for his repair bills," he said in a friendly way.

"I like to be left alone," replied Mark dryly.

"What was the shooting about?" asked Captain Wellbeloved, appearing with the red eyes and puffy eyelids of a man wakened from a sound sleep. As the owner of the barge Captain Wellbeloved was his own boss, and he set great store by his afternoon nap. "For God's sake, Mr. Niven, control yourself," he pleaded. "If you want to stay around, you should at least take more time off to rest."

"I'd never forgive myself if I let anyone catch me off guard." Mark didn't mention his $2,500,000 loss, having learned that no one would ever feel sorry for him.

The two men had to be content with his promise to be careful.

For the next few days Mark walked about restlessly, hardly ever letting go of his rifle. There was no word from the pilot of the plane he had shot at. Had the plane crashed or did the pilot have his own reasons for not lodging a complaint? A new fear was growing in Mark: he sensed danger like a dog, without knowing why.

One day his undefined dread made him take alarm at the familiar sight of the approaching helicopters. It was a bright afternoon with a warm south wind blowing, clearing the sky of clouds, and Mark could see the three dots as soon as they appeared on the horizon. The three dots were supposed to be there around four o'clock, when the transport helicopters and their police escort showed up, and it was nearly time for them: his watch said 3:45. Yet these dots, which had never bothered him before, made him nervous.

"They's a bit early today!" Coco called up from the deck, where he was nailing down a crate in the presence of the two Customs and Excise officers zealously taking note of every item brought from the sea.

Mark picked up his rifle, ran down from the bridge into the radio room two flights of steps below, and told the radio operator to ask the helicopters to identify themselves.

"Must be a tourist party," commented the operator, getting no response.

"I knew they weren't ours!" exclaimed Mark almost exultantly.

Still smiling, the operator took a look at the rifle. "Something's always going wrong with those radios. They just don't hear us."

"Try all frequencies, keep trying! And warn them that if they don't identify themselves or turn around, we'll shoot them down."

"They just don't hear us, Mr. Niven, I swear," begged the operator, beginning to get nervous. "If they heard you, they'd be only too glad to oblige, I'm sure."

"Do what you're told!" Mark snapped at him, then ran back up to the bridge, firing several shots in the air to raise the alarm. "Strangers!" he shouted. "Strangers!"

Apart from two divers still down with the wreck and a few people inside the various cabins, the crew were out in the open, and they turned to stare at their dangerous employer. Standing on the bridge in his ragged shorts and wide-brimmed straw hat, waving the gun over his head, he looked ready for anything. "Strangers! Strangers!"

"The way that guy carries on you'd think losing a few coins would make a real difference to him," drawled a young Texan who had so far pumped 72,247 gold crowns and escudos up from the sand and resented that the crew weren't allowed to leave the barge for a night out.

"Mr. Niven, it would be better for everybody's sake if you would put that gun down!" Lieutenant Dunsmore called across the few feet of water from the gunboat. "You've made it, you're on top of the world, don't spoil it for yourself!"

"Those people are raiders!"

"If they are, we'll take them out of the sky for you, don't you worry your head about it."

The police communications officer couldn't establish contact with the helicopters either, so Dunsmore ordered his men to ready their weapons, but only as a routine precaution: he was convinced of the deterrent power of his gunboat.

When the engine noise of the approaching helicopters suddenly broke through the hiss of the wind around them, Mark reloaded his rifle and once more ran down from the bridge and along the whole length of the barge, dodging to avoid cranes, suction pumps and the legs of resting divers, telling everybody to take cover in the water or inside the aluminum huts. The men obeyed him reluctantly: it was a good day for lying in the sun. The two Customs and Excise officers ignored him with studious disdain and went on taking notes. Coco, who no longer thought Mark was a fool, picked up a spare shotgun; Mark thanked him with a look, then signaled to the security guards to raise their rocket launchers.

"Mr. Niven!" cried Lieutenant Dunsmore, horrified by these preparations. "You can't shoot people just because they don't talk to you!"

"*You* shoot them down then."

"Do you want to be tried for murder?"

"Shoot them down!"

"The law cannot shoot first," replied the exemplary police officer.

Captain Wellbeloved came up to Mark, trying to say something, but Mark pushed him aside, and as the steel edges of the amphibious helicopters flashed in the sunlight like swords and the figures in the cockpits became visible, he aimed his rifle at the nearest cockpit. Just then an urgent voice came through the hitherto silent radio receivers, turned up to full volume on both the barge and the police gunboat: "We're tourists, tourists, tourists!"

Mark wavered for an instant, then called *fire!* and pressed the trigger.

In the helicopter cockpit the pilot's head jerked back as if he had been jolted and there was a sudden flash of flame from the engine. The security guards did what most men commanded by a lunatic would have done: they pretended to obey, firing into the air, taking care not to hit anything. The first helicopter exploded and fell into the sea in huge blazing chunks. The other two helicopters sank the gunboat with well-aimed rockets, spilling the policemen and Lieutenant Dunsmore's corpse into the sea. Next they sprayed the barge with bullets, killing Captain Wellbeloved, a guard and a Customs and Excise officer; Coco fell with a leg wound. The rest of the men still on the barge jumped overboard, except for Mark, who was trying to hold off the attackers on his own.

What was he defending?

According to the Customs and Excise officers' scrupulous notes, later retrieved from the debris and gore, they had on board, crated for shipment, 378 gold bars, 1,647 escudos, a heavy gold chain with 12 links, 4 gold candlesticks . . . but the longer the list the more absurd it seems that anyone would risk getting killed for half of it, especially if he had a great deal more of the same stuff safely tucked away in the bank. But then, Mark fought back not because of the value of anything but simply because he had already given up more than he could stand. He was firing at the helicopter hovering over the barge when he was thrown to the deck with a bullet in his stomach. The helicopter tried to land on top of him to crush his body with its weight but, buffeted by a gust of wind, swerved and caught only his left arm.

'I was right!' he thought, as his mouth filled with blood and he lost consciousness.

The other helicopter landed amid the floating wreckage of the gunboat to cover the men in the water. "Stay in the sea and we won't harm you!" cried a girl with long blond hair and a round untroubled face, standing in the open doorway of the helicopter with a submachine gun. "We're against needless violence!"

The raiders wasted precious minutes collecting their dead and were disconcerted enough to grab only two crates of gold bars and the biggest sealed crate, which contained six cannonballs of some slight historic value, before they were forced to flee by the approaching transport helicopters. As the gang took off they showered the scene with paper: there were thousands of leaflets strewn all over the water and the barge, proclaiming

IT IS A CRIME TO BE RICH IN A STARVING WORLD!
TURN GOLD INTO FOOD!
LAND FOR MIGRANT LABORERS!
THE REDISTRIBUTION ARMY

After the funerals the salvaging continued under the direction of Captain Wellbeloved's son. With two new gunboats flanking the *Mississippi,* a helicopter gunship flying circles over the site, and armed Customs and Excise men aboard the barge, the work was completed without further incident.

THOSE who died in the attack on the barge had a rare destiny — few of us are struck down by a single bolt from the sky. Ruin is one misfortune after another, the fatal mistake is many mistakes, the fatal blow is many blows . . . and who can count all his enemies?

The day after the terrorist attack Vallantine, feeling vindicated for staying on in spite of his wife's entreaties, went to Darville and told him that he and Mark had been planning an exhibition of the treasures in Nassau to be organized and promoted by the Vallantine Gallery. He offered to proceed with the matter if the Bahamian government and Darville wished him to do so, and suggested that Darville contact a few museum directors who had dealings with his gallery, impressing the lawyer with his insistence that "no one should be allowed near those h . . . historic artifacts without immm . . . immm . . . impeccable references."

Darville wrote to all the seven museum directors Vallantine suggested, but Vallantine got to them first on the phone, asking them whether they would be interested in acquiring any of the celebrated treasures of the *Flora.* Darville's inquiry confirmed the likelihood of Vallantine's involvement, and as the museum directors were of course interested in adding valuable pieces to their collections, they did not wish to antagonize him. Although by this time the results of the Italian police investigations were well-known in the art world, even if the Italians weren't making much headway with their lawsuit, and the most charitable museum officials had to allow at least the possibility that Vallantine was a receiver of stolen goods, only two out of seven had the half-decency not to reply to Darville's letter at all. The rest wrote to affirm their high regard for John Vallantine and his gallery; they had had the pleasure and privilege of dealing with Mr. Vallantine in the past and were looking forward to the opportunity of dealing with him again.

Darville thought of himself as a cynical man: he would never have taken the word of a head of state for anything; but it did not occur to him that directors of world-renowned museums, honored guardians of civilization, would be prepared to aid and abet a criminal simply because they hoped that some good piece of business might come of it.

In late January an exhibition of the treasures and fittings of the *Flora,* navigational instruments, her anchor and cannon, together with pictures and models of merchant ships of the period, opened at Government House in Nassau. The gold bars and cannonballs taken by the Redistribution Army were missing from the display cases; also, hundreds of pearls, coins and gems listed on the manifest were not recovered or at any rate were never noted as salvaged. However, what remained filled several large rooms and the pages of color magazines all over the world. The 16,800 gold bars were displayed in a separate Bullion Room; it was Vallantine's own idea, and it was a great success. The Vallantine Gallery organized special weekend flights from all the major cities of the U.S. and Canada, bringing tourists "to swim and sun in the Bahamas and see the treasures of Lima.''

Before the opening of the exhibition, in accordance with Mark's contract with the government, every single object salvaged from the wreck was examined and priced by a committee of appraisers mutually agreed upon (Franklin Darville doing the agreeing on behalf of his incapacitated client). The signed inventory of the appraisers listed the *Flora*'s anchor at $800, the Cross of the Seven Emeralds at $710,000, the gold statues of the Madonna at $75,000 each. At the current price of gold (still only $35 an ounce), the total value of the find was put at more than three hundred million dollars ($335,127,100). It was indeed the richest find in the history of the seas, just as the headlines claimed.*

All this time Mark was lying in the Santa Catalina clinic. His left upper arm was crushed and the bullets had torn his stomach in several places. He was operated on repeatedly; much of his stomach had to be cut away, and with recurrent internal bleeding it was uncertain for weeks whether he would pull through.

*Mark Niven's record was broken some years later when Melvin Fisher, who found more treasure wrecks than anyone else, discovered the wreck of the *Nuestra Señora de Atocha* 34 miles off Key West, Florida. This Silver Fleet galleon, which went down in a hurricane in 1622, was laden with 47 tons of treasure valued at $600,000,000.

A Beautiful Idea

It's time I started living!
BENJAMIN CORMIER

SIR Henry Colville hated hospitals, and the Santa Catalina clinic was built to look as much as possible like a villa he had once owned on the Riviera, in the days when thousands of tourists went there instead of millions. Apart from the two public wards where the blacks of the island were treated free of charge to appease their resentment, the patients' quarters were not single rooms but well-designed apartments, with down-filled armchairs and sofas, loosely woven silk curtains and hanging baskets of ferns and flowers. Before the industrial age hospitals were built like cathedrals, to lift the soul: their splendid arches and domes, stone carvings, frescoes, paintings — works of art, intimations of immortality — gladden the hearts of the afflicted to this day. Most modern hospitals, on the other hand, are built without regard to the eye or the spirit, in apparent ignorance of the healing power of magnificent sights; their worst features are their depressingly bare walls, monuments of thoughtless cruelty, which encourage the sick to concentrate on their pain and fear. Sir Henry's clinic didn't match the Scuola di San Marco in Venice, but thanks to Sir Henry's donation of the less costly part of his Impressionist and Post-Impressionist collection, it had no barren vistas. Even the corridors, hung with paintings by Sisley, Pissarro, Eva Gonzales, Berthe Morisot, Mary Cassatt, Paul Rigor, Seurat and Signac, could have been mistaken for rooms in a good museum.

But nothing works for everyone. In spite of all the paintings and Provençal pottery, the marble floors, the fountains, the foliage, the striking furniture from Milan, Sir Henry decided on one short visit that the clinic still looked and smelled too much like a hospital, and never set foot in it again. He had a wing of his house transformed into a replica of the clinic's operating room, so that if he broke a bone in the bath or was shot by a terrorist, Dr. Feyer's team could look after him in his own home.

Mark's life, so singularly rich in lucky breaks, was saved by Sir Henry's foible. If the clinic hadn't been there, only three minutes by helicopter from the barge, he would have died; nobody believed that he could have survived the flight to Miami. About a quarter of an hour after he was wounded, he received a massive blood transfusion and a team of general, cardiovascular and orthopedic surgeons began operating on him to save his life and his arm. Drugged to the limit, drifting in and out of consciousness, he knew very little of the tortures his body was subjected to. The first thing he saw was Dr. Feyer's large face materializing out of a fog, telling him in a stern voice: "You're *verry, verry* lucky!"

In his waking moments, when there were no doctors around, Mark was comforted by the window. Unlike most hospital rooms, which have their windows on one side of the patient's bed so that he has to turn his head to see the sky, the tall windows of the patients' apartments in the Santa Catalina clinic faced the beds, and when Mark opened his eyes, he was greeted by a wild grape tree swaying in the breeze. When he blacked out, the wild grape tree blended with the forest of his dreams — there were storms in his head, bending the branches.

Then he had the joyful surprise of seeing his parents reunited; they were together, sitting beside his bed. The sick become children: he wanted to be held and hugged. "Hold my good hand," he told them. They could travel again, he thought, the three of them, with money — there would be no quarrels. He was happy, but then something happening in his body made him forget it. He saw his parents even when they weren't there. Threatened with extinction, the brain worked on its own to strengthen the will to live, playing back flashes of happy memories. Once — it may have been during a blood transfusion — he was back with Marianne, skin to skin, just as she contracted under him; her joy shot through his veins like fresh blood and he felt the throbbing of her belly against his heart.

For weeks he thought that she was back and they would never part — until he was awakened by tearing pain.

"You're verrry lucky to feel anyting!" shouted the surgeon, watching him with piercing eyes.

Dr. Attila Feyer missed the sounds of *th* and *wh* as confidently as ever, but there was no trace of the friendliness he had shown when Mark was a healthy hotel clerk. "I had to cut down on your drug intake, so you'll live with pain for a vile — and I don't vant to hear any complaints about it!" he boomed at the invalid with merciless ferocity, to remind him that he came from the same tribe as his fifth-century namesake Attila the Hun, the Scourge of God. A confirmed practitioner of medicinal rough manners, intended to inspire patients with contempt for their ills and bills,

Dr. Feyer towered over the bed like an impregnable rock of solid flesh, except for his soft triple chin, which quivered vulnerably on its own even while he stood still. "Your stomach is as good as new. Better. It's half the size it used to be. You von't be able to overeat, you von't be blocking your arteries vit fat. Don't vihmper! Tank your Maker. And tank your doctor — I vant to be rich, too, you know!" (Dr. Feyer frequently enraged himself with the idea that he wasn't making all the money he should.) "I lohst my country and you're going to help me to buy vun!" said the enormous political refugee threateningly.

Then Dr. Feyer explained that they had had to remove some of the damaged muscles from Mark's arm. "It von't be pretty to look at, and you may have to find somevun to cut your meat for you," he said, "but it's still better dan an artificial arm. And you can improve it vit exercise. As you grow older it vill hurt more and ve may have to tink again. But you could have been paralyzed and you are not! Dat is verrry verrry lucky!"

VALLANTINE too was lucky. While his unsuspecting adversary lay in the clinic, he could go about his business unopposed. In the great battle of intelligence and will-power which was shaping up between them, Mark started with the disadvantage of being at death's door. This is how people who create the wealth of the world end up with so little of it. It costs a great deal to do anything worthwhile — even to recover sunken treasure — and the doers are at the end of their tether, bleeding one way or another, by the time their work is done. That's when the parasites start living, bright and rested, fresh from their bath, ready to move in and take over.

All through January and February the art dealer was busy flying back and forth between New York and Nassau, doing his best to make the exhibition a success and winning the respect of everyone connected with the *Flora*. The proceeds were split between the Treasury, Mark, the Vallantine Gallery and the relatives of those who were killed in the attack on the barge, so that Vallantine was looked upon as a benefactor. Not surprisingly, Darville was delighted with the good man's offer to stage another exhibition in New York in the fall, this time with only Mark's share of the treasures. The terms could not have been more reasonable: a $500,000 advance and a 70%–30% split of admission charges in Mark's favor. Moreover, as Vallantine pointed out, a show in New York would assist the sale of any objects Mark might decide he wanted to sell. Darville agreed all the more readily because the Bahamian Treasury had exercised its *right of first choice* by choosing all the gold bullion, thus depriving Mark of the only part of the cargo which could be sold promptly anywhere at a fixed price. So far only one lot of eighteen diamonds and five emeralds had attracted an offer (from Cartier in Paris) that met the price determined by the appraisers, and an additional show in New York, the world capital of publicity, seemed an ideal way to attract the right buyers. Darville and Vallantine's lawyer worked out a contract, subject to Mark's approval once he was well enough to attend to business. Thus Mark's ruin was prepared for him in a perfectly open manner; everybody heard about it and nobody found anything wrong with it.

Out of caution and some kind of delicacy, the art dealer avoided meeting Mark's parents and began to frequent the clinic only after they left. Mark's mother returned to Amsterdam at the end of January; a month later his father had to fly to London, where he was making a film with Joanne Woodward and Sir Ralph Richardson. Mark's friends came to visit him regularly, but Sarah and Eshelby had jobs and other friends, Darville other clients, Weaver other guests. Vallantine came last but stayed longest. In the end neither parental love nor friendship nor professional solicitude turned out to be as steadfast as the devotion of greed. Vallantine kept Mark company for hours every day. He adjusted the pillows, rang for the nurse, or just sat in an armchair with an anxious, eager look, pleading for recognition. And Mark recognized him, of course: he was his old friend who had talked taxes with him.

"I'm h . . . here because I'm trying to ingratiate myself with you," Vallantine explained with a conspiratorial smile when the invalid, trapped in pain, too weak to carry on a conversation, looked at him with questioning eyes. "We've become partners while you were too sick to know about it, and I'd h . . . hate to have a partner who didn't like me. Besides . . ." he added in an agony of embarrassment, "I must confess that I told a terrible fff . . . fib. I told your lawyer that you wanted this exhibition in Nassau."

The old man snuffled and moved his hands in the air as if he were about to suffocate with guilt; he could lie not only with words but with his whole being. He appeared so embarrassed, so flustered about his *fib* (which after all had earned Mark, as he already knew from Darville, nearly three hundred thousand dollars) that Mark ended up thinking his partner was, if anything, too scrupulous.

Indeed, Vallantine didn't want to discuss business at all. "Seeing how well things worked out in Nassau, I've made another proposal to your lawyer about a nnn . . . New York exhibition, but I don't want to influence your thinking about it, he can brief you. You're going to pay him a fortune anyway, so let him work for it, let him do the w . . . worrying. Let's leave business to the lawyers!"

He preferred to entertain his sick friend.

"I wish I could have seen those soldiers of the Redistribution Army when they opened that h . . . heavy crate and found six rusty cannonballs!'' he exclaimed, making funny faces and dancing his bushy gray eyebrows until he succeeded in drawing a smile from Mark. ''You can't feed many migrant laborers with that stuff. Incidentally, the p . . . police think the leaflet was a ruse to send them running after political hotheads instead of professional criminals, but I think it's quite likely that your attackers were genuine idealists with the very bbb . . . best intentions — valiant, generous souls who killed Captain Wellbeloved and that poor policeman only because they wanted to pinch some gold for the hungry poor. All the same, I don't think those two hundred gold bars will be turned into bread just yet. A lot of mmm . . . money has to be spent before the Redistribution Army can get around to the itinerant farmhand with his empty bowl. First they have to pay for the h . . . helicopters and machine guns, the hideouts, the passports and all that. And whom are they going to sell the gold *to?* They'll have to deal with rich people, so they'll have to look rich and act rich — fly first-class, stay in luxury hotels, dress expensively. You can't talk about big money if you look poor. And they need to put sss . . . something aside for the future. Idealists must eat too — especially idealists! Who deserves a better life than those b . . . brave rebels? It's their duty to keep in shape for the next good deed. With the best will in the world, they can't avoid spending most of the loot on themselves.''

The art dealer paused with a twinkle, sailing his wit back to the subject of taxation to re-establish the bond of shared ideas and grievances. ''Terrorists are just the same as bureaucrats: most of what they ccc . . . collect turns into overhead profit.''

''John's a witty man,'' Mark said to his lawyer a few days later as Darville handed him one by one the museum directors' letters which confirmed his good opinion of Vallantine. Pleased with all that he heard and read about the Nassau exhibition, Mark showed no anxiety about the proposal for another one in New York.

He no longer worried about the treasures — or the bills Darville brought. The lawyer thought they should refuse to pay the appraisers' bill for $874,250 and go to court over it if necessary. ''They dump all their phone bills on us,'' he argued. ''All their calls to New York, London, Amsterdam — to their offices, even to their families! They expect us to pay for their liquor! We could challenge that.''

''Why bother,'' said Mark, shrugging his good shoulder. ''I can afford it — I have more than enough.''

''Not yet,'' Darville reminded him. ''These checks are drawn on your overdraft.''

''If Mr. Murray isn't worried, I'm not worried,'' said Mark. He signed the checks he had to sign, but his mind was elsewhere. He concentrated on breathing and enduring. There were tubes in his abdomen to drain the wounds, and as the wounds healed the tubes had to be withdrawn a bit more every other day. His arm hurt constantly. But the pain had a curious inward effect on him: it calmed him down.

He was filled with a kind of serenity — and all as a result of his suffering. When he had his last operation, his doctors, concerned about the effect of all the drugs, gave him what turned out to be less than sufficient anesthetic, and he was conscious when they broke the bone of his upper arm to reset it. When the bone snapped he felt as if everything broke in him. He was in such pain that he felt it had to be the end of his troubles. "Now it's really mine!" he groaned.

Dr. Feyer was bothered by this strange cry. After the operation he stopped to talk to the patient's friends waiting in the corridor; he glared at each of them from his lofty height, then tilted his head back to give more room to his wobbling triple chin. "He called out during the operation — he said someting vas really his!" he said significantly, pursing his lips.

"He must have been thinking about the *Flora* — he hardly ever thinks of anything else!" exclaimed Sarah with a sarcastic inflection in her voice.

"Isn't he rich?" asked Dr. Feyer, his high forehead filling with wrinkles of concern. "Is dere any doubt about his claim?"

Eshelby shook his head. "I hear the Treasury's taking all the gold bars, but he gets half the total value."

Dr. Feyer was not entirely reassured; he intended to bill Mark for the round sum of $500,000. "I don't like my patients to vorrry. Vy he insists dat it is *really* his?"

"Well, if he's feverish, poor boy," said Eshelby, hazarding a guess, "maybe he thinks the government will let him have the whole ship after all."

"Ch . . . children, children, you've got it wrong," stammered the art dealer, growing patronizing in his excitement, realizing that he had won. "That's not it at all! He's saying that his ship is really his because he's . . . sssssuffered for it. He studied for it, he risked his life for it, he paid taxes on it, he kkk . . . killed for it, he bled for it, he's *earned* it! He can relax — no one can steal it from him now. It belongs to him like his arm. It's a b . . . beautiful idea!"

The Contract

A cunningly planned fraud . . .
a piece of deft trickery.
BALZAC

PERHAPS nothing about Mark Niven's life is of such general significance as the way he lost his fortune. Few of us search for treasure
ships, fewer still find one, but we have all lost something through foolish trust, or will do so. True stories should be read like intelligence reports, word from a scouting party signaling the dangers ahead.

Mark had no warning.

"You made a mistake there," he was told seven months too late by
Bernard Jay Wattman, Esq., Attorney-at-Law. "Listen, a man has a shaky
voice, he blushes when he passes a mirror, he's full of noble ideas and
good feelings, he sheds tears for children, he hasn't dumped his old wife
even though he could afford to, he's witty and entertaining — all that
means nothing, that's personality. He can still cut your throat for two
cents — that's character."

Besides, explained the New York attorney, Mark was given a clue
right at the start as to what kind of man he was up against. "You knew
he was a little old lady who loved his doggie and took it everywhere
with him to cover the sidewalks with turds. You went into business with
a guy who is perfectly content to let his fellow men walk in shit and
you're surprised that you're in trouble?"

But when they first met there was no question of going into business.
As far as Mark knew neither of them wanted anything from the other.
He had chatted aimlessly with a loving husband and wife in the Terrace
Café; he didn't weigh his impressions of them. We all tend to form
opinions about casual acquaintances casually, because it doesn't seem
to matter whether we're right or wrong about them. Back in the Terrace
Café, why shouldn't Mark have assumed the best about a man with whom

he never expected to have any dealings? The trouble was that when the time came to deal with Vallantine, he thought he already knew him!

And he thought the contract that Darville brought to him at the clinic, the day the cast was taken off his arm, was just a formality.

"Do you want me to read all this stuff?" Mark asked, annoyed by the thick sheaf of long pages.

Darville nodded emphatically. "Yes."

"Is it all right?"

"You'll have to judge that for yourself, you're the one who has to sign it."

Freshly washed and shaved by the nurse, wearing a cream-colored silk robe and muslin pajamas brought by his mother, Mark sat behind an elegant little desk in a corner of his sitting room, staring at the terms and provisions of the agreement for the New York exhibition of objects owned by him. ". . . Mark Alan Niven hereinafter referred to as the Owner warrants the said objects are his property fully owned by him and his ownership thereof is uncontested by any person or persons . . ." Darville, who stood at Mark's side sorting papers for him to spare his left hand, insisted that he read every word of the contract to see whether there was anything that he did not approve of.

"Well, you're my lawyer, is it all right with you?"

Darville raised his eyes and his arms with his accustomed show of surprise. "Of course it's all right with me. If it wasn't all right with me, I wouldn't be showing it to you. I'm a fully trained lawyer, you know, not Little Black Sambo." Darville's training, however, called for long and complicated documents justifying high fees and leaving the uninitiated in ignorance and confusion. Negotiating with Vallantine and Vallantine's New York lawyer, he had done his best to serve Mark's interests, but it is fair to say that he had also thought of producing a sufficiently elaborate document to warrant an extra charge of forty-five thousand dollars.

After reading the first page for the second time Mark began to finger the rest impatiently, remembering Vallantine's advice to leave business to the lawyers. "If it's all right with you, why should I bother reading it?"

Darville's whole body sagged under the weight of the problem. "Because you have to understand what you're signing. Look, we've had this draft contract ready for you for weeks, but I refused even to give it to you until I saw you out of bed. Writing your name on a contract isn't doodling — you have to be very careful what you put your name to. Who knows, it may not say what you want."

252

"Well, there's nothing wrong with the five-hundred-thousand-dollar advance on the proceeds," said Mark. "It'll take care of Dr. Feyer's bill."

"He wants *half a million?*" Darville was shocked. "Doctors charge the earth!"

"That's for all the doctors, and I'm alive," Mark replied, scanning the opaque paragraphs without taking them in. He stopped only at Clause 24.

24. THE APPLICATION OF LAWS

This agreement shall be interpreted according to
the laws and statutes of the State of New York,
regardless of the place of its execution.

"What does that mean?" he asked Darville after reading the clause aloud. "What's so special about New York laws?"

"It simply means that if we had any dispute with John it would have to be argued before a New York court. His lawyer preferred it that way, and I saw no reason to oppose him."

Clause 24 was the whole point. In the Bahamas, Mark Niven was the biggest news since Sir Harry Oakes was murdered; he was the number-one taxpayer and one of the chief customers of an important bank; he shook hands with the Prime Minister; he boosted tourism, he had the power of a popular hero. In New York he was an already forgotten minor celebrity, the subject of a few old articles, nothing. Clause 24 proposed in effect that Mark should exchange his rights as a somebody for the rights of a nobody. He noticed the clause without guessing its true import, simply because he was wondering about his legal status in the States.

"I was a draft dodger, I might not even be able to go to New York,"

"You wouldn't have to, we could instruct an attorney from here," Darville explained. There he made his mistake! Familiar with the corruption of Bahamian courts, he assumed that in the unlikely event of litigation his client could only fare better in New York. Even lawyers have illusions about the legal process, especially in distant places.

"Oh, well, old John wouldn't do anything to annoy me," Mark said complacently, ready to move on to the next thing.

This was at the end of March; the Nassau exhibition had closed a few days earlier. With his share of the treasures back in the bank, Mark was free to accept Cartier's offer for the twenty-three gems, and he signed half a dozen papers in connection with the sale.

"You have a few more days to study the contract before John comes back from New York. So do it!" Darville said before leaving.

LIKE millions who sign leases, insurance policies, agreements to purchase, Mark didn't actually read his contract until it was too late. Darville's honest insistence that he should do so only reassured him that Darville was looking after his interests, and since Darville was a lawyer and he wasn't, what was the point of trying to find fault with his work? Mark was young, he still had faith in experts.

Next day Thomas Murray phoned from the Royal Bank to report that Cartier's check had gone through and, after retiring the overdraft and interest, Mark had nearly $1,500,000 in his account.

Overjoyed, he phoned his father in London. "Dad, I still haven't paid you back the money you lent me."

"What money?"

"Come on, Dad! You paid for me to come down here. You paid for my boat, diving equipment, everything."

"I'd rather you'd tell me about your arm."

"It's all right. Dad, what would you do next if money was no object?"

"Well, I don't have false pride when I talk to my son," said the actor. "I guess I would stage Kleist's *Romeo and Juliet,* with Ustinov and myself playing the fathers."

"What do you think, Dad, would a million be enough?"

The only part of the Vallantine contract Mark studied was the appendix: the 18-page inventory of his share of the treasures. This was the first time he saw a full list of what the government had left him. The gems he had already sold to Cartier were still listed, so he crossed them out. Then he began wondering, trying to decide what to give to whom, what everyone would like best. He felt so much better for having sent his father a million dollars that he wouldn't deny himself the pleasure of giving everybody presents right away, rather than waiting until after the exhibition in New York. He spent two joyous days poring over the list, crossing out things and phoning Mr. Murray, who promised to see to the safe delivery of the surprise packages to the recipients. Mark felt like Timon of Athens —

> *Methinks I could deal kingdoms to my friends*
> *And ne'er be weary.*

He was also generous to himself and phoned Mr. Murray (who truly earned the bank's charges) to ask for his first gold Madonna and the Cross of the Seven Emeralds to be sent to him at the clinic.

THE sight of the gold Madonna and the Cross of the Seven Emeralds in Mark's sitting room was a terrible shock to the art dealer when he returned from New York to sign the contract. He had been away to arrange for the transportation of the treasures and was counting on taking all Mark had. He could hardly manage a greeting and would not sit down.

"What's this ssssstatue doing here?" he asked in a shaky voice. "And the cross? I need them in New York!"

"Not these," said Darville, handing him a copy of the revised inventory for the New York exhibition.

Reading the shortened list, Vallantine felt a squeezing pain in his chest. The room went dark before his eyes. Was he having a heart attack? He fell back into a chair, and it took some time for him to assure the others that there was nothing wrong. When he recovered, he questioned Mark and the lawyer in an aggressive manner, forgetting all about his unassuming personality. "You can't g . . . give away five hundred gold doubloons to everybody, you'll ruin yourself!" he protested with trembling lips.

"Not to everybody, just to everybody who lost somebody on the barge," Mark corrected him, sitting on the sofa with his feet up, still tired from being out of bed.

"Captain Wellbeloved had several life insurance policies," said Vallantine, casting a murderous look at the statue of the Madonna. "They all had insurance. Plus you insured th . . . them yourself. I gave them a quarter of the proceeds from the exhibition at Government House! And even if I count everybody ttttt . . . twice, it seems that thirty thousand gold doubloons are still mmmmmissing."

"I'm giving them to Coco. He started up the motor of the boat to make a noise when I was in the water with two hammerheads. He probably saved my life."

"But you ppp . . . paid him wages!"

"Well, he ought to have a bonus," replied Mark abruptly. Beginning to resent the interrogation, he decided to increase Coco's reward. "I'm also going to give him a couple of diamonds."

"You c . . . c . . . can't just give and give and give — people don't do things like that!"

"I'm enjoying it."

"I don't say anything about the pearls you're giving to Miss Little, they're a fffffine idea. By all means, let Eshelby found a public library. The necklace to your mother, the cross — yes, give them away keep them, sell them — but p . . . *please* wait until after the exhibition! If we don't have an impressive collection, we can't attract people. I'm not sure I w . . . w . . . want to go ahead without so many of your star pieces. My advance offer was made on the understanding that we could display everything you h . . . have."

Darville raised his hands. "It was understood that the deal was subject to Mr. Niven's approval."

"I didn't expect him ttt . . . to —"

"I don't understand why you're upsetting yourself, John," the lawyer interrupted soothingly. "You told me you didn't even *want* a whole lot. You said you weren't interested in taking the government's share to New York."

"That would have been too mmmmmuch, but there is also such a th . . . thing as too little," replied the art dealer, trying to sound calm. But then his quavering voice rose again. "What happened to the mask? The mask! That Inca mask of beaten gold?"

"It belongs to the man who sent me to this island — the man who gave me a job here."

"And what about the biggest diamond earrings in the whole ccc . . . collection? They are nowhere on the list."

"I owe them to a lady in Genoa."

"Couldn't she wait a few months? Let her wait!"

Mark frowned. Through inexperience, illness, bad advice, he was drifting into a disastrous partnership — it was all settled in his mind, he wasn't even thinking about it anymore — but now, just before signing, his annoyance with Vallantine loosened the bonds of inevitability. He remembered that he could still say *no,* and began flipping through the contract. "I don't like this clause about New York laws," he said sullenly. "I don't want to go back to New York if we have any disputes."

Vallantine waved the objection away. "But we're not going to h . . . have any disputes! It's a clause of no ccc . . . consequences — it's only there to k . . . keep the lawyers happy."

Mark pushed the contract aside with a decisive gesture. "We're having a dispute right now. I think I won't have a New York exhibition after all."

"Wh . . . what?" The bushy eyebrows bristled with alarm. For a terrible moment Vallantine didn't know what he had been saying. He began sweating through the underarms of his light cotton jacket; in spite of the air-conditioning, his thick neck turned beet-red. Had he given himself away?

Just then Sarah rushed into the room, followed by Eshelby. There were loud cries of protest and thanks: Mark's presents had been delivered and his friends were berating him for his generosity. Mark beamed, forgetting all about the exhibition. Vallantine stepped aside, trying to efface his blunders with smiles.

Jolly and bouncy, certain that Mark had recovered from his meanness and they would be loving friends again, Sarah kissed him on the cheek and on the mouth. His tepid response brought back all her disappointment and humiliation. She turned away, touching her burning face, then glanced quickly at the others to reassure herself that they didn't know how she felt. "You know, Mark," she said pertly, "I don't know whether I should take those pearls. What are they, some sort of good-bye present? You're planning to go away and forget us! So it's *arrivederci Bahamas,* is it?''

"Come off it, Sarah, I'll be around," Mark replied. "Who else is going to cheer me up when I'm down?" he asked, less chccrfully than he meant to. He had convinced himself that Marianne would have no use for a cripple. He wanted to put the past behind him, he wanted to care for the people who cared for him. But the memory of Marianne's joy, the feeling of her belly throbbing against his heart, affected him even when he wasn't thinking of her, and the fond look he gave Sarah had no desire in it.

Cut to the quick, Sarah hated herself for the ice cream she had eaten that morning, and seeing Vallantine standing dejectedly by the wall, seized his arm as if it were a lifebelt. "What's the matter, you dear sweet man?"

The art dealer burst into one of his short little laughs. "What a nnnnnatural girl you are, Sarah, you could disarm Russia! I wish I had a daughter like you."

"What's wrong?"

"I'm in the wrong," replied the art dealer sheepishly, his eyebrows wilting. "I was mean, I'm getting crusty. Now that I've been watching you all laughing, I see that Mark's right. Nothing is as important as making your friends h . . . h . . . happy.''

"Mr. Niven's calling off the New York exhibition," Darville explained.

Sarah flopped into one of the low white leather armchairs surrounding a low glass table. "Poor John — I bet he doesn't trust you!" she sighed, pressing down the folds of her full skirt. "After all the trouble you went to! He's insufferable. You won't believe this, but when he found the wreck, he didn't breathe a word about it to Ken or me. He said we were his friends, he swore he couldn't have survived without us, and he went on lying to us just the same. He let us worry ourselves sick about him for weeks!" She shook her head slowly, trying to turn her anger into sorrow. "I don't mind, but what's going to become of him if he can't trust anybody? He might as well be a hermit in the desert. He's going to dry up completely — consumed by suspicion — you'll see!"

Before the raid on the barge, Mark had listened to Sarah's reproaches with equanimity: he had to do what he had to do and she was unreasonable. Now that he was more alive to pain he heard not so much her words as her hurt. "Of course I trust you. I didn't mean to lie to you. I'm sorry. I should have told you."

Vallantine nodded approvingly. Nothing could have suited him better than to have Mark worry about not being a trusting enough person.

"And that helicopter he shot down!" Sarah went on, getting more and more upset at the thought that she was making herself ridiculous. "He didn't *know* those people were raiders! They told him on the radio

257

that they were tourists, and he still shot them down! That's what every-body's saying. People mean nothing to him. Mark, didn't it bother you that you might be killing innocent sightseers?''

Mark kept squinting from frustration. ''I didn't kill innocent people. I felt absolutely certain they were thieves.''

''And what made you so absolutely certain, my dear boy?'' asked Eshelby eagerly, preferring a puzzle to an argument. ''Tell us.''

Sarah refused to change the subject; her round rosy face became oddly severe. ''All I know is, I don't want any presents from Mark. We're not close enough for that.''

''You're too h . . . h . . . harsh with him, Sarah!'' said Vallantine, taking her hand with a warm feeling of gratitude. ''He's such a good friend, he would have canceled our show and given up an advance of half a million dollars rather than hold back your pearls for a few months. So you mustn't be mad at him. I'm not mmmmmmad at him either.''

He let Sarah's hands go and, turning to Mark, raised his arms in sur-render, trying to make light of an embarrassing admission. ''You win, Mark. I could nnnnnever stand up to you — you're the stronger person-ality, that's all there is to it.'' He blinked helplessly over his half-moon glasses, then dropped his arms, reached into the inside breast pocket of his jacket and took out a certified check for $500,000, which he put down on Mark's desk beside the contract. ''We'll take whatever you lend us. We'll leave more space between the exhibits and make less look more impressive.'' Without waiting for a response, he turned back to Sarah with the courtly bow of an old-fashioned gentleman. ''So there's no problem, my dear. We can have our show and you can have your ppp . . . pearls.''

However, once Sarah had given way to her indignation, there was no stopping her, She kept turning her head to avoid everybody, then cast a fiercely scornful look at Mark. ''I don't want any presents from him. He's not the person I used to know.''

''I *did* know that those people were gangsters.''

''How? How could you possibly know?'' Eshelby asked encourag-ingly.

''Well, we'd been trying to talk to them on the radio for about five minutes, we kept asking them to identify themselves, but they didn't respond until they were practically over us. When they said 'tourists, tourists,' loud and clear, it must have made me realize that they could have talked to us from the beginning, so if they didn't, they had a good reason for it. I didn't think it through, but I kind of felt it instinc-tively . . .''

The argument about the shooting went on and on and on — it was too much of a good thing. Vallantine wished it was all over. He felt

258

dizzy, he couldn't stand the tension. There was too much at stake! He had two armored vans parked at the Royal Bank in Nassau; he had a rented plane waiting at Nassau airport to fly the treasures to New York. Were all the expensive arrangements for nothing? Could he lose out at the last moment? 'Sign, sign!' he thought, staring at Mark, trying to will him into doing it. But Mark hadn't so much as glanced at the certified check for $500,000 and seemed to have completely forgotten about the contract.

At last Vallantine's nerves gave way. "Children, stop ch . . . ch . . . chattering!'' he shouted, without meaning to.

There was a moment's silence. His harsh tone was so much out of character that the others looked at him with surprise. 'How that man sweats!' Eshelby thought with distaste. He wouldn't have had anything to do with the art dealer, but the gold Madonna shining on the table discouraged him from criticizing Mark's choice of a partner. ("So crazy is right!'' was the first thing he had said when they talked on the phone after the news of Mark's find was announced in Nassau.)

EACH curious look stabbed Vallantine like a knife. His shirt was soaked, Everything had been perfect and he had ruined it for the second time. He had lost his temper twice! Was he too old for all this? What could he say to revive the assumption that they had a deal?

"There might be ppp . . . problems we haven't discussed yet,'' he rushed on, improvising desperately. "Does Mark have a w . . . w . . . will, for instance? What if something happens to him while his treasures are under my care in New York?''

"I'm trying to explain to Mr. Niven that nobody can be as rich as he is without making a will,'' Darville replied in an acid tone. "So far he refuses. He doesn't think he needs one.''

"Why, that's just ttt . . . terrible!'' exclaimed the art dealer, seizing on a legitimate issue to explain his nervousness and demonstrate his absolute honesty. "He's still in the hospital, what if he has a relapse? What if the Redistribution Army come back to avenge their fallen comrades? I'm sssssorry, Mark, but to be brutally frank with you, these are things you have ggg . . . got to worry about! Whom will I return everything to — all those priceless artifacts! — if there is no will? Being responsible for them for a few months is all I can take.''

The art dealer grew more dignified with every word he uttered; he was lying himself out of his embarrassment. Good people find lying painful and awkward, but for the practiced liar it is a joyful experience; lying boosts his ego, raises his spirits, steadies his nerves, gives him a sense of superiority, a sense of being in command. He *knows* that what he is telling people is untrue, and they do not. "I can't go ahead with the exhibition if there is no will," Vallantine declared sternly. "I have to know whom to give it all back to if something happens to Mark."

"Nothing can happen to me," Mark said with an involuntary smile, his eyes brightening at the thought of his charmed life.

"Wh . . . what do you mean?"

"I was drafted — I could have been killed in Vietnam, but I got away. I nearly drowned, going crazy in the Atlantic, trying to dive to the bottom of the ocean . . . I fainted down there. But I came up. I was nose to nose with a hammerhead and nothing happened. So what are you talking about? Those terrorists were shooting at me at close range, they even landed their helicopter on me — and I'm still here. I'm so healthy, I can't even get fat!" Biting his lip, Mark raised his left arm a couple of inches. "I'm rich and I'll live to be a hundred." He no longer worried about hubris and no longer thought of canceling the exhibition.

Vallantine was adamant. "We never know what the fff . . . future holds. I don't want to get caught in a legal wrangle between your relatives."

"You should listen to John," interjected Darville.

"Listen to your legal adviser," commanded Vallantine in a firm voice. "He knows I have to know whom to give it back to."

"You might as well make a will, dear boy, or they'll talk you to death," said Eshelby.

"It's settled, then," ventured the art dealer, "We'll leave you alone with your attorney to work out provisions for your heirs, and tomorrow we'll sign our contract."

"I've no objection, so long as it's on my terms," said Mark regally.

"On your terms, nnnnnaturally."

Darville tried to hand back the gallery's certified check for $500,000 but Vallantine waved it away with a deprecating gesture. "Leave it with the papers, I'm sure Mark isn't going to cash it before we conclude the contract."

It was a heady and busy time for Mark. Everything conspired to cloud his judgment. Hardly had he been left alone with his lawyer when they were interrupted by an important visitor, ushered in by Dr. Feyer himself.

Oh, to Be Rich and Good!

Today, I will walk all the roads,
All the paths of the world.
EUGENE J. McCARTHY

THE visitor ushered in by the Medical Director of the Santa Catalina
clinic was a tall, slim, blond, blue-eyed, unobtrusively elegant individual in his thirties. He could have been a high official of the World
Bank or the UN Secretariat. Well-born, well-connected and well-placed,
Dr. Hans-Felix Habeler held a doctorate in zoology from the University
of Hamburg, and on his way to the top executive post of the World
Wildlife Fund, served as Sir Henry's private secretary. "Sir Henry sent
me to ask you to have tea with him this afternoon," he said to Mark
with the benign smile of a bearer of glad tidings. "Dr. Feyer tells me
that he has no objection."

"Perfectly true," the surgeon concurred, nodding with his head tilted
backward; his chin wobbled violently.

"It will be a simple occasion," Habeler added reassuringly. "You'll
have tea and biscuits and chat a little."

Mark was taken aback. 'So I'm going to have tea with the richest
man on earth!' he thought. He had never had a keener sense of the drastic change in his social position. "I'll be glad to have a chat with Sir
Henry," he said gravely. They were equals now, more or less.

"Sir Henry has tea at four-thirty."

"Tell Sir Henry I'll be there."

"I'll pick you up at four."

Mark was half offended. "I don't need a ride, thank you. I can get
there on my own."

"I'm sorry, I didn't mean to imply otherwise," apologized Dr. Habeler in the politest way. "But you must allow me to come for you.
You see, I'm responsible for you being on time."

During their conversation Dr. Habeler devoted his whole attention to
Mark's face without even a sidelong glance at Darville or Dr. Feyer or

261

the gold Madonna standing on the coffee table. Only on leaving did he relax his concentrated friendliness to exchange a few remarks with the others and look around. "I've seen the exhibition at Government House, of course, but each Madonna looks like the only one!" was his parting compliment.

"Interesting, no? He speaks English *vidout* an accent!" Dr. Feyer said before rushing after the secretary.

Having thought about his will and dictated his wishes to Darville, who promised to have the document drawn up for him to sign the following day, Mark spent the remaining hours until teatime reading about himself. The drawers in the built-in cupboards were full of old newspapers and magazines from around the world with reports of the discovery of the *Flora* and the raid on the barge, interviews, news stories and feature articles about the Nassau exhibition. There were stacks of them that he hadn't even seen yet, and he asked the nurse to put some on his desk. Fame multiplies for the multilingual: he read his own story in English, Italian, French, Spanish, and made out the gist of it in Portuguese, Dutch and German. He was pleased to find that most papers applauded his plans to save the rain forests of South America and to invest in oil-free cars "to clear the air". The Lima papers took note of his promise to establish scholarships at the Universidad de San Marcos, to honor his debt to Peru.

These vague plans which had served to bolster his self-respect while he had other things to do were acquiring an inner importance he himself was hardly aware of. Now that he felt secure in his wealth, he needed something new to aim at. It may be also that his concern for the human community was intensified by the melancholy conviction that Marianne would never come back to him and he was destined to live alone like his father.

An old issue of the *Miami Herald* which reported the attack on the barge put him on the front page along with Prince Charles. Before he found his true love and married her, the handsome and popular prince was rumored to be engaged to someone practically every month, and the rumor this time was that he had set his heart on a girl from California. Prince Charles's picture was no bigger than Mark Niven's — Mark was being treated on an equal footing with the heir to the British throne, the riding companion of his childhood dreams. He stared at the paper and *reigned*. He felt the weight of his responsibilities, the burden of his ignorance about the mechanics of power. It was time he started to be useful: he had to get down to work, but he needed allies, contacts. Would Sir Henry help him? Give him good advice, at least?

SIR Henry certainly kept an eye on everything. Mark was profoundly impressed by the billionaire's library — an enormous book-lined room, two stories high, with a gallery running around the second level, and long tables covered with newspapers and magazines in various languages, including Arabic. "Sir Henry reads about a dozen newspapers a day," explained the librarian, a tall Bahamian woman with wide-framed glasses. "There are only about eight thousand books on the shelves — the rest are bound volumes of magazines. We keep the newspapers for a couple of weeks and then put them on microfilm."

In danger of being late, they said good-bye to the librarian, and as they walked past the tables covered with magazines, Dr. Habeler pointed to Mark's picture on the cover of *Der Spiegel*. "Sir Henry was pleased to see his island in the news."

"Is it true that he's the richest man on earth?" asked Mark, wanting to be sure.

The secretary paused for an instant before offering a philosophical evasion. "Let's just say that when Sir Henry thinks about his personal affairs, he has to think about the world."

Mark nodded appreciatively. "A few months ago I wouldn't have known what you meant!"

The young millionaire about to meet the old billionaire felt the same sort of excitement as a newly commissioned officer meeting the Commander-in-Chief or a newly ordained priest meeting the Pope.

Tea was already laid for three in a cool, shady room off the library. Sir Henry stood in front of his chair to greet them, leaning on his ebony cane. An exquisite little man with a birdlike face and fine delicate bones, the 87-year-old billionaire still had his own thick white hair, his own white teeth and bright darting eyes like a squirrel's; he bowed to make up for not offering his hand, then lowered himself promptly into his high-backed leather armchair which made him seem even more diminutive. Mark was surprised to see that "the Grand Old White Man of the Bahamas" was a small person, and liked him for it.

"I don't talk to everybody on the island," said Sir Henry in a light but firm voice as he studied the young man's face with undisguised curiosity. "Some of my neighbors here think that all there is to being rich is stealing. But I'm interested in you. You're stubborn and you have the courage to work on your own. A young man who enriched the world with so much treasure at the age of twenty-one — you have possibilities."

Mark sat on the edge of his chair, not touching anything, and met the probing looks without flinching.

"You owe me ten percent of the *Flora*, twenty percent of your wealth, that's over thirty million dollars," announced Sir Henry, who liked people to be quite clear in their minds what they owed to him. "It was I who got your levy reduced from sixty to fifty percent." He tapped his cane on the marble floor to silence any noise of gratitude. "I want more than thanks," he said sternly. "I want you to return the favor: I want you to help those who are doing something well."

"I will, sir."

"So far I'm not disappointed in you. You fight back, that's important too. You're capable of killing your enemies — yes, you have possibilities."

Sir Henry rested his cane on the arms of his chair so that it was suspended across his lap, and took a sip of tea and an arrowroot biscuit, then began to question Mark about his education and his family as thoroughly as if he were interviewing him for a job.

"I have a heart of stone, you know," he said abruptly, cutting the young man short once he decided that he had heard enough. "Ask any charity, I'm the meanest man they know. I'm famous for my meanness." There was a flash of pleasure in the tiny old man's eyes as he noted Mark's surprise. "I don't believe in charity, charity multiplies the unfit. What we need is more gifted people — we need them as badly as we need leopards and elephants." He picked up his cane and tapped the floor peremptorily. "Let the soft-headed look after the feeble-minded! When your turn comes, give a hand to those who are capable of enriching the world. Nobody's going to need your help more than they do . . ." A founding member of the World Wildlife Fund, particularly concerned about the survival of leopards and elephants, Sir Henry believed that gifted people too were an endangered species.

Mark agreed, easing himself back into his chair. "I'm going to fund scholarships in Peru."

"That's not what I'm talking about," Sir Henry said crossly, raising his cane in a warning gesture. "Never give money to universities. When I was young I lost millions listening to learned advice! An illiterate fool can be a useful fool, he can wash floors, but a fool with a doctorate is deadly. Social scientists, terrorists, sociobiologists, Marxists, psychiatrists, charlatans of every description — all these parasitic hordes are coming out of universities. And do you know why? Because no amount of learning can cure stupidity, and higher education positively fortifies it. So no endowments, remember!"

Mark made an inward vow to keep his promise to the students of Lima, but didn't argue.

"I'm pleased to hear that you intend to do some good with your wealth," Sir Henry said, his light voice animated by the joy of scheming. The old billionaire had outgrown greed, but the chance of influencing the disposition of $150,000,000 could still enthrall him. It was for this reason that Mark had been invited to tea. "A hundred and fifty million is not a great fortune, but it can enable you to make some difference to the world."

"I hope to make some difference to the world," Mark said, and drank his tea at one go.

"Are you serious about rain forests?" Sir Henry asked sharply.

"I wondered if you might help me."

"You'd certainly need help. You'd be up against lumber companies whose agents poison forest tribes to clear the ground. You need more than money to get the better of such people . . ." Sir Henry had little difficulty in persuading Mark that, instead of wasting fortunes on a one-man scheme which had no chance of succeeding, he should rely on the organization and contacts of the World Wildlife Fund. Dr. Habeler would be his guide.

"And Dr. Habeler won't let you spend more than a few millions," Sir Henry assured Mark, pleased with his success as a fund-raiser. "You'll still have a great deal left for your own enjoyment — that is vital — and for doing other things."

When not doing anything else with his cane, Sir Henry was rolling it between the palms of his hands; for the past sixty years or so, this had given him the same sort of satisfaction that he had once derived from smoking. Playing with his cane, however, he seemed to have lost the thread of his thoughts, and he was getting annoyed. "So you lived in London!" he said accusingly.

"Yes, sir."

"London, the capital of Great Britain!" sighed Sir Henry. "To like London these days you have to like Arabs." He raised the ivory knob of his cane against Mark's chest. "Have you read the Koran?"

"No, sir."

The cane was withdrawn. "You're fortunate that you weren't reared on that stupid and vicious book. I suppose the Wildlife Fund would throw my money back at me if they knew I harbored such opinions, and if it got out I would deny it, but it's not true, you know, that all religions are equally good," the little frail man insisted severely. "You grew up in a civilization based on the Bible, on the Hebrew prophets, the Gospels, Greek and Roman literature and art. You have spiritual fathers like Aristotle, Erasmus, the artists of the Renaissance — you are a citizen of the Western world, you ought to do your best to protect it . . ."

To Mark's amazement, the oil billionaire approved of his plan to finance oil-free cars. "We're still doing well with our Arab friends, but I'm moving into land and microchips," he confided. "I don't like to depend on the mercies of Allah."

Dr. Habeler had been frowning through all this, pained to hear Sir Henry sounding off like a taxi driver. "I believe Mr. Niven's chief concern is the environment . . ."

Sir Henry gave his secretary an amused look. "Dr. Habeler will prepare a list of people for you to contact, and arrange some meetings when you're well enough to travel. If I were younger I'd give a push to those cars myself. The experts will tell you that the problem is the battery, but it isn't a battery problem, it's a financial problem. A question of power. We're talking about who will rule the world. For one thing, if we don't stop burning oil for transport, there won't be an Israel for long. Yes, whoever succeeds in replacing the internal-combustion engine will father a new Industrial Revolution — a new era of Western hegemony.'' He jabbed the air with his cane. ''The Western world ought not to become a province of Arabia!''

This last exertion seemed to have exhausted the impish old man; he put down his cane on the table beside him. It was evidently a sign. Dr. Habeler rose to his feet; Mark followed suit.

Sir Henry, remaining seated, reached out this time to touch his guest's hand. ''We didn't talk long,'' he said. ''But if you're bright, a few words will do. Go. I'll keep an eye on you.''

IMPRESSED by Sir Henry's interest in his client, Darville had developed qualms about his own conduct the previous day and took an air-taxi to Santa Catalina the following morning instead of waiting for the regular flight, in order to arrive ahead of Vallantine. He felt he shouldn't have allowed the discussion of a contract involving the lending of a hundred and fifty million dollars' worth of treasure to degenerate into a scene about Miss Little's grievances. It wasn't the time or the place for airing her emotional problems and he ought to have asked her to leave.

''Listen,'' he said to Mark, ''there were so many things going on here yesterday that I'm not sure you had a chance to tell me what you really-truly want. At one point you were calling off the exhibition . . . John was giving you a hard time — if you don't really like him, you don't have to go ahead with this New York deal, you know. Don't be embarrassed about changing your mind — I can get rid of him for you, that's what lawyers are for. A good lawyer is his client's stuntman, he jumps the hurdles for him. Until you sign the contract, there's always time for second thoughts.''

''It's nice of you to worry, Franklin, but it's OK,'' Mark said absently. ''No wonder John was upset — he was counting on a bigger show. He's a nice guy — look, he even left his check behind.''

All these were petty details compared to the tasks ahead of him. Solemn and taciturn, preoccupied with the awesome problem of ridding the world of internal-combustion engines, he signed his Last Will and Testament and then, without waiting for Vallantine's arrival, the contract for the New York exhibition. It is one of the most common forms of self-destruction: he was thinking of something other than what he was doing. ''By the time the exhibition is over, I'll be ready to sell some of the coins and start investing in a few projects,'' he said as he signed his name. While he had the pen in his hand he also signed the $500,000 check over to Dr. Attila Feyer.

266

Vallantine came and went, taking his copy of the contract. "I hope this will be the beginning of a lifelong association, Mark," he said as they shook hands on the deal. They would never see each other again.

In the afternoon Dr. Habeler came to the clinic to discuss the meetings he proposed to set up for Mark in Europe and South America. Mark was busy planning his new life based on the wealth which was already on Vallantine's plane. More than a hundred and fifty million dollars' worth of gold coins, plate, statues, altar vessels, pearls, emeralds were being flown to New York and Mark had nothing to show for them but forty-six neatly typed pages of legal-sized paper, which he put in a drawer to make room for Dr. Habeler's notes.

Sir Henry's loyal aide was offended by the young man's failure to express his respectful appreciation of Sir Henry's kind interest. "There must be millions of people who would envy you Sir Henry's friendship," he said with studied casualness.

"Yes, I'm sure you're right about that," Mark replied without special reverence, already used to his new privileges. "He's a bit of a racist, though, isn't he? Why is he so down on Arabs?"

Dr. Habeler objected with a cold blue gaze. "Sir Henry is probably the most envied man on earth."

"I don't doubt it!"

Later, when he was overwhelmed by his troubles, Mark wished he could have asked Sir Henry for help, but some weeks after they had tea together Sir Henry died in his sleep.

36

Phone Calls, Cables, Letters

Laws get to be very vivid
when you come to apply them to yourself.
MARK TWAIN

T HE first sound of disaster was a voice on the phone: the cool, in- solent voice of Vallantine's secretary. "Who should I say is call- ing?" she asked.

"Tell him it's Mark from Santa Catalina."

"Mark who?"

Mark had been in Europe, visiting his father in London, his mother in Amsterdam, Signorina Rognoni in Genoa and Bernini in Rome. He had grown accustomed to respect and recognition. When he dropped in on rehearsals of the Kleist play at the Queen's Theatre on Shaftesbury Avenue, the actors and actresses welcomed him with the generous en- thusiasm characteristic of artists: he was Dana's son who had made it all possible. The secretaries of the politicians and scientists Dr. Habeler had arranged for him to meet all knew who he was. He was a some- body. But a somebody who blew all his cash. He stayed in the best ho- tels, invested in Jessica's British Solar Glass, bought the patent to a battery-powered motorbike, and returned to the island impatient to sell his coins. He wished now that the New York exhibition was already over instead of just starting. This was September 2, and according to the con- tract the exhibition was to open by the first of September, though oddly enough there were no reports about it in the New York papers. Nor was there any explanation from the Vallantine Gallery. Mark had plenty of mail waiting for him at the Seven Seas Club: a note from Dr. Habeler saying that Mark could get in touch with him in Paris, a reminder from the Wildlife Fund people in Brazil asking when they could expect his contribution, more letters reproaching him for his great wealth and asking for some of it; but there was nothing from Vallantine. As soon as he settled down in his Florentine suite, he asked the operator to place the call.

"Niven . . . ? Mark Niven? Could you tell me what it's about?"

Mark was stunned. How could she ask what his call was about? They had his whole fortune, and she didn't know who he was?

"Just get me Mr. Vallantine."

"Just a moment please . . . I'm sorry, he isn't in his office."

"Let me talk to Mrs. Vallantine then."

"I'm afraid she isn't here either."

In the end a man who introduced himself as the Assistant Director of the Gallery came on the line, and explained that they had decided not to launch any major exhibition so early in the fall. When they had some news they would be in touch.

"Tell Mr. Vallantine to call me as soon as he gets back," said Mark, picturing his timid, blushing friend eager to please him. "I don't like this at all, tell him to call me right away."

"Well, I'll tell him, but Mr. Vallantine's a busy man, you know."

The phone went dead before Mark could recover enough to speak. He stood up and began to do his exercises: raising and lowering his left arm, he walked back and forth in his rooms, trying not to think. He was interrupted by Coco, who dropped in, looking cool and elegant in a linen suit, to tell him about his new life: he had started a nightclub in Nassau and planned to get himself elected as an Out Island MP. The sight of a man whom he had made rich revived Mark's spirits for a while, until Coco happened to mention that Vallantine had been back on the island a week earlier and had tried to borrow his thirty thousand coins for the New York exhibition.

"What did he say, when will the exhibition open?" asked Mark.

"He says right away. He buys me dinner here at the Club and offers me ten thousand dollars to lend him my gold pieces. I eat his dinner but I says to him, Mr. Vallantine, ain't nothin personal, but I wouldn't never trust no white man. He looked real mad."

Mark spent the evening with Sarah, Eshelby and Weaver: they asked him about his trip and he told them about his meetings, the rehearsals in London. He couldn't bring himself to mention his call to New York: he didn't want to sound paranoid. Vallantine was bound to call him back.

"Oh, yes, Mr. Niven," said Vallantine's secretary promptly when Mark called again in the morning. "We're all very busy, but Mr. Vallantine left word that you should write to him if you have any problem."

A man and his incorporated company are not one and the same thing; Mark, who imagined that he had entered into an agreement with John Vallantine, kept coming up against people he had not known existed.

VALLANTINE GALLERIES INC.
East 57th Street
New York, N.Y. 10020

Office of the Assistant Director

Mr. Mark Alan Niven   September 8, 1970
Seven Seas Club
Santa Catalina
Bahama Islands

Dear Mr. Niven,

We are at a loss to understand the reason for your calls and cables. There is even one here from your attorney in Nassau.

I fail to see why you are distressing yourself. Everything is proceeding most satisfactorily and you have no cause for alarm. The delay is due simply to the need to improve security arrangements at the Gallery.

In the meantime, we are proceeding with private showings, and I'm sure you will be glad to hear that we have already concluded several important sales. You will receive accounts and payments in due course.

Yours sincerely,
David Davies

"That sounds very reasonable to me," Sarah said when Mark showed her the letter. "You can't blame them for improving security. If John wanted to steal from you he would have gone to South America or somewhere, he wouldn't stay at his regular business address and have his people correspond with you. I lent him my pearls last week and I'm not worried. You know what? I'll ring him up for you and tell him to phone you so you won't be upset."

"They can't sell anything, that would be fraud," said Darville confidently on the phone from Nassau. "This man Davies is just playing the fool: We could invalidate the sales. They undertook to open a three-month exhibition on or before the first of September. For some reason they missed their deadline and now they're trying to distract us with this kind of shit-talk. Nowhere in the contract did we authorize them to sell so much as a single doubloon. Nowhere. All they have is Clause 18. It says, let me read it to you . . . quote: *In the event that the Owner —* that's you, the owner — *in the event that the Owner shall avail himself of the services of the Exhibitor as agents for the sale of any of the exhibits, the Owner shall pay to the Exhibitor a commission of six percent of the monies accruing from such sale.* Unquote. Clear as daylight. It's up to you whether you sell anything or whether you use them as agents.''

"I want my treasures back in the vaults in Nassau," said Mark.

"And we can do it. I got you a foolproof cancellation clause which empowers us to void the contract if they are in breach of any of the provisions. Failure to open the exhibition before or on the date specified is a breach. They're obliged to airship everything back to you within 48 hours if I send them a cable voiding the contract."

"Send the cable then!"

Ordinarily reminders of breaches of contract demanding restitution within 48 hours were simply ignored by Vallantine, but this time, with so much at stake, he immediately handed everything over to his attorney, who cabled Darville the following day.

> ATTENTION FRANKLIN DARVILLE ESQ. PLEASE BE ADVISED
> VALLANTINE GALLERIES INC. REFUSE TO TERMINATE AGREE-
> MENT AS THIS WOULD UNFAIRLY AND WITHOUT SUFFICIENT
> CAUSE PREJUDICE THEIR RIGHTS TO EXHIBIT AND SELL GOODS
> IN QUESTION FOR WHICH RIGHTS THEY PAID YOUR CLIENT FIVE
> HUNDRED THOUSAND DOLLARS.
>   WILLIAM T. MACARTHUR ATTORNEY-AT-LAW

"This man MacArthur is daring us to sue," explained Darville after reading the cable over the phone. "The only right they bought was the right to exhibit the goods between September and November. The 500,000 was simply an advance against your share of the admission charges for the exhibition. They certainly didn't buy the right to sell anything. All they have on that is Clause 18."

The mind fears nothing so much as confusion. Mark asked the lawyer to read Clause 18 again.

"Oh Lord," groaned Darville. "You know it by heart! You agreed to pay them six percent commission in the event you availed yourself of their services as agents, but as you did not avail yourself of their services as agents, they're entitled to nothing. The whole clause is meaningless, that's why I let them have it. The man knows that what he says is not true, and he knows that we know it."

"Then how could he send that cable?" asked Mark, uncomprehending.

"He isn't concerned with what we know," explained Darville. "What we know or what he knows has nothing to do with it. This is just his opening move. He's saying *this is our position, prove us wrong in court.*"

"But it's a self-evident lie!" To state a lie firmly, categorically and with great authority, undeterred by the fact that all concerned know it to be a lie, is one of the principal activities defined by the term *practicing law* — but Mark had never been involved in a legal dispute.

"In law nothing is self-evident."

Mark took a deep breath. "Will I have to prove that I found the *Flora?*"

Darville promised to send another cable threatening legal action.

Mark could not eat that day and woke in the middle of the night, clutching his head: the derogatory phrase "goods in question" burned in his brain. Vallantine used to call the treasures *marvels, priceless artifacts, historic relics!* He no longer had any doubt that the art dealer meant to rob him.

> ATTENTION FRANKLIN DARVILLE ESQ. I AM ADVISED BY VAL-
> LANTINE GALLERIES INC. THAT AS A RESULT OF ACTIONS TAKEN
> BY THEM PURSUANT TO CLAUSE 18 AND VERBAL AGREEMENT
> BETWEEN THE PARTIES THEY ARE NO LONGER IN POSITION TO
> RETURN THE GOODS IN QUESTION.
> WILLIAM T. MACARTHUR ATTORNEY-AT-LAW

"He's implying that it's all gone," Darville explained on the phone, as if this was exactly what he had expected.

Mark felt as though his stomach had dropped out. He had to wait until he got his breath back, and then he screamed into the phone. "What do you mean, *all gone?*"

"I guess he's implying that they've sold everything pursuant to Clause 18."

"But Clause 18 doesn't allow them to do that!"

"That's why they came up with this business of a verbal agreement. The reference to a verbal agreement means they're going to claim that Clause 18 means what they say it means."

"That's theft! Let's report it to the FBI — they must have a man at the American Embassy in Nassau."

"I'm afraid this is a civil case. What we have here from the legal point of view is two conflicting interpretations of a partnership agreement. They paid you $500,000 and we'll be arguing what it was for. We'll have to sue them ourselves. We'll tell our story, they'll tell their story, and the court will decide who is right."

"You said all we had to do was send them a cable and we would get everything back in forty-eight hours!"

"Yes, but they came up with this verbal agreement," sighed Darville. "They're testing the old adage *possession is nine-tenths of the law.*"

"I thought that was a joke. Is it true?"

"Well, possession gives them a certain advantage."

"You mean you let me hand my treasures over to Vallantine, knowing that he can do as he pleases with them?"

"Good Lord, I didn't know Vallantine was a crook! I checked him out with the directors of the best museums — you saw the letters. With

272

hindsight, I guess we should have handled this the same way as the Nassau exhibition. We should have retained possession — rented his gallery, hired him to handle display and publicity, and kept our own guards in charge of the treasures.''

"You're telling me this *now?*''

"I advised you to read the contract carefully before you signed it — I told you I wanted you to understand its implications,'' Darville reminded him calmly. He was in the clear.

"You charged me forty-five thousand dollars for that contract!''

"Now, Mr. Niven, there is no point in getting emotional about this. They won't get away with it, you just have to be patient. All you need is a good lawyer in New York.''

"I paid *you* to be my lawyer. I paid you almost three hundred thousand dollars to look after me!''

"And I've earned every cent of it — I can show you my time sheets. If you're not satisfied, you don't have to involve me any further.''

Within an hour of this conversation Mark had checked out of his $500-a-day suite at the Club and left his things at Eshelby's apartment, except for a suitcase of clothes. Eshelby offered to return the gold cup and diamonds Mark had given him, but Mark refused. He was by no means destitute; his first Madonna and the Cross of the Seven Emeralds, returned to the bank vaults when he left for Europe, were still there and could serve as collateral for loans up to a million dollars. Sarah, Coco and Eshelby went to the Santa Catalina airstrip to see him off and try to cheer him up.

"Hey, man!'' said Coco. He grabbed the air with his hands, then let it go. "Easy comes, easy goes!''

Sarah kissed him with a contrite look. "I'm sorry — I should never have introduced them to you. I wish I could give you the pearls, at least!''

"I lends you some coins if you asks.''

"I keep thinking of that disgusting sweaty man insisting that you should make a will because he just *had* to know whom to give it all back to if anything happened to you,'' sighed Eshelby. "Dear boy, I'll hold on to those diamonds and that gold cup for you, in case you change your mind. Don't lose heart. America is one of the few countries in the world based on the rule of law. You ought to be able to get back what everybody knows is yours.''

"I know,'' said Mark, embracing each of them with tears in his eyes.

He stopped over in Nassau to borrow money from Mr. Murray and to collect copies of the contract and correspondence. Darville handed over the papers in an expensive leather briefcase which he had bought specially for the occasion. "You're welcome to keep it,'' he said magnanimously.

Mark was so shaken that on the plane back to New York he did not once recall his panicky flight from his native city nineteen months earlier. Nor did he think of the danger of being arrested as a draft dodger. Seeing the police out in force at Kennedy Airport made him feel safer; he would have been shocked to be reminded that once he had thought of policemen as useless brutes. Now all his hopes were in the law.

Games Lawyers Play

Dare any of you, having a matter against another,
go to law before the unjust . . . why do ye not rather
suffer yourselves to be defrauded?

SAINT PAUL

I do not care to speak ill of any man behind his back,
but I believe the gentleman is an attorney.

SAMUEL JOHNSON

The law is a horrible business.

CLARENCE DARROW

MORE than twenty years earlier, in his student days at Columbia, Dana Niven had been friends with a quick-witted, funny, idealistic youngster called Bernie Wattman, who often invited him to his place in the Bronx. Bernie's father was a tailor with his own shop, and their small house had the air of contented poverty. The parents spoiled not only their children but also their children's friends. Never except in his own home did Dana Niven feel so much at home as at the Wattmans' place; indeed he would remember the son less vividly than the parents, who were overflowing with affection and good feeling and apparently found great joy in patting his cheek and feeding him. The friends lost touch after graduation, but when Niven was back in New York starring in *The Devil's Disciple*, Bernard Jay Wattman, Esq., came backstage one evening with his attractive wife to say hello.

They had supper together at the Russian Tea Room, and the actor was impressed by how little difference twenty-odd years had made. The successful New York attorney thought and spoke the same way as in his youth, except that he no longer hoped to rise to the Supreme Court of the United States. "I don't have powerful connections," he said. "I'm a lawyer for the underdog — I wouldn't work for the big corporations."

He even looked like his old boyish self: a pudgy, cheerful man with puffy cheeks and bright eyes.

"You haven't changed at all!" Niven exclaimed several times during the evening, and a couple of years later when he was tied down in London and Mark was in trouble in New York, it seemed natural to him to call his old college friend for help. Bernie promised to do his best for Mark.

Unfortunately, Bernie's unchangingly youthful look, his almost babyish glow that so many people found reassuring, were signs not of untarnished integrity but of a psychological regression, a moral malady that attacks even hitherto decent men and women around the age of forty. As moral beings, many people are destroyed in childhood and adolescence; nonetheless, there are multitudes of generous and compassionate young adults in every generation who renew hope for the future. But where are they twenty years later? Dana Niven, whose character had withstood the poison of unfulfilled ambition, the foretaste of death which is middle age, could not fathom what it meant for Wattman to live with the knowledge that the Supreme Court of the United States was beyond his reach and that if he didn't lose weight, as he didn't, he was a candidate for a heart attack. The older Wattman grew, the more he regressed into the self-absorption of a child: nothing was quite real for him except himself, his family and his things.

The fact that he kept up the liberal rhetoric of his youth, deriding the big corporations, worrying about minorities, civil rights, disarmament, concealed his transformation into a monster of egotism. If he remained a liberal, he was a liberal the way most crooks in New York are liberals, the way most crooks in Texas are conservatives — they fit in wherever they are.

Outwardly Wattman's law practice didn't change: he still represented underdogs — it was just that he represented more and more of them. He became one of those lawyers who, lacking rich clients, manage to earn a yearly fortune by taking on far more cases than they can handle. A gifted advocate, Wattman employed his talents chiefly in landing clients, parting them from their savings, and then doing as little as possible for them. Those who hadn't yet paid their dues found him always at their beck and call, but once he had collected his *retainer,* he looked at their files with the eyes of a busy man: which case could yield the most profit in the least time? He rarely went to trial with anything but a personal injury case in which he could display his client's missing limb to the jury. Those who had complicated cases or difficult opponents were shunted aside until they were ready to pay more.

Those who could not keep paying were eventually dropped; they deserved their troubles for not helping him to meet his expenses. He felt only annoyance when one of his discarded clients committed suicide in his reception room; he could not forgive the dead man for making a mess and causing him embarrassment.

Wattman spread human misery from a four-room office in downtown Manhattan which he shared with his partner, Marilyn Schon, Esq., who handled mostly divorce cases. There was the reception room where the secretary worked, a conference room for taking depositions and storing files, and a separate study and washroom for each partner. (Clients in favor were offered their attorney's washroom; the rest had to use the public one down the corridor.) In keeping with the underdog clientele, nothing was for show: all the furniture in the office was clean and new and plastic, offering no clue to what went on there. The suicide's blood-spots on the walls had been painted over many times.

MARK'S welcome could not have been more encouraging. "Mr. Wattman is in conference. I'll call him — he told me not to keep you waiting," said the secretary.

"Yes, it's urgent," replied Mark, who had taken a taxi straight from the airport and was still carrying his suitcase as well as Darville's brief-case, both with his good hand. He had hardly had time to put them down when Wattman came in.

"I was glad to hear from your father, but this is a terrible business," said the lawyer briskly, holding out both of his spongy white hands. His lips seemed to smile a little even when he wasn't smiling. "I'm tied up all day today. If you give me everything you have on paper I'll read it tonight and talk to you about it tomorrow."

Mark gave him Darville's briefcase.

"Good. I know how important this is, so be here at seven-thirty in the morning. We've got to start early — I have to be in court at ten."

At 7:30 in the morning the two of them seemed to be the only people in the building apart from the maintenance men.

"I want you to know how much I appreciate your making time for me like this," Mark said gratefully as they were riding up in the elevator. "I mean getting up at dawn for me."

"Aw, nuts," replied Wattman with a deprecating shrug. "My friends' kids are my friends. I wish I had better news for you, though. I don't think we'll be able to recover much."

Mark was suddenly dizzy, feeling how little he had slept. "What . . . ?"

"Haven't you read those cables?"

"If it's a question of their five hundred thousand, I'll pay it back!"

The lawyer shot a piercing look at him. "You still have it?"

"No, but . . ."

"Never mind, that's not your problem."

"Oh, that's all right then," said Mark, greatly relieved. "You're thinking of their claim that we had a verbal agreement, but it isn't true!"

"Nah . . . guess again," said Wattman as he unlocked the main door to WATTMAN & SCHON. "Do you want some coffee?" He led the way to his study, took an electric kettle from the cupboard, put it on the desk and filled it from a bottle of Evian spring water.

By a trick of memory this had a momentarily calming effect on Mark. "Are you worried about the agency clause? My lawyer in Nassau says that's a meaningless clause."

"They can spin a lawsuit out of it for years, that sounds pretty meaningful to me. But that's not it."

This was a new fright. Now Mark's arm was aching. "Do you think they really sold the treasures? Could the buyers keep them?"

"You have a worse problem than that," the lawyer said briskly, producing two mugs and placing them beside the kettle. "Come on, think! You can't guess? Try. There are three words in each of those cables which wipe out your rights for all practical purposes."

"Rubbish," retorted Mark, surprised and angry. He had come to hear how he was going to get his treasures back as quickly as possible. "There are no words that can turn my treasures into Vallantine's. Rubbish."

"So . . ." Wattman's smile broadened; dimples appeared on his puffy cheeks. Prompted by the whistling of the kettle, he put spoonfuls of instant coffee and powdered cream into the mugs and poured in the bubbling water. "Let's hear how you got into this fix," he suggested, pushing one of the steaming mugs toward Mark, then sat down to sip his coffee, to question, to comment. He had many ways of breaking in a client.

"What do you mean, Vallantine looked harmless?" he said at one point. "You can't tell how harmless a person is until you've seen his attorney. Vallantine's attorney would have frozen your blood."

Mark told his story and learned what a fool he had been; this is how most prospective litigants acquire respect for their lawyers' opinions. "What's wrong with those cables?" he finally asked, humbled.

"You mean those three words?" Wattman said merrily, back at his game. "I've given you clues. You still can't guess? You give up? It's the signature! William T. MacArthur."

"What's so great about his signature? He's just a lawyer like you, isn't he?"

"Just a lawyer?" Wattman seemed to grow thin from horror. "You call a member of PETER, BLACK, JEFFERSON, MACARTHUR, WHITMAN & WARREN *just a lawyer?* These guys are demigods like their namesakes. They specialize in corporate fraud. Anybody who steals in a big way goes to them for protection. They take up two whole floors of a skyscraper. Their office rent is $1,600,000 a year, if they haven't bought the building yet. How shall I put it to you? Just the other week Mac-Arthur was defending a couple of Wall Street brokers who had stolen two million from their investors. They kept the money, too, claiming it was all gone. The judge fined them $40,000, gave each a six-month suspended sentence, and complimented them on their distinguished attorney. That's not a bad deal, is it?''

"They couldn't do things like that every day."

"Well, it's expensive," Wattman conceded with a shrug. "MacArthur's fee must have been at least eight hundred thousand. And no doubt he expressed his thanks to the judge. They're members of the same clubs, so they were probably able to work out some invisible transaction."

"My case is different," protested Mark, getting up from his chair. "A judge may hand out suspended sentences, but he can't hand over to Vallantine what belongs to me. There are laws — you wouldn't have all those books on your shelves if they didn't mean anything."

Wattman heaved a deep sigh. "I know you won't believe this, but I have people coming in here every day — they want a lawyer, they beg for advice, and then they tell me all about the law!" He shook his head and added in a sharp voice. "Take your coffee, sit down and listen."

"Sorry." Mark took the mug, but was too tense to sit down.

"The law is like the Bible."

"That's good enough for me."

"And how many priests, rabbis, ministers agree on what the Bible says?" asked the lawyer, weary of explaining the obvious. "There are as many laws as there are judges. The law is what the judge says is the law — and that judge could be anybody. Anybody. You should think of this town as Chicago during Prohibition. That was before your time, it was even before my time, but you can read about it. Did you know that justices of the Illinois courts used to act as pallbearers at gangsters' funerals? Of course today no judge would carry a gangster's coffin because he'd be seen on TV, and the money to buy immunity comes from drugs not liquor, but the rest is the same. Poor Robert Kennedy used to say that organized crime spends more on law-enforcement personnel than the U.S. government —"

Mark interrupted, insisting impatiently that he had nothing to do with the Mafia and they had nothing to do with him.

"Yes, I'm sure all this sounds very remote to you, but you could find yourself at the mercy of Judge Aurelio, one of the late Frank Costello's chums. The FBI has him on tape agreeing to fix a trial for a fee. But they tapped his phone without a court order, so they can't prosecute him. The voters, members of your jury, could get rid of him — the transcript of the tape was in the papers — but they keep re-electing him to the bench. So this man is still on the state supreme court, waiting for you to go to him for justice.''

"There must be honest judges!''

"Sure there are — I know one in a lower court. He's so virtuous he thinks that men who go to prostitutes are depraved. Years ago, when I was just starting out in this business, I defended a girl who stole two hundred bucks from a customer. She admitted it to the police, so all I could do was make sure she got this Solomon to hear her case. Sure enough, His Honor refused to make an order against the girl. A man who picks up prostitutes deserves to have his wallet stolen, he said. Case dismissed. What do you think of that? A magistrate suspends the laws against theft because he disapproves of horny men. Supreme Court justices are more sophisticated, they wouldn't proclaim the doctrine of legal relativism in court, but they'll find theft quite lawful if they think you deserve to be robbed.''

"They can't all be fools or crooks!''

"Of course not! But they're all MacArthur's friends. Judge MacArthur, as they still call him, used to be a judge himself, you know. For years he was a vice-president of the New York Bar Association. He's big in local politics and has a lot to do with the selection of candidates for the bench — many state supreme court justices owe their lucrative posts to his support or lack of opposition. The rest of them are his dear old colleagues. His *pals*. The man's power is proverbial. The DA complains that theft is no theft, fraud is no fraud, when Judge MacArthur is defending.''

Bowed by these words of discouragement, Mark stared at the mug of coffee in his hand, with no idea that he was supposed to drink it. "Well, if you're so scared of MacArthur and his friends, I'll have to look for another lawyer,'' he said bleakly.

Wattman's eyes widened with surprise. "I'm trying to scare *you*,'' he said crossly, his puffy cheeks growing taut. "Most lawyers would promise you quick success, take a fat retainer and bankrupt you without so much as a word of warning. I'm not like that. I'd rather lose you as a client than leave you in ignorance about your chances. I guess you want me to cheer you up, improve your mood, but if I were you . . .'' He paused; his bright, darting eyes fastened on Mark. "If I were you, I'd prefer an attorney who levels with me, an attorney I can trust!''

Mark sat down again, exhausted, desolate, confused.

"Do you realize that all this is costing you nothing?'' asked Wattman, amazed at his own generosity. "If I charged you for reading your papers at night and advising you before breakfast, you would faint. You're getting special treatment, and it isn't just the money either. You think I get up at dawn for everybody?''

"I'm grateful, but I can afford to pay my way," said Mark, worried that the lawyer was so negative because he saw no money in the case.

'God, I could do this in my sleep,' thought Wattman. "No, no, you can't afford it," he said regretfully. "The law is for the rich.''

"But I *am* rich!''

"That's different . . ." Wattman closed his eyes and leaned back in his swivel chair. "How much do you have?''

"That's what it's all about! Vallantine is holding a hundred and fifty million dollars' worth of historic treasures which belong to me.''

Wattman opened his eyes. "Oh, you mean *Vallantine* is rich!'' He stared sadly at Mark to convey the full force of his disappointment.

"But even if Vallantine sold everything he can't keep the money. He has to pay me 94% of the proceeds.''

The lawyer looked, if possible, even sadder. "He has to pay you 94% of the proceeds like he has to return your treasures to you when you ask for them. He had no right to sell anything in the first place, so what makes you think he would cut you in on his illegal sales? These guys have more ways of robbing you than you could dream of. They can sell the whole lot to a corporation they set up in Liechtenstein, so you could never prove they sold the stuff to themselves, then claim they had to pay a million to a subagent — a real person, somebody like Vallantine's brother-in-law — and *then* deduct the 6% commission they're entitled to under the contract. How much would that leave you with from your fabulous fortune? Anyway, you wouldn't get it. You'd have to sue them for it — go to court against Judge MacArthur. These big crooks never disgorge a cent.''

Mark had a great longing to go berserk, to throw things and smash things, but he steeled himself to keep calm and stick to the point. "I'm rich all the same. I still have a gold statue and the Cross of the Seven Emeralds — they're at my bank in Nassau.''

"That's better. This cross with the emeralds . . . that rings a bell. How much are those emeralds worth?''

Mark grew wary, remembering Darville's bills. "Everything I have is in the bank as security — I've already borrowed on them, but I'm sure I can borrow some more.''

"Well, so far you're not spending anything, and you can keep it that way!'' the lawyer said harshly, sweeping the air with his arm.

"What do you mean?''

"I'm a family lawyer . . ." There was a pause to stress the significance of this. "I mean I'm the lawyer for my whole family. If any of my sisters, in-laws, nephews, aunts want to sue anybody, they come to me and they all get the same advice. Some years ago my dad, a hardworking tailor, had a case — a far stronger case than yours, a far stronger case — and I said to him: Papa, you fed and clothed me for twenty-five years, you sent me to summer camp, you put me through law school, you bought me my first car, thanks to you I'm a big-shot lawyer and drive a Rolls-Royce. Now it's my turn! This is my chance to repay your love and kindness. Your devoted son is a first-class attorney who will do everything for you that it's possible to do for a client, and I'm telling you, Papa, *forget it!*''

"You don't understand," Mark sighed despairingly, pressing his hand against his forehead as if to keep it from splitting open. "I don't want any big lawsuit, I don't want Vallantine to be punished or anything, I just want my treasures back."

"So . . ." Wattman tilted back and forth in his swivel chair with a what-am-I-to-do-with-you expression. "You want it fast, huh? Let's say I file a notice of action tomorrow. They have three weeks to answer."

Mark took a deep breath. "Three weeks?" To save money for his lawsuit, he had checked into a cheap hotel nearby which had big rooms and abstract expressionist paintings in the lobby but smelled of insecticide, marijuana and dogshit. "I'll wait three weeks if I have to."

"You'll be waiting for a *postponement,* kid. If I take your case, you'll have to promise me patience. I couldn't have you come here bothering the secretary every day, wanting to know what's happening. Most of the time nothing would be happening and I couldn't do a thing about it. Three weeks from now Vallantine's going to be busy. Six weeks from now his attorney's going to be busy. They just won't have time to attend to your complaints for months. Can you promise me patience? Please, don't spill the coffee on the carpet. Put it down. . . . Put it down! Thank you. Didn't your dad ever play Hamlet? Haven't you heard of *the law's delay?*''

"Vallantine can't just walk away with my fortune and then say he's too busy to come to court!"

"And why not?" asked Wattman mercilessly, watching Mark trying to clean the carpet with his handkerchief. "Are you familiar with the principle that a person is presumed innocent until proven guilty? Do you have any idea what this noble legal precept actually means?"

"Of course I do."

"Of course? It means that you — *you* — are a wicked liar maligning an innocent man. A respected citizen, a leader of the New York art world, pays you five hundred thousand dollars, and then you come here and call him a thief. Do you expect the law to violate his civil liberties, jump on him, ruin him, simply on your say-so? Your complaints will have to be looked into *very carefully* — and not in a hurry either. You must understand that all the law ever worries about is the danger of an innocent man being convicted. Or even needlessly bothered. The law doesn't

282

worry about the victims. The victims are supposed to be dead. Or they are mistaken. Or they're trying to ruin a good man for some personal reason. It's the same as with rape — it's always the victims who have to prove their innocence.''

"I was on television! All the New York papers printed reports about my discovery of the *Flora*. My contract with Vallantine says that I'm the owner — what is there to prove?''

Wattman threw up his arms. "How do I know? Am I a mind-reader? All I know is that MacArthur is going to come up with something. I didn't want to mention it, but I saw him at a fund-raising dinner last night and he says he knows you.''

"How can he say such a thing? I never saw him in my life.''

"That's the kind of guy he is. I suggested that we should settle this dispute peacefully; he said his client has done nothing wrong and so there's nothing to be settled. They mean business.''

"If it's this verbal agreement he was talking about — he wouldn't dare perjure himself like that before the court.''

Wattman's puffy cheeks were all smiles. "He wouldn't *dare?* Judge MacArthur? The chairman of the Committee for Legal Reform? You think a man could get that big in New York if there was anything in the world he didn't dare? I promise you, he'll think of something that will make you climb the wall.''

"I thought you lawyers were supposed to defend the innocent, or even the guilty, for some crime already committed, but this MacArthur's actually helping Vallantine to rob me. He's as much a thief as Vallantine!''

"Exactly. I'd say half the cases before the courts are about ongoing crimes, and they're kept going by lawyers. They're there to make sure that Vallantine or whoever can take a piece out of you today and another piece tomorrow.''

"Aren't they ashamed?''

"Whatever for? They're doing their job. They're being loyal to their clients.''

"We had no verbal agreement, I didn't authorize any sale —''

Wattman cut him short with an impatient gesture. "How do I know that? Never mind, you've convinced me. How do we prove it in court?''

"Darville can testify that the contract covered everything.''

"Good point!'' Wattman raised his eyebrows and thrust forward his lower lip appreciatively. "MacArthur won't want to argue that a fellow attorney is lying. You have the makings of a competent client. I'm impressed. So if MacArthur comes to court in six months' time with his story about a verbal agreement, we hit back with a sworn statement from Darville. We'll win the first round — but then MacArthur starts asking for postponements again,'' he sighed, his lips still smiling. "We'll have to wait another six months and in the end he files an answering affidavit which ignores everything we have said and everything *he* has said, and serves us some brand-new nonsense which we'll have to refute. And then there are the interrogatories, the oral depositions! That's what's called *discovery proceedings* — and they can go on for five to ten years.''

By then Mark was out of breath, even though sitting in a chair. ''My God . . . how could the courts allow that?''

Wattman tilted his head and looked at Mark with an innocent expression. ''You mean, why don't MacArthur's pals tell him — Bill, stop making money, let's be poor and serve justice?''

Mark twisted his body as if warding off a blow. ''I don't understand this — don't you want any clients? You could charge me whatever you want in the end!''

The lawyer shook his head with an unhappy expression. ''I couldn't wait that long, Mark. It would cost you a great deal, so think! I'd rather lose a fat fee than see you caught up in this hellish and expensive business.''

All this was routine. Wattman did his best to dissuade all prospective clients from going to court. What better way was there to demonstrate that he put their interests ahead of his own? What better way to justify himself ahead of time for his negligence? How could his clients reproach him for anything if he always started out by warning them that they would have no satisfaction? William Blake rhymed the point a long time ago:

> *A truth that's told with bad intent*
> *beats all the lies you can invent.*

Clever attorneys don't run after clients, they catch them by sending them away. They know there is very little risk that their warnings will be heeded. In more than twenty years of legal practice Wattman had come across few litigants who were prepared to accept defeat at the onset of their misery; as far as he could tell, people were driven to the law by intense pain or intense hate and were quite immune to practical considerations. It made no difference what he said. However, Wattman tried to be more persuasive than usual with his friend's son: he wanted the boy to listen, to be one of the exceptions. ''I want you to listen!'' he said, leaning forward with a solemn expression. ''This city's a jungle — run. You're only twenty-one. A lawsuit can eat up the best years of your life, and at the end of it you can still lose.''

''I'm not going to give up what's mine!''

''I'm not making any impression on you,'' sighed Wattman plaintively. If Mark listened, he deserved to get away; if he didn't he deserved to be cleaned out. ''This is a fateful thing, why don't you go back to your hotel and think it over?''

284

"I can think right here, thank you," replied Mark impatiently. The more Wattman tried to dissuade him, the more Mark believed he had found a lawyer he could trust, who would do his best for him.

"Don't be stupid! You still have that cross and gold statue and maybe a few more keepsakes you were too shy to mention — your little hoard could keep you going for the rest of your life. Hang on to it, don't waste it on litigation. You're young and you have enough for a long and care-free life — you can study, travel, pick whatever profession or career you want without having to worry about how much it pays — what more could you want?"

There was a buzz on the intercom, followed by the secretary's voice reminding the lawyer that it was 9:20 and he would be late for court. "I can tell you how to be happy, Mark," he begged in a hurry. "Forget you ever found a treasure ship!"

Mark had heard all the words, but to understand them he would have had to be capable of realizing that everything he had done since Toledo had never happened. He would not give up anything.

Wattman got to his feet, ready to run. "So you instruct me to go ahead? All right, but don't forget, you've been warned!"

"I've always been lucky!" replied Mark, raising his bad arm to prove it.

Wattman nodded, then picked up a briefcase from the row of brief-cases on a shelf and waved Mark out ahead of him. He stated his terms in the elevator. "I'll tell you what I'll do . . . I won't charge you any-thing as long as the case is hopeless. You won't pay for failure. But if we're making real progress, against all odds, I'll ask for a lot. Is that fair?"

NEXT day Wattman applied to the Supreme Court of the State of New York, County of New York, for a preliminary injunction to prevent Val-lantine from selling the treasures still in his possession. Granting the motion, the court ordered: "The chattels shall not be removed from their location, transferred, sold, pledged, assigned or otherwise disposed of or permitted to become subject to a security interest or lien until further order of the court."

Following this WATTMAN & SCHON issued a summons against John Vallantine & Vallantine Galleries, Inc., hereinafter called Defendants, on behalf of Mark Alan Niven, hereinafter called Plaintiff, and filed a complaint recounting the history of Plaintiff's discovery of the *Flora* and appending all relevant documents and correspondence, not least Plain-tiff's agreement with the government of the Bahama Islands, which granted Plaintiff ownership of the treasures subsequently entrusted by him to Defendants. Wattman argued that the contract between Plaintiff and Defendants was entered into for the sole purpose of enabling Defendants to exhibit the aforesaid chattels between September 1 and November 30 of the current year, which Defendants failed to do, while at the same time refusing to return them, claiming they were no longer in a position to do so, and refusing to honor the cancellation clause of the contract. Accordingly, Wattman asked the court to put an end to "this brazen attempt to defraud a person of his property". Specifically, he requested that the court

a.) declare null & void Defendants' unauthorized sale of any and all chattels owned by Plaintiff,

b.) declare the contract between Defendants and Plaintiff null & void on the ground that Defendants had failed to open the exhibition on or before the date specified in Clause 3 of the contract,

c.) declare Defendants' $500,000 advance on exhibition receipts forfeit to Plaintiff for the aforesaid reason,

d.) order the immediate restitution of all aforesaid chattels to Plaintiff.

In his answering affidavit on behalf of the Defendants, William T. MacArthur, *duly sworn,* solemnly affirmed that Mark's complaint was "an act of breathtaking mendacity in view of the indispensable help and generous financial assistance Plaintiff had received from Defendants." The former state supreme court justice could hardly believe his eyes when he read that Plaintiff had "the temerity to accuse his benefactor of fraud".

Fraud in this case was practiced only by Plaintiff, who "shamelessly" claimed sole credit for the discovery of the *Flora* although it was the researchers employed by Vallantine Galleries who had traced the probable location of the wreck and it was John Vallantine who had sent Plaintiff to Santa Catalina, providing him with funds to purchase his boat and diving equipment — this in addition to the $500,000 advance on exhibition receipts, which was "a good deal more money than a young man with no trade or profession could expect to earn in a lifetime".

This large payment, MacArthur argued, proved Defendants' good faith and enabled Plaintiff to wait in comfort for the opening of the exhibition, admittedly delayed. Ignoring his own cable implying that Vallantine Galleries no longer had the goods in question, MacArthur claimed that the postponement of the exhibition gave no grounds for voiding the contract or forfeiting the advance, and "only an unconscionably greedy, ungrateful and litigious person" would use such unavoidable delay as a pretext for legal action, "wasting the time of the Court".

Accordingly, MacArthur asked the court to dismiss Plaintiff's complaint as "completely spurious, mischievous and groundless".

Summoned to another early morning conference at Wattman's office, Mark sat in a chair holding Judge MacArthur's sworn statement, pale as death. He didn't utter a sound as he read, but his whole body trembled as if he were shivering from cold. When he finished reading the defense statement, he began tearing it up, page by page. "It's not enough for them to rob me, they have to abuse me too!" he said in a low, hoarse voice, throwing the scraps of paper on the floor.

Wattman put his hand involuntarily on his copy of the document. "Listen, you're not here to mess up the place. What I want to know is what evidence we have, if any, to disprove their allegations."

The physical discomfort of sitting in a chair while exploding inside became unbearable: Mark stood up and began to walk about the room, gesticulating wildly, in the manner of people who are so agitated that they feel they must move their arms and legs or they will die. "So Vallantine's my benefactor! I'm the one who's unconscionably greedy! Isn't there a law against perjury?"

"I *told* you MacArthur was going to think of something that would make you climb the wall. You've got to take this in your stride. So he's abusing you, big deal. What do you expect him to do, praise you? Once they rob you, you become their enemy. You're trying to get back what they stole from you — you give them no choice, they have to do their best to discredit you. That's what lawsuits are all about."

"MacArthur's lying under oath, that's perjury. You ought to be able to put him in prison for that!"

"Boy, you're a wild one. I can see you won't be much use to me on the witness stand. Look, if I were to accuse MacArthur of perjury, I'd be disbarred. Lawyers never perjure themselves — that's one thing they never do. You've got to get this into your head: our whole legal system is based on the truthfulness of lawyers. Attorneys are officers of the court, they never lie. They are misled by their clients."

This explanation, in spite of its clarity, made no impression on Mark; he could feel only the violence done to his memory. "Perjury's perjury," he insisted. "MacArthur swore out a statement that Vallantine financed my search for the *Flora!*"

Wattmann spread his arms with a triumphant grin. "He was misled by his client."

It was pain that made Mark see reason: his arm was hurting from tearing the paper and gesturing so violently and he was forced to sit down again. "Well, if you want proofs — my father paid my way to the Bahamas and gave me the money to buy my boat and my diving gear. He can testify to that."

"Does your father keep records? Canceled checks or the like? . . . He gave you cash? We've got a problem there."

Mark took a deep breath and continued doggedly. "The man who sent me down there wasn't Vallantine, it was a vice-president of North–South International right here in New York. I'm sure he wouldn't mind testifying about it. He's a nice guy — I got drafted and he sent me to the island to save me from Vietnam."

"I don't think I would want us to go into that," Wattman said hurriedly. "Forget that you were a draft dodger. I'll try to keep it out of the case. You just gave me another headache."

"I've got lots of witnesses on Santa Catalina — friends who can swear I never laid eyes on Vallantine till he came to the Seven Seas Club."

Dissatisfied, Wattman pushed up his little button nose with his index finger. "If they're your friends, their credibility can be questioned. If they're not such good friends, they may be too busy to come to New York when you need them. Witnesses can be bought, murdered — even die of natural causes."

"Well, then," Mark replied with apparent calm, "I'll bring a speargun to court and shoot the bastards."

Wattman sighed, then sat in silence for a while, watching a cloud pass by the window. "There's one more thing," he finally said, rousing himself from his reverie. He got up and came out from behind his desk to put into his client's hand the untouched mug of coffee he had made for him. "I didn't want to tell you this, because you were upset enough as it is, but MacArthur warned me against you."

"What do you mean?" asked Mark, taking the mug.

"I'll wait until you drink your coffee," said Wattman. "That's the way. Drink up. Good. Well, now. MacArthur says you're crazy."

"I don't understand."

"He says you're mentally unbalanced."

Mark stared at his lawyer with disbelief. "How could he say such a thing?"

"He knows you, remember?" Wattman took the empty mug from Mark's hand and put it back on his desk. "You appreciate that once there is any question about your mental competence, your testimony becomes valueless, and Vallantine's home with the goodies."

"I'll kill him at the hearing!"

"They would dearly love you to try. Listen to me. The only way I allow you to come to court is if you promise to shut up and behave coolly, calmly and reasonably, as if the whole proceedings had nothing to do with you."

"And then they'll think I'm normal?" asked Mark, trying to cheer himself with his own poor wit.

VALLANTINE didn't attend the hearing at the Manhattan County Courthouse, 60 Center Street, but Mark finally had a chance to lay eyes on the legendary Judge MacArthur of PETER, BLACK, JEFFERSON, MACARTHUR, WHITMAN & WARREN. William T. MacArthur was a big man with a high, domed brow and bald head. When not speaking in his powerful, even voice, he was totally immobile. His wide, flat, almost featureless face seemed to have been set in clay. All through the hearing Mark tried to catch his eye, wanting to exchange looks with the man who claimed to know him so well. But MacArthur looked over Mark's head when glancing in his direction, and even when their eyes met, his clay face remained as impassive as ever and his pale eyes gazed at Mark as indifferently as at the usher.

Remembering Wattman's warning, Mark held back his bitterness and rage; indeed, he couldn't have helped sensing that any expression of emotion would appear insane in the rarefied atmosphere of the courtroom. The usher at the door was as remote and dignified as Justice F in his chair. Every officer of the court seemed to wear a robe of manners, a mantle of chilling professional rectitude that was meant to elevate the bearer above the vices of prejudice, favoritism and greed. When you look at us, they seemed to say, forget what you know about the frailty of human nature: we are Justice made flesh.

The court's ruling on the motions had an aura of majestic impartiality by virtue of giving a bit to each of the litigants. Justice F rejected MacArthur's plea to have Plaintiff's complaints dismissed and held that Plaintiff had *grounds for action;* on the other hand, Wattman's request to the court to void the contract between the parties in accordance with the cancellation clause was also rejected, "in view of Defendants' alleged contribution to the finding of the *Flora* and their considerable investment in the upcoming exhibition . . ."

"Well, we got the court's leave to sue," Wattman explained to Mark afterward over lunch in a Chock Full o' Nuts near the courthouse. "What bothers me is that neither MacArthur nor his pal on the bench had anything to say about sales. Vallantine still has possession of the goods — he might disobey the injunction — I'd better file a motion to sequester." Once again Mark offered to pay, but the lawyer just shook his head. He wouldn't take anything until he saw a chance of winning. A few days later he presented another motion requesting that in view of the dispute Defendants be ordered to deposit the treasures with the court.

The clerk of the court, who sets dates for hearings and thus exercises considerable influence over the lives of both criminals and victims, assigned the motion, presented on the 18th day of November, for hearing on the 26th day of January. Learning of this delay, Mark left the hotel and rented a cheap one-room walk-up on St. Mark's Place, just off Third

Avenue. The apartment had a slanting floor, cockroaches and mice, but the street was named after his patron saint and he was beginning to feel the need for heavenly intervention. On the 25th day of January, the day before Wattman's motion was to be heard, a junior of PETER, BLACK, JEFFERSON, MACARTHUR, WHITMAN & WARREN presented an affidavit to the court requesting a postponement of the hearing because Defendants' attorney had to be in England at the time, to give a lecture at Cambridge on the American Constitution, and therefore holding the hearing on the said date "would deprive Defendants of the benefit of their regular legal counsel".

The court granted a three-week postponement, then several further postponements for other reasons, as a matter of course.

Who Cares?

Intellectual disgrace
Stares from every human face,
And the seas of pity lie
Locked and frozen in each eye.
W. H. AUDEN

DANA Niven blamed himself for Mark's involvement with Vallantine. The boy was lying wounded, helpless, in the clinic, and he
had left him to manage a fortune on his own! He should have stayed by
his bed day and night, screening everybody who came near him. The
actor had many excuses to draw on if he had been so inclined: he had
left the island because he believed that Mark didn't need him; since Mark
had proved him wrong by finding the *Flora,* the proud father was convinced that his son was smarter than anyone, including himself. But what
were parents for if not to protect their children? Niven's remorse was all
the more painful for the fact that he saw his life as a series of duties to
perform — as an artist, as a father, as a human being — and he could
not forgive himself for failing in his duty to his son. His success in London with the Kleist play only made him feel more guilty, since it was
Mark who had paid for it. When he heard that the second preliminary
hearing, which was only to establish where the treasures were, had been
postponed for the fourth time, he caught the first plane to New York,
hoping that his reputation and contacts would enable him to raise such
a hue and cry that Vallantine would be forced to hand the treasures back.

From Kennedy Airport he took a cab straight to the office of the managing editor of a New York daily, an old classmate from Columbia.

"What you're telling me is very interesting, but it isn't news," said
the managing editor, more intrigued by Dana Niven's presence in his
office than by the ins and outs of a lawsuit: according to the latest edition of the paper lying on his desk, Niven was on the other side of the
Atlantic having a big success with Ustinov in a German play — and
here he was, staring at him with bloodshot eyes full of parental anguish

and jet lag. Actors *were* different! This one had been killing his stage son in front of an admiring audience every night, and then thought nothing of walking away from the applause and rushing to the other end of the world on a fool's errand, trying to drum up publicity for his real son. And with what intensity! The managing editor was a father too, and he knew he wouldn't have done it.

"For an actor who loves the stage, you left it in an awful hurry!" he said jokingly to get rid of the disconcerting sense of admiration he felt.

"It's just for a few days." The actor shifted impatiently in his chair. "I have a great understudy. Anyway, I'm hoping that you'll do a big exposé on these crooks and I can fly back tonight."

"I'm sorry, Dana, but this doesn't involve any public issue — I couldn't justify covering it."

"What could be more of a public issue? No one's property is safe if Mark can be robbed like that! How could you hope to hang on to your house or your wallet if people can borrow a famous fortune for exhibition and then just keep it?"

"If I understood you correctly," the managing editor replied, drawing squares within squares on the edge of the proof page in front of him, "they can't just keep it, the issue is before the courts. The court will say whether they can keep it or not. And frankly, I don't think Judge MacArthur would be involved if Vallantine didn't have some right on his side."

The actor's tired, bloodshot eyes became young with the light of withering contempt. "You always speak frankly when you say something you couldn't possibly mean?"

The managing editor laughed a little and pressed the button to signal his secretary that he was ready for the next piece of business. "Well, maybe I don't quite mean it. But we've already published a piece on the Italian government's lawsuit against Vallantine. If we did an article about another lawsuit of his, it would look like we were conducting a personal vendetta against him. He could sue us for victimization. Besides, we don't usually report legal disputes until they come to trial."

"My son won't last that long!" exclaimed Niven in a harsh voice. It was a strange sound of reproach and remorse.

NIVEN hadn't warned Mark of his coming; he wanted to surprise him. But it was he who got a surprise when he saw the miserable walk-up his son was living in.

"You can't stay in a place like this!" he said. "It's awful."

"I like it here."

Dead tired from the transatlantic flight and his fruitless meeting with the managing editor, Niven decided that he would do at least one thing for his son before going to sleep: he would get him away from St. Mark's Place.

"Pack everything, we're moving out!" he announced with all the bravado he could muster.

"Where to?"

"To some decent hotel until we find you a decent apartment. You wouldn't want your poor old dad to climb all those stairs every day or sleep on that alarming bed, would you?"

"You can go to a hotel, Dad, but I'm staying. One of these days I'll have to pay legal fees."

Niven sat down on the bed, setting the springs squeaking. "But we have so much money! You gave me a million dollars, remember?"

"I didn't give you money to take it back," said Mark fiercely.

"You're not poor, you know! You bought patents, you have shares in Jessica's firm — these are things you can sell. You can have all the money you want. What's got into you?"

Mark gave his father a bitter look: he would never understand him! "I'm poor until I get back what's mine."

"I know what's wrong with you. It's this terrible place — it keeps you depressed."

"No, it doesn't — it keeps me busy!" replied Mark with a sudden grin, pointing to the walls and ceiling.

They were freshly painted, the windows looked as though Mark had just washed them, but the sunlight pouring through them only showed up the dirt in the cracks between the slanting floorboards and the cockroach scuttling behind the ancient refrigerator.

They argued, but not for long: Niven gave in with a sigh. "Well, if you're not coming with me, I'm staying here. I'm not going to desert you again."

Mark remembered and reached out to hold his father's hands. "You mean we'll ride the same donkey?"

"Sit down beside me, I'm too tired to get up."

Mark sat down on the bed and they embraced and cried and were happy.

"We'll wash dishes together again!" said the actor.

Once Niven had slept himself out, he called Wattman, who, anxious to have his old friend off his back, agreed that publicity could only help their case and that Niven should contact everybody he could.

"Dana, haven't you heard about libel laws?" asked the producer of a talk show. "If somebody grabs your wallet on the street and you shout *stop! thief!* the thief doesn't run away, he turns around and sues you for libel." The producer, who had taken Niven to lunch by way of apology for not helping, explained that no television program would dare to broadcast anything defamatory, however true, about a client of PETER, BLACK, JEFFERSON unless quoting an actual court decision. "Of course you can slander innocent people without connections, but criminals in high places have a right to their good name. Why are you so surprised? Every political system has its method of protecting crooks. The Russians have censorship, we have libel laws.''

"MacArthur doesn't need libel laws, he's in with every power group in New York. Nobody's going to annoy *him*," commented a columnist whom Niven had taken to lunch.

Niven refused to understand. "How come you guys are so tough with the President of the United States but you can't write about two crooks right here in New York?"

"That's the problem, they're right here," the columnist replied. "The President isn't here and he doesn't have much to do with the fortunes of your paper. It's the same all over the country. Newspapers can flay the gang in Washington day in, day out, because they don't depend on federal money. They live on local money, so they tell you more about the White House than about City Hall. I can attack the head of the CIA, spit on the President, that's freedom of the press, but it's not so easy to write anything embarrassing about a powerful law firm in the same town, or the owner of a department store which places full-page ads in every issue. There are exceptions of course, and this case may be one of them, but only when it comes to trial . . ."

The actor's reputation won him a meeting with everybody: people were friendly and sympathetic and took great pains to explain why they couldn't help.

"MacArthur's the least of your problems — you're up against the spirit of the age," said a magazine publisher. "These days nobody sees anything wrong with cheating and stealing. Crooks are the heroes of our time. By the way, didn't I see you playing a charming con man on television a few weeks ago?"

"That was an old movie."

"Old, new, there are an awful lot of films around with beautiful actors playing stylish, clever, amusing bank robbers, swindlers, jewel thieves — David Niven, Paul Newman, Robert Redford, Sean Connery, Belmondo, Peter O'Toole, Dana Niven . . ."

"That's entertainment! Nobody takes it seriously."

"You meet a lot of people who believe in honest dealing?" asked the publisher, affecting surprise.

"Listen, you publish a straightfoward, factual report on this outrage, and you'll see — they'll be shamed into giving the treasures back," Niven persisted. "Vallentine and MacArthur are public figures, they have to think of their reputation."

"We couldn't make the slightest dent in their reputation, and they know it. That's my point. When people's heads are stuffed with images of superattractive criminals, crime has to do with sex appeal, not shame. Evil can be done and can be seen to be done."

"You print an exposé on this and I'll never play a charming crook again!"

The publisher touched the actor's arm with an apologetic gesture. "Please don't take it personally. A few more movies glamorizing criminals are neither here nor there. Anyway, it's the same with books. Did you read *Thorn Birds*? That moving love story of a poor girl and the absolutely wonderful priest who defrauds her and her family of their multimillion-dollar inheritance? She knows about it, of course, but she loves him just the same. The whole disinherited family is ecstatic about this saintly man who relieved them of the burden of an immense fortune. Thieves can have everything, even their victims' love."

"You're making this up."

"You flatter me. But I have a better one for you. This piece of garbage is called *Rage of Angels,* and tells the inspiring story of a beautiful, brilliant, idealistic young woman lawyer who has affairs with a Mafia boss and a future President of the United States and employs her legal talents in getting professional killers and heroin dealers out of jail. You're assured on the last page that she will 'go on searching for the elusive thing called justice.' That's what letting murderers loose on society amounts to, a search for justice, elusive justice! The book's full of gangsters of every sort and description but the only person described as *lacking compassion* is the district attorney who's trying to put them away. And I'm not talking about some crazed would-be writer's pathetic efforts which nobody reads but his family — I'm talking about the biggest best-sellers of the decade! More money is spent pushing this vicious nonsense than on promoting the complete works of Mark Twain. Or on the promotion of all the good books that were ever written, for that matter. And that's fraud too — we're robbing people of their senses. Of course, it's also true the other way around — we give the reading mob what they want . . ."

"The question is, will you do anything on this fantastic story of a New York art dealer simply keeping a hundred and fifty million dollars' worth of treasures which don't belong to him?"

"Look, I make my living reading the public mood," protested the magazine publisher. "The only way I could have this *Flora* business written up would be as a funny story, recounting what an idiot your son was and how brilliantly Vallantine conned him out of everything. Nobody identifies with somebody who earns money with a lot of wear and tear and hard work. People don't dream about making a fortune anymore — they dream about stealing one. We would have to have a story to the tune of *Never give a sucker an even break.* Now that's America, that's the world, that's what people want to hear!"

"What did you expect, the man's lawyer is Jefferson of PETER, BLACK, JEFFERSON, MACARTHUR, WHITMAN & WARREN," said Wattman, who hosted a dinner in the actor's honor that evening at his house on Bank

Street in the Village. "After you mix with media people the courts don't look so bad."

"How can Mark be so patient," sighed Niven. "I'm going mad."

The guests at the dinner, mostly lawyers and their wives, were disappointed: they had been counting on hearing inside stories about Hollywood, Broadway, the West End, and the actor talked about nothing but his son's case, making gratuitously offensive remarks like "I'd hang all the lawyers who work for crooks!"

"You're a great actor, your place is on the stage, get back to your play in London," Wattman told his old friend as he drove him home at midnight. "Don't worry, I'll win this case even against MacArthur — but we have to take it one step at a time."

MARK hadn't gone to the dinner party; he hated people watching how awkward he was with his left hand or asking him how he had got mixed up with Vallantine. He stayed home worrying about his father making a fool of himself, complaining to lawyers, as if they cared!

When the actor came in, he wavered as if he had lost his sense of balance and sounded slightly drunk, though he didn't touch alcohol as a rule. "Are you still in mourning?" he growled, seeing Mark lying on his back staring at his freshly painted ceiling. "Why don't you go somewhere and do something? I've been telling you since you were a kid that you should forget about those stupid treasures!"

Mark bounded off the sofa, feeling guilty, for he had meant to spend the evening reading, but that only made him angrier. "You want me to leave everything with Vallantine?"

"Yes!" shouted Niven, falling on the bed. "You should handle thieves like a Franciscan monk. Didn't you hear about Brother Juniper when we were in Italy? Do you remember what he did when a thief snatched his hood on a cold winter day?"

Mark didn't reply, hoping his father would fall into a drunken sleep, and the actor was quiet for a while, but then suddenly raised himself on his elbow. "Brother Juniper ran after the thief, caught him and gave him his robe as well. Please take it, brother, he said, you must need it more than I do. And I bet that shivering Franciscan was a happier man than you are!"

Mark had been glad that his father cared enough to come, but now he suddenly found his presence so intolerable that he couldn't bear to look at him. He realized that once his father got around to blaming him, he would have no peace. He had lost one of the great fortunes of history and he wasn't even allowed to be upset about it! "Please, Dad, go back to London," he begged. "You were on top of the world there!"

"I'd be happy to go, more than happy, if you would only have the sense to start living again!'' the actor said bitterly, falling back on the bed and pulling a blanket over himself.

Mark tried again in the morning. "You look terrible, Dad — you can't even get a proper sleep in that bed. There's no point in wasting your time here being miserable.''

"You're worse off on the sofa,'' Niven replied, trying to rub the ache out of his lower back. "We've got to stick together. I can't let them ruin you. I want you to get back your fortune and start leading a happy life. Don't worry, I'm going to find somebody who will make a fuss for you.''

Mark winced. "You can't do anything to help, Dad. All we can do is wait for the trial.''

"So why don't you go back to college and study while you wait?'' Niven asked, careful to sound more amicable on the subject than the night before. "Nixon's ending the draft, the war is winding down — you're flying in and out of the country and nobody bothers you — I'm sure your sins are forgotten, you could go to college right here in the States.''

"I study on my own — I'm reading.''

". . . I'll go back to London but I won't leave you here moping,'' Niven insisted when he finally gave in. "Come with me! See some plays. There are so many great actors you've never seen in action! Dinsdale Landen, Anton Lesser, Robert Urquhart, John Normington, Felicity Kendal . . .''

Realizing that his father would never leave without him, Mark accompanied him back to London and did his best to appear interested in all sorts of things. He went to the theater every night, but neither great plays greatly done nor Jessica's glowing reports about the prospects of British Solar Glass could raise him from a state of restless depression. He was back in New York in ten days, afraid of missing the next step in the proceedings.

Nothing happened for months.

THERE were times when Mark felt that he was going crazy with anxiety, wondering where his treasures were. Did Vallantine still have them? Had he obeyed the injunction? Or had he disregarded the injunction and sold them? Were they still in New York, or had they been shipped to Rio or Geneva? Were they in Jeddah? In Hong Kong? And how much longer would he have to wait before he got them back?

He bought a television set to bury his mind in it; watching the news, he happened to see a replay of the opening of the Spanish Cortes. It was an impressive sight, a magnificent chamber filled with rows and rows of dark-suited deputies, who sat upright and dignified until a group of rebel officers armed with submachine guns burst in and started shooting. The chamber emptied in an instant; the sea of heads disappeared from one moment to the next as the elected representatives of Spain dived for the floor, ducking under their seats. There was only one who did not jump for cover: a young man, too, it seemed, though the newscaster identified him as the former prime minister. Arms folded and head high, Adolfo Suarez sat quite still and looked straight ahead with a slightly scornful expression: he wouldn't get down on all fours, not even for his life! This display of pride and courage made a tremendous impression on Mark, and he was distracted from his misery for days, wondering whether he would have been man enough not to crawl. Later when he heard that King Juan Carlos had made Adolfo Suarez a duke, Mark remembered that he used to see himself as a prince and made an effort to summon up his own spirit of *noblesse oblige*. He phoned Santa Catalina and asked Eshelby to send the suitcase filled with letters people had written to him after he found the *Flora*. When the suitcase came, he spent several hours every day reading the begging letters (some of which made him feel he didn't know the meaning of misery) and answering them, apologizing for the delay and explaining that in the interval he had lost his fortune. To those who made him feel that his own problems were trivial by comparison he promised help when he had recovered his treasures, and he bought a school exercise book in which he made a list of the writers' names and addresses and particular circumstances, so that he would be able to keep his promises to them when he got his money back. He knew peace only when he was thinking of other people or concentrating on the arm exercises the physiotherapist at the clinic had taught him. At least his arm was improving! He even invented an exercise of his own. He flung his arms wide, then clasped his shoulders as hard as he could as if squeezing somebody to himself. It was after one of his exercise sessions that he called his old girlfriend Martha, now in her third year at Columbia. They got together for a while: she was outraged by the fraud, by the perfidy of Vallantine's attorney, she pitied Mark, she tried to comfort him with love, but in addition to all his other afflictions he had become insufferably boring. Finally she grew impatient with his constant complaining and left him.

People caught up in lawsuits are lost to the world.

Games Lawyers Play (Cont'd)

Corporations are increasingly turning to high-priced law firms
which, by legal maneuvering, obfuscation and delay, can
effectively void almost any contract . . .
ADMIRAL HYMAN G. RICKOVER

Where there is law there is injustice.
TOLSTOY

To pay workers for their time rather than their performance is to pay
them to be slow and inefficient. This truism is frequently cited when
the low level of industrial productivity is discussed, yet time-wasting in
factories is as nothing compared with the rampant time-wasting in the
business of the law — and for the very good reason that nowhere else
can it be made so profitable. The postponements Mark had to suffer and
eventually pay for were and are the very essence of the legal process,
an unbreakable tradition sustained by the blood, vaporized brain and
shredded nervous system of each generation of litigants. Attorneys are
paid by the hour, and thus even the simplest legal disputes, which sensible advisers could settle at one meeting, take years to resolve. Speed
may be essential to runners, generals, speculators in commodities, but
lawyers grow rich through delay.

The second hearing in the case of *Niven v. Vallantine,* originally
scheduled for the 26th day of January, was finally held on the 18th day
of October. At the hearing Justice F granted Wattman's motion and ordered Defendants to deposit "the chattels at issue" with the court, within
seven working days. Evenhanded Justice F also granted MacArthur's
cross-motion arguing that the exhibition was in abeyance because of the
proceedings initiated by Plaintiff (in other words, it was Mark's fault
that there was no exhibition) and ordered Plaintiff to deposit with the
court the Defendants' $500,000 advance on exhibition receipts until such
time as the court decided whether he was entitled to keep it or not.

Mark didn't have the $500,000, but that was the least of his problems. He was watching MacArthur, waiting for his response to the order to surrender the "chattels at issue."

Could he produce the treasures?

There was a slight crack of a smile in the broad clay face — so slight that possibly only Mark noticed it. "For our part, Your Honor," said the great attorney in measured tones, "we're ready to comply with Your Honor's order immediately." With this, he bent down to whisper to his assistant, who got up and left the room. After a few tense minutes, during which time everyone stared at the door at the back of the courtroom, four security guards rolled in two dollies stacked with steel containers and parked them in front of the bench. Justice F ordered the marshals of the court to take charge of the containers and declared the hearing closed.

Mark and Wattman didn't move from their place until the courtroom had emptied except for the marshals. They were the last to get up and go to the front to take a closer look. There were nine containers on each dolly, each container measuring eight cubic feet: that was all it took to hold what was worth by then, with the dramatic rise in the price of precious metals after President Nixon cut the tie between gold and the dollar, approximately $170,000,000.

"I'll leave this one to somebody else to figure out," Wattman declared, shaking his head.

The steel containers still bore the unbroken seals of the Royal Bank in Nassau. Vallantine not only hadn't sold the treasures, he hadn't even unpacked them.

THE art dealer restrained himself on his attorney's instructions.

At their very first meeting on the matter, MacArthur warned him not to touch the disputed goods until there was a legal determination for their disposal. "Any tampering with those things before the court grants you leave would be taken by most judges as a personal insult. So don't preempt judgment. We'll have to play this by the book if we want to win." Vallantine did as he was told, placing the sealed containers in the vaults of the Irving Trust Company.

Litigants, even clever crooks, assume that their legal representatives are on their side, forgetting that most lawyers, like most people, tend to represent their own interests ahead of anybody else's, and if their interests do not coincide with the client's, it is the client who must bear the difference. William T. MacArthur had always conformed to this basic rule of attorney-client relationships. He charged Vallantine a yearly retainer of $200,000 to keep him out of jail, plus fees and disbursements for each lawsuit, and under this arrangement did his best as a defense attorney. However, when something as big as the *Flora* came along,

MacArthur's problem wasn't how to rob Mark for his client's benefit, but how to rob them both. Of course he didn't suggest a readjustment of fees as long as his client was in actual possession of the treasures and had the option of fleeing the country with them. The great attorney waited patiently for Wattman to make the obvious move to have the treasures sequestered, and then made no serious attempt to oppose him.

At one of those dinner parties where lawyers and judges mix and are not supposed to discuss their cases, Justice F asked MacArthur what he thought of Wattman's motion. "It was a clever idea — I don't have any effective argument against it," MacArthur replied. "That's why I keep asking for postponements."

The postponements, costly as they were, kept Vallantine from complaining — he was persuaded that they were meant to "wear down the enemy". In fact they were meant to wear him down as well: the uncertainties of delay were just as hard on him as they were on Mark, indeed harder, for he was older. By the time the containers had to be surrendered, he was in no shape to run even if he had wanted to. This was the reason for MacArthur's odd little smile at the hearing: once the treasures were sequestered by the court, his client became totally dependent on him to get them back.

It was time to discuss a readjustment of fees.

Vallantine was summoned to his attorney's office, where everything was designed for the purpose of making big figures sound small. To begin with, it was a huge room of expensive Manhattan space with three long, low couches and many armchairs and tables of all shapes and sizes. MacArthur didn't smoke; clients who did could stub out their cigarettes in solid gold ashtrays. A few law books lay on various tables, but there was only one narrow bookcase in the room; the library of PETER, BLACK, JEFFERSON, MACARTHUR, WHITMAN & WARREN was one of the most extensive in New York, and if MacArthur needed more books, an usher brought them in.

Most of the wall space served to display intricately patterned, richly colored hand-knotted silk carpets and rugs from the royal workshops of the Safavid dynasty of the 16th and 17th centuries, the golden age of Persian carpetmaking, when no design was ever duplicated. A hunting carpet filled the eye with dark blue, black and brown lions, leopards and men on horseback chasing white stags and spotted deer across an orange field bordered with cloud bands, palmettes and flowering scrolls. Several vase carpets bloomed with magical plants, while many small rugs teemed with genii, trees and mythical birds and beasts. Behind MacArthur's desk hung a modern but equally striking lion rug of silk and white wool from the reign of the last Shah of Iran. Even a client who knew nothing about carpets would have known that MacArthur owned an almost priceless collection. A top New York attorney might be content with a modest home, but his office must always be opulent: Whitman of the same firm had a Rembrandt on the wall to tell clients that their attorney could think only in terms of fortunes and was rich enough to dismiss anyone who wouldn't meet his terms.

"This ruling today isn't the end, John, it only means that I'll have to work harder," MacArthur boomed cheerfully when Vallantine entered his carpet shop, but didn't get up to greet him.

"So you ddd . . . don't think everything's lost!" sighed the aging art dealer, lowering himself into one of the leather armchairs.

MacArthur returned to the document on his desk, picked up his pen and crossed out a word. "Nothing's lost, but it's a new situation," he said, giving only half his attention to his client. "I've written you a letter about the new fee structure I'm proposing."

"Wh . . . what do you mean?" asked Vallantine, feeling his heart hit him.

They were interrupted by a gray-haired secretary who had wrinkles in her face but none in her dress; she brought in a tray with a Georgian silver tea service and Sèvres porcelain cups. MacArthur waved *no* to refreshments and pointed to Vallantine as the man to serve. "Is my letter to Mr. Vallantine ready?" he asked her.

"Miss Delano's sorting the copies," she replied, filling the client's cup, then left unobtrusively.

The art dealer sipped his tea in silence, waiting for the letter from his attorney, who — a busy man — was studying another case at his desk. "She won't be a minute, John," said MacArthur, glancing at his victim. He enjoyed seeing people sweat. Like many large, stolid, impassive men who seem immune to feeling, he had profound inner thrills; he felt the tingling of a million nerves in this thick flesh when someone was going to pieces within his field of vision. The crooks he defended stayed clear of the penitentiary, but they didn't go unpunished.

The secretary returned with copies of the letter setting out the new fee structure, handing one to her boss and one to Vallantine, smiling at him encouragingly like a nurse at a patient before his operation.

"Read it, John, and ask me if there's anything you don't understand," MacArthur said with immense calm.

The carpets were perhaps less impressive than a Rembrandt, but just as intimidating: confronted by so much wealth on the walls, how could Vallantine argue that MacArthur ought to work for less than a $3,000,000 fee? The lion behind the desk, surrounded by radiant peacocks, looked ready to leap. Or so it seemed to Vallantine when he read the letter. MacArthur also proposed to take 50% of the treasures as a bonus if he succeeded in getting them back; the division was to be based on the Nassau inventory paid for by Mark, which was now on file as one of the documents of the lawsuit.

"I don't h . . . have three mmmmmillion!"

"You own that fine building with your gallery, you can borrow on that," the lawyer advised in an indifferent tone.

"It sssssseems to me that if I g . . . give you half of these historic relics, these priceless artifffffacts," Vallantine protested, his head shaking as much as his voice, "I shouldn't have to pay so much in c . . . c . . . cash."

The former state supreme court justice nodded approvingly. "That's a reasonable objection, John. I can see how you arrived at it." He raised his head and ran his fingertip along his jawline in a thoughtful manner. "But the fees must be commensurate with the difficulties," he sighed. "If I were to represent the Plaintiff in this action, I'd do it for $500,000 and no percentage, but you must appreciate that getting the court to release to you what this young man claims is his property is a far more involved business. You and I know that you're entitled to it, but it's not so easy to prove in a court of law." He raised his eyebrows to suggest what could not be said. "I may have expenses I wouldn't even want you to know about."

"Maybe I could raise a mmmmmillion."

MacArthur's colorless eyes turned to ice; the clay face congealed. "If you'd like another lawyer to represent you, John, of course I have no objection."

"Nnnnno!" Vallantine cried out, terrified. He understood only too well that without the former vice-president of the New York Bar Association, all he would get from the *Flora* was a prison sentence.

"I'm already preparing my next move — the interrogatories for the Plaintiff. However, I don't wish to influence you unduly. This is your decision, John. Is half a loaf better than none?" MacArthur spread his hands in a self-deprecating gesture: he didn't claim to have all the answers. "Take the letter home and talk it over with Shirley."

"WE haven't won the case yet, but Vallantine's already lost it," Wattman said to Mark as they left the Center Street courthouse. Flashbulbs were popping in front of them like fireworks: the Supreme Court of the State of New York taking charge of a $170,000,000 fortune was *news*.

Mark smiled for the photographers, gave a V-for-Victory sign, then let Wattman usher him into a taxi. This time the lawyer took him to Lutèce, which Tom Wolfe had recently dubbed a Status Lunch restaurant. The rarefied atmosphere of the place, the silent obsequiousness of the waiters, reminded Mark of his days as a clerk at the Seven Seas Club, and for the first time since things started to go wrong, he reflected how high he had risen in the world. It was good to be worth $170,000,000! The maître d' led them to a corner table and two waiters appeared to pull out and push in chairs for them; Mark acknowledged their services with a dignified nod.

When the wine list was brought, Wattman insisted on ordering champagne to celebrate the sequestering of the treasures. "I guess I was too skeptical, Mark — our system works!" he exulted. "I don't care how much of a teetotaler you are, today you're going to drink. You have an attorney who has prevailed over Judge MacArthur in court! That's more than the Manhattan District Attorney can say!"

Wattman was only sipping the champagne; he was getting high on food. With eyes sparkling, puffy cheeks glowing, pudgy hands stuffing buttered rolls into his mouth, he talked about the case all through lunch. "I'm quite comfortable about our chances of winning," he declared, feeling more comfortable every time he swallowed a buttered roll. He had buttered rolls even with his fifty-dollar *filet de sole*. Did Mark remember MacArthur's cable to Darville claiming that Vallantine was in no position to return the goods in question? With the goods in the court's vaults, it was crystal clear now that MacArthur's cable was a lie.

"Now you have your proof that MacArthur's as big a crook as Vallantine!" exclaimed Mark, his voice shattering the exclusive quiet of the restaurant and alarming the maître d'. He got drunk on half a glass of champagne.

"MacArthur certainly slipped up there," agreed the lawyer, hushed but joyful. "I can use that cable to try to destroy Vallantine's credibility with the jury. I can say: Our reputable art dealer is an inveterate liar who even deceives his attorney!"

"What do you mean? You have proof that they're *both* crooks," insisted Mark.

"Let's not get carried away," said Wattman, seized by gloomy second thoughts and putting down a buttered roll halfway to his mouth. "MacArthur will argue that he said Vallantine was in no position to return the goods in question because he'd already promised to sell them to a Liechtenstein corporation and felt *morally bound* to honor his commitment. MacArthur is too good a lawyer to get into a lie he doesn't know how to back out of. All the same, not everyone will believe him . . ."

There were still years of work ahead, motions, cross-motions, Wattman explained; they weren't home yet, but he would hand over his other cases to his partner and devote himself full-time to destroying the people who were trying to ruin his best friend's son. He might hire a young lawyer to assist him.

"Can you imagine how Vallantine is feeling?" asked Wattman.

"Miserable, I hope."

"And our big-shot former judge who shall be nameless?"

"I'll bet he doesn't look so dignified right now!" said Mark, his eyes shining with hatred. "I could watch him die. He's worse than Vallantine. He robs me and abuses me for a *fee.*"

"Don't underestimate him — I'm sure he's doing it for millions and millions."

"May he entrust them to a crook!" said Mark, with his voice lowered in response to the disapproving looks but his spirits soaring.

"Not a chance."

"All right, let him be mugged every day. Let him learn what it feels like to be robbed!"

"May he be disbarred!" Wattman raised his glass. "Let's drink the enemy's blood!"

"To the last drop!" said Mark. "On to victory!"

They clinked glasses and drank, comrades in arms in the battle of depositions, postponements and judgments. They were having a whale of a time.

"Do you remember the deal we made?" Wattman asked while waiting for the waiter to bring back his charge card.

"You said you didn't want anything until you made real progress, but then you would want a lot," replied Mark promptly.

The lawyer's eyes widened with surprise. "I appreciate your remembering. You have no idea how rare it is to find a reliable client!"

"I'm very grateful that you've carried me for nothing all this time, and I'll be glad to pay," was Mark's cheerful reply. His fortune was out of Vallantine's hands — what else mattered?

"Now that we're making headway, I think it's fair to charge you for the work I've done so far. $200,000 strikes me as a nice round figure. And I want an outrageous sum for the rest of the case, but it'll cover pretty well everything. I'll pay for most of the disbursements, all the motions, regardless of how many there are — that way you can be sure *I* won't be responsible for any delays. The fee I'm asking will also cover the trial. Though of course I'll also want a bonus when you get the treasures back." These last words were uttered in a grave tone. Wattman appeared to have sobered up completely by the time he reached into the inner pocket of his jacket: he too had a letter for his client.

Mark took the envelope nonchalantly, but grew pale when he read what was inside.

"Anything wrong?"

"No, no, I'm all right."

"By paying for everything in advance," Wattman explained in a subdued voice, "you make sure that I devote myself to your case full-time instead of running around trying to earn a living."

"That's all right, I understand," said Mark, attempting a smile. "I'll pay, I don't want anything for nothing."

THE late editions of the papers carried stories about Justice F's ruling and a summary of the Plaintiff's claim to the treasures, and Mark could see his picture on the front pages again, just as in his days of triumph.

"Now that he's got the case into the papers — which was something *I* couldn't do — he's bound to win," Niven commented on the phone. "And lawyers' fees are always in relation to what they're getting for you, so I guess we can't complain." He wanted to return all the money he had left after the production of the play, and the certainty of success gave Mark the strength to accept — but only as a loan — half of the million he had so grandly given to his father. He also sold back to Jessica the few shares in her company that he could afford to buy, and spent grim days selling the gold Madonna and the Cross of the Seven Emeralds, his first and last mementos of the *Flora*.

A week after their triumphant lunch at Lutèce, he handed his lawyer a $500,000 check (the amount of Vallantine's advance, to be deposited with the court as ordered by Justice F) and a $1,100,000 check for Wattman's past and future legal fees.

Prepaying his lawyer for all the work yet to be done was a foolish thing to do, even though Mark did it with his father's approval. They had long talks on the transatlantic line because Niven, feeling guilty about his sins of omission in the past, had begged Mark not to make any decision without talking it over with him, but the actor — who valued so many things more highly than money that he would have returned the gift of half a million dollars just as willingly to a stranger as to his son —was the wrong person to advise on the wisdom of paying a lawyer in advance. "If he's going to work for you full-time," he said, "it makes sense for him to ask to be paid the whole lot at this stage." This is the sort of absurd reasoning that makes homeowners pay for plumbing and roof repairs that never get done. It is not in human nature to exert oneself for something one has already got. To pay in advance is to believe in gratitude.

In their signed letter of agreement, Mark also undertook to pay further undetermined sums in the event of any unforeseen and extraordinary complications in the case, and to give Wattman a bonus of $2,500,000 the day he regained possession of the treasures.

"The bonus is your insurance," said Wattman as he put the checks in his desk drawer. "You can be sure I'll do my best to earn that extra bit. I'll move on this with full speed."

This reassurance, which amounted to dismissing a payment of $1,100,000 as a thing of no consequence the moment it was received, struck Mark as somewhat odd, though it took him time to realize why.

ATTORNEYS deal in wool and their clients are the sheep that are shorn. Once Vallantine and Mark had both paid what they could reasonably be expected to pay, their legal representatives saw no point in writing affidavits to each other and making innumerable court appearances about an issue which they could settle between themselves on the squash court at the Athletic Club.

"You're a brilliant lawyer, Bernie, you should be on the bench," MacArthur said before they started playing. "Didn't you try to get on the ballot once? I seem to recall the reform Democrats were backing you against Justice Aurelio."

Wattman stepped back to show his surprise and to avoid being dwarfed by the big man. "That was fifteen years ago! I didn't think anybody remembered."

"I remember everything. And I can see into the future." MacArthur was looking straight into Bernie's eyes to show that he wasn't trying to be funny. "You'll be elected to the state supreme court one of these days." The great attorney had sufficient influence in the political and professional organizations involved in selecting candidates to be able to read his colleague's horoscope even without knowing under what sign he was born.

"The plaintiff's father is a friend of mine," replied Wattman, squeezing the squash ball in his hand as if to test the strength of his refusal.

"I understand. That makes it difficult." MacArthur slowly lowered his big head and remained immobile for a moment, paying silent tribute to friendship. "Still," he went on, "you'd have to work very hard, Bernie. For years. And every case is a gamble, I don't need to tell you that. You could waste a lot of precious time and lose out in the end." Seeing that he had scored, MacArthur proposed that they start hitting the ball, and returned to the subject only at the end of their game. "Life is so short, Bernie!" he lamented, mopping his shiny dome with a towel.

"It certainly is," panted Wattman, half dead and sweating like a pig after ten minutes' exercise.

They had several discussions about *Niven v. Vallantine*, and in the end Wattman decided not to risk a certain judgeship for the uncertain bonus which depended on his winning the case after a hell of a lot of work. They closed the deal in the corridor of the Center Street courthouse, where they were both attending to other cases. It looked to people passing by as though the two attorneys had happened to run into each other and, having a few minutes to spare, were exchanging pleasantries — which in a way they were.

"So you see me on the bench, do you?" asked Wattman jokingly.

The clay face remained serious. "Absolutely. I give you my word."

"I'll need time. . . . We'll have to play it out."

"Of course. I'll prepare the interrogatories."

The illustrious members of the bar, so well versed in spelling out everything in contracts, saw no need to put their understanding on paper. Never for a moment did Wattman doubt that MacArthur would keep his promise. The most accomplished perjurer, the most infamous defense attorney in the whole city of New York, who bribed judges, suborned witnesses as a matter of routine, was also famous for his dependability in his dealings with his colleagues. William T. MacArthur's word was his bond. It was precisely for this reason that he could obstruct justice so effectively. Wattman would not have sold out his client if MacArthur had not been so reliable.

What a strange, terrible proof of the power of truth and plain dealing! A man cannot be successful even in the business of corruption unless he can be trusted.

40

Games Lawyers Play (Cont'd)

"I call that man an outcast,"
Kohlhaas said, clenching his fist,
"who is denied the protection of the laws!"
KLEIST

IGNORANT of what the attorneys were doing, Mark was watching his phone waiting for good news. After the sequestering of the treasures, the stories in the papers, his lawyer's optimistic assurances, and above all, the raising of $1,600,000 for court deposit and legal fees, so that all that he had left from the fabulous treasures of the *Flora* was less than $8,000 in the bank, he couldn't help feeling that he was on the brink of regaining everything. He had ruined himself to win his case, and as expectations match sacrifices, he lived in a state of hectic euphoria. When the secretary phoned to say that Mr. Wattman was coming to see him — something the lawyer had never done before — Mark thought he was coming to announce that Vallantine had decided to give in rather than continue to waste time and money on a lawsuit which he was bound to lose. It's the worst poison of litigation, wild hopes mixed with a little misunderstanding.

Not supposing for a moment that his client could be overconfident — worried, rather, that he might become suspicious — Wattman came to see Mark simply to demonstrate how hard he was working for his fee. However, having gone to the extraordinary length of making a house call, he saw no need to be polite. "I didn't think to ask whether you had an elevator in this building," he grumbled, out of sorts and out of breath after climbing the four flights of stairs to the apartment. "I couldn't have made it with my coat on. . . . What a place!" he exclaimed with disgust, looking around for a safe spot to put his cashmere overcoat, which he was carrying over his arm.

Pale, tense, dying to hear about the return of his treasures, yet not wishing to appear impatient, Mark took the coat and hung it in his clothes closet. "Sit down — I'll make coffee." He went to the kitchen end of

309

the room and filled a pot with water, but then forgot to switch on the stove.

"I think I'll stand," declared the lawyer with a horrified glance at the stained and greasy sofa. Fussily fastidious, afraid that some dirt might settle on his shiny skin, he even stood on tiptoe for a moment to have as little contact with the place as possible. "Do you mean to tell me that your father stayed here?"

"What did you expect, we spend our money on lawyers."

"Tsk, tsk, tsk, you're making jokes at your attorney's expense!"

"I thought it was at my expense."

Wattman laughed appreciatively. "Gallows humor, eh?"

"What's happening?" Mark asked in an unsteady voice, caring little for jokes, including his own. "Are they giving in?"

The question made the lawyer stare with wide-eyed surprise. "Not quite, but we're making progress."

Mark grew paler hearing that it wasn't the end, but quickly settled in his mind for progress. "Great," he sighed. "Thanks!"

"I've brought you some homework." Wattman put his briefcase on the table and opened it with the flourish of a magician. "We got the interrogatories from your old friend Judge MacArthur. We have the right to question Vallantine, but only after they've questioned you, so this is a step ahead."

"I see . . . fine." Somewhat hesitantly, Mark took the thick sheaf of legal-sized paper and glanced at the top page. "What's this? *List all the schools you attended!*" He laughed incredulously. "Don't tell me that's what I've been waiting for!"

"We'll have our turn but we have to let them go first — in a lawsuit Defendants are the ladies, they go first through every door."

"They want me to list my exam results . . . all the jobs I ever had . . ." The insatiable curiosity of the men who were robbing him struck Mark as less and less funny. "They must be putting us on!" he seethed, feeling singled out for special insult.

In this he was mistaken. Anyone who gets involved in a lawsuit will receive a set of written questions aimed at discovering everything the other side wants to know about him. These interrogatories, part of discovery proceedings prior to trial, are supposed to be confined to what is relevant to the dispute; but nothing of course is as relevant as anything that might serve to discredit the litigant in the eyes of the judge and jury. So interrogatories tend to be more personal and wide-ranging than anyone innocent of the workings of the law could possibly imagine. MacArthur's assistant, Elliott T. Sanborn III, a bright young attorney fresh out of Yale Law School, hadn't overlooked anything that could put Mark in a bad light or discourage him in any way. Interrogatories also tend to be long; boring the other party to distraction is almost as important as intimidating him. Elliott T. Sanborn III had prepared altogether 357 questions for the Plaintiff.

Mark lost his temper halfway through them. "What's this garbage got to do with anything?" he exploded, slamming the document on the table. Being alone most of the time with no one to talk to, he had a lot of unused emotions in him, and now they all turned into rage. "Are you telling me they can rob me of a fortune and then ask me how well I did at school? This is what makes MacArthur such a big legal scholar that they invite him to England to lecture on the law? I paid you over a million dollars, and now you bring me a bunch of stupid questions like that?"

"That's the way it is, suing is work," replied Wattman, unmoved. "I can't tell them what schools you went to! Just get yourself a typewriter and knock out the answers. When you've finished, we'll go over them. We have to be careful, you'll have to repeat every word under oath."

Mark was so incensed that he felt dizzy. "I'm not going to tell them about my school marks under oath!" he shouted, very much the man who had paid $1,600,000 to assert his rights.

"Why, what was wrong with your school marks?"

"I'm not going to let those monstrous crooks rob me and then play games with me! How come guys like that aren't in prison?"

All this was raving as far as Wattman was concerned, and he watched Mark with a disdainful air, convinced that he had made the right decision. Even if he had got Mark's fortune back for him, a person who got carried away by his feelings so easily couldn't possibly have held on to it. To stay rich, people must be nearer to the dead than to the living; they can't afford to get carried away by anything. "They know what they're doing," the lawyer said coolly. "You apparently missed the questions which require you to say whether you have ever committed an indictable offense."

Mark grew quiet, just as he was expected to. He understood what Wattman meant only because of the threatening emphasis the lawyer gave to his remark. "How come MacArthur knows about it?"

Wattman made a face and spread his pudgy hands to show that he wasn't holding anything. "You and Vallantine were such friends, maybe you told him. The main thing is that they know about it."

"Nobody cares about draft dodgers any more. I've gone through passport control several times and nobody's ever bothered me."

"It's because of your arm!" exclaimed Wattman with the excitement of sudden illumination. "They think you're a cripple. That's why they don't look you up in the book."

"They look everybody up, but my name isn't on their list."

"There you are, there's inefficiency for everybody. Vallantine's not the only one who gets away with breaking the law!"

"It's different," Mark protested, his indignation giving way to anxiety. For the first time the fear he had felt on the stranded plane came back to him.

Wattman started nodding violently to express his agreement. "Yes, you're in worse trouble than he is," he declared in his righteous voice when he had stopped nodding. "You're a fugitive from justice. A criminal on the run. If I were you, I wouldn't be too eager to condemn people for flouting the laws of the land."

"You're right, it's childish of me to complain," said Mark abruptly, twisting his bad arm to work himself free of a sense of doom. "This is a fight to the death. There's no point in whining about it. I'm going to answer the questions — but you told me you'd keep this draft thing out of the case."

"I said I would try to. And I *am* trying. Your answer to every incriminating question will be: *my attorney has instructed me not to answer.* And I'm going to write to MacArthur telling him that these questions are not relevant — you'll get a copy of my letter." The puffy lawyer beamed; he was almost floating with satisfaction. "So don't tell me I'm not earning my fee."

It took Mark a bleak month's work to answer the interrogatories. The 357 questions were so many poisoned darts meant to induce frustration, fear and self-doubt. "Get him to tell his whole story, so we'll know what we're up against," MacArthur had told his assistant, and along with everything else, Mark was asked to describe all his meetings with Vallantine, when and where they took place, what the art dealer said to him, what he said to the art dealer, etc. etc. etc. Methodical in all his undertakings — and getting curious himself about what had happened — Mark tried to remember every minute he had spent with the Vallantines, and made his replies as exhaustive as possible. The more questions he answered, the more he understood what a fool he had been. He had just about finished when Wattman's secretary called to tell him to come to the office right away.

Learning from his disappointments, Mark had steeled himself for a long struggle and made his peace with the fact that nothing decisive would happen for years. "I'm sure it can wait," he told her. "I'll drop by in a couple of days and bring the interrogatories with me." He didn't even ask why Wattman wanted to see him; he was teaching himself not to expect too much.

"Oh, you can forget about the interrogatories!" she said cheerfully. "There's a breakthrough, Mr. Niven. They want to settle."

Mark tried not to believe it and he didn't, then he did — up in hope, down in despair, his soul on a swing. "What's the breakthrough?" he asked, out of breath, when he got inside his lawyer's study.

"WHAT breakthrough?" Wattman, sitting behind his desk, twisted his little button nose and looked cross.

"Miss Orloff said there was a breakthrough."

Wattman switched on the intercom. "Miss Orloff, would you come in please?"

"Yes, Mr. Wattman?" asked Miss Orloff brightly, closing the door behind her.

"Did I tell you there was a breakthrough in *Niven versus Vallantine?*"

A motherly blonde with fair skin, Miss Orloff blushed terribly. "No, but you said they wanted to settle, so I assumed . . ."

"They made a settlement proposal, yes, but I wouldn't exactly call it a breakthrough," Wattman went on when he had sent Miss Orloff out in tears. "I certainly don't wish to claim that there is reason for celebration. They offer to let bygones be bygones, each party pays his own costs, and they pay you $300,000 to dispose of all claims you may have against them."

"You mean on top of returning the treasures?"

Wattman shook his head energetically. "No, no, no. They mean to keep everything. You would clear $300,000, that's all."

Mark looked blank; his mouth worked as he tried to steady himself to speak. "That doesn't make sense. That's less money than I deposited with the court a few weeks ago! And they must assume that I paid you a lot. So why waste time making a proposal like that?"

"Do I have to spell it out for you?" asked the lawyer impatiently, drumming on his desk with his fingers. "It's meant to wear you down. They let you sweat over the interrogatories and then they make this offer to impress upon you how little they think of your chances. They're trying to drive you to despair." He paused and glared at Mark, waiting for him to make a scene.

Mark was too shocked even to raise his voice. "What did you tell them?"

"I talked to MacArthur, I told him he's crazy. But he thinks you've spent all your money and 300,000 might be quite a fortune to you in your reduced circumstances." The lawyer pursed his fleshy lips. "Who knows, he could be right, I don't want you to blame me afterward, complain I spoiled your chances to settle. Of course, I could probably talk the money up for you . . . maybe to a million, a million and a bit," he added petulantly, convinced that a young man without any special skill or talent who lived with cockroaches ought to appreciate any respectable amount, yet knowing full well that nothing but the whole caboodle would satisfy him.

"You didn't tell him to go to hell?"

"Sit down, you make me nervous. I told him I would talk with you and let him know your reply."

"You didn't tell him to drop dead?"

Wattman raised his hands: he was just a messenger. "If that's your reply, I'll pass it on. But I can't make decisions, I'm only your legal representative. I have to do what you tell me to do. My job is to give you all the facts, all the options. If we go to trial MacArthur plans to make a lot of your past. It's not just that you were a draft dodger. . . . He tells me that you threw a rock at poor Hubert Humphrey."

"It wasn't a rock, it was an apple. Not even a whole apple!"

"It makes no difference."

"I wasn't even arrested. The police looked at my library card and let me go. I've answered all the questions about it the way you told me to — my attorney instructed me not to answer."

"And I've written MacArthur a letter, as I said I would," the lawyer said emphatically, with an upward glance to make sure his client didn't miss the point. "I wrote him that none of these matters is pertinent to the present action." He flicked through the papers on his desk with incredible rapidity, extracted the letter, handed it to Mark, and leaned back in his tilting chair to watch him reading it. Like most basically lazy people he was inordinately proud of any piece of work he managed to do. "You can keep it, that's your copy," he added generously, but then sprang forward to get back to business with a frown. "What was that you said, the police took your library card?"

"They took it but they gave it back."

"How long did they have it?"

"I don't know, a few minutes."

"A few minutes. Oh, my God!" cried Wattman in an anguished voice, pressing his hands to his puffy cheeks and staring at Mark with a tragic look. Hoping to scare his obdurate client into some sort of settlement, he got up and began to pace the floor with desperate steps. "If they took your library card, your name's been fed to the computers. The FBI and the Secret Service have you on their lists. You're the client every lawyer dreams of . . . I'm going into court to ask the jury to award treasures worth $170,000,000 to a draft dodger and potential presidential assassin!"

Mark looked at his lawyer with burning eyes, without really observing him. Any doubt cast upon the return of his treasures could throw him into a panic, but no matter how frightened he was, he knew what was his. "Your letter says none of this has anything to do with who owns the treasures."

"Yes, but whatever I say, MacArthur will find a way to acquaint the jury with your crimes. I'm telling you, I won't enjoy losing this case."

"Are you working on the interrogatories for Vallantine?" asked Mark, getting angry. "Are you asking him about *his* past? The Italian government's lawsuit against him? Have you put us down for trial?"

"Are you so anxious to go to trial?"

Mark shook his head like a boxer warding off a blow. "What do you mean? I already paid you for it. You told me you could destroy Vallantine's credibility with MacArthur's cables."

"I said I could attack it. Right, we go to trial," Wattman agreed ominously and sat down again. "And let's say we're lucky. We get an honest judge who would love to see MacArthur lose a case, and we even get a jury of decent people. More: they're not only decent, they're intelligent. Why not, it's possible. The only problem is, the foreman of the jury lost his son in Vietnam. You didn't think of that, did you? There could be several Vietnam veterans on that jury. They're going to *hate* you . . ."

Suddenly Mark couldn't bear to listen to another word. He wanted to escape, he felt an urge to crash through the window. He even got up, ready to break his head against the glass, but as he looked out he was stopped by a fleecy lamb of a cloud floating toward him. It was a clear December day and the office was high enough to give him the illusion that he was out in the open sky with the cloud. There was another world, immense, bracing! He felt free in the blue sea of space, remembering the sky in the mirrors in his room on the Ile Saint-Louis, the sensation of happiness, the old conviction that life was worth living. Such flashes of mystic communion with the universe keep people sane; how often we are saved by the sky!

"I'm not afraid of the jury," he said, when he felt strong enough to face his lawyer again. "There's such a thing as a sense of justice."

"That's a very exceptional sense," came the testy reply. "In twenty-odd years of legal practice I've met very few people with a sense of justice. Most of the judges and jurors I've run across judged by their likes and dislikes, and I can assure you, nothing appeared more just to them!"

"Even if the jurors hate me," Mark stubbornly insisted, "they can't ignore the fact that I'm described as owner of the treasures in all the documents."

"And I'll tell them so repeatedly. I'll explain that it's their duty under the law to discard their prejudices, their personal likes and dislikes. Justice F will instruct them that they must be swayed only by the facts of the case. That's what trials are all about, facts. Right? Wrong. Trials are about power. When you go to trial you're placing yourself in the hands of strangers who have the power to do you a good turn or a bad turn. Once you go into court, your gold is neither yours nor Vallantine's, it belongs to the judge and jurors and they can give it to you or to that stuttering crook. That's the basic fact. As for the other facts . . ." Wattman shook his head with an air of profound dissatisfaction. "Do you know anybody who's swayed by facts? About anything? I used to go to school with your dad, Mark, so I've been around for quite some time, in and out of court, and I'm telling you: people use facts as excuses to justify whatever they want to believe. When Vallantine testifies that you had a verbal agreement with him which entitles him to 120% of your treasure find, the jurors will have the choice of believing this nice helpless elderly gentleman or believing you — *you,* a cowardly deserter who wouldn't fight for his country, for liberty, for the rule of law, but who now expects the courts to make him the richest young man on earth. I'll tell you a fact. That big stone in Washington honoring the Vietnam War dead has 58,022 names engraved on it. Each of those young Americans died doing his duty to his country, and you expect their grieving relatives to hand you a fortune for shirking yours? There's a star-spangled banner in that courtroom, you know.''

During this long speech Mark was looking out the window, but this time it didn't work. "What do you want me to do?" he asked, clenching his fists. "Kill myself?"

"Never mind, never mind," Wattman said hurriedly, not wishing to go that far. He didn't care for another bloody mess in his reception room. "I'll argue that your transgressions have no bearing on the issue. There's no reason to despair, even murderers have property rights."

"If you don't believe you can win the case, you can give me back the fee I paid you and I'll look for another lawyer."

Wattman grew pink, his eyes widened with sadness: he was hurt. "I was just trying to remind you of the dangers, all right? I'm a trial lawyer, I cut the evidence to fit my argument, satisfied? We might have a jury packed with former anti-war activists — parents whose sons went to Canada to avoid the draft — and they'll give you back your gold, the $500,000 advance, and throw in Vallantine's little dog in punitive damages. Anyway, the outcome of the trial is neither here nor there — the loser will appeal, and that's another few years." Seeing that the idea of a settlement hadn't worked out, he bounced back as the fighting attorney. "Go and finish the interrogatories, and I'll work on the questions for Vallantine."

Mark left the lawyer's study drained of all feeling, but he felt guilty when he saw Miss Orloff's reddened eyes. He was ready to cry himself. "I'm sorry, I didn't mean to get you into trouble."

"It's very nice of you to say so," she said with a forgiving smile. "I didn't mean to disappoint you."

Only then, as he turned away from Miss Orloff, did Mark realize that the reception room was full of people. They had been there when he arrived but he had been too preoccupied to notice them. "Are all these people waiting for Miss Schon?" he asked apprehensively.

"Oh, no, this is one of Mr. Wattman's busiest days!"

The waiting clients all looked like people in mourning, and they glared at him resentfully: he had jumped the queue. It finally dawned on Mark that Wattman had no intention of working for him full-time: his fate depended on a man who had tricked him.

A FEW days later, early in the afternoon, the Vallantines were sitting in their upstairs office at the Gallery, each with a copy of Mark's deposition in reply to the 357 questions. Shirley Vallantine sat on the couch; her desk had been taken over by MacArthur's assistant, Elliott T. Sanborn III — a tall, lean young man with large square glasses, who was questioning and coaching them about the various points raised by the Plaintiff's answers. "I refer you to the answer to question 171," he said slowly to give them time to find the right passage. "Mr. Niven claims that one of the reasons why he entrusted the treasures to Mr. Vallantine was that Mr. Vallantine's father was an actor like his. Any comment?"

"You can sssssee that he's making it up," said Vallantine, moving his giant eyebrows. "My father was in the insurance business."

Elliott T. Sanborn III nodded approvingly. "Right. Either Mr. Niven is lying or he thinks that everybody's father is an actor. Let's make a note of that," he concluded thoughtfully, making a note.

"He's mmmmmaking it up. If we hadn't helped him to find the *Flora,* he would have never relinquished c . . . c . . . control to us. I don't deny he could have done b . . . better for himself, but if he's intelligent, he can learn a lot from this experience. He'll th . . . th . . . thank me for it one day."

The young attorney raised his head: he was so surprised that he stopped pretending he was on the team representing the innocent party. "Do you really mean that? Can you imagine this poor kid being grateful to you?"

Vallantine looked back with a stern and defiant expression: a brave old soldier who would not retreat under fire — a brave old crook who always stood his ground on the witness stand. "Why not? I did him a fffffavor. I taught him how life works."

"Yes, if he finds another treasure ship, he'll know what to do with it," commented Sanborn without bothering to hide his contempt. He was a churchgoing Episcopalian who thought of himself as an exceptionally honest person; he wouldn't have had people like the Vallantines as friends, but this didn't prevent him from helping his firm's client to perpetrate a monumental fraud. This was his profession. His work. His job. Theft and fraud are considered grave crimes in New York as much as anywhere else — that is, if they are committed on the weekend, on one's free time as it were. But if committing or abetting crime is one's regular employment, one's way of *making a living,* then it is perfectly all right.

Just the same, Sanborn III's air of moral superiority did not appeal to the couple. Shirley Vallantine said nothing but looked daggers at the conceited underling who dared to be insolent to the best and dearest man in the world. As for the art dealer, he didn't care for the offhand manner of New York attorneys toward their clients who paid them fortunes; he believed that people for whom he had to raise three million dollars owed him some respect. "What was that you said, Elliott?" he asked testily.

Unperturbed by the flying sparks of wounded pride, Sanborn III straightened his glasses and looked at the art dealer with an uninvolved expression. "I said if the poor kid finds another treasure ship, he'll know what to do with it."

"Exactly!" Vallantine's eyes flashed and his eyebrows grew bigger as he affirmed the truth of the sarcastic remark. There was no doubt in his mind that he had been good for Mark. "He's only twenty-t . . . two years old and he's already learned how to take care of himself. And he has mmmmme to thank for it."

Yet such is the delicate nature of self-deception that when the clueless receptionist phoned from downstairs a few minutes later to report that a Mr. Niven was asking to see him, Vallantine knew for certain that Mark had come to kill them all. "Tell him we're not in!" he told the girl and, slamming down the phone, shouted, "Mark's here, lock the door!" Before either of the other two could move, he ran to the door and bolted it himself.

"Why the excitement?" asked the lawyer.

"Oh, God, he has an automatic rifle!" wailed Shirley Vallantine, standing up and clasping her hands together. "He shot several people who came near his wreck."

"He's a k . . . k . . . killer and he came to k . . . kill us!" stammered the art dealer. "Call the police . . . no, don't!" he gasped, and collapsed on the couch, breathing heavily and clutching his chest, trying to get at the pain.

His wife sprang to his aid, loosened his tie and unbuttoned his shirt; he touched her arm to thank her and begged her in an almost inaudible voice to find out whether Mark had left the gallery. She obeyed to quiet him, rushed to the phone and soon was back, taking his hands, saying, "He's gone, he's gone!" She wanted to call the doctor, but he wouldn't let her. "Don't bother, dear, only my j . . . jaw hurts now, and that can wait for the dentist," he said jokingly to calm his wife.

Sanborn III, however, was beginning to feel ill. He knew of two attorneys who had been killed by litigants in civil disputes, and he didn't want to be the third. "You mean you got involved in this business with a maniac who settles disputes with an automatic rifle, and you forgot to tell us?" he asked, and picked up the phone to relay this most important news to his boss.

"YOU'VE got to get out of town, out of the country," Wattman told Mark a couple of hours later, having climbed the stairs to his client's apartment for the second time. "Get your things together, I'm driving you to the airport. I'm not going to ask you what you were doing at the Vallantine Gallery today, I don't want to know about it, but they're very upset and MacArthur tells me if you're still here tomorrow they're going to report you to the police as a deserter and have you arrested. And that won't help our case at all, I assure you."

"How can anything help me when my own lawyer says he's going to lose my case?" Mark retorted bitterly, sitting down on the sofa. His eyes had the tired look of a man who had been in too many places of worry and anxiety; he had no intention of going anywhere. Prison was no threat to him. "I don't care if I'm arrested. I'm going to fire you and you'll have to give me back my money. If I have money I can get myself another lawyer even from jail."

"What are you talking about?"

"You told me you won't enjoy losing the case!"

Wattman threw his coat on a chair and puffed out his cheeks to express his irritation. "I said we might lose out with the jury. It's my duty to warn you of possible setbacks like that. But I also told you that it won't make any difference who wins at the trial, because the loser will appeal. So we're bound to win in the end. Come on, I'll help you pack, and I'll settle with the landlord for you."

Mark didn't move. "You have too many clients!" he exclaimed angrily. "I paid you a fortune to work on my case full-time and your office is full of people."

"And they're kept waiting whenever you need me," Wattman replied triumphantly. "You must have misconstrued our agreement. I meant I'd work on your case full-time whenever the need arises. And I will, believe me. I'm the guy who's going to get an extra two and a half million when you regain the treasures, remember? But of course," he added, raising his button nose and casting a contemptuous look at Mark, "you can go and look for another attorney if you want to. I'm not sure I want a client who trusts me less than I trust him. If I remember correctly, I worked for you for over a year and got the treasures out of Vallantine's hands before I asked you for a cent. And don't forget, $200,000 of the fee you're talking about was paid for work already done — I'm surprised you overlooked it. So . . . I'd gladly pay you back $900,000 as soon as you got another lawyer to look after you. We certainly won't have an argument about this."

Mark had the right idea but allowed himself to be talked out of it. Unable to conceive that he could be totally irrevocably robbed of the treasures, yet lacking self-confidence, he could not have been more susceptible to bad advice. Shaken in his suspicions by Wattman's offer to return the money, he didn't know what to think or say, and Wattman made the most of this hesitancy.

"The trouble with you is, you have no patience!" he said, locking his gaze into Mark's. "I told you this case would take years, so be a *mensch* and face up to it. Go somewhere and start some sort of life. You can't do anything here except get yourself arrested . . ."

Wattman talked a great deal and had to repeat his offer to return the $900,000 before convincing Mark that he should stop being paranoid, leave the case to his lawyer, to his father's friend, and go somewhere safe to await developments. Longing for fresh air and the sound of the waves — for the wide sky over the sea, unobstructed to the edge of the horizon — Mark flew to Nassau the following morning.

Each Man Is His Own Victim

Why didn't he reflect?
Why wasn't he more observant?
ITALO SVEVO

THE spirit of thievery thrives on a resolute disregard of the bond between people and their possessions. It is assumed that there is an
absolute gap between the owner and what he owns, so that when a thief
lifts a man's wallet he is not really touching him. Yet women who come
home to find that their house or apartment has been burglarized while
they were out speak of feeling raped, and many otherwise healthy old
people die because they're bereft of some object stolen from them. Clearly
they were bound up with their possessions, things were part of their psychological makeup.

Things grow into the soul. This remarkable phenomenon can be best
observed as part of the general process of aging. The older people get,
the more they are attached to their things; as their passions, their hopes,
their hair, their teeth desert them, the more they cling to what they are
left with. But even the young keep back what they can from the days
that rush past: what child hasn't once kept a broken toy? It is as if each
cherished object were a photograph capturing a moment irretrievably gone.
Things embody something of the years that drift away and evaporate like
smoke. Possessions are proof, concrete evidence of all that has disappeared; to rob a man of what he has is to rob him of his past, to tell
him that he didn't live, that he only dreamed his life.

From the moment he realized that Vallantine meant to keep the treasures, Mark was in a spin. Hadn't he lost Marianne because of the *Flora*?
Hadn't he given up half of the treasures to the Bahamian government so
that he could keep the other half? Hadn't he fought the Redistribution
Army? What were his wounds if he wasn't the richest young man in the
world? The more the *Flora* cost him, the more it meant to him. Once
he had risked his life for the treasures, they were as dear to him as his

life. He needed to get them back as much as he needed to keep his sanity. And that much would have been true even if Vallantine had blasted his way into the Royal Bank and taken the treasures by force. But Mark had *given* them to him!

Con men are the worst kind of thieves, for they rob their victims not only of their possessions but also of their faith in themselves. Such theft ought to be a capital offense — Vallantine certainly felt that he had done enough to be killed for it — but it isn't often that the victims strike back: they have lost the self-respect so necessary for righteous revenge. The Vallantines were never in any danger from Mark. He had gone to the Gallery to talk to them, to see whether they couldn't come to some kind of agreement between themselves, without the lawyers. It didn't even occur to him that he might harm his enemies. Brooding on his own gullibility, he had come to hate himself more than anybody else. When he thought of murder he thought of suicide.

No doubt Mark's self-hatred made it easier for Wattman to manipulate him. It is not difficult to influence someone who fears that he is an idiot. There came a time when Mark couldn't understand how he could have left Wattman in charge of his case even when he no longer quite trusted him — but how could he have acted wisely when he no longer trusted his own judgment?

Back in the Bahamas, he went to Santa Catalina only for his boat, and settled in Nassau. Still a Bahamian resident with all the rights of a citizen (rights dearly bought), he set up in business with the *Il Saint-Louis*, ferrying people from the hotels to the reefs. The finding of the *Flora* was still news in the islands, mentioned in every brochure, and sometimes his passengers asked him what he knew about the famous treasure wreck, but he never confessed that he had anything to do with it: he was convinced they would only laugh at him. Whenever he saw Franklin Darville or Tom Murray on Bay Street, he crossed the road to avoid them.

One day he saw Eshelby in the lobby of the British Colonial and tried to walk past him with downcast eyes, but Eshelby noticed him and grabbed his right arm. "Hey, young man! What is this? Are you snubbing me? Are you so rich and famous that you don't recognize your old friend?"

"It's like the first time we met, I didn't see you," Mark lied, trying to make a joke of it.

"Yes, that's how we met, bumping into each other!" replied Eshelby with a sigh. It seemed to him that Mark had aged a decade since they first met. "How's your arm?"

"Fine, thanks."

Surprised that Eshelby remembered his bad arm, Mark nonetheless tried to get away, but Eshelby, wanting a full report from his young friend whom he looked on as a kind of pupil, insisted they have lunch together. They were halfway through their meal in the hotel restaurant before he managed to learn that the lawsuit still wasn't resolved and Mark was earning his living ferrying snorkelers to the reefs. Eshelby was amazed. Did Mark need the money? "My dear boy," he said, "you may have forgotten, but I'm still holding that gold cup full of diamonds that you left with me. They're here in a safe-deposit box in Tom Murray's bank, we can go and get them right now."

Mark looked at Eshelby with angry pride. "I didn't leave them with you, I *gave* them to you. I thought you'd have a library for poor kids by now!" he said, his hands moving restlessly over the table, shifting the fork, rolling the napkin. "I don't need anything. I'm rich. I'm worth over a hundred and seventy million dollars. . . . Anyway, I want to hear about you."

Eshelby tried to argue but, seeing that Mark took his offer of help as an insult, thought it better to drop the subject and told him that he was on his way back from Canada and had come into Nassau to pass the time between planes.

"How big is Canada?" asked Mark with sudden intensity. "How many square miles?"

"I don't know, but too many — far too many!"

"Come on, you're a teacher, you must know the figure — tell me!" Mark demanded, more alive and interested than at any other time during their conversation. "Never mind, I'll look it up," he said impatiently, as he saw he was not going to get an answer.

"You might as well ask me how high is Mont Blanc!"

"I know that — it's four thousand eight hundred and ten meters high."

"You take my breath away, dear boy . . . how on earth do you happen to know a thing like that?"

"I'm reading a book called *A Million Facts*."

"I thought you'd be reading Stendhal, Balzac, Tolstoy, Swift, Sterne, Defoe — anybody who makes sense of life!" exclaimed Eshelby, still trying to save his friend with books. "You can read modern writers if you want to, I don't mind — Kafka, Bulgakov, Thomas Mann — Thurber, Waugh — Graham Greene, Philip Roth, Günter Grass, Garcia Marquéz — but what will a million facts do for you?"

"I can tell you how big the North American continent is," Mark countered.

"Please don't!"

"It's eight million square miles."

"And what do you know when you know that?" Eshelby sighed. "Facts have no meaning. You might as well watch television."

Mark shrugged defensively. "It's a good book. When I read it I don't have to think. I mean I can relax."

"Exactly — facts are mental tranquilizers," said Eshelby, unable to conceal his contempt for anything that puts the brain to sleep. "I can't believe you really need that sort of stuff at your age," he added with lessening certainty. Maybe it was best for Mark not to think of anything but the height of mountains until he got his treasures back.

Misinterpreting Eshelby's sudden hesitant silence, Mark winced and bit his lip. "You think I'm a fool."

"Don't be silly. I'm sure nobody thinks you're a fool — not since you found the *Flora*!"

Mark snatched the bill from the waiter's hand, a millionaire insisting on having his own way, and before leaving he promised to fly to Santa Catalina one day and collect the things he had left with Eshelby. But he didn't show up or call.

He wanted to avoid everybody until he had his treasures back and could look people in the eye without feeling ashamed of himself. He worked hard at his ferrying business, and when not working he hid out in Loft House, a fine old guest house in the center of town with thick walls, high ceilings, large, pleasant rooms and good old worn and faded furniture. The French windows of his room faced a great expanse of big, bright, leafy plants: destined to be flattened a year later to make way for Nassau's first skyscraper, Loft House had an overgrown garden as dense and luxuriant as a tropical rain forest. It was by the window looking out at this wild greenery that Mark seated himself to peruse *A Million Facts*.

His social life consisted of small talk with his elderly English landlady at Loft House and long conversations with his father on the transatlantic phone. In a heroic effort of filial love, he always tried to sound cheerful and confident. His father didn't quite believe him and sent him Fortini's *Nuova Vita di San Francesco* to read. The moral genius of the 13th century, in love with poverty, was an expert in aversion therapy and quite successful in instilling in his disciples a physical revulsion to gold. He once ordered a monk who had touched a coin to put it between his teeth and press it into a pile of stinking dung. Later on Mark would come to grasp what Saint Francis meant, but at the time he was trying to read the book his own aversion therapy was far from complete and he thought Saint Francis was crazy.

When Wattman sent the Defendants' interrogatories, in which Vallantine had been trapped into some mutually exclusive lies, Mark went wild with joy and wrote his lawyer a letter of thanks and congratulations and thought of him with affection for weeks. Then nothing more happened for months. He often thought he would die if he had to wait another day.

Yet he never doubted that he would win the case. The religious ideas of his childhood helped him to endure his frustration as a well-deserved punishment for getting involved with Vallantine. He was atoning for his stupidity, and once he had suffered enough, he would have God for a friend again.

He had been living at Loft House for about six months when, coming back from the harbor one hot afternoon, he found a letter waiting for him on the table in the dark, cool hallway.

WATTMAN & SCHON
– Avenue of the Americas
New York, N.Y. 10014
May 22, 1972

Mr. Mark Niven
Room 2, Loft House
Nassau, Bahamas

Dear Mark,

Niven v. Vallantine

I am sorry to have to advise you that it now appears that your claims against the Vallantine Gallery are not as strong as they at first appeared. The new facts that have come to light require a far more extensive preparation for the trial than we anticipated; you will appreciate that your own violations of the law, for instance, make the case a great deal more complex.

I refer you to our Letter of Agreement in which you undertook to pay Wattman & Schon additional sums in the event of unforeseen complications. As such complications have unfortunately arisen, I am sure you will wish to comply as promptly as possible by remitting the requisite sum of $100,000 to our firm, so that we can proceed with all due speed.

Best regards,

Bernard Jay Wattman, Esq.
Attorney-at-Law

Without consulting anybody to seek what he felt was bound to be useless advice, Mark got out his secondhand typewriter and — muttering, cursing, shaking his fist at the walls of his room — wrote and rewrote his reply, which he mailed at two in the morning.

Dear Bernie,

You must think I'm an idiot, writing me a letter like that! You know very well that I know there are no new facts in this case. You undertook to handle it up to and including the trial for $1,100,000, which I paid you in full. I can't believe you too are turning out to be a crook! How can you keep your license to prac-

325

tice if you don't do the work you've been paid for? You can go to jail for that.

I don't understand you. You stand to gain $2,500,000 when you win the case! Even if you *are* a crook, it makes sense for you to go ahead and earn your bonus instead of trying to squeeze me now for another $100,000 which I don't have.

You've done good work for me so far, so get back to it, get us a trial date, prepare us for trial, and I'll forget you ever wrote me that ludicrous letter.

He felt that his own letter was so effective — so tough and to the point — that Wattman couldn't possibly have an answer to it. He was convinced that the lawyer had no choice but to earn the money he had already taken and sheer greed would compel him to take the case through trial and win it to earn the bonus. All the same, to make sure, he called Wattman two weeks later. He wasn't surprised that Wattman didn't come to the phone — he was getting used to people becoming unavailable as soon as they did something dirty — and besides, Miss Orloff was cheerfully positive: yes, Mr. Wattman had received his letter and was working on the case. Whenever Mark called, Miss Orloff was full of reassurance: Mr. Wattman was busy on his behalf and things were moving ahead. If there is a hell, there must be a special pit reserved for nice, sweet, charming, intelligent secretaries who have spent their niceness, sweetness, charm and intelligence on covering up for their bosses.

All Mark needed was patience.

One day in February of the following year, the third year of his lawsuit, there was a thick, long, narrow envelope waiting for him on the hall table at Loft House. Inside he found an *Order and Judgment,* signed by Justice F, and twenty-four pages of enclosures.

The court had dismissed the lawsuit, released the sequestered treasures to Vallantine, and awarded Vallantine the $500,000 advance on admission receipts which he had paid to Mark at the signing of the contract.

Mark read the enclosures on the plane to New York, trying to understand what had happened. There were several letters purportedly sent to him by Wattman. In the first, Wattman noted with regret that Mark had lost confidence in him and, as he could not reasonably be expected to work for a client who called him a crook, he asked Mark to find himself another attorney to represent him. In the next letter Wattman complained of Mark's failure to reply and urged him once again to find another attorney, as the case was coming up for trial. It appeared from the other papers that *Niven v. Vallantine* Index No. 1580/70 Calendar No. 70932 had duly come to be heard at Trial Term, 1C Part X, held in and for the County of New York, but that instead of judging the issue of the ownership of the treasures, Justice F had heard Wattman's motion to be *relieved as counsel for the Plaintiff* and a cross-motion by MacArthur for an order *to return the sequestered chattels to the Defendants* and *to dismiss the action with prejudice.*

Wattman's motion to the court complained of the Plaintiff's paranoid suspiciousness and abusive language, of Plaintiff's failure to respond to all entreaties to find himself another attorney, and of Plaintiff's failure to show up for the trial even after being duly notified.

William T. MacArthur's cross-motion for the Defendants asked the court to release the sequestered goods to Defendants and to dismiss the case, as it was evident from the submission of the Plaintiff's own attorney that the Plaintiff was an unbalanced and abusive character who had a propensity to accuse everyone who came in contact with him, and his absence from the proceedings clearly showed that there was no substance to his charges.

There was more, but it all added up to the *Order & Judgment* in which

. . . due deliberation having been had thereon; and upon reading and filing the memorandum decision of this Court dated the 1st day of February 1973; and upon all of the papers and proceedings heretofore had herein; it is

ORDERED, that the Motion by Plaintiff's attorneys to be relieved as counsel and to protect their liens is granted; and it is further

ORDERED, that Defendants' Cross-Motion to return the sequestered chattels to the Defendants and to dismiss the above-entitled action is granted, the action is dismissed with prejudice and the Clerk is directed to enter Judgment accordingly.

Despair is cold air growing around the heart. Mark didn't scream and thought that he behaved normally, but the U.S. Customs men at Kennedy Airport spotted his strange look and shaking hands and searched him for drugs. They finally let him go, though not without misgivings.

WATTMAN made no difficulties about seeing his former client, but received him standing in the middle of his private office, very much on the alert. "You were warned not to start this action!" he exclaimed, upbraiding Mark before Mark could say anything to him. "You were told to forget it!"

Taken aback by the lawyer's accusing tone, Mark pulled the long envelope containing the Judgment and enclosures out of his coat pocket and held it up, as if wishing to remind him of what he had done. "What

327

are these letters you're supposed to have sent me? You didn't send me any of these letters!''

Wattman didn't blush, he didn't have the skin for it, only his puffy cheeks grew taut. "There you go again, making unfounded allegations!" he complained dolefully. "That's what it's all about, the way you go around making totally absurd accusations against everybody who tries to help you. . . . It's not *our* fault if you didn't get our letters. The postal service is appalling. If you'd had a clean record and could have stayed in New York, you would have known what was going on. We're not responsible for your problems as a fugitive from justice . . .''

Mark watched with horrified fascination. It was difficult for him to conceive that the shiny-faced man who was berating him with such confidence was the same man who had betrayed him. "OK, give me back my $900,000 from the $1,100,000 I paid you."

Wattman raised his eyebrows and backed away a little to flex his muscles. "So . . . you evidently haven't read the *Order & Judgment:* the court granted our motion to protect our liens. That means we are entitled to be paid for all the work we've done for you. We've been carrying this case for over two years, you know!" The pronoun *I* had disappeared from his vocabulary; he held the corporate identity of WATTMAN & SCHON in front of him like a shield.

Mark was so sick of him, he didn't want to argue. "Fine. Give me back $800,000."

"According to our agreement you were obliged to pay an additional fee and you breached this agreement by refusing to comply, so whether we ought to return any part of our fee is a moot question."

Mark uttered a sound between a laugh and a howl.

"We may owe you *some* money," Wattman added hastily. "But I can't discuss this with you, you're not a rational person. Get yourself another lawyer and I'm sure we'll be able to resolve the matter."

"But why? Why did you give up the case? If you're so keen on money, how come you didn't want to earn the $2,500,000 bonus?"

"Money isn't everything," replied the future justice of the Supreme Court of the State of New York with magisterial dignity.

"What about your reputation?" argued Mark, still half hoping that he would wake up from his nightmare. "When you won the case you would have been a famous lawyer."

"And what if we didn't win?" asked Wattman. "You're always so sure of winning!" Satisfied by this time that Mark didn't have a gun, he sat down behind the desk. "Your case was dismissed with prejudice, you know. That means you forfeit your $500,000 security and you owe Vallantine damages as a result of the injunction. I don't know what they'll be but with MacArthur in charge I'm sure the sky's the limit."

Mark was saved from doing something violent either to the lawyer or to himself by the sudden thought that he must not tell his father how his old college friend had turned out. If only Sir Henry were still alive! He wiped the sweat from his face and neck, realizing for the first time that he was in a hot room and still wearing his heavy coat.

"So . . ." said the lawyer with triumphant malice, watching his former client's attempts to collect himself. "You're always so sure of winning. And what makes you so sure we would have won?"

"I'm going to get the treasures back because they're mine," said Mark, his eyes flashing, gaining new strength from the desire to show he wasn't beaten. "Everybody knows they're mine!"

Wattman shook his head pityingly. How much time he had wasted trying to explain things to that obtuse kid! "Mark, the trouble with you is, you don't understand that evil is stronger."

MARK spoke to people, walked through doors, went up and down in elevators, crossed streets: he was like a hunted animal, mortally wounded but still running. Some time later he found himself in a reception room in the U.S. Department of Justice building in Lower Manhattan. He was waiting to denounce himself to someone.

In the way that a tormented mind seizes on any idea, he had come to feel that he deserved to be ruined because he was asking for the protection of the law while showing no respect for it. He no longer thought that being a draft dodger or a deserter (he wasn't sure which he was) had nothing to do with his case. If he wanted his country to protect him, then he should pay the penalty for breaking its laws. He was *looking forward* to going to prison. Once he paid his dues, they couldn't deny his property rights. They couldn't refuse him his treasures then!

He wanted to be punished and protected. The profound justice of such an exchange seemed so self-evident to him that he thought it would be almost automatic. He didn't have to wait long: observed talking to himself, he was shown almost immediately to the office of one of the assistant district attorneys. Mark, who couldn't avoid looking in a mirror from time to time and had come to think it natural for people to look worn and haggard at twenty-three, was taken aback to find Authority looking like a college freshman, but the boyish Assistant District Attorney, who was in fact twenty-eight years old, was reassuringly serious and businesslike. He listened attentively to Mark for a few minutes, then rang for a shorthand typist. "We'll deal with the draft business later," he said while they were still alone. "First I want you to tell me all about this *Flora* case, that's more complicated."

An elderly man carrying a narrow shorthand typewriter came into the office, placed his machine on a small table and put a roll of paper on it, unrolling enough paper to wind onto an empty spool at the other end of the spindle. The Assistant District Attorney swore Mark in and as Mark talked the old man typed, with the paper rolling from one spool onto the other. Using Mark's copy of Justice F's *Order & Judgment* with enclosures as reference, the Assistant District Attorney asked questions about the original fraud, the course of the lawsuit, about Bernard Jay Wattman, Esq., and William T. MacArthur, Esq., and Mark was allowed to talk for hours about what was killing him.

At the conclusion of the deposition, which took up several rolls of paper, the elderly shorthand typist left the room and the Assistant District Attorney looked at Mark with an embarrassed air. "I really admire what you did, you know," he said. "I mean finding the *Flora*. I read about it in the papers at the time."

"What happens next?" asked Mark, his heart beating faster.

"Well, nothing, unfortunately," replied the attorney with a sheepish grin. "Wattman told you the truth, we've never managed to put any of MacArthur's clients in jail. We're trying, but so far we're only wasting the taxpayers' money. I don't think my boss would like us to get involved in yet another case with that invincible carpet merchant."

"Aren't you people going to take it over?" begged Mark. "I told you I'm willing to go to prison. You can arrest me."

"If you want to be arrested I'm sure you could find somebody in this building to arrest you, but then you'd only be released on your own recognizance. The word is that Nixon's going to resign or be impeached and the next President will probably declare some kind of amnesty for guys like you. Under the circumstances I'd feel rather foolish wasting time and money arraigning you — especially as we can't prosecute half the crimes we know about —"

"You mean you won't do anything?" interrupted Mark.

"What *can* I do?" Seeing how upset Mark was, the young man came out from behind his desk to stand beside him. "This is New York, Mr. Niven. If we could worry about your kind of crime and your kind of grievance, I would envy myself!"

Mark took a deep breath. It seemed to him that he had always known there was no help. Why had he come to this place? Nobody made any sense. "Then why did you bother?" he asked bitterly. "Why did you get me to testify? If you knew you couldn't do anything."

"We'll keep your testimony on file. It might tie into something someday, and then we'll hit them with it. Not that you'll have to wait for that . . ." There were still ten days to appeal Justice F's *Order & Judgment*. He thought he might even be able to suggest a couple of up-and-coming attorneys, friends of his, who would take on the case without initial payment . . .

Mark was suddenly overcome by deadly fatigue. He had lost interest in lawyers, in the treasures, in the world, in himself. Words of encouragement filled him with loathing. Those who despair, despair of everything. The light went out of his eyes; he stared dully into empty space as if looking at something inside him. Like Sultan Assid in *The Thousand and One Nights*, he conceived life as a great wrong.

A Wife's Coughing

A virtuous woman
who loves her husband should always act
in perfect obedience to his wishes and desires
as if he were a kind of divine being.
                        KAMA SUTRA

As far as Kevin Hardwick was concerned, his wife and Mark Niven were still lovers. He watched them making love on the deck of the *Hermit* at least once a week. Next to his office on the top floor of the HCI Building there was a screening room where the company's television commercials were shown for his approval, and it was here that he screened Masterson's film after his secretaries had left for the day.

It was his secret vice. The film, now also on a videocassette, was hidden in the most secure place he had, the same place where he kept the records of the bribes he paid, in the secret compartment of his wall safe at the office, where everything was wired to burn in 3000-volt heat if the lock was tampered with. The wall safe itself was concealed behind the oak paneling. Hardwick was far from shy — there were occasions when he had a woman on the sofa in the same room without bothering about the doors — but he never watched the film without locking himself in.

Every time he watched it some previously unobserved detail, a new act of vile betrayal, leaped into his eyes. Insulted and enraged by what the couple were doing to each other, rolling naked on the deck mattress as if he didn't exist, blinded to everything else by his wife's visible pleasure in making her lover grow in her mouth, he failed for a long time to notice the smile bursting out on her face at the mere touch of her lover's hand. Once he noticed it, it never stopped rankling him.

He tested her whenever he could: surprised her by taking hold of her hand and watching her expression. Later, alone with his video set, he played back the tape to compare the smile that lit up her face for the younger man with the blank looks she gave him.

HARDWICK had counted on killing that relationship during the winter his wife spent on a safari farm in Kenya: her boyfriend couldn't come into their home through the box, and she was too far away to hear about the ambush at sea; she couldn't feel sorry for him and rush back to sit at his bedside. There was nothing in Kenya to feed her infatuation, and Hardwick had some tolerable nights with her on his flying visits to the safari farm. At least she submitted, the bitch, even if she made a big fuss about swallowing and clearing her throat afterward.

Besides, the young stud had got what was coming to him. "It took some time, my friend, but when you say the word I get up an army," Vincenzo Baglione told Hardwick at their meeting in a Denver hotel suite after the attack on the barge. Baglione explained that he had "thought up" the robbery at sea to disguise the fact that they were after the actor's son, and to make sure no one would ever think of connecting Hardwick to the event, he sent his people out as a bunch of crazy terrorists armed with guns and leaflets. "I lost five of my men to oblige you, Kevin," the Chicago crime boss said mournfully. "But we took care of the kid for you. He got a squashed arm and he's full of holes — he ain't dead yet but he's as good as dead. I done my bit." In fact, Baglione had absolutely nothing to do with the people who called themselves the Redistribution Army — all he knew about the raid was what he read in the papers — but like most successful organization men he knew how to take credit for other people's work.

To Hardwick everything seemed to be in order. The film was pushed to the back of the wall safe, and he could devote his energies to his business. At the time he was directing the transfer of several HCI plants to Third World countries where his advisers thought people would never know enough to worry about pollution. (His trips to Kenya to see his family were also working trips.) He was so busy that when his family came back in the spring they were home for several days before he had time for Marianne.

One afternoon, passing by the open door, he saw her standing in the playroom even though the children weren't there. She looked pensive and withdrawn, as if she had all kinds of thoughts in her head. "Wake up," he told her, putting his arm around her waist and reaching up to fondle her breast. He wanted her most when she appeared to live in a world of her own. "Is anything wrong?"

"No."

"Then let's screw," said the husband, who didn't waste time on preliminaries unless he absolutely had to.

In bed Marianne was docile, even eager. She had heard from Joyce, who heard it from Fawkes, that Mark had been in Dr. Feyer's clinic, laid up for months with gunshot wounds, while they were in Africa, and she was punishing herself by doing for her husband everything she hated, without his having to ask. 'What did Mark think when he didn't get a letter from me, not even a get-well card?' she asked herself despairingly. 'He must hate me, he must despise me. No, he doesn't despise me, he doesn't think of me at all.' Her mouth was sore, but she wanted to feel pain. Hardwick was delighted: she was starting him up a second time.

She would never have any sex life, she told herself, if she waited until she could enjoy it. And she *should* try to enjoy it; didn't the wives on the island look healthy and satisfied, even though their husbands were old and disgusting? If other wives could do it, so could she. Just forget her feelings. There was such a thing as animal pleasure, pure sex, everybody said so. She felt a wave going through her.

But the next time, the next morning, she started coughing and choking, and more violently than ever before. She had to run to the bathroom to vomit. It was while listening to the sound of her throwing up that Hardwick realized *as good as dead* wasn't as good as dead. When he got to his office he looked at the film again: she wasn't choking with her boyfriend! This was when he began to watch the film regularly, when he began to think of her affair not as something in the past but as something that was still going on, in her heart at least. She was cheating on him and he was not going to let her get away with it. He was going to teach her that she belonged to her husband. Every time he watched the film he became more convinced that he was right to press her, to insist, to make her do it, and that there was nothing wrong with her except her attitude.

BUT she would not become more tractable, and when she found a pretext, she turned openly hostile. She started baiting him about an old memo that some disloyal employee had stolen from the files, photocopied and mailed to the *Tribune*. The memo advised against dumping dioxin into Lake Michigan

> . . . because of future complications in the event of claims of contamination against us.
>
> To put problematic waste into shallow wells is preferable. The original cost factor would be low and there would be no future expense involved. It is considered impossible to determine the course of subterranean streams, and therefore, responsibility for any contamination could not be fixed . . .

The memo, prepared by a young attorney in HCI's legal department, had not been followed up by any digging (Hardwick made the deal with the Illinois Safe Transport Company instead) but what put the four-year-old document even on network television news was Hardwick's note in the margin, intended only for the memo's author. "I like your thinking, you've got a raise!"

All this was made to look even more incriminating by the fact that Hardwick had promoted the same young lawyer to the top post in his legal department just before the memo was leaked to the *Tribune* — possibly by another lawyer in the department who was annoyed at being passed over.

What could Hardwick do to rid himself of the odium of rewarding employees who had bright ideas about saving company money by poisoning the tap water?

To respond in a dignified and authoritative manner, he first of all renamed his chief public-relations man *education specialist* (an inspired designation which caught on like wildfire in the chemical and nuclear industries), gave the newly christened hack a raise and sent him into battle. HCI's education specialist immediately called a press conference at which he first of all explained that the wells were never built — this was true — and the memo and Mr. Hardwick's comment on it were "exercises in gallows humor", and then gave a detailed account of HCI's measures and expenditures to control hazardous waste, claiming that no other chemical company spent as much on pollution control as HCI. He pointed out — and this was also true — that HCI was spending more than three million dollars *every year* on salaries and benefits for employees whose job was to purify HCI discharges and "thus improve the quality of the air and water people use". The press conference was followed by a spate of press releases on HCI Clean Earth Products, and many of them got printed, owing to the controversy surrounding the firm. All in all, Hardwick felt he came out ahead, but Marianne used the incident to vent her frustrations on him, passing judgment on things she didn't understand.

When he came home on the day the memo was published and stopped at the door of the children's playroom to say hello, he found Marianne sitting on the sofa with Creighton leaning on her from one side and Ben from the other, listening to her read *Stuart Little*. "You want to come and listen with us?" Creighton asked his father, but Marianne greeted him with a look of burning contempt.

Hardwick, who had long ago resolved to spare his sons the hurt of parental tensions and arguments, gave them all a cheery wave and went away. He ignored his wife's ugly silence during dinner, thinking that he would calm her down in bed, and later when she was about to disappear into her dressing room he caught her arm to hold her back. "Come on, I'll cure your headache."

"You should be worrying about the headaches of the people you poison," she hissed at him, tearing her arm free. "No wonder we have to worry about letter bombs!"

Hardwick tried to explain that HCI's wastes were either detoxified at the factories or safely trucked away to government-approved disposal sites in Canada, but it made no difference: she was determined to put him in the wrong. "If you're not dumping poisons, then why did you make us stop drinking the tap water?"

"Because everybody's dumping. Or rather, we don't know who's dumping what. Are you blaming me for trying to protect you?"

She left him standing in the corridor and locked her door to keep him out.

"What kind of behavior is that?" he asked through the door.

STILL, there were the children, life had to go on, there had to be a compromise, some attempt at peaceful coexistence, and some weeks later Hardwick managed to coax his wife into bed again.

But just as he had got rid of her nightgown and was beginning to feel excited, she held him away with both hands to ask him a question. "When those ads of yours boast about HCI improving the quality of the air and water, what they really mean is that HCI plants are reducing the amount of poison they discharge, is that right?"

He rolled away from her without a word.

She took this for an affirmative answer. "That's exactly the same as if I started putting only half a spoonful of arsenic into your coffee every morning instead of my usual spoonful, and then claimed I was improving the quality of your coffee!"

"What is it you want?" sighed Hardwick, turning the light on so he could see her. "Do you want a divorce?"

She was busy getting back into her nightgown. "Aren't we rich enough to stop dealing in poisons?" she asked once she felt dressed. She sat up against the headboard and drew the blanket up to her chin. "Can't you get *out* of chemicals?"

"You mean right now, at midnight?"

She strained her eyes, trying to make him out from a great distance. "I don't see what's so funny about it. I just looked up the figures today: three out of every ten Americans have cancer. And that's not counting skin cancer."

"Marianne, what kind of pillow talk is this? Do men and women get into bed to discuss cancer?"

"Can't we ever talk?"

Hardwick got out of bed to put on his pajamas; he didn't feel like being naked either. "Of course we can talk," he sighed, switching his mind to discussion. "We have a higher incidence of cancer than we used to because medicine's curing everything else. And because of the fallout from atmospheric nuclear tests in the 50s and early 60s. HCI had nothing to do with these things. It's your cousin James you should be worrying about — he's mixed up with the French, selling nuclear technology to Iraq and Pakistan. Anyway, if it isn't Iraq or Pakistan or India, it'll be the Russians or us, or the Chinese, the French, the Libyans, the Argentinians . . . give them all a chance and *somebody's* going to push the button. And you're blaming me because there are problems with pesticides and disinfectants?''

''James is a creep — that doesn't excuse *you.*''

''Please don't interrupt! Let me finish. I'm going to explain it all, but *listen.* Suppose a lot of our chemicals do turn out to have harmful side-effects. Closing HCI tomorrow wouldn't make the slightest difference. The other companies would simply increase production, period. The amount of stuff that gets into the water table would be exactly the same as now. Never mind HCI . . . if all American companies closed shop, it would still make no difference. The Japanese, the West Germans, the French, the English, the Swiss would all be delighted to take over our shrinking markets. The only consequence of my closing down the business would be that you wouldn't have a plane to fly you here, there and everywhere. Making you rich or poor, that's the sum total of the difference HCI can make to the fate of the world.''

Marianne lifted her chin defiantly. ''You're an important man — you could set an example that people could follow.''

Hardwick, who had been pacing around the bed, stopped to stare down at her. Had he married a stupid woman? Would his sons turn out to be stupid? ''You mean people would quit making money if I showed them the way?''

''So the Marxists are right! You capitalists are so hell-bent on profit that you'll destroy the world if you can make money on it!''

''Stop!'' shouted her husband, raising his hand. ''Wait, I want to show you something, wait!'' He hurried out of the room, ran barefoot down the stairs to the library, picked up an issue of *U.S. News & World Report,* bounded upstairs with it and rushed back into the bedroom, stubbing his toe against the doorsill.

''Marianne, are poor Neapolitan fishermen capitalists?'' he asked, not minding the pain. He was going to make this benighted woman understand the world she lived in. ''Poor Neapolitan fishermen who can't read or write or count — just the sort of people the Marxists think will save us all. Correct? Well, my dear, here's the story,'' he said, waving the magazine. ''There's an outbreak of cholera in Naples and it turns out that it was started by infected mussels, fished and sold by these poor, good, simple people. The hospitals are full of cholera victims, so the medical authorities ban the fishing and sale of mussels. And what do your poor, simple fishermen do? They demonstrate, they protest. They want to go on fishing and selling their catch and they want people to go on eating mussels even if it kills them.''

"But those poor fishermen can't do anything *else*. They can't make a living any other way. That's all they know, fishing.''

"Exactly,'' said Hardwick triumphantly. "And what else does your poor nuclear physicist know? All he knows is how to make warheads or reactors, and he wants to go on making them. Capitalism has nothing to do with it. Soviet scientists are exactly the same. They make less money than James but they earn a very good living and get a lot of professional satisfaction and a lot of standing out of it, Lenin Prizes or what not, so they want to carry on regardless. And that's why neither Russia nor the States will ever have enough bombs. They had enough megatons to annihilate each other three times over about twenty years ago, but they never stopped adding to their stockpiles, year in, year out — and they're always arguing for more! Listen to them twenty years from now, and they'll still see the need to go on doing what they're doing. Just like your poor Neapolitan fishermen.''

"But if you're right, nobody will be here twenty years from now!''

"That's my point,'' said Hardwick with a satisfied air. "Most of the authorities who write on these subjects assume that our species is a goner.'' He had never discussed the end of the world with a greater sense of well-being: the room was big, warm, familiar — it felt good talking — and he was cowing his wife.

"What will happen to Creighton and Ben?'' Marianne asked, staring at him with wide burning eyes. She was so shocked and revolted, she felt unclean, cold. "How can you dismiss their future so calmly?''

Taken aback, Hardwick glanced at the framed photographs of his sons on the wall, then sat down on the edge of the bed and lifted his foot to massage his sore toe. "I'm not talking about Creighton and Ben,'' he said, annoyed. "There's no reason to be morbid about this. We have a few generations to go if we're lucky. All I'm saying is that nobody will stop doing anything because of possibly harmful consequences. In the whole history of HCI we had two research scientists who wanted to quit on a matter of principle, and they're still with us. It's not in human nature to stop doing what you're good at doing. Nobody ever abandons a job or profession which works for him, no matter how dangerous it is for everybody else. There is no such thing as a human being who will say *I like what I'm doing, I'm good at it, I'm well rewarded for it, but I'll stop doing it because it may be harmful to my fellow men*. If you could find a hundred people capable of saying that — not in Chicago or the States but in the world — if there were a hundred such creatures among four and a half billion, you could say there was hope for the

338

human race. . . . But there aren't, and there's nothing I can do about it."

"You mean it's all right for you to poison people because it makes no difference? Doesn't it make any difference to the people who are poisoned? Doesn't it make any difference to you?"

"Can we go to sleep?" asked her husband in a pained voice. He got back under the blanket, stretched himself and yawned aloud, hoping she would stop baiting him if she didn't have to worry about him making love to her.

"I'm not sleepy," said Marianne with a nervous shiver. "You can't just talk about everybody dying and then go to sleep! You don't care, so you think nobody does. You're insane."

"Oh, God," groaned Hardwick.

"Why, isn't it insane to say that there aren't a hundred decent people in the world? There are millions of them. Hundreds of millions!"

"There are billions of them, my dear. Billions. So even if the human race survives everything else, it will still die of people. How often do I have to tell you that the earth cannot support all these rabbits?"

"I'm sick and tired of that obsession of yours," she said, throwing off the blanket and swinging her legs over the side of the bed to turn her back on him. "It's possible to grow enough food for twenty billion people."

"Sure, of course. Why not. If you use enough of our pesticides and herbicides that you're always complaining about. The problem isn't feeding people, the problem is what to do with the garbage. You complain about how we're fouling the earth, air, water right now — how do you think the world will look when there are twenty billion humans in it? Twenty billion people just *breathing* and *farting* would make the birds fall out of the trees."

"Very funny," she said, keeping her back to him.

"Well, we're already overheating the atmosphere. Why don't you listen to your husband for once in your life? I tell you, feeding, housing, transporting twenty billion people would produce more pollution than the earth could take. The problem is people. That's what you refuse to face. *Mothers* do more harm than chemical companies."

"How about fathers?"

"If you adopted all the measures the environmentalists are pushing, they wouldn't do as much good as a plague. We need about a billion people to die before childbearing age, from cancer or whatever, I don't care, if anybody is to survive."

"What if one of them is you?" she asked, turning to face him. "What if one of them is your child?"

"Well, you've got to be careful what you put into your mouth. It's the survival of the fittest. Survival of the best informed. Our kids don't eat shellfish. But you don't want them to be suffocated, do you? What we need is more and bigger disasters. You should be overjoyed whenever you hear about an earthquake or a famine. Who knows, maybe even a limited nuclear war . . .''

She ran out of the room, down the hall, and locked herself in her little bedroom next to the children's.

Hardwick didn't mind. 'You wanted a discussion, you got a discussion,' he thought. 'You'll stick to sex the next time.'

MARIANNE spent most of her time with her children and the rest doing volunteer work for music in Chicago and for Greenpeace. It was a settled thing in her mind that being happy with Mark had to do with their youth and everything that was going to happen to her had already happened. After nearly two more years, this was how matters stood with the family. In public, at dinner parties and receptions, in front of their children or servants, Marianne and Kevin Hardwick tried to behave as though there were nothing amiss between them, but whenever he surprised her alone in a room, she had a coughing fit. It got so that she didn't even have to see him. When he returned home in the evening, as soon as he came near enough for her to hear his footsteps or his voice, he could hear her start coughing, and he suffered the torments of the damned.

He also turned into a faithful husband. Watching the film regularly, he knew how free and easy his wife could be — and yet how shy, how repressed she acted with him! He became so obsessed with her *duplicity* that he lost all interest in other women.

And he wasn't feeling very well. Spending a lot of time coping with environmentalist paranoia both in his business and at home, he was quite proud of his ability to discuss megadeaths without sentimentality, but it all got to him in the end, when he caught cold on a trip to Cubatao and coughed up bloody phlegm on the return flight. Did he have bronchial cancer? Had he choked on the foul air of Cubatao once too often? He was seized by such terror that he radioed his doctor from the plane, and when they landed the doctor was waiting with his driver at the airport to take him to the clinic for a thorough checkup. It turned out that the blood in his phlegm came from his nose: he had had a nosebleed in his sleep, and the blood had run down into his throat. But he was not entirely reassured, and from that time on he was convinced that his failing sex drive, his loss of interest in women other than his wife, had to do with all the muck he breathed and touched and ate and drank.

One day his PR man came to see him with a news report about the spilling of eight tons of Canadian-manufactured uranium hexafluoride into the North Atlantic, and an Ottawa official's statement that the amount was insignificant compared with the four billion tons of uranium already dissolved in the world's seawater. "Next time any of those eco-freaks come to bother us about our solvents, I'll send them off to worry about radwaste and our holier-than-thou neighbors to the north," said the education specialist, rather pleased with himself.

Hardwick didn't respond as he usually did to this sort of talk. "Do you have any children?" he asked the man gloomily.

Some weeks later when he happened to look into the nursery at noon, the boys were having fish soup without shellfish for lunch, and Ben offered him a spoonful. Hardwick took it, swallowed it and said, "Good! Good!" But then he thought it had a funny taste, and told Joyce to take away the plates and call the cook.

"You make fantastic bouillabaisse, Henri, and nobody's more sorry about this than I am, but I'm afraid we just can't risk eating fish in any shape or form," he said regretfully. "You'll have to make do with meat and poultry from the farm."

The cook didn't argue, but Creighton protested, "I want fish, I want fish."

"You can't have fish. It's not safe."

"Why not safe? It's safe!"

"It's not safe," explained Hardwick patiently, "because it comes from Lake Michigan."

"No it doesn't, it comes from an ocean."

"It's *not* safe, because it comes from the ocean or a lake or a river or a stream," the father said, "and I don't want to hear another word about it. Satisfied?"

"Daddy should have been a doctor," said Creighton when they were by themselves again. "He always worries about health."

Hardwick *knew* that he was overreacting and began to hate environmentalists, including his wife, more than ever. They not only hindered him in his business, they were turning him into a neurotic. Even so, the morning he discovered a blackish mole on his chest, he broke out in a sweat. It looked like a mole, it probably was a mole, but what if it wasn't?

What if it was malignant?

Was he one of the three out of every ten?

THE security measures regarding the mail remained in force. Everything addressed to 11 Bellevue Place was redirected first to HCI's security department and then up to Hardwick's office, where he checked it over before having it delivered to the house. (By then he wanted to read *all* his wife's mail, no matter whom it was from.) But whether it was the post office or HCI's security department or Hardwick himself who slipped up, one day Marianne received an unopened letter from Santa Catalina.

Dear Marianne,

I hope you haven't forgotten your fellow islanders, because we need your help. Our mutual friend was found yesterday lying half dead in the bottom of his boat, anchored at the spot where he found that cursed wreck. Lopez, our Haitian fisherman, brought him in and he's now in the clinic. Dr. Feyer says he was almost completely dehydrated and hadn't taken food for at least a week. He assures me that the young fool will live but I think he needs more than intravenous feeding. As you may or may not have heard, he was robbed of his famous treasures, and this apparently gave him the bright idea of starving himself . . .

Here Eshelby gave a lucid, concise three-page account of Vallantine's swindle and the subsequent lawsuit, which Marianne had to read three times before she could understand it.

. . . I suspect only someone with both money and connections could get the better of those high-powered crooks, and that's why I thought of you, dear girl. I tried to call you when our friend was shot but you were in Kenya, and I hear you've been in many places since . . . I realize you're having lots of fun all over the world, but however glamorous and eventful your life may be, what could be a more joyful thing to do than saving a friend?

A New Life

To live is to feel, to experience powerful emotions.
STENDHAL

The mortal sin of happiness . . .
GEORGE FALUDY

O NLY Fawkes knew they were coming. He was waiting for them at
the airstrip with the old station wagon and dropped Marianne off
at the clinic before driving Joyce and the children on to the house.

Waving to Ben until the car disappeared, Marianne took a deep breath
of the benign air before entering the clinic; it was the best time for weather
in the Bahamas, a mild summer day in early March. Once inside, she
walked up to the reception desk and asked to speak to Dr. Feyer.

"Certainly, Mrs. Hardwick," the nurse said and hurried away down
the bare-walled corridor. (Sir Henry had willed the clinic to the residents of the island, with a trust fund to keep it going, but the heirs had
taken the paintings.)

"Lovely lady, ve haven't seen you for so long!" boomed the large
namesake of Attila the Hun, his white coat flying, his triple chin wobbling, as he rushed forward to greet her. "Is anyting wrong?" he asked
gravely, pressing both her hands, and was relieved to hear that she had
only dropped by to see Mark Niven, if he was well enough to receive
visitors. "Yes, he's much better. He's verry, verry lucky! Ve vill have
her up and around in about a veek. But don't upset her, please. He is
depressed." He nodded several times with a mournful air. "He lohst
her fortune, you know, poor boy. Yes. Ve are not charging him anyting
dis time. Be nice to her! I mean be nice to him."

"I'll try to be nice to him for your sake, Doctor," Marianne replied,
her voice as even as she meant it to be. She was wearing a high-necked
cotton dress with a long skirt that covered most of her body and contrary

343

to her usual custom had put on a lot of makeup, so that if she blushed or turned pale, Mark wouldn't notice.

The news of her visit brought forward several doctors and nurses, bowing and smiling, remembering the old gossip, and the shade of knowing superiority in their attention made Marianne's spine stiffen.

"Let me show you to his room, lovely lady," urged the director of the clinic with passionate seriousness, bending his enormous body and pointing with his huge arm.

Even as Marianne hurried down another corridor, trying to keep up with Dr. Feyer, she was willing herself to look calm and distant. She was determined to show Mark that she had forgotten the past just as much as he had. She was offering to help him in the same way she would help any acquaintance who was robbed as he had been. Moreover, she was doing a favor, not to him, but to EAGLESON, LICHTERMAN, PERROT & BERGIN, her father's New York lawyers who were also hers. They were delighted that she was thinking of bringing them a new client. Mark didn't need to feel obligated to her — he could go on hating her if he wished to. She didn't want to renew their affair. Not for anything would she tell him that she was getting a divorce. Dizzy in anticipation of seeing him again, she tried to steel herself against his bright dark eyes. As Dr. Feyer held the door open for her, she entered the room with her head held high — only to stop short, stricken with surprise.

The handsome, vigorous young man she had held in her arms had turned into a stranger, with hollow cheeks, bitter lines around his mouth, gray flecks in his dark hair. The eyes were the same, but they looked at her from a well of misery, sunk deep into their sockets. All the way from Chicago she had been wondering why he had never written to her and trying to think of some way of finding out whether he was committed to the girl from the Club, but once she saw him she knew everything that mattered. There was no need for him to tell her that he had sent her twenty-three letters and a cable or that he had never found anyone to take her place: her first sight of him told her that he was alone, without love or hope. He lay inert in bed and his haggard face gradually acquired a strained expression, as if he had to make an effort to remember her. She burst into tears.

Emotion is strength. Mark, who a moment before had felt he might never get on his feet again — and was terrified by her sudden appearance, completely at a loss what to say to her in his shameful condition — could not bear to see her cry and leaped out of bed to hold her and calm her. He kissed her hands, her throat, her wet cheeks, and they embraced as if they were all alone. "Oh, Mark," she begged him, "we must never leave each other again!"

Dr. Feyer agreed to release his patient into Marianne's care with strict instructions about diet, and murdering genders as ever, admonished them to remember that she was still very weak and far from ready to lead a normal life. Mark left the clinic on his own feet but, as if to prove Dr. Feyer's point, was about to faint on his way to the car and would have fallen if Fawkes, who had driven back to pick them up, hadn't caught him.

When he had been put to bed in the guest cottage he remembered so well, Marianne brought the children over from the main house to visit him. Though inches taller, they were the same slender kids he knew, with golden skin like their mother and expressive, serious faces. Creighton's hair had darkened to light brown but Ben's was still blond and he had acquired a sprinkling of tiny freckles across the bridge of his nose. The anxious look that came into their eyes when their mother said that Mark was joining the family moved Mark to swear eternal friendship to them in his heart. He remembered his own hurt when his parents had parted.

"Nobody ever talked about you," said Creighton, eager to impart information without thought of its effect. "We didn't talk about you either."

"Are you sick?" asked Ben.

"No, I'm not. In a couple of days I'll be able to run around with you and play all the games you want. Have you still got my peacock?"

"He died," said Ben tragically in his deep voice.

"Oh, I'm very sorry," exclaimed Mark, using it as a pretext to reach out and take Ben's little hand, and then Creighton's as well, to make sure he didn't feel left out.

"Do you worry about health?" Creighton asked him, scowling.

"Oh, no, I don't worry about anything."

He dozed off when Marianne left with the children and woke up only when she came back into the room. She had just heard from her attorney in New York that this was the next-to-last day to appeal against the dismissal of the lawsuit, and she started talking about it, but he refused to listen. He didn't want to be reminded of the treasures. "Why do you want me to think about everything that made me want to die?" he asked bitterly, the lines around his mouth growing deeper.

Marianne didn't argue. Leaving him with an excuse about the children, she went back to the main house and sent a cable signed *Mark Niven* authorizing EAGLESON, LICHTERMAN, PERROT & BERGIN to act on his behalf. This well-meant forgery was a new experience for her; she was wild with the idea that she was saving Mark's fortune for him. Evidently nothing would have been done without her! Her eyes shone so brightly that Joyce thought she and Mark had already made love.

When Joyce tried to question her, she just shook her head and laughed, but she kept saying to herself "he needs me," and this made up for the years of separation and misunderstanding. She had a man for whom she could make all the difference in the world. She ran back to the cottage and slipped into bed beside him, taking care not to wake him up, for he had fallen asleep once again.

In the next few days she spent a lot of time watching him sleeping. The dark circles under his eyes grew lighter every day, his bones lost their sharpness, the lines around his mouth disappeared, and the gray flecks in his dark hair made him only more strikingly handsome as his face grew young again. Taking very good care of him — feeding him, loving him, fussing over him — she couldn't help feeling that he was becoming a little her own creation.

"I was sick of hoping, sick of hating, sick of fighting over things," Mark told her one day as they were lying side by side in bed, holding hands. "And when I woke up at the clinic and realized I was still alive, I wanted to die more than ever. . . . If you hadn't come back, I'm sure I would have found some other way of killing myself. I owe my life to you."

Even if he hadn't said it, Marianne would have believed it: with him she had the same joyful sense of her own significance as she had with her children.

Yet, though Mark claimed everything she did made him happy, when she told him one morning that she had cabled the lawyers in his name telling them to go ahead, he gave her such an angry look that she went cold, thinking he didn't love her.

"I'm tired of making a fool of myself," he told her. "What would I do with a fortune? I couldn't handle the simplest arrangements for an exhibition. The worst that can happen to you if you have nothing is that you starve, and I've tried that, I can do it."

"You're only talking this way because you're run-down," Marianne argued. "You did some sensible and useful things with your money and you'll do many more. I'll help you. Not many people can cope on their own. Your only trouble was that you were alone." She kissed one of his scars, but he drew away. She jumped out of bed. "All right, let's not talk about it. Come on, get up, stop brooding. Let's go over to the house and have breakfast with the boys."

Mark turned on his stomach and let his head hang over the side of the bed to avoid looking at her. Her naked body appeared especially soft in the half-light, and he didn't want to want her. "You go. You shouldn't be wasting your time with a loser."

"Come on, don't be childish. Look at that sun!" she said, stretching out her arm to cut one of the thin shafts of sunlight coming through the louvered shutters. As she folded the shutters back and turned herself around to give herself a shower of sunlight, a salty breeze swept into the room carrying the sound of the waves, the dry rustle of palm trees, the cries of gulls. "We could go sailing!" she said, grabbing a T-shirt and starting to pull it over her head.

Mark didn't move. "I don't feel up to doing anything. I shouldn't be here. I should have been left to rot in my boat."

He got into such a black mood that Marianne, remembering Dr. Feyer's warning, was afraid he might try to commit suicide again. All keyed up to go outdoors, she sighed, closed the shutters, threw her T-shirt in the corner, climbed back into bed and, putting his hand on her breast to calm herself, waited until she lost her eagerness to go out and do things. Then she pressed her whole body against his, to transmit her love to him, to make him desire her, to raise his spirits. She woke his strength, brought him up from despair, and they joined forces.

ARMED with the cabled authorization, Samuel Lichterman of EAGLESON, LICHTERMAN, PERROT & BERGIN applied for a two-week extension to prepare Plaintiff's appeal against Justice F's judgment dismissing *Niven v. Vallantine,* and for an order extending the sequestering of the treasures. Justice F himself granted both extensions at an extraordinary hearing.

Lichterman moved so quickly that MacArthur couldn't make time to go down to the courthouse; he sent his assistant Elliott T. Sanborn III instead and had to content himself with talking to Lichterman on the phone and dressing down Vallantine in his office.

"You didn't tell me everything, John," he said angrily when he had the Defendant among his carpets.

Having expected to repossess the treasures that very day, Vallantine had just learned from Sanborn III that an extension had been granted to the Plaintiff upon the intervention of one of New York's most powerful and prestigious law firms. Devastated by this terrible news, he had come to MacArthur's office to hear an explanation, not to give one. "Wh . . . what dddd . . . didn't I tell you?" he stuttered pitifully.

"You didn't tell me the Plaintiff was related to Montgomery Steel."

Vallantine made an effort to laugh. "He c . . . c . . . can't be! He's just an actor's sssssson."

"You mean you didn't know," commented the former judge contemptuously.

Taking a handkerchief from his breast pocket, Vallantine wiped his face and his thick, sweaty eyebrows slowly and deliberately as though he never wanted to move on to the next moment.

"What is this Mark Niven like? I think he was at one of the hearings but I don't recall him." MacArthur ruined his clients' victims without bothering to take a good look at them even when they met in court, unless he had some special reason to worry about their appearance. "Is he handsome?"

"I sssssuppose so. He's young. . . . Why?"

"He's involved with one of the Montgomery girls."

Vallantine sighed heavily. "Bill, all I know is that I paid you three million dollars and you get h . . . half of everything when we get it back."

MacArthur thought about this for a moment, kneading his fleshy jaw, then nodded with a determined air. "Don't worry, John, we're going to fight them. I don't like to be pushed around. We'll stall. I'll drag out the case and wait for the romance to break up."

A WEEK later Mark stood in Samuel Lichterman's office on Park Avenue, bending over an otherwise bare desk to sign a detailed agreement authorizing EAGLESON, LICHTERMAN, PERROT & BERGIN to represent him in his case against John Vallantine and the Vallantine Gallery. The agreement specifically stated that Mark was not required to make any payment in regard to either costs or fees until he regained possession of the treasures.

"This is such an interesting case that I'm sure there are many attorneys in town who would have agreed to act for you on similar terms," Lichterman told Mark, taking care not to look at Marianne as he said it.

A tall, urbane, youngish man with a well-cut suit and a trim dark beard, the attorney seated himself on the windowsill rather than behind the desk: it was his way of suggesting that there was nothing formal, mean or tedious about the kind of law he practiced. Most of his clients were rich but he wasn't in thrall to things and was content with a good life. The steel-framed Vittorio Fiorucci posters on his office walls had greater artistic than monetary value, and he got more joy out of opera and books — indeed, from records and paperbacks — than some of his colleagues got from owning apartment buildings or yachts, and consequently could afford to reject cases which offended his conscience. He wouldn't have represented John Vallantine, though he wouldn't have accepted a client in Mark's circumstances either, if it weren't for the Montgomery connection.

"I don't see why you'd want to bother," said Mark after signing the authorization. "All the judges are MacArthur's friends."

Lichterman laughed. "That's all right, we know people too."

Frowning, Mark sat down. He found it almost impossible to concentrate on anything having to do with the treasures, and was getting involved in another lawsuit only because Marianne insisted. Nonetheless, a well-trained client, he offered to tell his whole story.

"You don't need to tell me anything. It's all in the contract and the interrogatories."

"Great." Mark twisted in his chair so that he could see Marianne's profile. Though he had always known that she was beautiful, only in the last few days had he come to realize how important that was. He couldn't understand why he had ever despaired. The existence of the universe was fully justified by the graceful line of her neck, the way she crossed her legs and listened to the lawyer with a serious face.

Lichterman explained that the appeal he was preparing was based on the grounds that Mark had had no legal representative when Justice F dismissed his complaint. "I had a talk with MacArthur on the phone," he went on. "He's not too happy."

"What did he say?" asked Marianne.

"He offered to settle."

"Yeah, I know," Mark interjected. The mention of MacArthur's settlement offer had jolted a painful memory. "They're offering three hundred thousand dollars."

"No, no. Not to us. He offered to give back half the treasures."

"What did you say to him?" she asked.

"I told him, no, thanks, we want it all. And costs."

Marianne rewarded the lawyer with a sexy smile. "Good for you, Sam."

'Why is she smiling at him like that?' thought Mark, annoyed. He knew he didn't want to come to New York and get involved with lawyers again.

"What are you going to do about the money Mark paid to Wattman?" Marianne asked Lichterman. "I'd hate to see that man profit from getting our case dismissed."

The expression *our case* prompted Lichterman to cast a quick involuntary glance at Mark, which he tried to cover by adjusting his glasses. "Well, he sent me the files and he may return about half of what he was paid, but I'd rather not pursue it if you don't mind. The rumor is that he's going to be appointed to the bench, and we don't really like to go out of our way to make enemies of judges. Anyway, Wattman's fee is part of Mark's costs, so we'll take it out of Vallantine."

"What happens next?"

'No, she isn't really interested in him,' Mark decided. 'She's only interested in what he's saying. Who would have thought she could be so businesslike? How straight she sits!' It was at the back of his mind that he would have to pull himself together eventually — he couldn't let her take care of him for the rest of his life — but he told himself he was still convalescing. Who could blame a sick man if he just sat and watched?

Feeling by the prickling of her skin that Mark was staring at her, Marianne tossed her head, and he fell to wondering how many months it would take for her shining ash-blond hair to grow long again.

"It's a pretty straightforward case, but with PETER, BLACK on the other side, it could take a couple of years," said Lichterman, bringing the meeting to a close. "You can go back to your island, lucky people, and forget about the whole sordid business. Just don't get married until I get you your divorce! Kevin is very cooperative, it's going to be an uncontested divorce, you've agreed on joint custody, so all that remains for me is to negotiate a reasonable division of property.''

"I told him on the phone that I don't want anything except the place on Santa Catalina and the letters Mark wrote to me. And the cable he sent me the day he found the *Flora*."

As they were standing at the door about to leave and Marianne asked for copies of all the affidavits, Mark held up his hands in horror. He didn't want her to go through what he had gone through! It wasn't worth it. What was the point of being very rich? "Mr. Lichterman, I don't want you to build up Marianne's hopes," he said firmly. "Wattman is supposed to be a pretty good lawyer, and he didn't think the case was worth his while."

Lawyers can be as vain as teenage girls: Lichterman's eyes flashed through his glasses at the suggestion that anything Wattman said or did could have any bearing on what he, Samuel Lichterman, could do. "Ah, yes. Good old Bernie. . . . He's not a bad trial lawyer, but what he really likes to do is sit in his office and harangue his clients. Did he tell you this place is a jungle?''

"Yes!" exclaimed Mark, stepping back from the threshold. "How did you know?"

"You've got to watch out. When someone tells you you're in a jungle, he means he's going to eat you.''

"He also told me the trouble with me is, I don't understand that evil is stronger."

"Ah!" Lichterman tilted his head back and raised his arms heavenward. "He forgot about chance!"

WHILE their mother was in New York, Creighton and Ben were with their father in Chicago. There were moments when Marianne wondered anxiously whether Kevin would send them back, but he was as good as his word. Indeed, the abandoned husband was acting with greater consideration than his wife had thought he was capable of. "It's true that I kept the letters, but I wanted to see whether I could make our marriage work," he had told her on the phone in the conversation which she mentioned to Lichterman. "I'm sure neither Creighton nor Ben would blame me for that. I don't think even your father would blame me for that. Anyway, that's all water under the bridge. I think the chief thing now is to have a divorce which allows us to remain friends and minimizes the shock for the children. They'll keep us together for the rest of our lives no matter what we do, so we might as well be a happy extended family.''

Hardwick even promised to return Mark's letters and the cable if he could only find them; he was magnanimity personified.

He vented his anger on Baglione, with whom he set up a late-night meeting right in Chicago, in his office on the top floor of the HCI Building. The two men met without aides or secretaries; Hardwick also arranged for Baglione to evade the night watchmen. "Sorry about the inconvenience, Vincenzo, but I don't want anyone to testify to some congressional committee about what might turn out to be our last meeting," he told the wizened mobster after offering him a seat, while he himself went to the window and stood there with his hands in his pockets and his back to his guest, admiring the panoramic view of illuminated skyscrapers. "I wonder whether you would consider selling me back your interest in our Brazilian company. I'm also willing to cancel our contract with your trucking company."

"What is this, Kevin?" asked the pre-eminent gangster, who had come expecting to hear about his share of the new HCI insecticides and herbicides plant going up on the Greek coast west of Athens. "That's no way to talk with friends."

"We're friends," agreed Hardwick, turning to face the blundering old hood, "but we're bad luck for each other, Vincenzo. I know you meant well, but I need friends who can get rid of my enemies."

Baglione pulled back his little head and hunched up his skinny shoulders. "Them people who was giving you problems with your family life? You still remember them? All them people is dead or dying! We fixed that photographer for you, he went over a bridge — there's a guy who got his back broken on your say-so. And that gumshoe, we checked him out, he fixed himself with booze, gave himself cirrhosis of the liver. He must be dead by now, but if he ain't you wouldn't want to bother with him — why put him out of his misery? We took care of your wife's friend — Christ, we shot him up, we landed a helicopter on him — we lost five of our own people getting that guy killed —it ain't our fault if he's still alive." The old mafioso couldn't have sounded more hurt, more unjustly treated, if he really had been behind the Redistribution Army's attack on the barge. "He's a cripple, Kevin, he's out of the picture, ain't he?"

"I appreciate all you've done, Vincenzo, but he isn't out of the picture, he's living openly with my wife at our place on Santa Catalina, and my children are with them, too."

"That's news to me," said Baglione, shaking his head. "I'll look into it."

"I want my family back, Vincenzo."

Baglione kept nodding sympathetically, all the more so as he was still determined not to kill the actor's son. He got up, thrust his sharp, solemn face forward to stare at Hardwick in a meaningful and straightforward manner, then closed his eyes and slowly nodded his head again. "We'll give it another try, Kevin. We'll try and get him out of your way."

"What do you mean, *try?*"

Baglione opened his eyes and stared silently at Hardwick. He had already made up his mind what he would do. He would send two men over from Miami to Santa Catalina; they would play a couple of tricks on the kid, try to scare him away from his girlfriend, phone him a couple of times, tell him they'd kill him if he didn't leave, and if that didn't work, they'd take a potshot at his leg to show they were trying. A botched murder attempt was as far as Baglione would go to placate his vicious business associate. "All we can do is try," he said plaintively. "This guy would already be dead if he would die easy. We'll do our best, but if he survives what we do to him, then God's protecting him, and I wouldn't raise my hand a third time against a guy like that. You oughta respect God's will too, my friend. Enough blood has been shed over this already. This here is the last time we'll talk about it. I don't want you to question our friendship again."

The tone of Baglione's voice made Hardwick realize he had gone as far as he could go. "It's a deal," he said, extending his hand and bending from the waist with a show of deference to white hairs and wisdom. "Now when do you want to take a look at our new plant in Greece?"

They talked business, but Baglione kept thinking of the actor's son. He became quite fond of the boy whose life he was saving; he felt like a producer putting on a show!

Two days after this meeting in Chicago, the *Ile Saint-Louis* disappeared from the Hardwicks' dock on Santa Catalina.

The boys rushed into the cottage shortly after breakfast to report that Mark's boat, which he had promised to give them as soon as they were old enough, was gone. He ran with them down to the dock, where Fawkes stood watching the water and holding up the thick mooring line, evidently cut with a knife or a cutlass.

"You said we could have your boat and then you let somebody steal it!" Creighton accused Mark with scornful resentment.

"For sure it was a Haitian," Fawkes commented, shaking his head. Haitians are the black underclass for the black Bahamians, blamed for all unsolved crimes and flu epidemics.

"Are you upset?" asked Ben.

Mark shrugged, hardly remembering how he had once hated being robbed. "One less thing I own, one less thing I have to worry about."

"But it was *our* boat!" Creighton protested, offended by Mark's lack of concern.

To get their minds off the boat, Mark challenged the boys to a race along the beach.

A couple of days after the disappearance of the *Ile Saint-Louis,* by which time only Creighton was thinking about it, Mark happened to be by himself in the living room of the big house when the phone rang. It was a person-to-person call from Miami for Mark Niven. "Speaking," he said to the operator, and heard the coins dropping.

"Is that Mark Niven?" asked a heavy male voice.

"Yes."

"A guy about twenty-three?"

"Yes. Who is this?"

"The guy who found that treasure ship?"

"Yes, yes. What do you want?"

"You keep hanging around that woman and you'll find yourself dead," growled the hoarse voice.

It happens every minute of the day and night: people are minding their own business and then suddenly a stranger materializes out of nowhere and says *I'll kill you!* Where could such a creature have sprung from? Mark felt the same surprise, shock, incredulity as any other victim. How could he be listening to all this insane nonsense? "Are you sure you've got the right number?" he asked. "Are you sure you're talking to the person you want to talk to?"

The voice was offended. "Remember your boat? We sunk it a hundred yards from the dock. We shot it full of holes and you didn't hear a thing. We done it to show you we mean business. You want to live, you forget about your girlfriend and get off the island. Alone. Without her. Make sure. We're watching you. If you take her . . . don't try it. We'll kill you, see?"

A chill went through Mark as it dawned on him that he was listening to a live caricature of a human being, just the sort of person who actually could be a hired killer. Hired by John Vallantine. He assumed that the threat was meant to part him not from Marianne but from her lawyers, so that MacArthur could get the case dismissed again. Otherwise, why would the man mention the *Flora?* "Listen, tell Vallantine I'm bored with all this hassle about the treasures," he told the voice. "Tell him I've had all the fights about them I'm ever going to have. I have better things to do. He can take them and stuff them as far as I'm concerned. Tell him to speak to the lawyers. I'll accept whatever he proposes."

"What the fuck? I ain't speakin to nobody," said the voice, thick with anger, the fear of confusion. "We're already paid, see?"

Shaken and bewildered, Mark wanted to talk to Marianne, but when he found her she was curled up with the children on a sofa reading them *The Prince and the Pauper.* She gave him a glowing look and wiggled

353

her toes to greet him, and he sat down on the floor beside them. As he listened to her expressive voice, so full of drama and compassion, his fear ebbed away and the call no longer seemed so ominous. It could have been a crank or some vengeful member of the Redistribution Army who just wanted to spoil his day. 'If this thing was serious, I'd be more worried about it,' he thought, becoming fascinated by the way Ben kept stroking his mother's bare arm with absolute concentration.

Later, when Mark was alone with Marianne in bed — stroking her arms, her breasts, her thighs, her belly — he had no words to waste on some moron's crazy idea of parting him from the loveliest woman on earth. There was a moment when he might have mentioned it, but just then she drew him down, wanting their whole bodies to touch. When he entered her, she didn't let him move; it was her greatest joy, she said, just to have him inside her. Since she had discarded her diaphragm she could feel him reach the mouth of her womb. But they still weren't close enough. It was the sense of incompleteness which grows with passion: they couldn't get close enough even when he was thrusting into her as deep as he could go. They were trying to become one flesh and blood — and Marianne hoped that it had already happened.

When they had to rest and Mark was once again wondering what would be the right time to tell her about the threatening phone call, she told him she had missed a period. She felt almost certain that she was pregnant.

That settled it. He wouldn't have upset her for anything.

She phoned Lichterman in New York to ask him to speed up the divorce, and Mark phoned his father in London. He planned to phone Lichterman as well, when Marianne wasn't around, to tell the lawyer to call off the lawsuit and let Vallantine have everything, but he wanted to provide for his son (he had no doubt that he would have a son), and when talking with his father he agreed gladly to take the remainder of his investment in the Kleist play as well as the profit. "You'll have enough for yourself and my grandchild, and even some for your stepsons and your rich intended, and you can still go back to university," said Niven, wanting them to come to London.

"Dad, you'll never change!" exclaimed Mark, but all the same, he was thinking of getting back to his history of Peru. It is the same with every threat people can't do much about, whether it is the threat of nuclear war or an anonymous phone call: Mark had resolved not to think about it; he had put it out of his mind.

The lovers decided to share their great news about the baby with no one on the island except Joyce and Eshelby, who had given up the camera shop and taken the opportunity to return to the teaching profession as the Hardwick children's tutor.

Taking the announcement with uncharacteristic solemnity, Eshelby asked Marianne to stand up and allow him to feel and listen.

"It's too soon — *months* too soon!" she protested, laughing.

Eshelby was adamant. "I'll feel something!" he insisted, with the passion of a homosexual whose paternal longings were aroused.

"Oh, well, I don't mind," said Marianne cheerfully, quite pleased that the new child, still unformed, was already exciting curiosity. She pushed her chair back, got up, and unzipped her skirt for Eshelby, who was standing in front of her with his hands at the ready. He stroked her flat little abdomen with a circular motion, slowly and gently, then bent down and put his ear to it with an intent smile, trying to hear the pulse of new life.

Getting jealous, Mark reached out fiercely to pull him away, but was stopped by Marianne's look. 'Oh, well,' he thought, calming down, 'there's no harm in it, I guess.' He thought what she wanted him to think.

"I hope, my dears, you won't deny me credit for this child," said the former teacher as he straightened himself out. "If I hadn't written that letter to Marianne she wouldn't be pregnant."

"You'll be the baby's godfather, Ken," she said. "All three of us will be forever grateful to you."

MARIANNE was at the clinic with her obstetrician, Dr. Paul Harlock, who had come from Philadelphia to examine her, when Mark received the second phone call.

"How come you ain't looked for your boat yet?" the thick voice asked angrily. "We're watching you, see?"

"Did you talk to Vallantine? Did you tell him he can have whatever he wants?"

"You kidding? What valentine? Listen, I told you before, get away from that broad or you're dead for good. This is the last time, see?" The receiver was slammed down before Mark could ask any more questions.

Fighting rising panic with purposeful activity. Mark put on his mask and flippers and went snorkeling in the little bay in front of the Hardwicks' beach. The *Ile Saint-Louis* was lying on the sandy bottom in about ten feet of water, riddled with small holes.

Should he call the police in Miami? The island's only policeman? What could they do about anonymous calls and a wrecked boat? And even if he and Marianne went to Washington and got FBI protection, what difference would it make? If all the police forces of the United States couldn't protect President Kennedy, what protection could they have?

Should he make a run for it with Marianne and the boys?

If these gangsters were watching him, if there were so many people involved that the caller in Miami knew he hadn't gone to look for his boat, how could he avoid being followed wherever he went? Even if he and Marianne left the island separately, how could he be sure she wouldn't be followed?

The next thing he knew he was throwing things into suitcases and Creighton and Ben were watching him from the door with curious faces. "I thought we might go to London," he explained.

"OK, guys, let's go!" shouted Creighton, beginning to march up and down in the room. "I want my own passport this time!"

The boys liked the idea of travel, but their mother didn't. "Why so soon?" she asked Mark when she came back from the clinic.

"I don't want to fly in the first three months," she explained to him in bed later in the afternoon. "It's too easy to lose a baby in the first three months."

"I thought maybe I'd go ahead, find us a place," Mark suggested hesitantly.

"Could you leave me?" she asked him, shocked, and drew away to look for the answer in his eyes. "No, you couldn't," she said, laughing.

"I'm sure it wasn't easy for your husband to give you up," Mark said later. "If he read my letters and kept quiet about them all those years, it must have been because he wanted to keep you. He couldn't help loving you."

Marianne didn't believe it. "He was always bored with me. I think it was only because of your letters that he got interested in me again. Out of spite. He knew I wasn't happy with him."

"You're only saying that because you don't want me to be jealous," said Mark, getting jealous again. "You enjoy sex so much, you two must have had a great time together."

"I hate him — he stole years from us!" Marianne exclaimed, getting so angry that she had to sit up. This pacified Mark, who nibbled her nipples to coax her back to him. "With you I feel clean, I don't have to pretend," she whispered into his ear. "I can let myself go and do whatever I want."

'Her husband's trying to scare me away,' Mark decided. 'And if he *has* hired some goons to kill me, what can I do? Run away? How could I get up every morning knowing that I abandoned Marianne to save my skin? If there was a firing squad right here and they gave me the choice of leaving her or being shot, even then what else could I say but *Go ahead, shoot!*' She had never felt him so big and so hard inside her. Later, when they were resting, he went on thinking in a less exalted mood. 'We could try to disappear together — but even if we managed to get away from here and hide out somewhere, Hardwick could start an international police manhunt for us, saying we kidnapped his children. Do I want to spend the rest of my life in hiding?' He considered briefly the possibility of denouncing Hardwick to the police, but who would believe him? What proof did he have? In any case, whatever he did, it would involve upsetting Marianne, risking a miscarriage — and most likely for nothing. If they wanted to harm him, they would have already done so. They wouldn't be playing games, sinking his boat and making phone calls. Hardwick was just making him sweat a little, to have his revenge.

"What are you thinking about?" Marianne asked, sniffing his neck.

"The hammerhead shark I ran into once," Mark replied.

"You see, I was right to be worried!"

"But I got away," Mark replied, laughing triumphantly, and told her about the putrefied head, the rows and rows of teeth.

Remembering his past courage gave him confidence. The world was full of gangsters as the sea was full of sharks; should he spend the rest of his life shaking? He had risked death every day for the *Flora,* which had brought him nothing but agony. Would he be any less brave for the woman he loved and his son? In her arms he felt certain that his luck would hold and he would survive. He would tell Marianne all about it when the baby was born. He foresaw the day when he would be as old as his father and would be able to tell his son the whole story of the mysterious telephone threats, the harsh, sinister voice, the sunken boat riddled with bullet holes, and how he didn't let them scare him. He would set an example to his son and his stepsons, teach them that they must not let themselves be consumed by fear and worry.

Practicing to be a father, he spent a great deal of his time with the children, sitting in on Eshelby's classes with them (he thought that he too would become a teacher) and running races with them on the sunny beach, usually in the afternoon after the tide went out, when the sand was firm yet elastic, bending under their bare feet. The dogs led the race, clearing the ground of terns, followed by the children and then Mark, who took care to come last but right at their heels, to spur them on. Creighton was not so considerate: he would give Benjamin a few feet's head start and then catch up and pass him every time.

Marianne, who was bored by all strenuous physical activities except sailing and making love, used her pregnancy as an excuse to stay indoors reading and listening to music; Joyce sometimes joined in the sand races or sat on a stone bench, playing the role of spectator and cheering section. Finding her functions greatly reduced with the arrival of Eshelby and Mark, she couldn't wait for the birth of Marianne's child or, preferably, the advent of a man good enough to marry, but in the meantime she kept up her spirits and cheered on the racers as if she were a crowd. She happened to be sitting on the stone bench at the time the two men appeared from behind the curve of the shoreline and she was the only one who saw them. They were walking calmly and unhurriedly; they meant no real harm. Their instructions were to shoot into the sand near the young man's feet and then go back to Miami. The dogs were running in the opposite direction, toward the next point on the beach, followed by the boys and Mark, pounding along the springy sand. Ben, in the lead but hearing Creighton close behind him, was running desperately, straining ahead, crying, "Let me win, let me win!" and not looking back, but Creighton, turning around to protest to Mark that it wasn't fair, saw one of the two men raise a gun and fire and saw Mark's shoulder wrench and his T-shirt suddenly fill with blood as he crumpled to the ground.

Screaming, "Don't look! Don't look!" Joyce got to Ben before he had time to turn around and lifted him up to cut off his view with her body. Pressing his head to her chest, she ran for help, still screaming *don't look, don't look!*, while Creighton remained rooted to the spot, watching the blood-covered body sliding toward the sea and the two men hurrying away to board a motorboat which came around the curve of the shoreline. He was still there, as motionless as the flock of terns which had settled down on the sand again, facing out to sea, when Marianne, followed by Fawkes and Eshelby, came running from the house a few minutes later.

Mark was conscious when Marianne knelt beside him, and he looked at her with his eyes full of life and intelligence, which gave her hope. "Don't leave me, Bozzie," he whispered in the voice of a frightened child as the ambulance men from the clinic eased him onto a stretcher.

Marianne clutched his hand all the way to the hospital and kept looking into his eyes until some catastrophe happened inside him and he lost consciousness.

"Not again!" Dr. Feyer had exclaimed with disbelief at the phone call from the Hardwick house, but when he saw Mark brought in on the stretcher he shook his head despairingly. "Oh, vell, dis is de last time."

Marianne, still clutching Mark's hand, had to be separated from him by force as they wheeled the stretcher into the emergency room. "They can't save him without me!" she screamed at the nurses who were holding her back. "If he knows I love him, if he feels my hand, he'll come back!" She was hysterical, wrestling with the two nurses who were keeping her away from the emergency room. "I promised I'd stay with him. He asked me not to leave him and I promised I wouldn't. He doesn't want to die alone. Nobody should die alone . . ." The doctors lost Mark on the operating table.

358

NOBODY was responsible for the murder.

The goon who aimed into the sand wasn't sufficiently familiar with the weapon he was using. "It was the fucking gun," he told the other man, who was cursing him as they sped away in their motorboat. "It fucking jumped on me," he complained, disgusted, throwing the guilty weapon into the sea.

Kevin Hardwick was horrified. John Fawkes phoned him in Chicago to tell him that a guest of Mrs. Hardwick's had been killed and she was at the clinic under sedation. And they didn't know what to do with the boys, Fawkes said: Creighton, who had seen the shooting, hadn't spoken since it happened, and Benjamin wouldn't stop crying. The news that his sons might have received lasting psychic damage from witnessing a murder so shocked and frightened Hardwick that he couldn't feel he had any connection with the event. He flew immediately to Santa Catalina, and when he learned from Joyce that the boys had actually been in the line of fire, he began to curse murderers and stupid criminals so violently that she took the children away, trying to cover their ears.

Baglione felt genuine grief. "Them reporters complain I got too much power," he said to his brisk, bright young aide fresh out of college. "They got no idea how hard it is to get anybody to do what you want them to do. Everybody who works for you is so fucking incompetent." The aide listened with an appreciative smile to show that he wasn't worried about any of this applying to *him*. "Nobody's got too much power. It don't matter what I tell them, people will do their own stupid thing." He felt sorry for the young man who was dead; he had a kind of fellow feeling for him — they were both victims of the same fatality, the incompetence of underlings.

This is the mystery of our age: people get killed but there are no murderers.

44

A Kind of Immortality

Where is my father?
DUMAS

WITH the reopening of the lawsuit and the disposition of the treasures looking uncertain once again, despite all his efforts and his
enormous investment, Vallantine felt both poor and foolish, and this
double misery made all his ailments worse. Sluggish, dyspeptic and short
of breath, the art dealer no longer had the strength to get up first thing
in the morning; attended by his wife, he took his pills and breakfast in
bed and lingered among the pillows to scan the papers before rising to
the challenge of taking a bath. So he was still in bed when he read the
brief agency dispatch about the murder of the once-famous treasure hunter
on Santa Catalina.

"John! What is it?" demanded Shirley Vallantine, alarmed by her
husband's sudden change of color. Even Daisy sensed that something
was happening; she jumped on the bed, very agilely in spite of her short
legs, and nuzzled against her master's hand.

"I think I'll get rid of my ulcer," he replied in a shaking voice, and,
taking a deep breath, read the report aloud.

His wife listened suspiciously, not daring to trust the good news. "What
if they got it wrong? What if he's just wounded?"

"The death of the plaintiff means the end of the lawsuit, Shirley,"
her loving husband explained patiently. "Dead men can't sue."

"What about his relatives?"

"An actor with one half-successful picture behind him? He doesn't
have the kind of money lawyers want."

"But the Montgomery woman is rich!"

"She's out of it. Her boyfriend's dead — she'll be busy looking for
another one."

For some reason this remark convinced her. "So he was murdered,"
she marveled.

"'You can ssssee that we weren't the only ones who couldn't stand him.''

"So he's dead, he's dead," she kept saying, and as the news reached the depths of her soul, she raised her arms and cried out, "It makes you believe in God! Oh, John, we can lead a normal life again!"

"And with a much broader financial base," rejoined the ailing man, feeling cured, and jumped out of bed. "I'd better call Bill. It's time he started to earn his extortionate fees."

"I saw the *Times,* John," MacArthur told him before he could say anything. "I'm just dictating the motion for dismissal."

However, while the motion for dismissal was being typed MacArthur received another phone call, this one from an assistant to the Manhattan district attorney, who informed him that, acting on a sworn deposition from the late Mark Niven, they were considering indicting his client John Vallantine for criminal fraud and conspiracy to commit murder.

"What am I supposed to do with this piece of information, Mr. Hamilton?" asked the former judge sternly. "Tell an innocent man to flee the country?"

"You're his attorney, Mr. MacArthur. I called you simply as a matter of professional courtesy."

"You people over there waste too much of the taxpayers' money on unfounded allegations."

The district attorney was just someone to play procedural games with, but there were other callers.

Before noon a prominent if not pre-eminent figure in organized crime in New Jersey phoned to say he was disturbed by reports that a poor American kid who had found a shipful of gold had had it all taken away from him.

"You're talking about a poor dead kid, Leo," MacArthur argued. "So why shouldn't it go to a nice guy who's still alive and who helped him to find the ship? I can tell you, Vallantine's a good man. He isn't just a client, he's a friend of mine."

"Yeah, sure, Bill, I understand. But the only thing Jack Vallantine had to do with that ship was steal it from the kid."

"What? How can you say that?" asked MacArthur in a voice filled with shocked surprise. The shock and surprise were genuine: how did the old man know?

"Alive or dead, the kid's being cheated," brooded the elder statesman of the Hoboken docks. "It ain't just, it ain't lawful, it ain't fair."

When Mark had used words like *just, lawful* or *fair,* he had sounded naive and ridiculous, but the same words carried great weight coming from the mouth of a man who commanded a private army raised from the profits of murder, extortion and the sale of heroin. Not that this warlord of America's medieval secret society meant to sound threatening.

He had been a terror in his youth but had mellowed with power and it was years since he had ordered so much as a glass of water, though he might say he felt thirsty. All he ever did was think aloud, express an interest, tell people how he felt about things.

"I certainly appreciate you calling me, Leo," the former vice-president of the New York Bar Association assured him. As a result of Leo's call, he decided not to do anything about the case until he knew what was going on.

A couple of days later a former partner of PETER, BLACK, JEFFERSON, MACARTHUR, WHITMAN & WARREN, who had left the firm to become head of the Criminal Justice Division of the Department of Justice, called to warn MacArthur about a libelous rumor going the rounds in Washington. "Somebody told the Attorney General that you've been helping to defraud a twenty-three-year-old youngster of a treasure ship he discovered down in the Bahamas, and now the boy's been found murdered, for Christ's sake! I told the AG it's inconceivable that you'd get mixed up in a thing like that. But what's going on, Bill? I thought you had political ambitions!"

After getting rid of his former partner MacArthur was sifting through the papers that had just been placed on his desk, wondering how the phone calls connected, when he came to a document issued by EAGLESON, LICHTERMAN, PERROT & BERGIN: Lichterman had filed a notice of continuance of *Niven v. Vallantine* on behalf of Niven's heirs. Reading the notice put MacArthur in a furious temper. "Call that crook and tell him to come in at five!" he barked at his secretary over the intercom, forgetting in his anger that she couldn't possibly know which crook he was referring to.

AT five on the dot Vallantine entered his attorney's carpet-hung office. "Hello, hello," he sang, his eyes twinkling and his bushy eyebrows dancing.

MacArthur stood erect behind his desk, a massive, motionless figure. His broad, colorless face looked frozen, his eyes were hostile; he was as solemn and ominous as if he were wearing a judge's robes. "Mr. Vallantine," he told his happy client coldly, "you have a good chance of spending the rest of your life in prison for fraud and murder."

Uncomprehending, Vallantine sank into one of the chairs. "Shhhh . . . shhhhh . . . surely you don't think th . . . that I . . . ?"

"You had a powerful motive. Right now the District Attorney's drawing up an indictment against you. He may not have sufficient evidence to charge you with killing your victim, but it'll be in the back of his mind. The judge, the jury, the newspapers, they'll all look at you as the man who's getting away with murder — you can be damned sure they won't let you get away with anything else.''

"I'm sssssorry, but you c . . . c . . . can't talk to me like this,'' Vallantine stammered with dignified indignation. "It won't do, it w . . . won't do.''

The attorney remained on his feet to emphasize that the whole business shouldn't take more than a couple of minutes. "You don't want a single coin from the wreck, Mr. Vallantine. I have a statement here which you will sign. You renounce all your claims to the treasure as backer, investor, agent and exhibitor. You renounce all your claims, period.''

"I'm sorry but you just can't t . . . t . . . talk to me like this. You can't tell me you can't win a case against a ddd . . . dead man!''

"Well, he's doing a lot better than when he was alive.''

"I don't believe in ghosts,'' the art dealer said firmly, without tripping over a single consonant.

"The dead have a way of getting back at you, Mr. Vallantine.'' MacArthur glared at his client. "That is why, speaking for myself, I would never have anybody murdered.''

"I didn't murder anyb . . . b . . . body,'' protested Vallantine, shaken and shocked at being accused for the first time in his life of a crime he had not committed.

"Well, everybody seems to agree that you did.''

"A man is innocent until proven g . . . g . . . guilty!''

"There's such a thing as carrying a good principle too far,'' the former judge declared sententiously.

"I don't under . . . sssssstand.''

"I'll tell you what *I* don't understand,'' continued MacArthur with some bitterness. Other things being equal, he preferred to be on the winning side. "I really don't understand how a guileless young man who was so badly advised throughout this whole business got around to making a will. But he did make one, and a very clever one at that.''

"A w . . . will?''

"Yes, a will. Do you know anything about it?''

"I ddd . . . don't remember,'' stammered Vallantine, instinctively repeating what MacArthur had taught him to say whenever he was in danger of giving a self-incriminating answer.

"Once you sign this statement renouncing all your claims,'' MacArthur went on, "I'll try to make a deal. They get the goods without further litigation and in return they agree not to press charges. I don't promise anything but I might be able to keep you out of the penitentiary.''

The inventor of the Cape Breton Gold mine could not accept that he had worn himself out and ruined his health for nothing. "I paid you three million dollars over and above your retainer for g . . . getting the treasures," he protested, his face turning reddish blue, then pale again. "You can't tttt . . . t . . . talk to me like this. This is no way to account for your fff . . . fee."

An ordinary man might have been embarrassed by a reminder that he had pocketed three million dollars he had no intention of earning, but the great attorney simply moved to a higher moral plane where money meant nothing. "I'm talking to you," he said reproachfully, "the way an aggrieved attorney talks when he discovers he's been fooled by his client." This was his accounting: he had been fooled; he was aggrieved. He would think twice before accepting another three million dollars. "You lied to me, Mr. Vallantine!" he thundered. "You lied to me about everything!"

Vallantine had no stomach for sorting out the lies; there was too much at stake. "I'm a ruined mmmman, I can't affffford to let go."

"If you are a ruined man, as you say, it was very foolish of you to put everything you had into this lawsuit. You should have instructed me to seek a settlement."

As his client went on arguing, explaining, begging, the great attorney eventually had to sit down and explain patiently that he had no choice. "I don't want to go into details, but you have somehow managed to get mixed up with all the people who can put you inside for life *and* the people who can gun you down in the street. It is not possible to appeal against both the Justice Department and the Mafia."

"All right, then, if I have to surrender everything, you should return your fee."

"I beg your pardon?"

"Mmmmmost of it."

This outrageous demand brought the attorney to his feet again. Over six feet six inches tall, he grew even taller with dignity: he was now indeed the judge, the vice-president of the New York Bar Association, member of the Ethics Committee, a majestic upright whale of a man, looking with annihilating contempt at a client who was wholly evil.

"Mr. Vallantine, this is the last thing I'm going to say to you," he said slowly and deliberately. "It is not enough to be a clever crook, you also have to be lucky."

Unspirited, undone, betrayed to beggary, Vallantine didn't know how he got home. His wife hurried to meet him at the door of the apartment.

"What happened?" she gasped, staring at his gray face shiny with sweat.

"We lost everything," he replied thickly, clutching his chest and forcing the words past his throat with difficulty.

"Oh, John!" she wailed, her hair and her glasses askew. "I knew it.

I knew it! I told you I didn't like that lunatic when we saw him on television, I told you not to get mixed up with him.''

"Shhhhhirley!" he shouted, losing patience for once with his loving wife, then wavered, dying on his feet, a victim of his own crimes. Many thought, though, that he had an unmerited easy death.

THE wicked, too, often do good — albeit for evil reasons, or out of sheer ignorance.

The man responsible for recovering half of Mark's fortune for Mark's father was Kevin Hardwick, whose wife stood to inherit the other half. The will that Mark had dictated to his Nassau attorney Franklin Darville on Vallantine's insistence left half of his estate to Marianne Montgomery Hardwick, "so that if anything happens to me she will know that I never stopped thinking of her and wishing we were together.''

As soon as Darville heard of Mark's death he called the Hardwick house, where a maid informed him that Mr. Hardwick was there but Mrs. Hardwick was in the clinic and could see no one. Wanting to do his duty, and perhaps also do himself some good, and knowing nothing about the divorce proceedings under way in the States, Darville decided to fly to Santa Catalina anyway and show the will to the husband. The bequest made it clear that Mrs. Hardwick had had an affair with poor young Niven, but what of it, the Nassau lawyer reasoned with worldly wisdom — her husband would have no time to worry about that when he learned that there was a danger of the family being robbed of an inheritance worth at least a hundred and fifty million dollars. Darville would not have associated such a primitive feeling as jealousy with a Harvard-educated industrial leader.

Mr. Hardwick was as businesslike about the will as Darville had hoped he would be, wanting to know all about the *problems* to be solved and difficulties to be faced in recovering the treasures from Vallantine. In the end he told Darville to call Lichterman and instruct him to carry on the lawsuit on behalf of the heirs. "I'm glad you came to see me, this sort of thing is men's work,'' he said to Darville when he dismissed him. "We'd better spare my wife the details. You call her lawyer and I'll do my best to speed things up.''

Ever since hearing that his wife's lover was dead Hardwick had been uneasy about meeting her face-to-face (he hadn't visited her at the clinic), and he was quite content to go ahead with the divorce, but he didn't intend to let Vallantine rob her of a fortune which would eventually be passed on to his sons, and when he returned to Chicago he became the most dedicated champion of his dead rival's rights. Baglione, who thought better of Hardwick since it appeared that he had also had financial reasons for wanting his wife's lover out of the way, was of course glad to help, as were Hardwick's elected representatives, Washington bureaucrats, people who spent their lives putting things right. Hardwick was far from knowing everyone who mattered — he was still too young for that — but he was a considerable power in his own sphere, with friends who called other friends, and in this corrupt manner justice was made to prevail swiftly, as it never is when things are done in the normal, lawful way.

Marianne heard the news when she got home from the clinic and phoned her husband to ask him to send the children back. "I'm glad at least you had a boyfriend who seemed to appreciate you," he told her in his gallant executive manner. "Since you don't need the money I'm setting up a trust fund for Creighton and Ben with it — all it needs is the steel cases from the court and your signature. They're lucky kids — with two parents like us, they're going to end up very, *very* rich."

"They're rich enough already," replied Marianne. "Whatever Mark left to me will belong to his child. I'm going to transfer everything to the baby."

"What baby?" asked Hardwick at the other end of the line, fingering a sort of welt on the back of his neck. "What child, what are you talking about? Does he have a child?"

"Not yet, but he's going to have one. I'm three months pregnant."

For a moment Hardwick knew that it was he who had Mark Niven murdered: the stranger from the film came up close and struck back at him. "As if there weren't already enough people in the world!" he said with disgust, slamming down the receiver. He hoped the baby would be stillborn.

MARIANNE gave birth to Mark's daughter on the 20th of October at her parents' farm in Bucks County, in the same bed in which she herself had been born, and her parents saw the baby when she was only a few minutes old. Ditha Montgomery laughed and cried from joy and excitement, but her husband eyed the crumpled red creature with evident distaste: "Of course," he said to his daughter, wanting to get things straight from the start, "you realize that I won't be able to love this child as much as I love my legitimate grandchildren."

It was as if the baby had heard this vile remark, for as soon as she was old enough to focus her huge eyes and reach out for what she wanted, she singled out her grandfather for special attention, and within a matter of weeks had turned him into a babbling idiot walking on all fours. "Abababababababa," he said to the child; "ooooooooohhhhhh" or "aaaaaaaahhhhh," she replied. They conversed like this for hours every day.

366

This brilliant but unfeeling man, who had missed his chance of becoming human as a father, acquired the gift of affection as a grandfather. It happens to many people: they have to grow old before they are ready to love. Creighton Montgomery delighted everyone with his change of heart, and none more so than his son Everett, who was appointed acting chairman of Montgomery Steel, to enable the chairman to spend more time with his *little orphan.*

"What he'd really like is to bury me," Marianne told her sister Claire on the phone. "Then she'd be a full-fledged orphan and he could have her all to himself."

She often broke down unexpectedly, crying about Mark, and talked to the baby about him when they were alone. "Your daddy loved us very much," she kept telling Zoé, as if she knew that Mark wouldn't leave them even to save his life.

Dana Niven first held Zoé Elizabeth Ditha Claire Barbara Alice Amy Andrea Niven in his arms in an old tavern in Marseilles, where he was shooting a film in accordance with the terms of Mark's will. Half of the treasure had been left to "this excellent father and brilliant actor, on the condition that he produce a new film version of *The Count of Monte Cristo* with himself in the title role, to win the worldwide success and stardom which should rightfully have been his from the beginning."

"All those names," he said to the mother, without taking his eyes off the baby, who gazed back at him equally attentively with his son's bright dark eyes. "I bet they were Mark's idea."

"Yes, he wanted lots of names," Marianne replied, involuntarily touching Niven's hand, seeing that he too had fallen in love with her daughter. "Only he thought we would have a boy."

"And which of her names do you actually use?" he asked, trying to make the baby laugh by blowing her downy hair.

"Zoé," Ben answered promptly. "We call her Zoé. Do you like her, Mr. Niven?"

"Do *you* like her?" countered Niven.

"I love her," declared Ben in his deep voice. "I love her up to heaven. Up to outer space!" And he raised his arm above his head to show how high that was.

They were sitting around a heavy carved oak table, part of the film set: Creighton Montgomery had brought the whole party over in his own plane, with his little orphan's bodyguards, and her nanny, Joyce, and the boys' tutor, Ken Eshelby, to make sure that they didn't fall behind with their lessons. Creighton Hardwick, now a tall and handsome nine-year-old, wasn't speaking; he hadn't spoken since the day of the murder. But he listened intently to the conversation and kept looking around, evidently fascinated by the actors in their makeup and colorful costumes.

It was a rich scene. Dana Niven, like all true artists, had no vanity, and he had used Mark's fortune to assemble a company of great actors and actresses without worrying about whether they would outshine him. Vittorio Gassman was there from Italy, in the guise of Jacopo the smuggler. David Niven was giving one of his finest performances as the wealthy, urbane, good-hearted shipowner, M. Morrel. Everybody was dressed in the festive Sunday best of 1814 — English and American actors doing one of the things they liked to do most, playing Frenchmen, thus bearing witness to the glory of France and the unity of Western civilization. Such an assembly of acting geniuses may not have appeared in one film since *Les Enfants du Paradis* was filmed thirty years earlier in nearby Nice.

In spite of his vast wealth, old Montgomery had never been in the same room with so many great men — although it would be too much to say that he appreciated the honor. He was watching Niven and the baby with a jealous rage he found ever more difficult to control. The two bodyguards kept their hands in their pockets, as much on the alert as if they had been among a band of brigands. When a wild-looking smuggler with a knife in his belt came up and put his arm around the boy who couldn't speak, trying to draw him away to tell him jokes and make him laugh, the two detectives sprang forward and grabbed him and would have thrown him on the floor if Marianne hadn't screamed at them to leave Signor Gassman alone. An immense silence descended on the set. The actors and technicians were staring in horror at the two men who didn't know who Vittorio Gassman was.

"I'm sorry, you must forgive them," Montgomery said to Gassman. "They're under terrible pressure. They know that if anything happens to any of the children, they'll have to deal with me. This world is full of people who think that kidnapping and chopping up children is a way of making money. If you had been making this film in Italy, we wouldn't have come to see you. This is a civilized country — here they still have the guillotine." (Years later Montgomery nearly had a heart attack when he heard that President Mitterrand had abolished capital punishment, putting France off limits to all members of the Montgomery family.) "I wouldn't take my granddaughter to a place where somebody could kidnap her, cut off her ear to make sure we paid ransom, murder her, and still be considered a human being with the right to watch television."

This tough speech, delivered in the tone of a bully, set Niven thinking about the great gulf between himself and the Montgomeries. He was attacked by sudden anxiety, wondering what the baby in his arms would be like when she grew up. Would she be an arrogant, unfeeling rich girl? Without thinking he drew her closer to him; he was overwhelmed by the desire to bring her up, to be a father to her, and began looking with new eyes at Marianne, wondering about his chances of marrying the mother to keep the child. The idea wasn't quite as mad as it might sound, for the scene Niven was playing was his wedding reception in which he was supposed to be nineteen years old. And indeed, with makeup and everything, he didn't necessarily look older than twenty-five. Sensing the tension in him, the baby became restless and wanted to go to her mother, and Niven reluctantly handed her over with a choking sensation of loss. He had only had one child, and he was dead.

"You'll have her again this evening, remember," Marianne reminded the actor, sensing that he was in need of consolation.

"Yes, of course."

They got talking about how soon Creighton might regain his powers of speech. "It would be nice to know how they will all turn out," said Niven.

"They'll be fine," said Montgomery gruffly to rebuke the implied criticism in the other grandfather's concern.

"Don't ever shout at her," Niven said to Marianne. "I used to shout at Mark all the time. Every day I think of the years we were together and the good times we might have had, and all I did was jeer at him and criticize him. How can you make up for that?" He reached out for his granddaughter again, as if wanting to ask her forgiveness. But the director went down on his knees, pointing to his watch.

As this book goes to print, Dana Niven's film is playing in cinemas everywhere, a joyful spectacle of great performances. It is not yet known how the children will turn out or when the world will end.